GOING TO TOWN
AND OTHER STORIES

GOING TO TOWN
AND OTHER STORIES

by Yuri Kazakov

Compiled and translated by
Gabriella Azrael

HOUGHTON MIFFLIN COMPANY · BOSTON
The Riverside Press Cambridge
1964

First Printing

HAPPINESS and its nature, suffering and how to overcome it, moral duty to the people, love, the attainment of self-understanding, attitudes to work, the vitality of vile instincts — these are some of the problems that occupy me . . . I do not think that literature immediately and automatically influences the life of man and his moral condition . . . At the same time I do believe in the educational power of literature. And I think a writer who all his life preaches man's goodness, truth, and beauty does after all elevate the moral qualities of his contemporaries and of posterity . . .

YURI KAZAKOV

Contents

Contents

THE SPIRIT OF THE FOREST

Kabiasy 269
Fog 279
Antler House 285
Teddy 296

A CRY FOR HELP

Going to Town

EARLY one morning Vasily Kamanin was walking along the road to Ozerishche. His boots were muddy, his swarthy neck long unwashed, his yellow-flecked eyes cloudy, and his face from his chin clear up to his eyes covered with gray bristle. He was straining forward, and his walk was uneven, as if his legs were trying to break away from his body. A cold wind was blowing down his back. Endless ridges of plowed land lowered on either side of him. Between the ridges water glittered darkly — it had been raining all week. On both sides of the road the red-brown, mud-spattered sorrel trembled in the wind.

The night before Vasily had been drinking heavily with his in-laws. Today his head was aching with a hangover, his whole body aching with the rheumatism he always got in bad weather, and the saliva in his mouth tasted repulsive. Vasily spat, raised his heavy head, and stared ahead glumly. But there was only the muddy unpaved road, dark cheerless haystacks and stretching out to the horizon, a low gray sky without the least bit of light or hope of sun. Vasily looked down, trying to find a dry spot; then, absorbed in thought, began to walk carelessly again, dragging his legs, his thin body bent forward.

Vasily Kamanin lived in an old house on the outskirts of Mokhovatka. Before the war, when Mokhovatka had been a large village, Kamanin's home had been near the others. But when the Germans retreated, they'd set fire to everything, and everything had burned to the ground except Kamanin's house which had by some miracle, remained intact. After the war the village had been rebuilt away from the site of the former village and Vasily found himself on the outskirts. They had proposed moving the house, and Vasily had intended to, but somehow it had never been done, so he remained apart.

One after the other his three daughters had married and gone to live in town. The house was empty and Vasily began to take on more and more work on the side. He was a good carpenter, and he made a lot of money, but as the years had passed he'd begun to be bored, and had taken to drinking and beating his wife in dark, drunken fits.

For a long time Vasily hadn't loved his wife Akulina. Before the war he happened to have been recruited to work on a large construction project in the city, where he had worked for a summer, and since then, he'd never abandoned the hope of moving to the city.

Each year in the fall, when there wasn't much work, he'd be overwhelmed by longing, and lie for long periods in the yard with his eyes closed, oblivious to everything around him, thinking about city life. He couldn't stand city people, he considered them parasites, but city life — the parks, the restaurants, the movie theaters and stadiums — he loved them so much that they were all he could dream about.

Several times he actually planned to go, and had even sold the cow, but Akulina had whispered to him in bed about the land, the family, economy, about how she would die of loneliness in the city. And he had thought it over, and stayed.

Everyone on the collective farm knew about his passion for the city and laughed at him about it.

"What, you haven't left yet?" they'd ask him.

"He who laughs last laughs best," he'd answer with a gloomy smile, inwardly cursing his wife.

In the spring Akulina got sick. They thought at first that she would get over it. Then Akulina started going to the medical center where she took the powders, medicines and evil-tasting concoctions prescribed for her, believing that they would cure her. But the cure didn't take place. Instead, she got worse and worse. Then they tried their own private measures. Old crones with bags of magic waters and root brandies became constant callers at their house. But they didn't help either. Her eyes and temples grew hollow, her hair fell out, and she began to waste away, losing weight with incredible rapidity. People who had recently seen her healthy would stop now on seeing her and stare. It was frightening to sleep with her; she was so thin and groaned so in her sleep. Vasily took to sleeping on the hay in the yard.

He'd spend whole days in the field haying, arguing with the foreman, pulling at his dark bushy eyebrows whenever he thought of his wife, who he was more and more convinced was about to die. In the evenings he'd cart home the hay and the seed bags given out in advance for the next day's work. He'd arrive home tired, his face burned brown, sit down on a bench, resting his chapped hands on his knees, and stare gloomily at his wife.

Frighteningly thin, with a fixed stare in her dark dry eyes, but still pretty, Akulina would be setting the table. Then she'd lean against the wall, breathing hard through her bluish lips. Her face would be covered with sweat.

"Vasya!" she'd plead. "In the name of Christ, take me to the city! Take me! I'll be dead soon probably . . . I have no strength left. I'm so sick, Vasya!"

Vasily would eat his soup in silence, afraid to look at his wife, afraid to reveal his inner thoughts.

"Take me, Vasya," Akulina would say quite softly, sliding to the floor. "I can't eat anything, it all comes back up. I can't even take milk now. Our animals, Vasya, I've got to look after them, and it's hard. If I could ride it would be easier. Inside me everything's burning, burning up! Take me, let a professor look at me. I don't trust anyone around here any more. It's terrible, terrible!"

So at last Vasily was going to ask the chairman of the collective farm for a horse for his wife, and at the same time request that they be released from the collective farm altogether.

He was in a bad mood. His head ached with his hangover, and with his hatred for his wife, for the foreman and for his neighbors. He cursed, and tried to figure out the best way to ask the chairman for permission to live in the city.

2

An hour later, when Vasily got to Ozerishche, he was so tired his legs were giving way under him.

The chairman's house stood out for its size, its fenced-in porch, its iron roof, its large yard covered not with hay like the rest, but with wood chips. Dark shapes of beehives stood under the apple trees in the garden. Wiping his feet carefully, Vasily squinted at the beehives, thinking, I should have raised bees, there's good business. But then he coughed, remembering why he had come, and feeling uncharacteristically nervous and constrained, he opened the door into the dark passageway.

The house was messy and dirty, and smelled of boiled milk and sour cabbage. There was a sewing machine on the table, scraps of material on the floor, and the wiring from the lamps to the radio was hung with socks. The man of the house was not at home. His wife, Marya, a tough swarthy wench with a firm backside, was squatting near the stove, her legs spread wide apart, rattling the oven prongs. Her face was flushed.

"Hello," Vasily said sullenly, taking off his cap. "Where's Danilich?"

"What's on your mind?" Marya asked just as sullenly, not looking up.

"I have some business with him."

"He's in the fields, went at daybreak."

"Will he be home soon?"

"He said for breakfast, but I don't know . . ."

"I'll wait then," Vasily said firmly, and sat down heavily on a bench facing the stove.

He got out some makhorka and would have liked to smoke, but Marya didn't like smoking in the house, so he put his pouch away. He didn't feel like smoking anyway. His body felt disgustingly weak, and his head was humming.

Vasily's head nodded and he became lost in thought. He thought about his wife dying soon, about having to build her a coffin, and about how it would be best to get good boards ahead of time. He'd have to kill the ram now because the in-laws would just love having it for the funeral feast.

Then he started thinking about selling the house and the garden plot, to whom and for how much, and where would he go then? First he'd go to his oldest daughter in Smolensk and from there he'd see. He'd saved some money, thank God; maybe he could look for a little house somewhere in town.

Then he began to pick out the most convincing things to say to the chairman so he would have no objections. Everything worked perfectly, in his mind; the chairman couldn't possibly have anything against it.

"Why did you come?" asked his hostess, putting the tongs in the corner and sitting down at the table.

Vasily was so absorbed that he didn't realize at once that he was being asked a question. Squinting as if he were only half awake, he looked at Marya's ruddy face, at her full lips, her impudent, slightly bulging, blue eyes.

"My wife's sick," he said at last. "I've come about a horse to take her to town. And then, some business of my own."

"How old is Akulina?" asked Marya without much interest.

"How old?" Vasily thought a minute. "Well, figure it out. I'm fifty-five and she's two years younger."

"Oh," was all she said.

She said nothing more for a while, absorbed in her own thoughts. Then she leaned over the sewing machine, bit off the thread, spread out the material and a steady even whirring filled the house.

Vasily closed his eyes again. He wanted to stretch out on the bench, cover his face, and not think about anything, just fall asleep. The thought of having to wait for the chairman, talk to him and prove that it was impossible for him to go on living on the collective farm, then of having to walk that foul road back to Mokhovatka, chilled and disgusted him. He felt a pain between his shoulder blades and the skin on his chest tightened.

Vasily was soon lost in the whir of the machine, not thinking a thing, and was startled when heavy footsteps sounded in the passageway and the owner of the house entered the room.

He had a strong build, and a small pale face covered with fuzzy whitish tufts, like the *skoptsy*.* He'd been on horseback, and as he leaned over to look at something out the window, he frowned and rubbed his thighs.

Vasily turned to look: a boy was leading a tall bony stallion with a clipped tail along the fence. The horse spread its legs apart and threw back its head.

"Well, how was it?" Marya asked loudly, going to the hearth and taking up the tongs again.

The chairman, still leaning over, turned his head in his wife's direction and started to say something, but seeing Vasily, stopped and offered him a cold, clammy hand. Then he crossed the room, heaved the sigh of a terribly tired man, and sat down, his back to the window, and began to pull off his boots.

Rubbing his bare feet, he looked at his wife, his face gradually taking on a private, drowsy expression. Vasily looked at Marya carefully as she moved the pots and pans on the stove, her powerful back straining, and thought in spite of himself, Pretty smooth, all right!

"Well, how are things with you?" asked the chairman. "You haying?"

"We are," Vasily answered quickly, looking away from Marya. "But we won't be able to finish any time soon. The rain came at

* Castration sect.

a bad time, everything's wet. And there aren't enough people. They're all sitting at home."

The chairman frowned. "What's the matter with that foreman of yours? How many times has it been said that we've got to get the hay in? Waiting until the rains came! Wait till I get to that foreman!"

The chairman looked at his wife and took a deep breath. Vasily coughed and squirmed on the bench.

"Ready soon?" the chairman asked his wife.

"On time," Marya answered absently.

Vasily was in agony. His host hadn't asked why he'd come and his request was an awkward one to initiate. All that phrasing that he'd figured out while he was waiting vanished suddenly, and he began to feel sick again. The important thing now was to get himself some hair of the dog and go to sleep.

"A correspondent from the regional paper and I looked over Bukatinsky field," said the chairman, brightening up. "The flax looks good. He promised to do a story on our girls."

Without turning around, he grabbed a crumpled ball of newspaper from the windowsill behind him, tore off a scrap, stretched out his right leg to get at his makhorka, and started to smoke.

"You don't say!" said Vasily as if he were amazed, hurriedly lighting up himself. "Doing a story! Well that's their business . . . stories."

"You're smoking me out," Marya said sulkily. Banging the door open, she went out into the yard.

"Why did you come to see me? What's your business?" asked the chairman, following his wife with his eyes, and smiling at Vasily.

Vasily shifted his legs, settled heavily, and bent his head.

"My wife's sick," he said. "I want to take her to town. But the road's so bad, the cars can't move. I need a horse, Danilich."

"A horse?" The chairman groaned and scratched his head. "Has she been to the medical center?"

"She has, but I think she needs an operation."

"All right, it's too late today, but I'll tell them tomorrow to give you a horse. You'll go in the morning."

"And my health has gotten kind of bad too," Vasily began again, pulling a long face. "Can't you drop in on me sometime?" he interrupted himself, remembering that such matters aren't settled without a drop of something to wet the throat. "I've got some home-brewed beer, my daughter sent me a package of sugar from town. Our beer's not so bad, pretty good in fact, my wife made it the other day, not bad at all. We also have some nice pork fat to go with it, eight pounds of it from the pig . . . Come on over!"

"I could probably do that," said the chairman, smiling.

"But I've decided, Danilich," Vasily took up again happily, "to leave the collective farm for good."

The chairman stopped smiling. "What do you mean by that?"

"Well this," said Vasily, looking away and gathering his courage. "Well this. I haven't any desire to work here any more. My wife's sick, my daughters write, they invite us. Why stay here? I decided a long time ago. The old chairman gave me permission, just ask anyone! Let other people work, I've had enough. I can always find myself some carpentry work in town. But here I can't."

"What do you mean can't?" The chairman looked at Vasily as if he were seeing him for the first time. "Have you forgotten the ruling of the board?"

"What do I care about the board?"

"Don't give me that. No work? This fall we're going to build a new cowbarn. Isn't that your work? Then we're going to do the club over. Isn't that work for you? And lay the forcing beds . . . that's not work?"

"That's true, but let others do it. Don't hold me. I'll go anyway. I know my rights."

"You know? And do you also know that there aren't enough people on the farm? Do you know that?"

"That doesn't concern me. It's your business to see that no one runs away from the collective farm. People don't run away from something good. But I want to live, I'm not such an old man that I have to lie on the stove to keep warm. What have I got from the collective farm? Culture? There's not even a place to drink!"

"You live badly, is that it?" The chairman's tone was vicious, his face beginning to go yellow. "You've killed yourself working I suppose?"

"Don't get smart with me," said Vasily, pulling his eyebrows. "Don't start getting snooty! I've gotten where I am by my own hard work. You're not going to get anything but snow out of this farm this winter!"

"So other people should work and struggle, but you're going to town?"

"My wife's dying!" Vasily's head was ringing and he caught his breath. "I have to get her to town. How can I?"

"We'll give you a horse." The chairman got up.

"Meaning you won't release me?" asked Vasily, also getting up.

"Have you gotten rich suddenly?"

"Oh I've got so much I don't know what to do with it."

"To be sure." The chairman gave a loud sigh. "A skilled workman can always make something extra. Build us a cowbarn, then a club, the seedbeds, and then we'll see."

"A cowbarn? What else do you want?" Vasily made an indecent gesture.

The chairman turned toward the window. "This conversation is finished. Now get out! You know the decision of the Party. Are you literate enough to read it? Well that's it. We'll call a board meeting, and talk about it there."

"All right," Vasily pulled his cap down over his eyes. "All right, you mother-f——. We'll see! We'll find a noose that fits around your neck!"

Slamming the door, he stumbled out into the passageway and lumbered across the porch. Snorting with shame, grinding his tar-stained teeth, he walked quickly down the street, scaring a chicken that had settled near the wattle fence.

"We had our talk, you mother-f——," he muttered, wiping his dripping face. "It was obviously no talk to have without a pint of something!"

The whole way home he was sorry that he'd come without that pint.

3

The next day, having been drinking his home brew since early morning, Vasily went to the horse barns and came back half an hour later on a horse. Tying the horse to the porch, he brought some hay from the yard, filled the cart and stamped it down, and as an afterthought, gave some to the horse. Then he went inside. He had decided the night before to kill the ram — it was market day in town and the ram had had a cough for the last two weeks.

Ordering Akulina to pack, he took his long narrow German knife and went out again. He had trouble getting the ram, an old black brute with a white spot on his neck, out of the shed. He held back, trembling, and wouldn't budge.

"You suspect something?" Vasily muttered, giving him a nasty smile. He rested a minute and then grabbed the warm twisted horn. The ram watched the open door gloomily.

"Well say your prayers," said Vasily, falling on the ram, digging his knees into his soft side, and grabbing the muzzle. The ram kicked and slipped free. Wheezing, Vasily got on top of him again, and twisted his head back until the white spot was exposed. Then clenching his teeth, he took aim, and plunged the knife with unnecessary force into the spot. The ram quivered and went soft under his knee. Red-black blood gushed from the gaping wound, covering the straw and manure, staining Vasily's hands.

A slight tremor ran over the body, the eyes flickered and went dark. The calf, coming out of its corner sniffing curiously, snorted suddenly and battered several times against the wall.

Vasily got up, threw away the knife, and carefully got out his tobacco pouch. Without taking his eyes off the ram, he rolled a cigarette in his bloody fingers, slobbering on the paper.

The ram twitched and stretched, his eyes completely closed now, his back legs pumping so hard that after a minute the whole body was moving rhythmically, as if it were running along gaily, scattering the straw and chicken mess.

When the ram had quieted, Vasily hung him on a rack and began to shear him quickly and accurately, cutting through the bluish skin to snip the leg tendons.

Cutting the steaming stomach open, he took out the warm liver, cut off a chunk and munched on it noisily, staining his lips and chin with blood.

Akulina came out on the porch in clean clothes, carrying a bundle. The bundle was a change of linen in case they put her in the hospital. Scrambling into the cart she opened her umbrella and waited for Vasily, looking around tenderly at the dark fields and the river below, as if she were saying a last farewell to her home and village.

A little later Vasily entered the yard, cradling the ram's sheared and bundled carcass.

Putting the ram in the front of the cart, he went to feed the livestock and lock the house. Akulina suddenly became aware of the sweetish scent of freshly killed meat. She'd always loved the smell. It always pervaded the farmhouses on holidays. But she didn't like it now, and she covered her nose and mouth with the edge of her scarf.

Having had a little more beer and locked the house, Vasily came out on the porch, tightening his belt. He'd shaved and washed that morning, and now he'd changed his shirt. He looked fresh and gay.

"Vasya!" said Akulina. "Look see, how pretty. I'll probably die in town. It's terrible to leave. My heart is heavy."

Vasily looked out at the dark haystacks, the black plowed fields, the river, the roofs of the village, dark with rain, and spat, and said nothing.

Then he untied and bridled the horse, forcing its lips open, straightened the hay in the cart, and sat down and flicked the reins. The horse was startled and jerked forward, and the cart swayed into the wide ruts.

Akulina sat behind, her hands across her chest, gripping her shoulders, looking tenderly at the houses on either side of her, at the birch trees, the ash trees already covered with saffron clusters.

She looked around and recalled her whole life spent on the collective farm: her youth, her marriage, her children, her love for everything growing stronger and sharper with the realization that she might never see her native village or her dear ones again. Tears streamed down her hollow cheeks. All she really wanted was to die at home and be buried in her own graveyard.

Some women passing at that moment in the street stopped and looked at her, silently nodding their heads. Akulina smiled a stiff embarrassed smile through her tears and nodded back, a nod so enthusiastic and low that her head nearly hit the edge of the cart.

Vasily urged the horse on. His ruddy face was strained with expectation and joy. He was thinking how he'd leave his wife at the hospital, go to the market, sell the ram, drop in on his relatives, and then go off to that restaurant near the station.

He'd sit there and drink a weak beer, and watch the trains passing outside the window. A waitress in a white apron and cap would wait on him, the orchestra would play, and there would be the smell of food and the smoke of good cigarettes.

And there in town, when he'd gotten his relatives' advice, he'd decide how to proceed, the easiest way to move from the collective farm to town, and how to get the best deal on the house and the garden plot.

Here Comes a Dog!

THE pale glow of the summer sunset had long since died out, the luminescent street lamps of cities deserted by the lonely hour had shot past and been left behind, and the bus escaped finally onto the broad flat highway. With a mournful, monotonous whir it tore along smoothly and triumphantly in the darkness, its windows whistling, rocking slightly on the curves, throwing its city and country lights far and wide.

In the beginning the passengers had talked, rustled their newspapers and magazines, and done some drinking — straight from the bottle — and eating and smoking. Then they began to settle down, adjusting their seats, leaning back, putting out their bright, milk-white reading lights, rolling their heads on the headrests, trying to get to sleep. In an hour or so, the warm, stuffy bus was dark. Only the blue floor lights on the aisle were still on. Beneath them hummed the oily highway and the crazily spinning wheels.

Only Krymov and his neighbor weren't sleeping.

Krymov, an engineer from Moscow, wasn't sleeping because he hadn't been away from Moscow in a long time and he was just too happy. He was happy because he was going to spend three days fishing in his own special, private place, because his rucksack and spinning reel were lying down below in the dark baggage compartment that smelled so strongly of apples, along with the rest of the suitcases and bags. He was happy finally because he'd be getting out at dawn at the fork in the highway, and he'd go through the wet meadow to the river where happiness awaited him — the brief happiness of a passionate fisherman.

Unable to sit still, he shifted around in his seat, looking out into the impenetrable darkness flying past, stretching his neck to peer over the driver's shoulder, past the windbreak, at the flatness of the highway.

His neighbor wasn't sleeping for some reason either. She was sitting quite still with her eyes closed but she was biting her lips, which in the darkness seemed almost black.

There was one other person on the bus who was not asleep — the driver. He was monstrously fat, hairy and unkempt, and his body bulged out fiercely through his clothes. Only his head was small, and so smoothly and lustrously combed on either side of his straight part that it glistened in the darkness. His powerful hairy arms, naked to the elbow, rested quietly on the steering wheel. He was as calm as Buddha himself, holding nothing higher than his passengers, his highway, his space. He was a dark silhouette against the pale lights on the dashboard and the light reflected from the road.

Krymov felt like smoking, but not wanting to disturb his neighbor, he decided not to go up ahead to the smoking section. He got out a cigarette, leaned over, and furtively snapped on his lighter. He inhaled deeply and a thin wisp of smoke disappeared in the darkness beneath his feet.

"Do you have a cigarette?" he heard his neighbor whisper. "I want a cigarette badly."

Krymov leaned toward her slightly as he got out another cigarette and as he did so looked at her face closely, but all he could see was a pale blotch, with dark holes for her lips and eyes, and straight hair falling to her shoulders. He gave her the cigarette and snapped the lighter again. She too smoked furtively, cupping the lighted cigarette in her hands, making them look transparent, but still Krymov could see nothing but a straight nose, her cheekbones, and soft eyelashes.

"Oh that tastes good," she said, inhaling and leaning toward him. "Is this an Aromatic? Thank you, they're strong."

She was wearing a strong sweet perfume, and there was something besides gratitude in her whisper, as if she were saying "Please talk to me, introduce yourself, I'm so bored." And Krymov was swept by the frivolous mood of the traveler, when one feels like talking playfully, dropping mysterious hints about oneself, when one's voice quivers in a pretense of great candor, when one's hand brushes one's neighbor's as if by accident, when in order to feel her hair on one's face, one pretends to look at something out the window, never quite managing to pull back.

His heart was pounding and his nostrils quivering when he remembered the deeper, ineradicable happiness that awaited him in the morning, and his passion subsided.

"This is nothing," he whispered with quite a different kind of animation. "You're not really smoking on a bus or at work at the plant. But in the morning, by the side of a river, you know, when the fish are jumping and you're not getting anything, and suddenly you get one! You pull it out, take out the hook, throw it on the grass, it flops around, ekh! That's when you have a smoke, a real smoke!"

"You're a fisherman?" she whispered.

"Inveterate fisherman." Krymov stretched and wrinkled his nose with pleasure. "I'm an engineer, months on end I don't see a river, thanks to my work — I'm in production, factory production, not one of your workshops, no sitting around. You want to know the last time I went fishing? In May! And it's now July. I'm a good worker, they depend on me, and when they finally gave me three days off it's an off season for fishing. Oh well, pretty soon I'll get my vacation, then I'll get my fill!"

"Where are you going?" she asked, and again Krymov sensed something strange in her whisper, some unasked question.

"Just to a little spot," he muttered evasively. He was superstitious about these things. "Why aren't you sleeping, do you get off soon?"

"I go to the end of the line. You say you have three days, when are you coming back?"

"Tuesday."

"Tuesday? Wait a minute, Tuesday." She thought, then sighed
and asked, "Why aren't you sleeping?"

"I have to get off at four o'clock." Krymov pushed up his jacket
sleeve and studied his watch. "Three hours to go. No, I don't
want to sleep. It's better not to, because then you're not sleepy
and drowsy when you're fishing."

The driver looked around, and then back at the road. He
seemed undecided about something. Then he cautiously put out
his hand and turned on the radio. It blared, and quickly turning
it down, the driver began switching to various stations. First one,
a second, and a third, all broadcasting either muffled foreign lan-
guages or else folk music, none evidently being to his taste. Finally
the weak sound of jazz rose up out of the noise and the
driver dropped his hand. He smiled so broadly that even from behind they could see his puffy cheeks moving out toward his ears.

It was a quiet, simple tune, with one melodic line shifting from
the piano to the saxophone, to the trumpet, to the electric guitar.
Krymov and his neighbor were silent, each listening attentively,
each thinking his own thoughts, each swaying in rhythm with
the bass.

From time to time they passed trucks parked by the side of the
road for the night, standing there strange and lonely and still. It
was as if something earth-shaking had happened and all the drivers
had gone off, leaving on only the tiny roof lights to burn as long
as the batteries held out.

Once in a while they passed other inter-city buses. Long before
they passed, a haze of light would quiver on the horizon, then a
twinkling point of light would appear in the distance, growing as
it came nearer, doubling and tripling until it became five powerful
headlights which would suddenly flash off and on again. The two
buses would slow down and stop. The drivers would lean out
and talk for a minute, the motors smoking in the slanting rays of
the headlights. Then the buses would lurch and a minute later

they'd be tearing along again in the darkness on different sides of the road.

I wonder where she's going, Krymov thought. I wonder if she's married. Why did she want a cigarette so badly? Just because or is she unhappy?

Then he forgot all about her and became absorbed in the road, the sunrise, and thoughts of the three days he would spend by the river. He was afraid his tent was beginning to leak, which would be bad if it rained, worried that the bus might be delayed for some reason and that he might miss the morning fishing.

He grew tired of these pleasant little problems and again his neighbor commanded his attention. She was quiet now, lying with her head back and her eyes closed. But whenever he looked straight ahead at the road for any length of time, it always seemed that when he turned back she was half turned toward him, and her half closed eyes were following him in the darkness.

Who is she? he wondered, but decided not to ask, trying instead to guess from some of the things she had whispered to him. He hadn't really looked at her earlier, because he hadn't been interested, but now he hoped that she was pretty.

"Let's have another cigarette," she whispered suddenly. "And talk to me. We might as well, we're not sleeping."

Krymov was surprised to feel a note of irritation in her voice, but docilely handed her a cigarette. What can I talk to her about? he wondered, slightly annoyed. She certainly is strange!

"I'm thinking about women," he said, "how you can not like hunting and fishing when it's such a great feeling! It's not only that you don't like them, you don't understand them and see no meaning in them whatsoever! Why is that?"

She shifted around in the darkness, pushed back her hair and wiped her forehead.

"Hunting is murder and a woman is a mother, so murder is doubly wrong. You say it's nice to watch a fish flop around, but I think it's horrid. But I understand, that is to say I understand that you don't hunt and fish out of cruelty. Tolstoy for example was tortured by the idea of death after he'd been hunting. And so was Prishvin . . ."

What's she talking about? he thought dejectedly, looking at his watch. "An hour and a half to go," he said happily.

His neighbor put out her cigarette, pulled up the collar of her raincoat, and leaned back, facing away from Krymov, tucking her legs up under her.

Sleepy, all of a sudden, he decided. Well it's about time. I don't like the kind of chitchat you have on the road! It's a good thing I'm not married, he thought suddenly. She'd have been like this one, pronouncing me a murderer, reading moral lectures . . . You'd go out of your mind!

But something was bothering him and though he put his mind on fishing, he couldn't feel the same tremendously deep joy he'd felt earlier.

Up ahead the driver leaned over, one hand on the wheel, and fished around on the floor without taking his eyes off the road. Then he straightened up, and began fussing with something on his knees, still holding the wheel with his left hand. Krymov watched him with interest. Then the driver put a bottle to his lips, threw back his head and drank. Then he sighed, threw back his head again and took another drink. Krymov could see his neck swelling and tightening as he swallowed.

What's that he's drinking? Krymov wondered. Beer maybe? No, he can't when he's driving. Oh, lemonade. Now if we can just go a little faster!

He remembered the mess tin and coffee in his rucksack and he suddenly longed for some coffee.

It was just beginning to get light, but the foliage on the trees was still dark, and the few houses that flashed by in the fields seemed startlingly white by contrast. Krymov's mouth was dry from smoking and he was thirsty but his mood improved when he managed to stop thinking about his neighbor. He thought about his place by the river, about the mist on the river. He craned his neck to look at the road up ahead.

The driver put off the headlights and they could see the sun coming up. From minute to minute it grew lighter, and everything came sharply into focus, the mileage markers, the signboards, the road signs, even the western horizon.

They'd passed the 250-mile mark when the driver turned and looked inquiringly at Krymov. Then he nodded. A minute later he decelerated and turned onto the side of the road. Turning his head abruptly, he ran his eyes over the meadow. About seven hundred yards from the highway stood a black line of willow trees.

In low gear now, the bus went slower and slower, the hum of the tire treads deepening and quieting to a mutter, and then dying out. Only the crunch of the sand under the wheels bespoke the fact that the bus was still moving. Everything was quiet. The driver dropped his hands from the wheel and stretched luxuriously, running his hands over his body. Then he yawned and opened the door. He got off and began rattling around underneath in the baggage compartment.

"Excuse me," said Krymov, getting up quickly and tapping his neighbor's shoulder.

"What?" She jumped. "Already? You're getting off? Good luck! What do you say, 'three bags full'!"

Three bags full of bad luck! Krymov said to himself superstitiously, and went up forward. The first thing he looked at when he jumped off was the meadow, and then he turned back to the bus. It was standing, long and enormous and dusty, its overheated tires and motor sending warmth into the morning chill. The baggage compartment on the right side was open. Moving aside suitcases and bags, Krymov found his rucksack, and finally, his rod, and the driver slammed the compartment shut and locked it. Then he went around the front of the bus and disappeared in the woods.

"So here's your little spot!" a voice came from behind him. Krymov turned and saw his neighbor. She'd gotten out and was standing by the bus, pushing back her hair, looking across the meadow. She was pretty and reminded him of some movie actress, but Krymov had had enough of her already.

"Well give me a last cigarette," she said, coming up with an embarrassed laugh. "You were awfully good to put up with me. I was torturing you with requests all night!"

When she bent over the lighter, her hands and lips were trembling so that she couldn't get the tip of the cigarette to the flame. What's the matter with her, Krymov wondered, glancing at his rucksack. Perhaps I'd better go.

"You're lucky," she said, looking around appreciatively. "You'll have three days of peace and quiet." She stopped and listened, picking some tobacco from her lips. "The birds are up. Do you hear them? And I have to go to Pscov."

Should I go or not? he thought, without listening to her. Leaving now would be awkward. I'll wait until the bus leaves, they can't be staying here long, he decided and lit a cigarette.

"So," he said, in order to say something.

"You know, I've often dreamt of living in a tent. Do you have a tent?" she asked, looking at Krymov sideways. And suddenly her face was sad, the corners of her mouth turned down and trembling. "But I'm a city girl, and it's just never worked out."

"Hmmm," said Krymov without looking at her, squinting down the empty highway toward the woods where the driver had disappeared.

She turned, frowning and sighing, and bit her lips as she threw away her cigarette.

At that moment a dog came out of the bushes by the side of the road and ran along the highway, crossing it at an oblique angle. The dog's curly coat was wet with dew on his stomach and paws. The dew on its muzzle and whiskers glistened in the light from the east.

"Here comes a dog!" said Krymov absently, not thinking about anything in particular. "Here comes a dog," he repeated in a slow singsong, the way one repeats a line of a poem that comes back out of nowhere.

Businesslike and purposeful, the dog ran without looking to either side. It was so quiet they could hear the click of its claws on the asphalt.

Finally the driver came out of the woods, and back onto the highway. He whistled to the running dog, but it didn't come. As he approached the bus, he looked as if he were seeing it for the first time. His boots were covered with dew, and there was even dew on his hairy arms. He stamped his feet noisily, shaking off the dew, and went around the bus, checking the tires. Then he climbed aboard.

"Well, thanks for the cigarettes," the girl said, climbing on.

"Good luck," Krymov muttered, stooping for his rucksack.

The motor roared, the bus lurched, and he caught a glimpse in the light of that unhappy face looking at him for the last time. Giving a feeble wave, he smiled vaguely, climbed down the embankment and set off for the river.

Here comes a dog, here comes a dog, he sang to himself as he crossed the meadow, matching the rhythm of the words to his footsteps.

He stared at the sky and the glistening meadow in childish delight, filling his lungs with air. Only one thing worrying him now: someone might already have beaten him to his place.

When he reached the river he jumped down the low bank onto the sand and looked around anxiously. There wasn't a single footstep in the sand. The shaded, narrow river, full of rocks and pools and sandbars, was winding lazily around the meadow.

Krymov quickly unpacked his rucksack and got out his coffee, mess tin, and sugar. He scooped up some water, collected some dry kindling and started a small fire. Then he drove two spikes into the sand, hung up his mess tin, and sat down to wait.

There was the smell of smoke, and the wet riverbanks, and the distant smell of hay. Krymov sat, frightened by his own happiness.

He couldn't have imagined being so happy about the morning, the river, about the fact that he was alone.

Coffee first, and then cast, he decided, and began oiling his reel, watching the river and keeping an eye on the fire at the same time. The water in the mess tin was just beginning to boil.

"Here comes a dog!" he intoned repeatedly. "Here comes . . . Coffee now, cast later . . ."

A pike splashed loudly in the reeds on the other side of the river. Krymov jumped up, perspiring, and located the spot instantly. Great rings were circling out into the water.

No, cast now, coffee later, he decided, threading his line and attaching his favorite lure, a silver one with a red feather. The pike splashed again in another place, and a little roach skittered along the bank.

Wait a minute, wait just one minute, he thought triumphantly. Here comes a dog, and he fastened the reel to the rod.

The water in the mess tin was boiling, bubbling and hissing over the edge, raising a cloud of steam. Krymov looked at it, and took it off, licking his dry lips. Hell, at least I can have some coffee, he thought, squinting vigilantly at the river and opening the coffee can. He stuck his nose inside, took a sniff, and sneezed.

"Ekh, you," he said aloud, and laying his rod across his knees, he began to make coffee.

The sun rose higher and higher, constantly changing the colors in the reeds; tendrils of mist swam over the water, and the leaves glistened as if they'd been lacquered. Back in the meadow and close by in the willows, birds were darting around, singing their various songs. The first breath of a wind rustled through the reeds, bringing the warm, bittersweet scent of the woods.

Krymov was totally happy.

He fished all day, reveling in his solitude, and went to sleep in his tent. But he woke up suddenly in the night for some reason, so he started a fire and made coffee, whistling as he waited for the sun to come up. The next day he went swimming and he swam to the other side and climbed in the reeds, breathing in the smells of the swamp. Then he dove back in and bathed. When he was worn out, he lay blissfully in the sun to dry.

So he spent three days and two nights. On the evening of the third day, sunburned and thin and light on his feet, with two pike in his rucksack, he went back to the highway, lit a cigarette, and waited for the bus to Moscow. He sat leaning against his rucksack, his legs spread apart, happy and at peace. He looked across the meadow for the last time, at the tops of the willow trees in the distance, and imagined the river, flowing quietly under the willow branches, and it occurred to him that it had now become a permanent part of his life.

Trucks, milk trucks, enormous gray refrigerator vans bearing the "Volga" make, tore past him down the highway, red in the setting sun. Krymov watched them contentedly, looking forward already to city life, lights, newspapers, work, imagining the hot greasy smell of the factory tomorrow, the noise of the machines, and thinking about his friends.

Then he thought vaguely about getting off here at sunset three days before. He recalled his traveling companion and how her lips and hands had trembled as she tried to light a cigarette.

"What was the matter with her?" he muttered, and suddenly he caught his breath. Prickly heat passed over his face and through his chest. He felt suffocated and vile, his heart was tight with pain.

"Ai-ai-ai!" he muttered, spitting. "Ai-ai-ai! How could I? What kind of a rat am I? Ai-ai-ai!"

Something large and beautiful and melancholy hung suspended over him, over the fields and the river, a thing of excellence, remote, but full of understanding and pity.

"I'm nothing but a rat!" Krymov groaned, breathing hard and rubbing his sleeve. "Ai-ai-ai!" And he beat his knees painfully with his knuckles.

Morning Calm

THE roosters had just begun to crow sleepily, the house was still dark, his mother had not yet milked the cow, and the herd had not been driven to pasture when Yashka woke up.

He sat for a long time on the bed, staring at the steamy, pale blue windows and the gradually emerging gray shape of the stove. Sleep is sweet just before dawn, and Yashka let his head roll back on the pillow, hardly able to keep his eyes open. But he pulled himself together, and began to stumble around the room, hanging on to the benches and chairs, looking for his old pants and shirt.

Yashka ate some bread and milk and taking his fishing rod, went out on the porch. Fog had wrapped itself around the village like a great feather quilt. The nearest houses were visible, the ones beyond them just dark patches, and farther on, near the river, nothing was visible at all. It was as if the windmill on the hill, the fire tower, the school, and the woods on the horizon had never existed. Everything had hidden and disappeared, and Yashka's house seemed to be the center of a secluded little world.

Someone had gotten up earlier than Yashka, because there was hammering down at the blacksmith's; the sharp metallic sounds cut their way through the foggy shroud all the way up to the invisible granary and came back again faintly. It seemed as if there were two people hammering, one loudly, one softly.

Yashka jumped down off the porch, shook his rod at the rooster that ran between his legs, and trotted cheerfully to the granary. There he found a rusty knife and began digging. He turned up some clammy red and violet worms almost immediately. Whether they were fat or thin, they were equally prompt in getting back underground, but Yashka managed to grab them and nearly fill a can. Covering them with dirt, he ran down the path, fell over the wattle fence and raced to the shed where his new friend Volodya was sleeping in the hay loft.

Yashka put two dirty fingers in his mouth and whistled. Then he spat and listened. All was quiet.

"Volodka," he called, "get up!"

Volodya stirred in the hay, moving and fussing around for a long time, and finally slid down clumsily, tripping over his untied shoelaces. His face, rumpled with sleep, was as blank and lifeless as the faces of the blind. There was hay in his hair and, evidently, down his back, because he kept pulling at his scrawny neck, twitching his shoulders and scratching his back.

"Aren't you early?" he rasped through a yawn, and swaying, caught himself on the ladder.

Yashka was irritated. He'd gotten up a whole hour earlier, dug for worms, collected the rods, and this skinny runt was the sole reason he'd done any of it, if truth be told, so he could show him the fishing spots, and instead of enthusiasm and gratitude, "You're early!"

"For some it's early, some late," he answered sourly, looking Volodya up and down contemptuously.

Volodya looked outside and brightened up a bit, his eyes shining as he began hurriedly to tie his shoes. But the morning had already been spoiled for Yashka.

"You're going to wear shoes?" he asked scornfully, studying the big toe on his bare foot. "Galoshes too maybe?"

Volodya didn't answer, blushing as he set to work on his other shoe.

"Well of course," Yashka continued, venting his spleen, leaning the rods against the wall. "At home in Moscow I guess you don't go barefoot."

"So what?" Volodya looked up at Yashka's wide, nasty grin.

"So nothing. Run home and get your coat."

"All right I will!" Volodya said through his teeth and got even redder.

Yashka felt depressed. There'd been no reason to get mixed up in this thing. Kolka and Yenka Voronkov — professional fishermen — already admitted that there was no better fisherman on the collective farm than Yashka. Just show Yashka the place and it was like shaking apples from a tree! So this kid came up yesterday so polite, "Please, please . . ." What should he have done, hit him or something? So he'd had to get mixed up with this city boy who'd probably never seen a fish, and was going fishing in his shoes!

"And put on a tie," Yashka taunted with a hoarse laugh. "Our fish get insulted if you come without a tie."

Volodya finished at last with his shoes and left the shed, staring blindly straight ahead, his nostrils quivering with resentment. He was ready to call off the whole thing and burst into tears, but he'd waited so long for this morning! With Yashka dragging along behind him, the boys walked down the street without saying anything or looking at each other. As they walked through the village, the fog backed up, revealing more and more houses, the shed, the school, and long rows of milk-white farm buildings. Like a stingy host, it revealed all this just for a minute, and then closed in behind them.

Volodya was miserable. He was angry with himself for the way he'd answered Yashka and for having been awkward and pathetic, and angry with Yashka. Trying to quench his unpleasant feelings in bitterness, he said to himself, All right, I'll show them if they make fun of me. I won't let them laugh. Big deal — going barefoot! It takes a lot of imagination! But at the same time he was looking with candid admiration and envy at Yashka's bare feet and his canvas fishing bag and his patched fishing pants and gray shirt. He also envied Yashka his sunburn and the special way he walked, with his shoulders, shoulder blades and even his ears swinging, considered especially chic among the village boys.

They passed an old green well.

"Stop," muttered Yashka, "let's have a drink."

He went to the well, grabbed the chain, brought up a heavy bucket of water and raised it greedily to his lips. He wasn't particularly thirsty, but there was no better water anywhere to his mind, so every time he passed, he drank some with enormous pleasure. The water spilled over the edge of the bucket and splashed his bare feet. He curled up his toes, but went on drinking and drinking in great noisy gulps.

"Here, have a drink," he said to Volodya at last, wiping his lips on his sleeve.

Volodya wasn't thirsty either, but in order not to anger Yashka any further, accepted the bucket and meekly took a few swallows, the nape of his neck contracting with the cold.

"Well, how was it?" Yashka asked confidently, when Volodya turned away from the well.

"Pretty good," replied Volodya, shivering.

"It probably isn't that good in Moscow, is it?" asked Yashka, screwing up his eyes nastily.

Volodya said nothing, taking a breath through clenched teeth, and giving him a conciliatory smile.

"Have you ever been fishing?" asked Yashka.

"No, I've just seen them fishing on the Moscow River," Volodya admitted quietly and threw Yashka a timid glance.

The confession softened Yashka a little. Rubbing the can of worms, he said casually, "Our gang saw a sheat fish in Pleshanski pond yesterday."

Volodya's eyes lit up. "A big one?"

"You bet! Two yards long, maybe even three. It was hard to tell in the dark. The gang got frightened, thought it was a crocodile. Do you believe me?"

"You're kidding!" Volodya sighed rapturously, clasping his shoulders; it was evident from his eyes that he believed it absolutely.

"You think I'm kidding?" Yashka was astounded. "If you want, we can go tonight. What do you say?"

"Can we?" Volodya asked hopefully, his ears reddening.

"Why not?" Yashka spat and wiped his nose on his sleeve. "I've got the tackle. We'll get sea devils, loach, there's even some chub there still. Two o'clock this morning, we can grub for crawlers, build a fire. You coming?"

Volodya suddenly felt extraordinarily happy. At last he could appreciate how good it is to get up early. How glorious and easy it is to breathe. How he wanted to run full steam ahead down the road, jumping and yelling for joy!

What was that funny tinkling sound behind them? What was that sharp musical sound in the meadow suddenly that sounded like a thin string being plucked again and again? When had this happened to him before? Maybe it hadn't. But why did this feeling of joy and happiness seem so familiar then?

What was sputtering so loud in the field? Motorcycles? Volodya looked questioningly at Yashka.

"That's a tractor," Yashka said importantly.

"A tractor? Why is it sputtering?"

"He's fixing something. It'll be going soon. Listen. There! You hear? It's running. There, it's going. That's Fedya Kostilev. He's been plowing all night. Took a short snooze and back to work."

Volodya looked in the direction of the tractor. Then he asked, "Do you always have fogs like this?"

"No, sometimes it's clear. Later on, toward September, you'll really see some fog. Go fishing then, and you really pull them in!"

"What kind of fish?"

"What kind? All kinds. There's carp, and pike . . . let's see. Perch, roach, bream. And tench. You know what tench is? Tastes like pork. And fat! The first time I saw one, I really gawked!"

"Can you get big ones?"

"It depends. One time you'll get ten pounds and the next time just enough for the cat."

"What's whistling?" Volodya stopped to look up.

"That? A flight of teal. They're ducks."

"Uh-huh, I know. And that?"

"Thrush. They're in the mountain ash in Auntie Nasta's garden. Have you ever trapped a thrush?"

"Never."

"Mishka Kayunenok has a net, you wait, we'll go trapping. Thrushes are greedy birds. They can fly over a field and get worms out from under a tractor. Stretch a net in an ash tree, hide somewhere, and wait. You'll have five of them in your net before you know it. Stupid things. But there are some that are sensible. I had one this winter that could do anything. It took water like a steam engine."

The village was soon behind them, the low-lying oat fields stretched out endlessly all around, and they could barely make out the dark rim of the forest up ahead.

"Is there still a long way to go?" asked Volodya, several times.

"We'll be there soon, it's right nearby. Let's walk faster," Yashka answered each time.

They climbed a hill, turned right, dropped down into a hollow, took a path through a flax field, and suddenly, the river opened up before them. It was not a large river, with shrubs and willows growing thickly along its banks, rushing noisily over the shoals and spilling over into deep dark pools.

The sun had finally come up; a horse whinnied softly in the meadow, and suddenly everything around grew light and warm; the dew was distinct on the fir trees, but the fog was on the move, thinning out, reluctantly revealing the haystacks standing dark against the smoky background of the woods. The fish were running. Heavy splashing could be heard in the pools, and the disturbed water lapped along the banks.

Volodya was ready to start right in fishing, but Yashka kept on walking along the bank. They were wet to the waist with dew when Yashka finally whispered "Here!" and climbed down to the water. As he stepped, he accidentally sent a wet clod of earth rolling down the bank and some ducks flew out of their hiding place, one after the other, flapping their wings, over the river and into the fog. Yashka slid down and hissed like a goose. Volodya wet his dry lips and slid down after him. Looking around, he was struck by the gloom reigning at the pond. It smelled damp, muddy, slimy; the water was black; the willows nearly blotted out the sky with their wild growth. Up in the meadow where the sun had warmed things up, the blue sky was shining through the fog, but here by the water, it was damp and gloomy and cold.

"You know how deep it is here?" Yashka rolled his eyes. "There's no bottom."

Volodya drew back a little and shivered. A fish jumped on the opposite side.

"No one around here will swim in this pond."

"Why not?" Volodya asked in a faint voice.

"It sucks you under. Just put your feet in and it's all over. The water is like ice, and pulls you right down. Mishka Kayunenok says there are octopuses down there."

"Octopuses are . . . only in the ocean," Volodya said hesitantly and drew back farther.

"I know that, only in the ocean. But Mishka saw one! He was going fishing, goes past here, he looks, a tentacle is sticking out of the water and groping around the bank. Mishka ran all the way to the village. He was probably lying though. I know him." Yashka finished abruptly, and began unpacking the rods.

Volodya cheered up, and Yashka, the octopuses already forgotten, was looking impatiently at the water. His face wore a strained and tragic expression every time a fish splashed.

He unreeled the rods, handed one to Volodya, poured some worms into a matchbox, and nodded toward the place where Volodya should fish.

Yashka cast, and holding the rod in both hands, stared impatiently at the cork. Volodya cast right after him but got his rod caught in the branches. Yashka gave Volodya a dirty look, and cursed him in a whisper. When he turned back to his own cork, all he could see were little concentric rings moving out into the water. He tightened the line immediately, and moved his hand gently to the right, enjoying the elastic pull of the fish down below. Then the line slackened and he yanked an empty hook from the water. Yashka trembled with rage.

"Got away, eh? Got away did you?" he hissed, his wet fingers slipping a new worm on the hook.

He cast again, and fixing his eye on the cork, he gripped the rod firmly, expecting a bite. But there was no bite, and there was no more splashing to be heard. Pretty soon his hand grew tired and he carefully ran the rod into the wet bank. Volodya watched Yashka and ran his rod into the bank also.

The sun had finally risen high enough to peep into their gloomy fishing hole. The water began to sparkle blindingly. Drops of dew shone on the leaves, the grass, and the flowers.

Volodya frowned at his cork, then he turned and asked uncertainly, "Maybe the fish have gone to some other hole?"

"That's for sure!" Yashka snorted. "The one that got away scared all the rest. And it was such a good one. My arm was almost pulled off. It could have weighed at least two pounds."

Yashka was ashamed of letting the fish get away, but being human was inclined to ascribe the blame to Volodya. Give me a real fisherman, he thought. Fish alone or with a real fisherman. That's the only way. He was going to pick on Volodya, but suddenly reached for his rod instead. The cork had moved slightly. Pulling hard, as if he were pulling a tree out by the roots, he slowly pulled the rod out of the bank, and picked it up, balancing it carefully. The cork tipped again, and went over on its side, where it stayed for a moment before righting itself. Yashka took a deep breath, and squinting, he saw Volodya getting up, looking quite pale.

Yashka was hot, drops of sweat rolled down his nose and upper lip. The cork quivered again, went halfway under on its side, and finally disappeared, disturbing the water ever so slightly. For the second time Yashka moved forward, tightening the line, trying to straighten the rod. The cork quivered, and the line traced a curve. Yashka got up, took the rod in his other hand, and when it gave a strong jerk, he moved his hand to the right. Volodya was at his side, his round eyes wide with despair, calling in a thin little voice, "Come on, come on, come *on!*"

"Get away!" rasped Yashka, and took several steps backwards.

Just then the fish leaped out of the water, flashed on its side, slapped its tail, raising a pink fountain of water, and darted back into the cold depths. Yashka, the rod jammed into his stomach, stepped all the way back and shouted, "Get away I said!"

Finally he brought the tired fish to shore, jerked it out onto the grass, and fell down on top of it. Volodya's mouth was dry, his heart pounding furiously.

"What have you got?" he asked, squatting down. "Show me, what is it?"

"A *bream!*" Yashka's voice was ecstatic.

Cautiously pulling the large wet fish out from under his stomach, he turned his broad happy face toward Volodya, and started to laugh, but suddenly his smile faded. He was staring horrified at something in back of Volodya. He jumped up, shouting, "The rod! Look!"

Volodya turned and saw that his rod was slowly slipping off a clump of earth into the water. The line was caught on something. He jumped up, stumbled, and reaching for the rod on his knees, managed to grab it. He turned his round pale face to Yashka.

"Hold on!" Yashka shouted.

But at that moment the ground under Volodya slipped; he lost his balance and dropped the rod, his hands clasped together incongruously as if he were catching a ball. Then he yelled and fell into the water.

"You fool!" cried Yashka. "You bungling idiot!" He jumped up and grabbed a clump of earth, ready to throw it at Volodya when he surfaced. But as he watched the water he suddenly froze, experiencing that exhausting sensation of a dream: three yards from shore, his arms thrashing in the water, his pale face thrown back, his eyes bulging, Volodya was gulping and going under. He tried to shout something, but all that came out was a gurgled "waaah."

He's drowning! Yashka thought, horrified. Dropping the clump of grass and wiping his sticky hands on his pants, he backed away from the water, feeling weak in the knees. Suddenly Mishka's story about the enormous octopuses on the bottom of the pool came back to him, and his chest and stomach went cold with terror: an octopus must have Volodya. The ground slipped under his feet. In a dreamlike trance, he climbed slowly up the bank without turning around, hanging on with trembling hands.

Pursued by Volodya's terrifying sounds, he ran through the meadow toward the village, but after about ten feet he stopped as abruptly as if he had fallen. Running away was out of the question. No one was around, no one to call to for help. Yashka searched convulsively through his pockets and bag for some kind of tow line; finding none, he inched, white-faced, back to the fishing hole. When he reached the bank, he looked down, hoping that everything would be all right, but expecting the worst. Volodya was almost completely submerged, with only the top of his bristly head showing. He was no longer thrashing. The head went under and came up, went under and came up. Without taking his eyes off the bristly head, Yashka undid his pants, yelled, and slid down. Pantsless but still dressed in his shirt with his bag slung across his shoulders, he jumped into the water. In two strokes he had reached Volodya and grabbed his hand.

Volodya clung to him, pawing him, grasping his shirt and bag, and pulled him down, all the while giving out that terrible inhuman sound, "waaah, waah." Water rushed into Yashka's mouth.

Aware that he was caught in a deadly grasp, he tried to get his face
out of the water, but Volodya was all over him, trembling, trying
to get on his shoulders, weighing him down. Choking, coughing,
gasping, gulping, Yashka saw red and yellow circles blaze up
with blinding strength before his eyes, and he became terror-
stricken. He realized that Volodya was drowning him, that this
was death. Gathering his remaining strength, with a noise as inhuman as Volodya's, he floundered, kicked Volodya in the stomach
and surfaced. Through the water streaming down his face, he saw
the bright flattened ball of the sun. Throwing off Volodya, he beat
the water to foam with his arms and legs and made for shore.

And only when he had hold of the weeds on the bank did he
come to his senses and look back. The churning water settled, and
there was no one on the surface. From land came several sprightly
puffs of wind, and Yashka's teeth chattered. He looked around:
the sun was bright, the leaves on the shrubs and willows
were glistening, a spider was happily sunbathing in the flowers.
A beaver sat up on a log, swinging its tail and looking glassily at
Yashka, and everything was as always, everything breathed of
peace and quiet, the calm of the morning was on the land, but for
all this, just now something horrible had happened — a person
had just drowned and it was he — Yashka who had drowned him.

Yashka blinked. Letting go of the weeds, he hunched his
shoulders under his wet shirt, took a deep fluttery breath, and
dove. Opening his eyes under water, all he could make out were
the vague greenish yellowish patches of weeds and light flickering
all around him. But down there — in the depths — the sun did
not penetrate at all. Yashka went deeper, swam a bit farther and
saw Volodya. He was lying on his side, one leg caught in the
weeds, his body slowly rocking, his round white face turned to the
sun, his hand moving as if he were groping his way along in the
water. It occurred to Yashka that Volodya might be pretending, lur-
ing him on so he could grab him when he caught up.

Completely winded, he made for Volodya, grabbed his hand,

closed his eyes, and quickly dragged Volodya's body to the surface. He was amazed how obediently it followed him. He surfaced and took a frantic breath, nothing mattering now but breathing and feeling his lungs fill up, breath after breath, with the wondrously clean, sweet air.

Hanging on to Volodya's shirt, he began to drag him to shore. It was tough going. Feeling bottom, he dragged himself and Volodya out, wincing at the touch of the cold body and the sight of the dead still face, feeling so tired, so unhappy . . .

Turning Volodya on his back, he began pumping his arms, punching his stomach, breathing in his mouth. He grew faint and out of breath, but Volodya was still cold and white. *He's dead,* he thought, overcome by terror. He wanted to run somewhere and hide, anything not to see that cold blank face.

With a sob of horror, Yashka jumped up and grabbed Volodya by the legs. With as much strength as he had left, his face turning purple with the strain, he began to shake him. Volodya's head knocked against the ground, his hair dragging in the mud. And just at the moment when Yashka, totally exhausted and out of breath, was about to drop him and run away, at that very moment, water gushed out of Volodya's mouth, he groaned, and his body moved convulsively. Yashka dropped Volodya's legs, closed his eyes, and sat down.

Volodya raised himself weakly into a kind of runner's crouch, and fell back again, coughing convulsively, spewing out water and writhing on the wet grass. Limply, Yashka crawled over and looked at Volodya. There was no one on earth he loved better than Volodya, nothing dearer than this pale frightened, anguished face. A gentle loving smile lit up Yashka's eyes as he watched Volodya, asking tenderly over and over again, "How are you, huh? How?"

Volodya recovered a bit, wiped his face, looked at the water, and stammered in an unnatural, hoarse, but remarkably strong voice, "How did I . . . go under?"

Yashka closed his eyes, squeezing back the tears that were pouring down his face, and started to sob: sob bitterly, inconsolably, his whole body shaking, choking in embarrassment. He was sobbing for joy, for what he had been through, that everything was all right, that Mishka Kayunenok was a liar and that there were no octopuses at the bottom of the pond.

Volodya's eyes darkened, his mouth gaped slightly as he stared at Yashka, bewildered and frightened.

"What's . . . wrong?" he groaned.

"I . . ." Yashka said carefully, wiping his face on his pants, and trying not to cry, "you were duh-drowning and I . . . had to . . . to save you . . ."

And he began to sob louder and more desperately.

Volodya blinked and frowned. Looking again at the water, his heart caught, and he remembered.

"I almost dud-drowned!" he exclaimed and burst into tears, clasping his thin shoulders, helplessly dropping his head and turning away from his savior.

The water in the pond had long since settled, the fish on Volodya's line had gotten away, the rod was floating by the bank. The sun was shining, the bushes were glistening with dew, and only the pondwater was still black.

The air had warmed up and the horizon shimmered in the warm currents. Far off, from the fields, from across the river, came gentle gusts of wind, smelling of hay and sweet clover. These smells, blending with the sharper, more distant smells of the woods, and the light warm wind were like the breath of an awakening earth, awakening and rejoicing in a bright new day.

The House under the Hill

BLOKHIN arrived in the regional seat just before dark. He got out of the car at the regional committee building and looked around. A light snow was falling, the street lamps weren't yet on, but from lighted windows the dark street was streaked with long, yellowish bands of light.

Having inquired of a passerby about a hotel, Blokhin went down a narrow little street and wandered around for a long time among the squat, bargelike buildings before finally finding the hotel, and knocked. Someone came down the stairs, but the door did not open. To Blokhin's inquiry about a bed, the person replied after a pause, "There isn't anything."

"Then where can you spend the night?" Blokhin asked, glaring at the dull gleam on the ancient copper doorknob. "And open the door!"

There was no answer. The person behind the door went back upstairs, the stairs creaking as he climbed, and Blokhin reflected nastily that he must be a very fat man.

Leaving the hotel, he brushed the snow off a stone, sat down, and thought his situation over. He had come to this little place from Moscow. Never having traveled much, he'd been too excited and happy and full of plans to sleep en route. From the railway station, it was still forty miles by car, and he had had to spend half a day at the station looking for a car going in his direction. He'd finally found one and here he was, tired, desperate, with no idea of what to do or where to go. His feet were beginning to freeze when he decided to hail down a passing girl. She listened to him in thoughtful silence and then led him down through some dark alleys lined with snow-covered houses and up a hill.

They soon found themselves in the warm and lighted House of Culture. It was noisy. Children were tearing around in the hall, peeping out of every doorway. Upstairs a wind orchestra was practicing, loud and shrill. A girl scurried into one of the rooms and pretty soon a man with a splendid beard came out into the hall, dressed like an old merchant, a great watch chain across his chest. The children stopped everything at once and threw themselves all over him.

"You want a room?" the man asked in a youthful voice, pulling at his beard and frowning. "If you'll wait just a minute, I'll take you."

He pulled off his beard, shook his fist at the children, and disappeared. Five minutes later he was back, dressed in a coat. He turned out to be a ruddy young man.

"Let's get out of here," he said with a mock sigh of relief. Blokhin decided this strange, pleasant little town would be an easy place to live in.

The young man led him past some wooden fences, a stone wall, a tea shop where some frostbitten horses were standing in the snowy hay, past some white houses with dark windows, telling him as they went along, boots squeaking in the snow, "The house is down there, right near the river. The room is nothing in particular, it's livable and all that, but the owner is a problem."

"How so?" asked Blokhin.

"Well . . . but you probably won't be here long, will you? This was just some business between me and her. You won't have any problem. Just pay her and don't bother her, and that will be that."

"Is it a private room?"

"Private. Are you here on a job?"

"Practical training."

"Practical training? In the House of Culture by any chance?"

"No, the library."

"Oh, too bad. Or I might have done something for you. Your bag heavy? Let me carry it."

"I'm all right, thanks. Anyone else live in the house?"

"A daughter."

"That's interesting. Is she young?"

"The daughter?" The young man was silent a minute. "She's young. Very young."

So that's it, thought Blokhin. A young girl. He probably went after her without any luck. And he began to feel happy and curious: he was going to a house where a young girl was living.

They went down into a ravine, through some black, sparsely scattered trees, turned left, and walked along under the overhanging precipice. To the right of them were shuttered houses, light gleaming here and there through the shutters, and beyond the houses, though they couldn't see it, they could sense the vast expanse of the snowy river.

"This is Landslide Street, so called," the young man explained. "The sides of the hill are always slipping, but these people go right on living here. They just close their shutters. As soon as it gets the least bit dark, they close their shutters. These people! The old devils all have their own wells. And they all have coffins and crosses stored in their sheds. They're afraid of rotting when they die, so they make sure they'll be in their own private grave under their own private cross."

"That's very interesting."

"Interesting to some people," the young man growled. He led Blokhin up to a large house with a high front porch. One half the house was dark, in the other half a soft light was shining in the window, lighting up a low-lying fence, its posts capped with little hats of snow.

"Well, there it is. I'll be going now. If it doesn't work out, drop back at the House of Culture, maybe we can fix you up. Drop around anyway, ask for Kolya Balaev. They all know me."

He began to whistle softly and long after he had disappeared into the darkness his whistling could still be heard. Looking around the porch, Blokhin found a broom and cleared the snow away. Then he knocked.

The door was opened by a girl in a dressing gown with a turned-up hem and rolled sleeves. She was breathing hard, her arms were dirty, and there was a lock of hair sticking to her face. Seeing Blokhin, she caught her breath, quickly checked her dressing gown, pushed her hair back and let him into the kitchen. For some reason she took a long time locking the door.

"Talk to Mama," she interrupted him in a tremulous voice when he started to explain, and with a deep blush she hurried out of the room.

Her mother came in, a thin woman with tight lips and a defeated expression. She looked as if something unhappy had just that minute happened to her.

"A room? We'll give you a room. Take a look." She opened a glass door and turned on the light. "It's a good room, a wonderful room, very clean. You single or married?"

"Single."

"A professor lived here last year. Before him, two engineers. It's a good room, warm . . ."

The room was cold and empty and smelled stale. Blokhin frowned.

"You're what . . . here for a long time?" the woman asked guardedly.

"For a month," Blokhin answered shortly, feeling a growing dislike for his hostess, and thinking about the girl who had opened the door.

"This room's a wonderful room, quiet. Just like a house in the country."

"How much do you want?"

"Well the Professor paid two hundred rubles. And he was almost never home."

"Two hundred?" Blokhin repeated with a frown. That was expensive.

"Not including firewood," she added hastily. "Are you going to be using firewood? Then I'll need more. With firewood, it'll cost a kopeck more. These are hard times."

Blokhin was finding this more and more unpleasant. After being on the road all day he just wanted a place to get warm, any place at all. And he really didn't have a choice, so he agreed. After all, he thought, what difference does she make? She has her life, I have mine. And I'm not going to be living here forever.

"All right, fine," he said. On the other side of the wall, something fell.

"Maybe you'll take a walk, while I get the room ready?" she asked, listening to everything that was going on.

Blokhin went outside and lit a cigarette, feeling lighthearted. He didn't particularly want to go anywhere, but he went down to the river and stood there, thinking.

Blokhin was twenty-six years old. He had finished the institute and was thinking more and more about marriage. But he couldn't imagine marriage without love and he had yet to fall in love. Lately this had begun to worry and even depress him seriously. It seemed to him, as to so many others, that nothing out of the ordinary was ever going to happen to him in Moscow, at the institute; in short at home. Home was commonplace and ordinary by definition. The extraordinary was to be found elsewhere, so he loved taking long trips. Every time he got ready for one, he was almost positive that something delightful was going to happen, that someone would fall in love with him. And though nothing ever had happened to him on his trips, he never lost faith that it would.

Looking now at the wide snowy expanse of the river, he fell to thinking about the girl who had been so embarrassed when she opened the door for him. The more he thought about her the more excited he got. Maybe this was the long-awaited moment, the extraordinary happiness he'd dreamed of. Who was she? What was her life like? He tried to remember her lips and her eyes and her face, but he couldn't remember anything. Just that she was pretty and that her embarrassment might have meant something important.

"Fine!" Blokhin said aloud and looked back. The windows of the house were aglow with gentle light. After Moscow everything seemed extraordinarily quiet and mysterious. Blokhin felt excited and gleeful. He finished his cigarette and flipped it into the air. It fell into the snow, but did not go out, and the place where it had fallen glowed for a long time with a delicate rosy light.

It's probably all right to go back now, Blokhin thought, and as he returned to the house he was smiling in the darkness and enjoying the squeak of his boots in the snow.

2

The floor of the room had been washed and a greasy gray pillow sat on the narrow iron bed next to the wall. His hostess came in. She kept turning her pale face uneasily from Blokhin to the wall. She seemed to be conscious of everything going on behind it.

"Do you need linen?" she asked.

"Of course," Blokhin answered, irritated, raising his eyebrows in an effort to communicate his dissatisfaction; his dislike of her was increasing by the minute.

The bed was made and there was a cloth on the table. Relaxing somewhat, Blokhin opened his suitcase and unpacked. He took out a book and tried to read, but he was bored suddenly. Reading wasn't what he wanted; he wanted some strong hot tea in a slender glass and someone to talk to.

Putting his book aside, he began to look out the dark steaming window, leaning on his elbows and listening to the wood crackling in the stove, thinking that only yesterday he was walking along the Arbat in Moscow, and now he was sitting in a strange house with people who didn't care about him or his past or his activities, and who would perhaps never think of him again after he left.

These reflections left him feeling sad and glum. He considered going to sleep, but he wasn't sleepy. He got up, circled the room, patted the stove, listened for a minute, and went into the kitchen.

Dressed now in a dark dress, the girl was sitting at the table embroidering. Seeing Blokhin she started, and moved as if she wanted to get up and leave, but she didn't; she merely dropped her head still lower. Blokhin looked at her, sat down at the table and asked in a low voice, "Where's your mother?"

"She's feeding the pig." She answered slowly, as if she hadn't immediately understood the question. Her voice was low and gentle. Her golden-yellow hair moved on her temples and a few curls fell across her face. A neat, straight part cut through the lustrous mass.

How old is she? he wondered. Eighteen, nineteen? He looked at the curls, the part, the thin neck, sorry that he wasn't twenty, sorry that he wasn't good-looking, experiencing the weary sensation of regret. He wanted to sit there forever, just looking at her. You may fall in love yet, he thought unhappily.

"Do you work or are you a student?" he asked.

The girl raised her head. Blokhin saw tiny freckles on her nose and forehead, a small red mouth, and bright, clear eyes, eyes which held their own, distant, strange, and for Blokhin, unattainable world.

"I work," she said in a sweet, trusting voice. "As a cashier. On the other side of the river. I tried to get into the institute, but they didn't take me. I prepared like crazy too, but it was a waste of time."

"Are you bored?"

"It's all right during the day at work. But at night it's very boring. I'm always alone. I don't go out much, just to a movie occasionally. Mama doesn't like to be left alone. So I embroider. I'm glad you took one of our rooms. I hate them to be empty. I was afraid you wouldn't like it here in this lonely place. What can you like about it?" She looked around the kitchen, her eyes darkening with distaste.

You, I like you, he wanted to say. But he said nothing.

"Have you ever been in Moscow?" he asked presently.

The girl shook her head without looking at him. Blokhin began to talk about Moscow. He spoke of the theaters, the institutes, the stadiums, his tone unconsciously assuming a more and more boastful note. The girl listened like someone listening to a fairy tale, her cheeks flushing and her eyes shining. Putting aside her embroidery, she leaned on the table and stared at Blokhin. He was embarrassed and bothered by her steady gaze, but his former depression and boredom were gone without a trace. He felt almost happy.

The dark, snow-blanketed town, its plump old-fashioned merchants' houses, the tea shop, the horses and sleighs, the smell of hay, manure and snow, the House of Culture, with the discordant sounds of its orchestra and its people running around in wigs, the dreams and conversations he'd had along the road, the wide lonely river and finally this house, with its unpleasant owner and her sweet trusting daughter—all these things began to seem strange and interesting and full of meaning.

"You're so lucky!" the girl said, frankly envious. "I was born here in the backwoods, and went to school, but I don't think I ever learned anything or lived at all."

Suddenly she gave him a sad, ironic smile.

"You just don't know how unhappy I was this summer. I was writing my autobiography. What's my autobiography? Three lines. I was born, I went to school, I worked in the garden and did the wash, I went berry-picking in the summer, and is that going to be it? I have nothing in my life. I go to the movies or listen to the radio: people are doing things, this one accomplished some great feat, that one went off to the virgin lands, people are busy with sports and studies, lights are burning at night, life is interesting, but I have nothing. Who told you about our room?"

"A young fellow brought me here. From the House of Culture."

"Oh, I know. Kolya Balaev, yes? Did he say anything?"

"No, nothing," Blokhin said and felt a stab of pain in his heart. "He didn't say anything. Why?"

"He used to live here. What a nice man! You see, I started participating in the theater circle, and we used to walk home together, talking and telling each other our dreams . . . But Mama . . ." The girl blushed suddenly. "Mama kicked him out. Just like that, kicked him out. And I . . . We don't even see each other any more."

"You loved him?" Blokhin asked with an effort.

"No," answered the girl thoughtfully. "No, I still don't know how love feels, but that . . . what we had wasn't it . . . Do you like our city?" she asked a minute or so later."

"It's a bit strange. Merchants' houses, horses, snow, darkness . . . It isn't like Moscow."

"Moscow," she breathed, her eyes darkening again. "Our city is old, eight hundred years old, and even the way of life is old. The only thing we have to be proud of is that some tsar died here. Something to be proud of! There's a movie, schools, a technical institute; in the summer everyone rides a bicycle, but even so everything is stagnant. It's a city of houses and merchants. Only they've taken all the merchants' money away so . . . So they all grow beards and sit around in the tea shop drinking tea. Everyone on our street is an Old Believer, Mama's one, she doesn't like people. Not far from here there's a meetinghouse where they get together to mumble and pray. I go there, but I don't believe any of it. I don't just to spite her! She wouldn't let me join the Young Communists. So here I sit with my embroidery. What's the use? I don't know. Why am I living?"

Tears came to her eyes, and she turned her face away quickly. Outside, a short rhythmic sound was heard, gradually coming closer. It sounded like the ticking of an enormous alarm clock.

"What's that?" asked Blokhin.

"That?" the girl said with a wavery sigh, looking out into the darkness. "The night watchman. He has a knocker."

"A knocker?" Blokhin repeated. He'd never heard one before. "What for?"

"I don't know," she admitted. "He knocks and knocks. Sometimes I think it's in my head."

Tock tock tock tock tock, the doleful sound faded off. Amazed and even a little frightened, Blokhin stared at the girl sitting in front of him, thinking how miserable it must be actually to live in this house.

"But how can this be?" he burst out. "It's impossible. This is one hell of a life! Why do you . . . Your mother I can understand. But your mother's an old woman. Her life is over, and it was a completely different life. She was born before the revolution and is used to this sort of life . . . But you? Talk to her, explain. Do you want me to talk to her?"

"Don't!" the girl pleaded. "I beg you, don't! It won't do any good. You think I haven't talked to her? Many times! But I'm alone here, with no one to back me up, and I've gotten used to it. I'm not the only one — if you only knew how many girls there are like me! We're all used to it. You see, we're marriageable — we have to be protected so we can be married off more profitably. If you only knew how hard it was the other time! Mama told you a professor lived with us — I heard her. She was lying. No one lived with us. They stay a week and leave, stay and leave. But I stay on and on and on. Sometimes I get so angry I'd like to tear the damned house apart, the sheep and piglets included!"

"So get out of here, get out!" said Blokhin excitedly.

"Get out? You think I don't want to? Of course, only where can I go? Who needs me? I have no education, no training, no family, no one in the whole world!"

There were steps in the hall. The girl stopped talking, and bit her lip. The woman came in. She set her pail down by the door, scowled at Blokhin and her daughter, took off her coat and went to her room.

"Will you have some tea?" she called out presently from her room.

"No thank you," answered Blokhin with an effort. His chest felt strange and tight. There'd been something unpleasant and shameful about their conversation that had left a bitter aftertaste. The girl was no longer looking at him but was rapidly running the needle through her embroidery, her small hands, rough from working in the cold, shaking. Unable to watch those shaking hands any longer, Blokhin got up and started for his room.

"Wait!" the girl said in a frightened voice.

Blokhin turned. Holding her hands to her heart, the girl managed to get up from the table and come toward him. Her cheeks and ears were burning, and it was evident from her eyes that she was also feeling ashamed.

"Why are you going?" she asked in a low voice, giving Blokhin a look that frightened him. "I told you all that because . . ."

"Tanya!" the woman shouted from the other room.

"Coming!" the girl called back, angry and frustrated, with a stamp of her foot. "Well, did you hear what I said?"

The woman's resolute footsteps were heard in the hall. The girl gave Blokhin a look of suffering and shame. "We'll talk again, all right?" she whispered quickly. He felt her warm childish breath on him as she left.

Blokhin went into his own room, closed the door without a sound, and listened a minute, holding his breath. Hell, he thought, starting to breathe again. What kind of life is this? It's a nightmare, an incredible nightmare! He tried to distract himself with thoughts of starting work tomorrow, thoughts about his affairs in general, but he felt feverish, he kept seeing the face of the girl. The poor girl's name is Tanya, he thought. We weren't even introduced.

A while later the woman knocked and entered cautiously. She touched the stove, straightened the tablecloth, sat down, and started complaining about life, widowhood, about the fact that the stores almost never had any sugar. Everything she had to say was tedious and trivial, and her voice was unpleasant. Blokhin was uncomfortable; he frowned, and said nothing. Then she began asking Blokhin about his job and family.

"So you live in Moscow?"

"Yes, in Moscow."

"You have a big apartment?"

"Small, one room."

"Oh, one room. You don't have an easy life either. Married?"

"Not yet."

"You making a lot of money?"

"I don't know."

"What do you mean you don't know?"

"Oh, eight hundred, nine hundred rubles."

"Eight hundred, hmmm." His hostess's eyes flickered and a barely perceptible look of contempt slid across her face. Breaking off her inquiries, she slipped out of the room.

Blokhin undressed quickly, put out the light, and lay down. He wasn't sleepy, and lay tossing around on the hard cold bed. Finally he got up and sat at the window, having a cigarette.

From the other side of the wall came the sound of whispers and sobs. The floorboards creaked, something bumped along the floor, and then someone went into the kitchen, took down the mug and had a drink of water. Outside, the rhythmic sound of the mallet was heard, coming and going.

When Blokhin fell asleep, he dreamed that some frightful creature was circling the house, knocking on all the walls, trying to get in. But there were enormous locks on all the doors and windows and so it was impossible.

3

The following day Blokhin awoke with a headache. The room had gotten cold during the night, and Blokhin's feet were frozen; the blanket was thin and inadequate. The mattress was so thin he could feel the bedframe through it, and his side hurt. The windows were frozen over. The house was quiet.

Blokhin dressed and went into the kitchen. There was a nauseous smell of boiled potato peelings. There was no water in the washstand and the samovar was cold. Blokhin went into the hall and tried a door. It was locked. He tried another, also locked. The third door opened into the shed, and Blokhin saw his hostess. She was combing the pig behind its ears, a gentle smile on her face. The pig was up to its ears in the pail, shoving it around, twitching its tail.

Seeing Blokhin, the woman frowned and went past him into the kitchen. She had great greasy boots on, a jacket, and an ancient scarf. Her clothes and hands smelled of manure.

"I didn't agree to carry water for you," she said. She thought a minute, counting aloud. "I'll have to ask two hundred and fifty for the room."

"And why is that?" Blokhin burst out.

"Why? Why? The bed linen has to be washed, the water brought and emptied. Why? You're burning electricity, a big bulb, one hundred watts, how much does that cost me? I haven't a printing press, I don't make my own money. And then, I'll have to ask you to smoke outside, you smoke a lot, and I get dizzy."

"Will you make me some tea?" asked Blokhin, turning red.

"Where am I going to get the coal? Coal costs money. I have to start the samovar early, but you sleep till all hours, I'd have started it ten times over waiting for you. I'm a widow, nowhere to turn to, no one to help me. I'm already sorry I let the room, you're a disturbing influence, by God."

Without a word, Blokhin turned and went to pack his things. The woman came in quietly and watched him for a while.

"So you're leaving, are you?" she asked finally.

His lips tight, Blokhin didn't answer.

"You know, I won't keep you. Don't try to threaten me. I can always find tenants right here, just pay me for the night, and good riddance. A professor lived here, he was grateful to me and even paid more than he owed . . . Some engineers lived here too . . . *They* were cultured . . ."

"So," Blokhin closed his suitcase and put on his coat. "There we are. I don't wish any further discussion. I spent one night. How much do I owe you? Seven rubles, or eight?"

"What do you mean *seven?*" his hostess blanched. "How do you figure seven? Didn't you take the room yesterday? That's two days. And because of you I will have to do the laundry. *Seven* rubles? And the pillow case too. Twenty-five rubles please!"

Blokhin took out ten.

"Take it," he said, sneering.

"What's this?" The woman's mouth dropped open. "Go ahead, take advantage of my kindness. I don't need your money. Get out, rob me, a poor old widow . . ."

"As you wish," said Blokhin, shoving the money into his wallet and glancing at her sideways.

A dark rough hand with dirty fingernails darted out, grabbed the money and clenched it.

"Are you proud of yourself? An educated person! What did you tell my daughter yesterday? You think she's an idiot? You planning on taking her away from her mother?"

"Daughter?" Blokhin started shouting. "You don't treat her like your daughter!"

"He thinks he's cultured, because he's finished the institute," his hostess shouted back without listening, getting paler and paler. "Shame on you. How can you show your face in broad daylight? You want to take over a stranger's house? Go get your own house. Holy Mother of God, forgive the miserable poor! You've dirtied my house, you disgusting anti-Christ! Get out of here! Go on, go on!"

Blokhin went out quickly through the hall and onto the porch. The snow squealed under his feet, the air was fresh and cold, and the extraordinary light of a February day was dazzling. But his spirits were as foul and low as if he had been caught doing something awful.

The tiny houses on the street, buried in snow, their windows sparkling, threw sharp blue shadows on the road. Amber piles of manure and scavenging ravens stood out against the bright sleigh-tracked snow, and up above on the steep precipice, overhung with snow, a few blue-trunked fir trees hung on by some miracle.

But Blokhin saw none of it, none of the beauty of the bright winter day. Puffing he clambered up the steep path to the top of the hill, leaving behind him a trail made by his dragging suit-case.

At the top Blokhin looked down at the blindingly white river and the house where he had spent the night. How am I going to see Tanya? Where can I meet her? I'll tell Balaev, he decided. He'll help me. Something has to be done. And his heart beat violently in shame and fury and love for the sweet timid girl. Suddenly he remembered why he'd come to the town, for practical training, and rage and bitterness overwhelmed him. Practical training! he thought irritably. Sitting in the library, making up catalogues, lists of recommended reading, totaling fines. While right next door a person is dying, while right next door there's a whole streetful of Old Believers. Who will probably be regulars at the library too! Practical training! That's where practical training is needed — down there!

He gave the house one last look of loathing and set off for the hotel. He didn't turn again, but he would have seen nothing if he had; the house was hiding under the hill.

THE STRANGE GIRL

Manka

It is eighteen miles from Vasintsy to Zolotitsa. There's no road, only a lonely path overgrown with grass and mushrooms. It occurs to Manka from time to time that if she hadn't walked this path every day with the mail, it would have been overgrown completely long ago, and she'd have been lost in the woods.

Manka is an orphan. "Papa died in a storm," she says, dropping her eyes and running her tongue over her lips, "and a year later Mama took her own life, she missed him so. She left the house one evening, ran down to the ocean and out on the ice; when she came to a hole, she laid her clothes in a pile and fell in the water."

And flushing, she winds up with a mumbled, "Mama was a wild one . . ."

And that same wildness, that same strangeness is in Manka. There's something intense and secretive in her silences, in her vague smile, in her greenish, perpetually lowered eyes. Four years ago, when they buried her mother, Manka stared at her feet, seemingly bored and indifferent. But suddenly she raised her lashes and looked around at the mourners, her eyes so strange and insolent that the men had coughed in embarrassment and the women were so frightened they stopped crying and turned white.

Manka has been working as a mail carrier for two years now. At seventeen she has probably covered as many miles as it would take to get to Vladivostok and back. But she loves her work. Her home is a lonely, unsightly mess: with no livestock, a roof with holes in it, long unrepaired, and a stove that hasn't worked for six months.

Tall, thin, long-legged, Manka walks easily and gracefully, and almost never gets tired. In the summertime her hair bleaches to a red-blond, her legs and arms turn brown, her face thins out, and her eyes become greener and more striking.

A soft ocean breeze blows in her face, and the distinct smell of seaweed brings a sweet pain to her chest. Toward August the tiny dark streams that run to the ocean, clogged with driftwood and gurgling with yellow foam, are lined with magnificent crimson flowers. Manka sometimes picks these flowers, great bucketfuls of them. Or resting in the shade of the blue-gray fir trees, stunted by the northern winter winds, she pretends she's a bride, and drapes herself with camomile flowers and blue-gray juniper berries.

Walking is sweet and easy for her when there's not much mail. But sometimes lots of packages and parcels and magazines come in and Manka has to put on her big bag and try to cram everything in.

"Well, my girl?" the postmaster's tenor rings out. "Will you make it? Maybe we should send for a horse?"

"This is nothing," she gasps, red-faced, moving her shoulders to get the bag into a more comfortable position.

After half a mile her back is breaking and her legs ache. On these days what fun she has with the fishermen at the fisheries. Things are so lively, there's so much laughter and cheerful talk as they slowly and painstakingly fill out their receipts. How they love their Manka!

"Hey you, girl!" they shout at her. "Throw down that bag and hurry up! Sit down and have some soup . . . Mitka, get a spoon!"

And tow-haired Mitka tears into the storeroom for a spoon, gives it a hasty wipe with a towel, and hands it to Manka with a slight bow.

"Get her some more!" they cry out from all sides. Manka sits down, blushing, eyes lowered, and tries not to eat noisily, grateful for their care and love.

After that she doesn't mind tramping along with the newspapers and mail; the straps no longer cut into her shoulders. After all, can't you see almost anything along the road and think anything you please? Manka has to deliver at three fisheries on the way to

Zolotitsa. At each one they're waiting for her eagerly; they never disappoint her. She arrives at the same time always, has her cranberry tea, tells the news, and delivers the mail. She reaches Zolotitsa sometime in the evening and spends the night. In the morning she goes home to Vasintsy, taking the return mail.

2

The first fishery after Vasintsy is called Vorona. There used to be four men and a cook living there but with the arrival of summer and the white nights, a fifth joined them, Perfilii Volokitin.

With black, closely cropped hair and a small, tough face, he'd been demobilized in the spring and lived a couple of months at home. He had planned to move to the city, but had started going with Lenka, the prettiest and naughtiest girl in town, whom the boys had fought over more than once. So he decided to stay and applied for work at the Vorona fishery.

He brought his accordion with him, and played it often, sitting gazing absently at the ocean. He was always gay and even-tempered, with the promptness and efficiency of a soldier, and he always volunteered for the heaviest jobs. Evenings he would shave, sew a bright-colored collar on his tunic, clean his boots, settle his cap on askew and go out to the club in town, never coming back before sunrise.

He was a fighter, a graceful and tireless dancer, a quick-witted and sarcastic talker. The first time she met him at the club, Manka gave him his letters and newspapers and immediately dropped her eyes and blushed. She began sleeping badly after that, either at home or in Zolotitsa, lying awake thinking about Perfilii for hours, remembering his face and voice, his words and laughter. With tears running down her face she imagined that she was living with Perfilii in a large new house with windows on the sea, and that they had everything they could want. Curling up next to the wall, she'd fall asleep finally, muttering to herself.

She was spending the night at Zolotitsa one night, in a warm stuffy room with eight other people — a team of carpenters — when she had a dream about Perfilii just before dawn. It was a vivid, extraordinary and shameful dream. Manka woke up, opened her wide green eyes, and sat up straight, unable to feel anything at first but her pounding heart.

The carpenters on the floor and on the benches were snoring, and outside the windows it was a glimmering white night. Silently sobbing and choking, Manka suddenly understood that she loved Perfilii. And she was overwhelmed with self-pity, hatred for her skinny, childish body, hatred for the beautiful Lenka; overcome by the thought that this was the end, that her whole life was ruined. And it was only at dawn that she went back to sleep, worn out and exhausted, her face wet with tears.

Going to Vorona after that morning was awful. She was afraid of giving herself away, afraid of the fishermen's coarse laughter. Her heart would drop on seeing Perfilii or hearing his voice and she'd tremble and shiver, her mouth gone dry and her chest tight.

She'd leave Vorona in a trance, more dead than alive, picking up speed slowly until by the time she had reached the woods she was almost running. Falling face down on the dry white moss, she'd cry for a long time, crying for joy, for love, for loneliness, for incomprehension. Then she'd lose herself in the woods, going any which way, smiling and talking to herself.

Sometimes she'd come out on the ocean and sit down on a stone, curling into a ball to warm in the sun. As she watched the sea gulls and the blue-green surface of the water, she'd rock herself and chant, "Little sea gulls, little sea gulls, take my love to him!" And her old grandmother, long since dead and departed, would come to her as in a dream, with her fairy tales, her mournful songs, her strange chant: *I, Manka, the slave of God, I am blessed. I make the sign of the cross . . . From door to door, from gate to gate I am going to the holy fields . . . And so he did yell and fell ill and burned in hell, and could neither eat nor see nor be . . . And* then she'd become frightened and her heart would pound and her palms sweat. How much she wanted Perfilii at these moments and how handsome and unattainable he seemed!

The ocean was smooth and still — just barely rising and falling, as if it were breathing. Light bright clouds stretched across the sky, blotting out the sun. But over there, over the gray hunchbacked promontory of rocks, where white fan-shaped rays of light fell into the sea, the sky was unbearably radiant and the sea swollen and misty. It was a fine, extraordinarily warm summer, full of the promise of joy . . .

3

Then one day in September, grown even wilder over the summer, Manka paused cautiously outside the Vorona fishery. The weather had been nasty since early morning: windy, and the sea disturbed and turbulent. There'd been a short downpour at dawn, and the house had grown dark with the look of autumn, the windows stingily reflecting the pale light. A lot of seaweed had washed up on shore that particular day, and a great number of wet crimson jellyfish and brownish yellow starfish lay about in the sand.

It was the feast day of the fishery's patron saint, and the evening before they'd netted a good salmon catch. Reluctantly the fishermen had loaded up the fish and delivered them to the fish collection point; then they'd gone on to the baths before going home for the night before the holiday.

Perfilii had gone along with everyone else. At the club that evening he listened to the accordion, showed off a little with it himself, put it aside in order to tell some jokes in an unnecessarily loud voice, nibbled on sunflower seeds, and had a drink with the boys outside. A queer look came into his dark handsome eyes, his voice slightly hoarse, growing more and more excited, he started running around shoving everyone into a circle, then, throwing back his small, peeling face, lazily closing his eyes, and stamping his squeaky calf boots, he calmly sang an obscene ballad, to joyous cheers from the boys and hypocritical scolding from the girls.

All evening long he anxiously, hungrily, followed Lenka's every movement; everything he did, he did for her. And when they were all kicked out of the hall so that benches could be set up and tickets sold for a movie showing, he found her in the crowd, grabbed her arm and led her out into the passageway. Dried-out husks crackled under their feet, and it smelled like a bathroom. Pushing her against the wall, his face white and his eyes half closed, he whispered to her, "Let's go to your house. What are you doing to me? Let's go sit at your house . . ."

"I can sit at home anytime," Lenka answered sharply, not looking at Perfilii, listening to what was going on inside.

"You mean you don't want to?" asked Perfilii, outraged and helpless, smelling her powder and her hair. "Have you found someone else? One of the fishermen? You'll be sorry! You'll cry your eyes out!"

"Let me be!" Lenka ordered, in a whisper, roughly tearing herself away. Without a glance at Perfilii, she went back into the club, slamming the door behind her. But Perfilii was only aware of her tempting little breasts, her strong eager hands, her hard pretty face, her thighs swinging invitingly as she walked.

He went out onto the dimly lighted street, into the refreshing cold, tore open his shirt, ripping off the buttons, pulled off his cap, and went home, quivering with shame and fury, his boots stamping loudly on the wooden sidewalks. Despite all his mother's efforts to dissuade him, he left again immediately, taking a bottle of vodka and some bread and lard. He went down to the ocean, got into a boat and was back at the fishery two hours later.

He went in, burning up after his furious rowing, lit a lamp and poured himself a glass of vodka. He drank it standing, grinding his teeth and wincing, his coarse hair, uncut since summer, bristling. Then he went out, sat on a log, lit a cigarette and sat for a long time, staring glassily into the darkness, at the freezing ocean, staring at the horizon where the crimson disk of sun swam and faded in the summer, and where now the rays of the first northern lights were beginning to quiver, flare up, and languidly die out.

And when Manka came in the next morning, disturbed by the unusual quiet, Perfilii was sleeping on his cot in the corner, legs spread, muscular stomach exposed, his head wrapped in his jacket. Hearing the door bang, he woke up, looked at her stupidly and rubbed his eyes.

"Ah, she's come," he said sullenly, going to the table, holding his head. "Any letters for me?"

"No," she said, sitting down, crossing her legs self-consciously, and taking a deep breath.

"No? So what did you bring?"

"Newspapers." Manka coughed and licked her lips.

"Newspapers." Perfilii looked gloomily out the window. "Storm's coming. Probably tear the nets. What are you doing here at the fishery? Everyone's gone, the sons of bitches, to have a good time!"

Slowly he got up and went for a drink from the pail, observing Manka's cowering figure.

"What's with you today?" he muttered, and throwing back his head to open his throat, he began to drink.

"With me? Nothing," Manka whispered, blushing crimson, and leaned down to smooth the dress over her knees.

"You live alone?"

"Yes."

"It must be boring," Perfilii answered without much expression, looking out the window.

"I get along." Manka made a weak gesture with her hand, coughed, got up, and went to the pail for a drink, enjoying the knowledge that she was drinking from the same dipper Perfilii had used.

"I've got to go," she said hoarsely, sitting down again and raising her frightened face to look at Perfilii. But Perfilii wasn't listening. He stared out the window without answering.

"Storm's coming," he said tonelessly. "A real bitch. Terrific winds according to the weather report."

Manka looked out the window too. The sea had darkened and was pounding the shore, and the wind was whistling in the drying racks. The foam-crested waves were coming in fast, one on top of the other, and an ever widening purple band rimmed the horizon.

"Storm's coming and they're out having a good time," Perfilii repeated bitterly, thinking about Lenka. Then he went behind a curtain and pulled on his waterproof pants and jacket.

"Where are you going?" Manka asked horrified. "Do you want to drown?"

"Where? The nets are out and they've got to be brought in," Perfilii muttered as he went out. Manka listened to the wind, her mouth hanging open. Then she looked out the window and saw that in the last minute the purple band had widened significantly. She tore out headlong after Perfilii. The wind hit her sharply in the face. Perfilii was busy fixing something in the boat when she came up.

"Well?" he turned toward her angrily. Without waiting for an answer, he started shoving the boat into the water.

"I'm going with you," said Manka, putting her shoulder to the boat.

"What is this, some kindergarten game?" he shouted as the boat budged and scraped in the sand. "Get back inside."

"I won't!" Manka's white fingers clung to the side of the boat. "What, haven't I seen the ocean before?"

"All right, hop in!" shouted Perfilii with a kind of gay desperation. "Get in!"

Manka jumped in easily, and holding on to the sides, made her way to the back. Red in the face and up to his waist in water, Perfilii bent over for one last shove. Then he threw himself up on the side on his stomach, rolled in, grabbed the oars and started rowing. In a minute they were rising and falling smoothly with the waves, headed out for the black posts supporting the nets, two hundred yards from shore. Manka hung on tight, licking away the salt spray from her lips, the wind tearing at her hair. I forgot my scarf, she thought. Oi, we're going to drown! The wind is blowing so strong! Oi! And she looked rapturously at Perfilii's red, determined face, thrown back into the wind.

At the first net, not daring even to look at the threatening black band, they hurriedly began to pull up the posts and get them into the boat along with the nets. Manka was pulling on the netting and bailing by turns, and soon her arms and legs were breaking, her dress drenched, and her strong thin thighs, uncovered and exposed, were blotchy from the cold. The edge of her pink underpants was showing; she was embarrassed but she just didn't have time to pull down her dress. Perfilii wasn't looking at her anyway: the posts had been firmly driven in and every time he pulled one out, the boat rolled. The waves were rising; they had to hurry.

Fifteen minutes later, with all the netting in, they headed for shore. The boat began to sink. Perfilii pulled frantically, watching something approaching from the ocean. Manka was facing the shore, bailing out water, afraid to turn around.

"Stop it!" Perfilii shouted wildly. "We can't make it to shore, we have to turn around. We can't make it from here!"

Dumping out all the netting they'd been dragging to shore, they turned again toward the ocean. Manka was facing the ocean now, numb with fear. Neither the sky nor the clouds nor the ocean in the distance were to be seen, everything was foggy and there was something vague and black and wanton, wild and exciting. Only the crests of the waves shone out coldly and cruelly white in the darkness. They barely made it through the wind to the second net rack. Perfilii arched and threw himself back with every pull, and Manka's arms were breaking.

And again, when Perfilii clung to the posts and pulled, the boat rolled. When the nose came up, the boat went over on its side, and Perfilii's head and arms disappeared from view entirely. Her eyes round with terror, Manka could see only his straining back, his bent legs, his shiny wet boots. With a jerk, the post pulled free and Perfilii fell back, pulling the net into the boat. There were several salmon and some silvery little fish darting about in the net, but Manka and Perfilii paid no attention.

And finally the real storm came. The water was whipped to a lather, the spray was flying, the wind from shore was one continuous roar, and a monstrous wave moved over the sand, threatening to engulf the fishery. The water turned a chocolate brown. The second net was almost entirely in, and only the post farthest to the right remained when the boat was taken by a wave, pitched up nearly vertical, thrown down on its side, and capsized. Manka found herself under the boat, stunned and gasping for breath.

She understood nothing there in the darkness except that she wanted light, air, and to see Perfilii. Her head was being battered against the seat and her feet were tangled in the sinking net. God, oh God, droned in her head. Oh Mamochka, I'm through, I'm through!

Something scraped against her leg. She kicked, grabbed hold of the seat and pulled herself up — there was still a little fishy-smelling air up there in the bottom of the boat — and began to yell. Then once more rough cruel hands slid along her legs and grabbed her thighs and pulled her down. Choking and spluttering, Manka pulled away like a frenzied animal, but she was dragged up roughly and painfully and shoved against the bulging ribs of the boat. Spewing out water and straining his bare bony back, Perfilii clambered up on the keel, and pulled Manka up after him.

"What were you doing, playing around under the boat?" he shouted in relief right into her ear, holding her tight against him as he gripped the slippery keel. "Hang on! We're going toward shore!"

Choking and spluttering on the moist salty wind and spray, blind with tears, Manka hung on to the keel with one hand and Perfilii's neck with the other, and fainted.

"Now now," Perfilii yelled in a high teasing voice, scraping his boots on the bottom of the boat. "We'll live. If you don't live on the sea, no troubles will you see!"

And the sea roared like a huge ferocious beast, the overturned boat on its back, and reared up, bringing the boat closer and closer to shore. Within half an hour, the boat was dancing in the roaring surf, its round sides glistening. The waves would take the boat, hurl it toward shore, and break. Then, surrounded by the hissing foam, the boat would be sucked backwards, slowly at first and then faster and faster, only to be taken up once more and thrown toward shore.

Suddenly it was quiet. The hiss of the water being sucked back into the sea could be heard, but the rumble rising up in the distance sounded like an approaching train. Perfilii looked around and almost let go of the keel: a twisted, ominous wave was washing down on them. Before the boat could crest it, it hit the boat, turned it right side up, and roared on over the sand. The last Manka could remember was her legs and arms being wrenched loose, and then being carried somewhere, her face, her back and her elbows scraping in the sand.

She came to on shore. Perfilii was kneeling beside her, holding her head. Embarrassed, Manka pushed him away and sat up, pulling her dress down over her bare legs. There were spots before her eyes and she felt nauseated and dizzy.

"Still alive!" Perfilii rejoiced. "Wait a minute, I'll be right back . . ."

He stumbled across the sand to the place where the glistening boat was spinning in the surf, went in up to his waist, and grabbing the boat, pulled it up on shore. Then he went back into the whispering muddy-white wash for the netting. Doubled over, legs trembling, he dragged it to shore also. Panting, the tops of his boots and the edge of his jacket flapping wetly, he came back to Manka. She was still sitting, unable to get up.

"Well? And what's the matter with you?" he said in cheerful mock reproach. "Never mind," he shouted, bending and giving her a worried look. "Here, hang on to my neck, I'll carry you."

But Manka turned away and stood up, reeling drunkenly, a guilty little smile on her pale face. They walked side by side. Perfilii put his arm around her thin shoulders to support her, his boottops squeaking as he walked, growing more and more animated. Looking out to sea, he talked and laughed, at himself, at Manka, at the storm, as if just a moment before he hadn't been clinging to the keel, yelling his lungs out, as he watched the waves in horror.

4

Perfilii lit the stove in the cabin, changed his wet clothes and brought Manka some pants, a sweater, and a jacket. Then he went out into the passageway and stood smoking, studying his scratched and trembling hands.

"Will you be long?" he shouted presently.

"Oi! Just a minute!" Manka shouted back nervously, hurriedly tearing off the skirt and blouse that were stuck to her body. When she was dressed again, stumbling in the pants that were much too long for her, she put her hand on her still slightly heaving chest, made a wry face, and took a deep breath.

"Well?" Perfilii called again from the passageway.

"All right, you can come in!" Embarrassed by her men's clothing, she scurried around in confusion, gathering up her wet things, wringing them out and hanging them in the wind to dry.

"Well then," Perfilii said to her. "Come here, we're going to recover by means of the last word in science and technology."

He sat Manka down at a bench at the table, got the bottle of vodka he'd started the night before out from under his cot, and poured them both a drink.

"Let's drink," he said, looking at her affectionately. "Drink, drink! Pick it up and pour it right down — that's so as not to catch cold. To our happy landing!"

He drank first, took a deep breath, and poured himself some tea. Then Manka drank hers, coughing and shaking her head. The effect was immediate. She flushed and her green eyes began to shimmer. To her complete horror, she found herself with only one sharp and great desire: that Perfilii take her and kiss her.

And as he was looking at her, Perfilii suddenly stopped talking and went white. Pushing away his glass of tea, he stood up and moved quickly out of the cabin. He looked around, the shore was deserted. He came back, sat down nervously and began to stare at Manka, openly and hungrily: her face, her flaming cheeks, her damp curly hair, her golden eyelashes, understanding at last the reason for her silence, her strangeness, her perpetually lowered eyes, her hoarse voice. Outside the sea pounded threateningly, but inside it was warm and dry, the stove was crackling, the air fishy.

"How old are you?" he asked quickly, his voice dropping.

"I must go," said Manka in a faint voice, getting up and sitting down again.

"How old are you?" he repeated, trying to catch her eye.

"Nineteen," Manka lied, turning away and feeling her hands grow cold and her head start to spin. Suddenly her feelings of the summer came back to her in a cold wave — the tears, the secret shame of first love, the despair of those ghostly white nights — followed by a wave of quiet horror. Sitting beside her with those terrible eyes, Perfilii was destroying her dreams! What's happening? she thought. He's going to fall all over me! Oi Mamochka, what's happening? and she looked at him wildly.

"Ekh," he groaned desperately, pretending to be out of control of himself, and slid along the bench toward her. Taking her face in his hand and tipping it back, he closed his eyes and kissed her long and hungrily, his other hand running shamelessly over her skinny body. Manka went stiff and numb.

"What do you want?" she pulled herself away. "Damn you! What do you want?"

"I can't control my feelings," Perfilii muttered in confusion, rising, and trying to pull her toward him.

"You bully!" she cried, close to tears. "Go kiss someone else! Don't touch me! I'm . . . I'm nothing to you!"

"Manya! Manyusha!" he pleaded, confused and repentant. "Wait . . . I'll be good to you!"

"I'm nothing to you! Go kiss your Lenka! I haven't . . . I haven't even been kissed!" Manka brought out with an effort, and turned away breathing hard, and shaking all over. Taking off his jacket, she threw it on the floor. "Get out of here, damn it," she said in a low voice. "I'm going to work. I've got to work."

She changed her clothes, completely forgetting to be afraid that Perfilii might come in and see her. Shaking with anger and a vague feeling of revenge, she grabbed her bag and went out past Perfilii who was smoking and pacing in the passageway, her head down, without saying goodbye.

She was walking more calmly by the time Perfilii, bareheaded and in his stocking feet, caught up with her.

"Here, I had this," he mumbled, thrusting a piece of chocolate candy into her bag. "That's for the road. Don't be angry, Manya. Forgive me? Lenka and I are through!" he said desperately. "She's no good, a good-time girl."

"Go away," Manka said, not looking at him. "Leave me alone!"

"Are you coming to the club on Saturday?" he asked, walking quickly beside her.

"I have to work," said Manka, still looking away.

"Well, Sunday then!" Perfilii wasn't going to give in. "I have something to tell you. Come, Manya, huh?"

"I don't know yet," she mumbled, and quickened her pace. Perfilii stopped.

Oh, of course I'll come, you just keep waiting, thought Manka, dropping her head to listen to the sound of the sea falling away in the distance. He found himself an idiot, didn't he? What should I go there for? For the candy? She reached in her bag and touched the candy, but for some reason she didn't throw it away as she had intended. She walked along, clutching the candy in her hand.

At the turn she looked around, as if someone had tapped her on the back. Perfilii was still standing where he'd stopped and was looking after her. Seeing Manka turn, he raised his hand and Manka hurried on so fast she had to keep herself from running. After a quarter of a mile, she stopped and looked back cautiously. Then she turned off into the underbrush, into the golden-yellow birch trees, onto the moss. She lay down, face buried in her bag. Why did this have to happen? How am I ever going to deliver his mail to him now?

Her face was burning and her head swimming from the smell of Perfilii, a fresh, clean fisherman's smell. She saw the queer, wild look in his dark eyes and her heart stopped while she relived the day in all its fear, in all its joy, and in all its shame. And gaily, tauntingly, tediously, the crazy words of the chant came back: *And he did yell and fell ill and burned in hell and could neither eat nor see nor be . . .*

Unattractive

THE wedding party was in full swing. The bride and groom had gone off long since and the roosters were already beginning to crow, but there were still five lights burning brightly, the indefatigable were still hanging out the windows, there was still someone playing the accordion and the house was shaking with the heavy tramp of feet.

There'd been a lot to eat and drink, a lot of tears shed, a lot of singing and dancing. And always more vodka and more things to eat, always phonograph records of waltzes and tangos and Russian dances whenever the accordionist took a break, the noise and gaiety spreading undiminished across the fields to the river, until the whole neighborhood knew that they were celebrating in Novodvor.

Everyone was feeling good; it was only Sonya whose spirits were low. Sonya — a girl of twenty-six, thin, pale, with pronounced veins in her neck and sparse hair of an indefinite color — was sitting quietly in the corner. Her sharp nose was red from the vodka she'd had, her head was humming, and she was sick with shame. No one had noticed her the whole evening, everyone had been happy and in love, but not with her, no one had even asked her to dance.

She knew she was unattractive, and was ashamed of her thin body. Over and over again she had vowed not to go to places where there would be singing and dancing and people falling in love, but she could never resist. She came, hoping to find some kind of happiness.

No one had ever fallen in love with her, not even when she'd been a young student at the institute. No one had ever walked her home, no one had ever kissed her. She'd graduated from the institute and had come to work here in the country, where she had a room in the school. She spent her evenings correcting home-work, memorizing love poetry, going to the movies, writing long letters to her friends and feeling sorry for herself. In the past two years almost all her friends had gotten married; all that had happened to her was that her face had grown paler and her body thinner.

So she had been invited, more or less as a joke, to the wedding, and she had come. She had watched the happy bride closely, and shouted along with everyone else when the groom had kissed her, reflecting bitterly all the while that they'd never be celebrating *her* wedding.

She was introduced to the veterinary, Nikolai, a sullen young man with a sharp handsome face and crazy-looking eyes. They were seated together and at first he made some effort to pay at-tention to her. Sonya ate and drank everything he offered her, thanking him with a look she imagined to be full of affection. But for some reason Nikolai became more and more sullen, and soon began neglecting her to chat with someone across the table. Finally, he left her altogether to dance. Shouting, waving his long arms, looking around wildly at everyone, he stopped only to come back for more vodka. Then he went out into the passageway and didn't come back.

Sonya sat in the corner alone, thinking about her life, despising all these happy, contented, drunken, sweaty people, despising her-self and feeling sorry for herself. She'd made herself a dress not long ago, a very nice dark blue dress, and everyone had admired it and told her it was becoming. But the dress hadn't helped at all, everything was just the same.

2

At about three in the morning, miserable and totally forgotten, her cheeks flushed, Sonya went through the passageway and out onto the porch.

The houses were all dark, the village was sleeping. Everything was quiet, the darkness pierced only by the sounds of the accordion and the shouting and stamping of feet coming from the open windows where the party was still going on. The light fell in red patches across the grass.

Sonya's chin quivered, and she bit her lip, but it didn't help. She ran down from the porch toward the birch trees, white and sweet in the darkness, threw herself against them and burst into tears. Ashamed and afraid of being heard, she stuffed a scented handkerchief between her teeth. But no one heard her, the only movement was the slight swaying of the birch trees. That's enough now, Sonya said to herself, squeezing her eyes shut. No more now! You've got to go home! She wanted to leave, but when she swung away from the trees, her legs wouldn't support her. She stopped.

"Who's there?" someone behind her asked loudly.

Sonya held her breath, pulled her handkerchief out of her mouth, wiped her face on her shoulder, and turned around guiltily, holding on to the tree. It was Nikolai. He swayed, and grabbed her shoulder, trying not to fall. His hands were smeared with dirt.

"Oh," he said, obviously quite drunk, "it's you. I've . . . I've been in the garden."

He staggered and pressed up close to her.

"The son of a bitch invites me to his wedding!" he managed to get out. "I'll kill him! That's too much. Wanted to buy me a bottle. You stinking liar! You're not buying me a thing!" Nikolai gritted his teeth and swore obscenely.

"Do you feel bad?" asked Sonya, quite frightened. "Do you want some water?"

"Huh? He wants to rub it in."

He pulled away from Sonya and walked over to a corner of the house. Leaning his head against the wall, he gagged and hiccuped, wiping away his sticky saliva with his finger. Sonya began to feel sorry for him. She brought a bucket of water from the house and poured some over his head. He bent down submissively, snorting and blubbering something incomprehensible.

Then, his head dripping, he sat down on the porch in his shirtsleeves and had a cigarette while Sonya washed off his jacket.

"Do you feel better?" she asked gently, afraid of someone coming and seeing them.

"Somewhat. Why haven't I seen you before? I know everyone here."

"I don't go out much."

"Do you live in the school?"

"That's right."

"Do you want me to take you home?" Nikolai stood up, put on his jacket, shook his head and went inside for a drink.

"Why were you crying?" he asked when he came back. "Did someone insult you?"

Sonya's heart beat gratefully. She lowered her head. "No, no one insulted me."

"Tell me! If someone touched you, I'll break the stinker's ribs for him!"

Nikolai took Sonya's arm and they crossed the dusty road, and turned left onto a path that went past the fenced-in kitchen gardens. The dew had fallen and the grass was wet.

Suddenly Sonya felt like laughing. She hardly knew herself. She felt like putting her head on Nikolai's shoulder, but was ashamed of her desire, so when Nikolai staggered and drew her closer, she pulled away quickly.

"Listen, you're awfully drunk!" she said to him, in a tone of affectionate reproach, as she would to an old friend.

"Drunk!" Nikolai wiped his face. "What do you mean, drunk?"

They got to the school and went up on the porch. Sonya was at a loss as to what she should do: go in right away or stay. She wanted to go in, but afraid of hurting Nikolai's feelings, she stayed.

For some reason Nikolai seemed drunk again; he was gripping her arm, and breathing hard.

"Well, tell me something," she said, raising her pale face in the darkness.

"What's to tell?" he answered hoarsely, and kissed her, holding her so tight that her bones cracked. His lips were wet.

"Let go!" she whispered, pulling away. "Let go!"

This wasn't how she had imagined her first kisses but she wanted to love someone so much, wanted kindness so much that with one scared, submissive look, she forgave him everything. She pushed him away and drew him to her all in the same moment, sobbing helplessly, repeating, "Let go! Let go!"

"Be quiet!" he whispered, drawing her into the dark hallway. "Be quiet. What's the matter with you, you little fool?"

Pressing her to the wall and unbuttoning her dress, he ran his hands all over her body, pinching her, rubbing his face against her tiny breasts.

"Kolya, stop it, sweetheart! God, what are you doing?"

"Do you love me?" asked Nikolai, breathing hotly in her face. "Do you love me?" And he buried his face in her dress again.

"Don't, Kolya, don't!" she said, suddenly so desperate that he let her go.

Getting his breath, he coughed and lit a cigarette, examining her face in the light.

"All right," he muttered. "Don't get mad. Look here, meet me at the threshing barn tomorrow. Will you?"

"When?" Sonya asked in a whisper, trembling all over.

"About seven, all right? Will you come?"

"I'll come."

"Ahhh," Nikolai inhaled deeply several times, threw the butt away and ground it out with his heel. "Well goodbye!"

He kissed her again, dispassionately this time, went down the steps, and disappeared in the darkness. A minute later he started to sing. It was a crazy, drunken song.

Sonya moved cautiously around her room, drinking cold tea as she undressed. She went to the mirror dressed only in her underclothes and for a long time stood staring despondently at her face, her thin shoulders and protruding collarbones. My god, I'm a fright! she thought and shivered. I must start drinking fish oil. I absolutely must!

She sat down at the table and ate some butter straight from the dish. It tasted repulsive, but she thought of Nikolai and took several great spoonfuls. Then she put out the light and lay down, but she couldn't go to sleep. There were linden trees growing across the street from her home in Moscow and shadows played on the windows all night long. Here there was unbroken darkness outside the window.

"Is this love?" Sonya asked aloud, and turned toward the wall.

3

All day long the next day Sonya was not herself. It rained from early morning on. Dictating to her pupils, Sonya kept looking nervously at the puddles and the wet chickens running around in the rain. But the rain stopped, the sky cleared, and toward evening the cars going past the school left a trail of dust behind them.

After work Sonya sat down to write a friend. She wrote that a boy had seen her home yesterday and that they had a date today, but she didn't really believe what she was writing herself. By the time she'd finished, Sonya had decided that she was in love with Nikolai. She took the letter to the post office, came home and lay down, her face to the wall.

She wondered if Nikolai would come or not, and if he did come, how he would behave himself and what he would say. She was worried about what she would do if he started kissing her again. These thoughts upset her so that her hands were trembling when she started to dress.

She put on the same dark blue dress, curled her hair a little bit and put on some cologne. Her palms were sweating.

When she went out, she felt as if she were being watched from every window, that everyone must know where and why she was going. She was so embarrassed that she would have run if she could have.

She breathed more easily only when she reached the fields. It was warm, the road dusty, the sun dropping into a crimson haze. A tractor was standing at the edge of the field near the road. Smeared with grease, the driver was tinkering with the motor. Seeing Sonya, he straightened up, wiped his hands on his trousers, lit a cigarette and stared after her thoughtfully.

Going down into the river valley, where the mud trampled by the cows never dried out, Sonya became afraid that Nikolai might have come earlier and left without waiting. She started walking faster, then she broke into a run.

She stopped when the threshing barn came into view. Sonya was glad to see no one around. She caught her breath a minute, and then she took off her grass-stained shoes and wiped them off. It seemed awkward sitting by the side of the road, so she went behind the barn. It was warm there, and the walls that had been baking all day in the sun were still giving off heat.

A little boy with a fishing rod appeared and started digging for worms. Sonya blushed and went back to the road. People coming by cart from town stared at her, and just to spite her the boy stayed for a long time. Sonya began to feel warm. At last the boy had enough worms and left, giving her several knowing looks. He must have guessed! she thought, mortified. It's a good thing he's not one of my pupils. She hid behind the barn again, and picked a camomile flower. Its petals were crossed and strung like a racket. Sonya picked off the petals. "He's coming, he's not coming." It came out "he's not coming." The worst thing was that Sonya didn't know which direction Nikolai might take.

She got up, walked around the barn, took a look and hid again. By the time Nikolai appeared, she was a nervous wreck. He came up from the river, his hands in his pockets, a coat thrown over his shoulders. He looked at her closely as he approached, like a man who has forgotten something and is trying to remember, the expression on his face gradually changing to one of boredom. Finally he dropped his eyes and put out his hand.

"Greetings."

"Hello," Sonya answered, putting out her trembling hand, unable to raise her eyes.

"Have you been waiting long?"

"No."

"Hmm, let's go where it's cool."

They went inside the barn and sat in the hay, facing the road. The sun was setting, everything was growing dim and vague, and the shadow of the barn began to creep over the entire field.

"Did you get home all right yesterday?" asked Sonya, taking a quick look at Nikolai, and giving him a sympathetic, understanding smile.

"As usual." Nikolai yawned and took off his jacket. "Just didn't get enough sleep."

"You weren't very nice yesterday," Sonya said gently.

"How so? Did I hit you or something?" Casually, Nikolai leaned over and took hold of her, intending to kiss her, but changed his mind and nuzzled her neck instead.

"It'll be dark soon," Sonya commented, snuggling up to him submissively, listening to the hollow beat of his heart.

"Time to be cozy as peas in a pod, huh?" Nikolai jerked his head to the right. "No place here but that hut over there. Do you want to? We can lie down in the hut."

"There's no need to talk that way, Kolya," Sonya pleaded with a sigh.

"Ekh!" Nikolai burst out. "I'd love some sleep! Here, at least let me lie down."

He lay down, his legs sprawling, his head on Sonya's knees. He lay there for a while with his eyes closed, caressing Sonya's ribs.

"Why are you so thin?"

For a moment Sonya stopped breathing.

"It's just my constitution," she said finally, with a nervous smile.

"Constitution! You've probably got worms. Or you're sick with something. Like with livestock. Once they get sick, it doesn't matter how much you feed them."

Suddenly nothing mattered any more, Sonya's heart came up into her throat, and she swallowed several times, trying to get rid of an awful sensation of nausea.

"What were you swearing for last night?" she asked after a long pause.

"Oh," Nikolai frowned. "I've got a score to settle with him. The stinker took Zoika away from me, and married her. Did you see the bride yesterday? I used to go with her."

"Probably a lot of girls are in love with you?" Sonya asked wistfully.

"To hell with them!" Nikolai made a face. "I know about their kind of love."

"Why are you like that, Kolya?" Sonya asked quickly. "You have to believe in people! Look what fine people there are! You have to look for the good in them."

Nikolai turned his head away and spat.

"You don't believe in it?" she asked, her voice sinking.

"In what?"

"In the purity of man."

Nikolai burst out laughing. "How you women love to muddy the waters! Purity . . ." He turned over, yawned, and closed his eyes. His large lazy body, his strong neck, his hard good-looking face in the half light gave off such an air of satiation that Sonya was frightened. It seemed suddenly that all her conceptions of love and friendship and life had been worthless, the fabrications of literature. Real life was something different — cruder, simpler, more terrible — and she would have to submit to it.

Timidly, Sonya moved closer, and began to run her fingers through his hair, searching his face, growing more and more red and embarrassed.

"Kolya, do you want me to kiss you?" she whispered.

"Wait a minute . . ." He raised his head to listen. Then he sat up, rubbing his hands on his knees. There was a couple walking along the road, talking quietly.

"Hey!" he cried.

They stopped.

"Where are you going?"

"To a party . . . Who's that? Nikolai?"

"The very same. Where's the party?"

"Sosnovka."

They both lit cigarettes and went on, their lights glowing in the darkness. Nikolai watched them, then he looked at Sonya, a bored look crossing his face.

"Wait for me!" he called. "I'm coming with you!"

He got up hurriedly, grabbed his jacket, and threw it over his shoulders. Then he coughed and held out his hand.

"Well, so long! I'll see you again sometime." Holding on to his jacket, he turned and trotted down the road.

4

It was quite dark. A new moon hatched out on its side, and a clear mist spread over the fields from the river. Noises died out, except once there was the sound of someone running behind the barn — *top, top, top.*

Sonya sat there, her back to the wall, her face turned upward. She was shaking. She pulled her collar up around her neck, thinking that would help, but it didn't. She tried to cry, but the sound that was dragged up from her chest was so low and terrible that she frightened herself. Numbly, she sat on.

Finally she stood up; holding on to the wall, she rested a little and then started home. As soon as she got away from the river, the air was warm and dry. She took the dusty road, lighted now by the stars. The dust and hay smelled sweet. The milky way gave off such radiance that the haystacks, flax sheaves, and the shining stalks of unthreshed rye could be seen in the semi-darkness.

"Good-for-nothing!" wailed Sonya. "What a good-for-nothing!" That was all she could say, all she could think of. She went down into the wet river valley again, and came back up. The tractor that had been standing by the side of the road was now plowing in a distant field. The rays of its headlights were just visible, and the faint whir of the engine could just be heard.

Soon the darkened village came into view. Everyone was asleep already, only a few lights were burning. A great white dog ran out through the gate. When he saw Sonya, he ran around her, sniffing. I hope he bites me, Sonya thought furiously. But the dog didn't bite her. He only pawed the ground a couple of times, remembered something else, and went off into the darkness.

Sonya felt vile and unclean, innocence was gone somehow forever, and she was saddled for all time with shameful memories.

Good-for-nothing, Sonya kept thinking. How shameful! God, what a fool I am! What a miserable, pitiful fool! I believed in love. I dreamed it was pure and innocent. How shameful!

She went home, and without lighting a lamp, she groped her way to the table and burst into tears. In a few days she began to feel better. She tried not to think about Nikolai, and once more she hoped to find happiness.

STORIES OF LOVE AND PARTING

Autumn in the Oak Woods

I TOOK the pail to get some water from the spring. I was happy that night because she was arriving on the night boat. But I knew about that kind of happiness and how unreliable it can be, so I took the pail purposely, in the pretense that I was simply going for water, and not thinking about her arrival at all. Something too good had been taking form inside me all that autumn.

It was a blue-black night in late autumn, and I didn't feel like going out, but I went anyway. It took me a long time to get my lantern lit, and when it finally caught, the glass fogged over and the feeble patch of light flickered and flickered. But it stayed lit and finally the glass dried and cleared.

I purposely left a light on at home, so I could see the lighted window as I went down the leaf-covered path to Oka. My lantern cast a flickering light ahead of me and to the sides and I probably resembled a watchman in a railroad yard, except that under my feet piles of maple leaves rustled wetly, and even in the dim light of the lantern the larch needles looked golden and the barberries glowed on the naked branches.

It's terrible walking alone at night with a lantern. Your boots make the only noise, you are the only thing exposed by light; everything else is hiding and contemplating you in silence.

The light in my house vanished as soon as the path dipped sharply over the bank and lost itself in a disorderly jumble of fir and oak branches. The last tall camomile flowers, the tips of fir branches, and various naked twigs brushed against my pail, some noiselessly, some with a clear boom! boom!

The path became steeper, more twisted, more lined with birch trees, their white trunks stepping momentarily out of the gloom. Then there were no more birch trees, the path became stony, there was a fresh wind, and though I could see nothing beyond the patch of lantern light, I had the feeling of broad expanse ahead of me. I had reached the river.

I could already see the buoy far out to my right. Its red light had a twin in the reflection in the water. Then I saw the nearer buoy bobbing on my side and I could make out the outline of the whole river.

I walked down to the river through the wet grass and willow branches, to the place where the boat usually stopped if anyone was getting off in our remote neck of the woods. The spring was murmuring and gurgling monotonously in the darkness. I set the lantern down, went to the spring, scooped some water into the pail, had a drink, and wiped my face on my sleeve. Then I set the dripping pail next to the lantern, and began to watch the landing pier far down the river.

The boat was at the pier already, its green and red deck lights just barely visible. I sat down and lit a cigarette. My hands were cold and shaking. I suddenly thought if she's not on board and they see my lantern they'll stop, thinking I want to get on. I put out the lantern.

And it was dark suddenly, the river pinpricked by the buoy lights. The silence was resonant. At that hour I was probably the only one around for miles. Up on the hill, behind the oak woods, the little village was dark; everyone there had long been asleep. Only in my house, at the edge of the woods, was there a light burning.

I thought about the distance she had had to come, just to see me, sleeping or sitting by the train window talking to someone, all the way from Archangelsk. About how she'd been thinking all that time, just as I had, about our meeting. About how she'd see the shores of Oka that I'd described when I'd asked her to come. About her coming out on deck, the wind blowing in her face, bringing the scent of the wet oak woods. About her conversations en route, sitting down in the warm cabins, next to sweating windows, listening to explanations about where to get off and where to spend the night if no one was there to meet her.

Then I remembered my own wanderings in the north country, how I'd lived in a fishery and how during the white nights she and I had gone harpooning while the fishermen were snoring away in their beds. We would wait for low tide and then take the boat out to sea. She used to row without a sound while I searched the depths, looking through the seaweed for the outline of a fish. I'd let the harpoon down silently, jab the sharp white prongs into the fish's back and then I'd lean over and bring it out of the water. Flailing and splashing water into our faces, its terrible jaws agape, it would tie itself into a knot and straighten itself out again like a triton. Then it would writhe in the bottom of the boat for a long time, trembling in the grip of death.

And I thought about the year just passed, how happy it had been for me, how many stories I'd been able to write, and how many more, probably, in what was left of the quiet solitary days on the river, surrounded by nature as it faded slowly into winter.

The night was all around me. When I inhaled, the bright spark of my cigarette lit up my face and hands and boots but I could still see the stars. There were so many and they were so brilliant this fall that the river, the trees, the white stones along the shore, the dark rectangular fields on the hills were all illuminated in their smoky light. In the ravines it was much darker and more fragrant.

And I thought that the most important thing was not whether you lived thirty or fifty or eighty years, because whatever the number it wouldn't be much, and dying would still be horrible. The most important thing was how many nights you had in life like this one.

The boat had already moved away from the pier. It was still so far away that it was impossible to detect its movement. It seemed to be standing still, but the distance was growing between it and the pier. That meant it was moving upriver toward me. Pretty soon I heard the high roar of the diesel, and I was suddenly afraid that she wasn't coming, that she wasn't on the boat, and that I was waiting in vain. I thought of all the time and distance that had to be overcome in order for her to get to me, and I realized how fragile all my plans for a happy life here together were.

"What am I doing?" I said aloud, and stood up. I couldn't sit still any longer and I began to pace the shore. "What am I doing?" I kept repeating hopelessly as I watched the boat, thinking how odd I'd feel climbing back up with my water all by myself, thinking how empty my house would seem, wondering finally if we were really so unlucky that, after all this time, after all our failures, we weren't going to meet again, and thus turn everything to dust.

I remembered how three months ago I had left the north for home, and she had come unexpectedly from the fishery to see me off. As I got into the motorboat that would take me to the ship, she'd stood on the pier saying over and over, "Where are you going? You don't understand anything. You don't understand anything. Where are you going?" And sitting in the boat, amid the farewells, women's tears, the shouts of boys, and all kinds of noise, I had understood that I was doing something childish by leaving and I hoped, vaguely, to make it all right in the future.

I recalled a month after that in Moscow and what had happened to us there, but recalled it hurriedly, fleetingly, because it had been a bad time, and had just about finished everything between us.

The boat was now quite near and I stopped pacing. I stood at the very edge of the bank over the black water, unable to take my eyes off the boat, squinting and breathing hard in excitement and anticipation.

The sound of the motor suddenly dropped, the searchlight went on in the wheelhouse and a smoky beam of light played along the shore, jumping from tree to tree. They were looking for a place to land. The boat turned to the right and the intense light of the searchlight hit me in the face. I turned away and then looked back. On the upper deck a sailor was standing ready to let the ladder down over the side to shore. And next to him, dressed in a light-colored dress, she was standing.

The prow of the boat dug softly, deep into the sand. The sailor let the ladder down and helped her off. I took her suitcase, carried it back and set it down next to the pail, and then I slowly turned around. The searchlight blinded me. I couldn't see her at all. Then she was coming toward me, throwing an enormous flickering shadow on the wooded slope above. I wanted to kiss her, but changed my mind. Not standing in the light of the searchlight. We just stood there, shielding our eyes from the light, smiling tensely, watching the boat. The boat went into reverse, the searchlight swung around and went out; down below the diesel rang out and the boat moved quickly upriver, the entire length of its lower deck alight. We were left alone.

"Well hello!" I said in confusion. She got up on tiptoes, took a painful grip on my shoulders and kissed my eyes.

I coughed. "Let's go," I said. "God, it's dark. Wait, I'll light the lantern."

I lit it and again it fogged over and we had to wait for the flame to take hold and for the glass to dry and clear. Then we started off: I went ahead with the lantern and suitcase, and she came behind with the pail.

"That's not too heavy for you?" I asked after a moment.

"Go on, go on," she said huskily.

She'd always had a low, husky voice. She was tough and husky in general, and for a long time I hadn't liked it in her. Because I like sweetness in women. But now on the riverbank at night, as we followed each other up to the house, after all the days of anger and separation, letters, of strange and ominous dreams, her voice, her strong body, her rough hands, her northern accent, were like the song of a strange bird, left behind after the autumn migration.

We turned right, into the ravine where there was a narrow road up the hill, which someone had cobbled once, but overgrown now with nut trees and pines and ashberry. We started up, our lantern barely lighting the way in the dark, and a river of stars floated over us, strewn with black pine branches, alternately obscuring and revealing the stars.

Scarcely breathing, we reached the leafy path and started walking side by side.

I suddenly had the urge to tell her all about the place, about its wild life, about various minor incidents. "Take a whiff," I said, "doesn't it smell good?"

"Like wine," she said, breathing fast, trying to keep up. "I smelled it back on the ship."

"That's leaves. Now, come over here."

We left our things on the path and taking the lantern, jumped across the ditch into the underbrush.

"Should be here someplace," I muttered.

"Mushrooms!" she marveled. "Mushrooms!"

Finally I found what I was looking for. A place where the grass and needles and yellow leaves were scattered with white chicken feathers.

"Look," I said, shining the light. "We have a chicken farm in the village. When the chickens grow up, they let them go free. And every day a fox comes here, hides in the bushes and gets one as they wander past. And eats it right on the spot."

I pictured the gray-snouted fox to myself, licking and snorting, trying to get the feathers out of his nose.

"He should be killed," she said.

"I have a gun; you and I can go into the woods and maybe we'll be lucky."

We returned to the path and went on. The lighted window in my house appeared and I began to think about how it would be when we got there. Suddenly I wanted a drink. I had some berry wine that I'd made myself. I enjoy making wine: picking the berries in the woods, bringing them home, putting them through a sieve until they run out in an amber stream, and then pouring the juice in a bottle with some vodka.

"And at home it's winter now!" she said as if it were an amazing thought. "Dvina is frozen over except for a passage broken by the icebreakers. Everything is white but the passage, which is black and steamy. When a boat comes through the dogs run along the ice beside it. For some reason they run in threes."

She said "threes" with a northern accent, and I could see Dvina, the ships, Archangelsk, her village on the White Sea. The empty two-story buildings, the black walls, the silence and the solitude.

"Is there any ice in the sea yet?" I asked.

"There will be soon," she said, and thought for a minute, trying to remember something perhaps. "I'll have to go back by reindeer, if . . ."

She stopped. I waited, listening to her footsteps and her breathing. Then "If what?" I asked.

"Nothing," she said, in a slow husky voice. "If the sea freezes over, that's what!"

We stamped across the porch and went in.

"Oooo!" she said, looking around, taking off her scarf. Whenever she was surprised and happy, she made that low, drawn-out "ooo."

It was a little old house I'd rented from a Muscovite who lived in it only during the summer. There was almost no furniture, only some old beds, a table, and some chairs. The walls were rough hewn, and powdered white. There was electricity, a radio, a stove, and some fat old books I loved to read in the evenings.

"Take off your coat," I said. "We'll get the stove going."

I went outside to get some kindling for the stove. I was so happy I was beside myself; my head was ringing, my hands were shaking, I felt weak all over and needed to sit down. The stars twinkled, small and bright. There'll be frost tonight, I thought. That means the leaves will be gone by morning. Winter will be here soon.

Three slow hoots rose up and hung over Oka, echoing in the hills. A tugboat was passing down below, one of the few old steam tugs left. The new cutters and barges have high, short, nasal whistles. Awakened by the noise, several roosters at the chicken farm screeched out in a falsetto.

I cut some kindling, picked up some logs, and went back in. She'd taken off her coat and was standing with her back to me, rustling some newspapers around, getting something out of her suitcase. She had on a colored dress that was too tight for her. If I had taken her out somewhere in Moscow, to see friends or to a club, everyone would have laughed at her, although it was probably her best dress. I remembered that she usually wore tights tucked into her boots, with an old faded skirt on top, and it looked very good.

I put on the kettle and began to kindle the stove. Pretty soon it started humming and snapping, sending off the smell of smoke and firewood.

"This is for you," she said, standing behind me.

I turned and saw a salmon lying on the table. A splendid, pale silver salmon, with a wide dark body, and a jutting lower jaw. The house smelled of fish and the sea. And I had a yearning for wide open spaces again.

She was from the White Sea. She was even born at sea, in a motorboat, one white-gold night in summer. But white nights meant nothing to her; it's only the stranger who looks at them and goes crazy with the loneliness and the silence. It's only when you're visiting, torn away from everyone, forgotten by everyone, that you lie awake at night thinking, thinking, saying to yourself, Now, now, it's all right, it's just the white nights, you won't be here forever. What's it to you that the sun has stolen a slice of the sea, go to sleep, go to sleep . . .

But she? She slept soundly in her curtained-off room at the fishery, because she knew she'd have to get up in the morning, row out to the nets with the fishermen, bring in the fish, cook the fish soup, wash the dishes. And that was her life, every summer, until I came.

And here we were at Oka, drinking berry wine, eating salmon, talking and reminiscing. About how we used to go harpooning in the white nights; how we used to help the fishermen bring in the nets before a storm, gulping the salty water in our excitement; going to the lighthouse for bread; sitting with our shoes and coats off at night in the village library, reading all the newspapers and magazines that had come in our absence.

We reminisced about everything, but not about Moscow which was just a month afterwards, because that was our worst time.

I threw my coat on the floor, fur side up, and putting down the teakettle and some candy, we took our cups and lay down, by turns looking at each other, the coals, and the sparks skittering around in the fire. In order to make it last longer, I'd get up from time to time and throw more wood into the stove and when it caught and snapped, we had to turn away from the heat.

At about two o'clock I got up in the darkness, because I couldn't sleep. It seemed to me that if I fell asleep she'd go off somewhere, and I wouldn't have her next to me. I wanted to know she was with me all the time. Take me into your dream, so I can be with you always, I wanted to say, because we can't be separated for long. Then I thought about people who go away and whom we never see again — that they are as good as dead to us. And we to them. It's strange, the thoughts that come into your head at night when you can't sleep for joy or pain.

"Are you asleep?" I asked quietly.

"No," she answered from bed. "I'm fine. Don't look and I'll get dressed."

I went to the corner where the radio was and turned it on. I was looking for music but all I could find was static and muttered announcements. I knew there must be some, and I found it. A velvety male voice said something in English, and then there was a pause, and I realized they were going to play music.

I jumped when I heard the melody because I recognized it. Whenever I'm feeling especially good, or especially bad, I remember this particular jazz melody. It's not my kind of music, but there's an idea hidden in it. I don't know whether it's an idea of joy or of sorrow. It often comes back to me when I'm traveling somewhere, or when something has made me happy or depressed. I remembered that night in Moscow when we'd ridden and ridden and walked and walked, lonely and unhappy, and though I didn't hear one word of reproach from her, I felt ashamed.

She was leaving for Archangelsk after five horrible days in Moscow. Everything was as usual in a Moscow railway station: the porters were wheeling around on their baggage carts, bumping into each other, everyone was in a hurry, everyone saying good-bye, precious minutes flying. She was leaving, although she didn't have to, she still had time, several more free days. I was disappointed, bitter, angry with myself and with her. I thought how empty I'd be without her, drinking again, trying to cope somehow with unhappiness.

"Don't go," I said.

She just smiled and looked up at me, her eyes flickering. Her eyes are dark with green lights in them and it's impossible to tell if they are green or black. But at the moment she looked at me, they were black, that I remember distinctly.

"This is stupid!" I said. "First I leave the north, with nothing understood between us, and now you. How stupid. Don't go!"

"What more is there to say?" she muttered fiercely.

"You shouldn't have stayed with those relatives of yours, they were always at home."

"Who with then? At your place maybe? It would have been the same," she persisted. "What more is there to say?"

"Let's go to a hotel, you'll stay a few more days."

"The train's coming," she said, turning.

"No, stay, think for a minute. After everything we said in those letters, we can be alone together, just think!"

She didn't say anything for a long time, biting her lips, her eyes moving across my face. Finally, hurt and wistful, she asked, "And you'll be glad if I stay?"

I found it hard to breathe, and there was a lump in my throat. I turned quickly and entered her car, bumping and elbowing my way, and found her compartment, grabbed her bag and left. I still remember how the conductors standing by the train stared at us.

"Let's go," I said.

"What about my ticket?" she asked, her eyes shimmering, her mouth trembling.

"To hell with it!" I said and took her hand. We went out to the square and found a taxi.

"To the hotel," I said.

"Which?" the driver asked.

"I don't care which!"

The car started, and moved toward the glow of the city's lights, past railway stations, apartment buildings, crowds of people.

"Stop here, old man," I told the driver at a store, and got out to buy a bottle of wine.

I came back, tucking it into my pocket. I pictured us drinking it, sitting alone with raised glasses, looking into each other's eyes. I could actually taste it when we came to a hotel and I went in to the desk.

"We haven't any rooms," he calmly informed me.

"Any room will do, you understand, any at all. The worst or the best you have."

"We haven't any rooms," he repeated sharply, and grabbed in irritation for the incessantly ringing telephone.

She was waiting for me in the lobby, looking in awe at the tremendous columns and mirrors. And she looked awed by me too, as if I were lord and master of it all! We went back to the taxi.

"Take us to another," I said irritably.

She got in without a murmur, and we began driving around

Moscow. I dropped in on a friend to borrow some money and nearly asked him to put us up, but his sister had guests. I looked at them, the wine on the table, down at the cassock supporting all those feet in narrow moccasins, and I didn't ask him. But I took some more money.

"Have a drink," he said suddenly, intercepting my glance.

"No thanks, they're waiting for me."

An hour, two hours passed and we were still driving, driving and always the same thing, "no room." Coming out on the street, I looked up at the tall hotel and apartment buildings, story upon story, row upon row of windows, so many still lighted, and I thought of everyone sitting or lounging peacefully at this hour, listening to the radio, reading themselves to sleep, holding their wives in their arms, and there was a stab in my heart.

Worn out finally, we took her bag to the station, checked it, and walked off slowly to Sokolniki. It was twelve o'clock midnight.

"What are we going to do?" I asked with a laugh.

"I don't know," she said wearily. "Maybe we could go to a restaurant? I'd like something to eat."

"The restaurants are all closed," I said with another stupid laugh, looking at my watch. "Let's go downtown, and walk around."

We strode along, the way we used to walk the seashore in the north, when we didn't want to be late for the movie in the club which was six miles away. All lights were out except for one on the other side of the street. There were almost no people on the streets. Finally we got to Tverskii Boulevard and sat down on a bench.

"And your place is impossible?" she asked hopefully.

"Idiot! Why else have we had to walk all over town? And just where would you have my mother and father go?"

"All right, all right," she said. "Don't get nasty. I'm leaving tomorrow, there's a train in the morning. Then . . ." she sighed, "then you can come see us again sometime."

I took her in my arms. She pressed close and closed her eyes.

"We can just sit like this, can't we?" she murmured, shifting into a more comfortable position on the bench. "You're sweet, I love you, you dope, I was in love with you up north, you just didn't know it."

Sitting up for a minute, she slipped off her shoes, drew up her legs, and pulled her skirt down over them.

"My feet hurt," she murmured sleepily. "Shoes . . . I'm not used to them. Why don't people in Moscow go barefoot?"

Two policemen emerged from a back alley. Seeing us, one of them stepped into the light and came toward us.

"Move along, friend." For some reason he spoke only to me. "That's not allowed."

"What isn't allowed?" I asked as she fumbled in embarrassment, getting her shoes back on her swollen feet.

"No back talk! You heard me, move along!"

We got up and left. I began looking at the apartment house windows again, and kept seeing a room with a cassock. There was nothing else in that room but a soft pink light and a cassock.

"Listen, shall we duck into a doorway somewhere?" I asked uncertainly.

"Yes let's," she agreed, with a faint smile. "We can sit on the steps and I'll take off my shoes."

We entered a dark courtyard, went back to the farthest doorway in the corner, went in, closed the door behind us, and sat on the steps. She took off her shoes immediately and began wiping off the step.

"You tired?" I asked and lit a cigarette. "Poor thing, we haven't had much luck in Moscow."

"True." She rubbed her cheek on my shoulder. "It's a very big city."

We heard footsteps. The door opened and the janitress came in and saw us.

"You get out of here!" she shrieked. "Curses on the both of you devils, alley cats! Get out or I'll start blowing!"

And she pulled a shiny whistle out of her apron pocket. She had a mean, high cheekboned face. We went back into the court-yard, followed by the janitress swearing at us all the while. Back on the street, we looked at each other and burst out laughing.

"It's not much like your White Sea," I said.

"Never mind," she said soothingly, "let's just walk. Or shall we go to the station and sleep on the benches?"

"All right," I agreed, then suddenly something struck me. "Listen, I'm a dope, let's go for a drive. We can take a taxi, I've the money, and we can go fifteen miles or so, that's what we'll do!"

A taxi was cruising down the street. Coming home late at night, I always love to watch the taxis. They weave a charmed circle through the sleeping city, their vacant lights blinking. Those green lights always make you want to take off for somewhere far away.

We hailed a taxi.

"Out of town?" the driver repeated. "I'll take you for," visibly jacking his price up, "seven and a half."

"All right," I said. I didn't care.

The drive made me sleepy. The road was deserted. It was dark in the west, but the east was growing light, the sun beginning to come up. A steady wind was blowing outside, and the cab reeked of gasoline.

"Anywhere here?" asked the driver, slowing down near a grove of trees.

"This is as far as we're going. The outskirts all right with you?" he asked, looking at her.

We got out and shivered in the predawn cold.

"Half hour enough?" he asked, looking at me appraisingly. "I'm going to sleep. Wake me when you get back. Got a cigarette? Let me have it . . ."

He turned off to the side of the road and we went through the tall grass toward the woods. I was feeling damp and cold, nothing more. My suit grew stiff and heavy, my shoes were wet, and my pants lost their crease. I watched the dusky light in the woods, wondering what to do. She looked tired and sleepy and there were rings under her eyes. Suddenly she gave a great yawn and looked around blankly, as if she were wondering what we had come for.

"Back to the woods," she half muttered, and gave me a sudden hostile look.

Then I yawned too, feeling bored and irritable about not being home in bed, but out here in the damp and cold.

"I'm fad up," she said, in the midst of a yawn, huskily pronouncing "fed" "fad." "Oh God, what's the point, I don't want this, let's go back."

"All right with me," I said listlessly, and yawned again. "But let's drink this, or it'll go to waste."

I got out the bottle and tried to uncork it, but the cork was in very tight. So I shoved it inside.

"Drink," I said, handing her the warm bottle.

"I don't want any," she murmured, but took the bottle and with a sigh began to drink.

Two streams ran down her chin like blood. She coughed and gave the bottle back to me. I finished it and threw it away.

"Let's go," I said, feeling better.

We made our way back through the wet woods, through the ferns, across the rolling meadow, and all the way she held her dress up so as not to stain the hem.

"Why so early?" the driver sneered, looking at me. "You didn't suit each other?"

"Let's roll," I said furiously, barely able to refrain from hitting him.

We dozed on the way back, falling against each other on the curves, and I remember finding those contacts with her body unpleasant, and she probably did too. It was five in the morning and we had three more hours to kill before train time. I felt bad, the wine had gone to my head, leaving it heavy and loggy.

Those three hours were a torture, mainly because I couldn't go away, but had to stay with her to the end. We lasted it out somehow and then once more I was putting her on the train without knowing what to say. My head was splitting.

"All right then, write me," she said, taking the handrail.

I found the strength to put my arms around her.

"Don't be angry," I muttered, kissed her forehead, and made for the exit. I remember feeling surprised at how relieved I was when I left her, but somewhere deep inside it was sad somehow, my soul smarted with a hurt of some kind, and I was ashamed.

I dragged the coat over to the radio and we sat on it, leaning against each other. All these months I'd had the feeling of loss, and now what I had found was even better than what I had imagined.

The bass murmured elegaically, searching in the darkness for its counterpoint, losing its way in uncertainty, rising and falling, its slow pace reminiscent of the movement of the stars. The saxophone listened compassionately, but the trumpet rose up angrily again and again, the piano chords coming between them like the Revelation. And underneath, like a metronome, like time, the soft, hollow, syncopating beat of the drum.

"Let's not turn on the light, all right?" she said, looking at the little blinking eye on the green dial of the radio.

"All right," I agreed, and thought that I might never have a night like this again. I was sad that three hours of it had already passed. I wanted it to be starting from the beginning, so I could go down to wait with the lantern again, so we could reminisce again, and then be afraid again of letting each other go in the darkness.

She got up to get something, and looked out the window. "It's snowing," she said huskily.

I got up too and looked out into the darkness. Silently, the snow was falling. The first real snow of the year. I pictured the mousetracks that would be around the pile of brushwood in the woods tomorrow, and the rabbit tracks around the locust tree where rabbits like to nibble at night. I thought of my gun and I felt so good a quiver of joy ran through me. God, how good! How glorious that the snow was falling, that we were alone with music, with our past and with a future that might be better than our past, that tomorrow I'd be taking her to all my favorite spots, Oka, the fields, the hills, the woods and ravines. The night was passing, but we couldn't sleep. We went on talking in whispers, holding each other, afraid of losing each other. We rekindled the stove and stared into its fiery jaws, watching the red light reflected in each other's faces. At seven, when the windows were already growing light, we fell asleep. We slept a long time because there was no one in our house to wake us.

The sun came up while we were asleep, and everything melted, only to freeze again. After tea I took my gun and we went out. The winter light in our eyes was so white and the clean air so sharp that at first they were painful. The snow had stopped, but there was an icy, thin, almost transparent crust over everything. The cowbarn was steaming fragrantly and some calves were huddled near it, their hoofs clattering as if they were on a wooden bridge. This was because the wash water from the barn was running just underneath the upper crust of snow. Several of them, their curly gray flanks spread wide apart, were urinating over and over again, wagging their tails in enthusiasm, producing emerald patches of young wet rye in the snow.

We took the road. The ruts were smoothly frosted over but when our boots broke through the crust, there was a brown splash of muddy water. In the woods the last pale yellow dandelions poked through the ice. Needles, leaves, and the last of the mushrooms could all be seen frozen into the ice and when we kicked at the mushrooms, they broke off and skittered around. The snow under our feet turned gray and crunched loudly all around us, in front, in back, and to the sides.

From a distance the fields on the hillsides were a smoky green and looked as if they had been sprinkled with flour. The haystacks looked black, and the woods, naked and penetrable and dark, were sharply accentuated by an occasional white birch trunk. The aspen trunks were covered with a shiny velvet green, and yes, there was still some color on the wooded hill, the last unfallen leaves red-capping the trees. Through the woods the river could be seen and looked, at that distance, deserted and cold. We went down into the snowy ravine, leaving deep dirty prints at first, then clean ones. We had a drink from a spring near a chopped-down ash tree. Oak and maple leaves were settling thickly to the bottom of the spring box, and the tree stump, which had turned an amber color, smelled bitter and cold.

"Nice?" I asked and looked at her. I was amazed: her eyes were green!

"Nice!" she said, licking her lips as she looked around.

"Better than the White Sea?" I asked.

She looked at the river again and up the slope. Her eyes turned even greener.

"Well the White Sea . . ." she said vaguely. "We have, ah . . . But you have oak trees here!" she interrupted herself. "How did you find this place?"

I was happy, but I felt strange and fearful. This autumn had turned out very well. I lit a cigarette, trying to relax, exhaling smoke and steam. A tug coming from Aleksin appeared, cresting a wave swiftly as we watched. Steam poured up from its engines and jets of water spewed from the sides into the river.

When the tug finally disappeared around the bend, we climbed up through the woods, holding hands, so we could get another look at Oka from above. We walked in silence, in a dream that had brought us together at last.

Two in December

He waited a long time for her at the station. It was a frosty sunny day and he was pleased by everything: the crowds of skiers, the crunch of new snow which the city of Moscow hadn't yet managed to dispose of. He was pleased with himself: his tough ski boots, the woolen socks that came up nearly to his knees, his heavy shaggy sweater and Austrian cap with a feather, but most of all with his skis, his tightly strapped, excellent maple skis.

She was late as usual. There was a time when he would have gotten angry, but he was used to it now, and after all, it was probably her only weakness. So he leaned his skis against the wall, stamped his feet to keep from freezing, and settled down to watch the direction from which she would be coming. He wasn't feeling particularly happy, just relaxed, and it was pleasant and peaceful to think that things were fine at work, that everyone liked him, that things were also fine at home, that it was a fine winter — December looked like March, with the snow glistening in the sun — and most important, things were fine between them. The bad period — of fights, jealousy, suspicion, doubts, sudden phone calls and silences at the other end of the line when all you can hear is breathing and your heart aches — all that was over, thank God. Now it was something different, a peaceful, trusting, tender feeling — that was it now!

When she arrived finally, he looked closely at her, up and down, and said simply, "Well, well, you're here."

He took his skis and they walked off slowly. She was out of breath from hurrying, and needed to rest. She had on a red cap, from which a few locks of hair had escaped. Her dark eyes narrowed and sparkled whenever she looked at him, and her nose was already sprinkled with tiny freckles.

He dropped behind for a moment, getting out change for the electric train, and looked at the back of her. He thought how pretty and well dressed she was, and that she'd probably been late because she always wanted to look as pretty as possible. Those loose locks of hair were perhaps not as accidental as they looked. How anxious to please and dear she was!

"Feel that sun! What a winter!" she said as he bought the tickets. "You didn't forget anything?"

He shook his head. He'd probably taken too much, it seemed now, because his pack was quite heavy.

The electric train, crowded with packs and skis, was very noisy: everyone was shouting and calling to each other as they found their places and banging their skis about. The window panes were cold and clear, but the stoves and benches gave off a dry warmth, and it was good watching the bright snow outside the windows as the train began to move, listening to the quick gentle tap of the wheels underneath.

Twenty minutes passed and he went out on the platform to smoke. One of the doors had no pane. There was a cold wind on the platform and a sharp smell of frost and iron. The walls and the ceiling were steaming. The sound of the wheels was no longer a tap, it was a roar, and the rails echoed.

He stood smoking, looking through the glass door into the car, his gaze wandering from bench to bench. He felt a bit sorry for everyone because none of them, he thought, was going to have such a good time in the next two days as he was. He watched the girls, their animated faces, experiencing the same vague and bittersweet excitement he always felt when a young and charming girl passed him with someone else. Then he looked at *her* and felt happy. He saw that even here — among all these pretty, younger girls — she was still the best. She was looking dully out the window but her eyes were dark and her lashes long.

He looked through the paneless window at the sky, squinting in the frosty brightness and the wind. They were flying past creaking wooden station platforms, buried in snow. Sometimes there'd be a lunch stand, all painted blue, with a stove pipe coming out of the roof, puffing blue smoke. And he thought how good it would be to sit at one of those lunch stands, listening to the thin whistle of the electric train, getting warm by the stove, and drinking beer from a mug. In general, everything was excellent: the winter, the joy of having someone to love, the joy of knowing that the one he loved was sitting inside and that when he looked at her he'd receive a look in response! Oh it had been good, he admitted, those many evenings alone at home, when he hadn't had her, or the evenings spent aimlessly loafing around the streets with friends, philosophizing, discussing the theory of relativity and other pleasantly weighty subjects. But it had always been sad to come home. He'd even written verses which a friend of his had liked, because he hadn't had anyone either. His friend was married now.

He thought what a strange creature man is. Here he was a lawyer, already thirty years old, and he hadn't done anything in particular or created anything; he hadn't become a poet or any kind of a champion, as he had dreamed as an adolescent. He had so many reasons to be sad now, because his life hadn't amounted to anything, and yet he wasn't sad; his job, although it brought him no glory, didn't sadden or horrify him either. On the contrary, he was as satisfied and at peace as if he had achieved everything he'd dreamed of. He lived a normal life.

He was uneasy about only one thing at the moment — the coming summer. Every year in November he began to think about his summer vacation, planning where and how to go. This vacation always seemed so endless and at the same time so brief, that in order not to make a mistake or miscalculate, to be sure of picking the right spot, he planned everything in advance. All winter and spring he worried, inquiring about the good places, what the weather was like, what the people were like, how to get there. The inquiries and plans were, perhaps, more enjoyable than the trip and the vacation themselves.

He was thinking now about summer, how he'd go to a small river somewhere. Taking a tent with them, they'd take a canoe out on their little river like Indians in their dugouts. Then it would be goodbye Moscow and asphalt and law suits and consultations!

Then he remembered the first time they'd left Moscow together. They'd gone to a tiny town in Estonia, where, as it happened, he'd had some business. They'd gone by bus, stopping off that night in Valdau. Everything had been dark, but one restaurant with its lights on, where they'd had a glass of vodka and gotten drunk. He remembered how happy he'd been on the bus because she'd been beside him in the lonely night, leaning against him and dozing. They'd arrived at dawn and although it was the middle of August and rainy in Moscow, there the sun had been out, clear and bright. He remembered the little white houses with sharp red tile roofs, the many gardens, the isolation and quiet, the tangle of weeds growing between the stones in the streets.

They'd taken a clean bright room smelling strongly of apples which were lying to ripen everywhere, outside the window, and under the bed and bureau. There had been a busy market; they'd gone and together they had picked out smoked bacon, some honey bread, butter, tomatoes, and pickles (all fabulously cheap). And that smell from the bakeries, the incessant cooing of pigeons, the flap of their wings. But of all his memories, she was the most important — such an unexpected surprise, a complete stranger, at the same time so close and beloved. What happiness that had been, and how much more there could still be, probably, if only there weren't a war!

He had been thinking a lot recently about war; he hated it. But now, looking at the glistening snow, the woods, the fields, listening to the ring and rumble of the rails, he felt certain that there'd be no war and there would be no death. Because, he thought,

there are times in life when a man can neither think about evil
nor believe in its existence.

They went almost to the end of the line. The snow crunched
loudly under their feet as they stepped onto the platform.

"What a winter!" she said again, squinting. "There hasn't been
one like it in a long time!"

It was ten miles to his summer cabin, and their plan was to
spend the night, ski the next day and return that night on another
railroad. He had a small strip of orchard land and a cabin built of
logs, furnished with two beds, a table, some crudely made stools
and an iron stove made in Germany.

After he'd gotten his skis on, he jumped several times, clapping
his skis and sending up a powdery spray of new snow. Then he
checked her straps and they moved off slowly. At first they tried
to pick up speed so they could get to the cabin early and get warm
and rested, but the woods and the fields made it impossible.

"Look at the trunks on those aspens!" she said, stopping. "The
color of cats' eyes!"

He stopped too to look, and it was true — the tops of the aspen
trunks were a yellowish green, the exact color of cats' eyes.

The woods were pierced by slanting rays of smoky light. The
snow hung like a shroud on the trunks, and the branches of the
fir trees, freed of the burden, clapped their hands.

Up and down they skied, spotting a snow-covered village below
them from time to time. Every cabin had a stove going, sending up
smoke. The columns of smoke rose up toward the sky, dropping
suddenly, stretching, spreading, wrapping the surrounding hillsides in a transparent blue mist. Even when the village was a mile
or so away, they could smell the smoke. It made them anxious to
get home, so they could light their stove.

And so they followed the deep sparkling runner tracks over the
dung-spattered roads, and although it was December, there was
something springlike in the wisps of hay on the roads, the clear
blue shadows in the ruts, in the roads themselves. Spring was in

the air. Once they saw a black horse galloping on one of the roads toward a village, his coat gleaming, his muscles rippling, the ice and snow flying up under his feet. They could distinctly hear the crunch of his feet and his snorting. They stopped to watch.

Then a badly worried jackdaw swept past nervously, hurriedly followed by another. In the distance an interested magpie dove down, keeping an eye on them: what had they found? And again they stopped to watch. Bullfinches — looking like birds of the tropics against the ice and snow — swayed and chattered on thistles sticking out of the snow, and darted around busily, dropping seeds from their tough beaks.

Sometimes they'd come on fox tracks, following a regular though sinuous path through the hills. Then the tracks would turn and disappear in the snowy radiance. Going on, the skiers passed through aspen and birch groves, finding more tracks — rabbit or perhaps dog tracks.

There was something disturbing about those signs of secret nocturnal life, carried on in the frozen empty fields and woods. One was reminded of the glass of tea before the hunt, of guns and sheepskin coats, the slowly moving stars, of black haystacks where rabbits gorge at night and where, after sitting up on their haunches and sniffing, the foxes come to find them. One could imagine the crack of gunshot, the flash of light, the fragile echo breaking in the hills, the barking of the excited dogs in the villages, the glassy eyes of the rabbit, reflecting the stars as it lies stretched out on the ground, the great frost-covered ears, the warm weight of the carcass.

Down in the ravines and valleys, where the snow was deep and dry, the going was difficult, but the sides of the hills were powdered with fresh snow and there it was fine skiing. The woods on the farthest hills, on the horizon, glowed with a rosy light, the sky was blue, and the fields appeared to have no end.

So they climbed and descended, resting on fallen trees, smiling at each other. Sometimes he'd take her by the neck, draw her to

him and kiss her cold chapped lips. They said almost nothing
to each other, except for an occasional "Look!" or "Listen!"

The truth was that she was sad, distracted, and hanging back,
but he didn't see that. He thought she was just tired, and he'd
stop to wait for her. Catching up, she'd look at him with a pecul-
iar reproachful expression and he'd ask cautiously, as he knew
his companion didn't like such questions, "You're not tired? We
can rest."

"Of course not!" she would say quickly. "It's just . . . I was
thinking."

The sun was low, only the fields at the tops of the hills were
still light; the woods, the valleys, the ravines had been darkening
and disappearing for a long time. The two lonely figures moved
on across the endless expanse of woods and fields — he in front
and she behind, he enjoying the rustle of snow under her skis
and the tap of her poles.

Once the steady roar of a motor was heard up there where the
sun was dropping down in the rosy light behind the woods, and a
minute later a plane appeared. When the sun's rays broke over its
body, it was the only thing visible in the dark, and it was nice
watching it from below, in the silent frosty twilight, imagining
the passengers sitting up there thinking of the end of their trip,
thinking about being in Moscow, and the people who were to
meet them.

It was dark when they finally got there. They dropped their
frozen boots on the porch, unlocked the door, and went in. The
room was completely dark and seemed colder than it had been outside.

She lay down immediately and closed her eyes. She'd been overheated and perspiring from the exercise, and now that she was
cooling off, she was so shaken by a chill that she couldn't move. She
opened her eyes, looked up at the log ceiling in the darkness, then
down at the flame rising in the steaming chimney of the kerosene
lamp, and blinked — all the colors she'd seen that day, yellow-

green, white, blue, crimson, were swimming and shifting before her eyes.

He got some firewood out from under the porch, dumped it near the stove, crumpled some paper, lit the stove, and heaved a sigh of satisfaction. But nothing was of any help to her; she was not happy about having come.

The stove got red hot, the cabin warmed up, and it became possible to undress. He took off his jacket and shoes and socks, putting them near the stove, and sat in his undershirt, his eyes closed in contentment, scratching his bare feet and smoking.

"You tired?" he asked. "Get undressed."

And although she had no desire to move, only the desire to escape sadness and disappointment in sleep, she obediently took off her ski clothes, and hung her jacket, socks and sweater up to dry, keeping on only a pair of men's blue jeans. She sat down on the bed and stared at the lamp, her shoulders sagging.

He stuck his feet into his boots, threw on his jacket, took the pail and went outside. The pail began to ring melodically. Returning, he put the teapot on, rooted around in his rucksack, emptying it, and set out everything on the table and window sill.

She waited for her tea in silence. Pouring herself a mug, she sat munching on some bread and butter, warming her hands around the mug, sipping her tea and watching the lamp.

"Why are you so quiet?" he asked. "Wasn't it a nice day?"

"Yes, but I'm terribly tired now." She got up and stretched, without looking at him. "Let's go to bed."

"So that's the trouble," he said lightly. "Wait, I'll put on some wood, so the house won't get cold."

"I'll sleep by myself tonight, right here by the stove. Don't be angry," she added quickly, dropping her eyes.

"What's the matter?" he asked, suddenly remembering how sad and remote she'd been all day; remembering, he felt bitter, and his heart beat painfully.

He suddenly realized that he didn't know her at all — what she was studying at the university, who her friends were, what she talked about. He realized that she was as much a mystery to him now as she had been at their first meeting. That to her he was dull and insensitive because he didn't understand her needs, nor could he do whatever it was that would make her so continually happy with him that she'd need nothing and no one else.

And he was suddenly ashamed of the whole day, of this pitiful cabin and stove, of his own peace of mind, even of the sun and the snow. Why had they come, why was it necessary? And where was this damned, much praised happiness?

"All right," he said casually, and took a deep breath. "Sleep where you like."

She undressed without looking at him and lay down, covering herself with her jacket, and staring at the fire in the stove. He went over to the other bed, sat down, and lighted a cigarette. Then he put out the lamp and lay down. He had the terrible feeling that she was leaving him. Something, he didn't know what it was, had worked against their happiness, and it made him angry.

After a while he heard her crying. He got up and looked at her across the table. There was enough light from the stove to see by, and he saw her lying on her stomach, looking at the blaze, her unhappy face wet with tears and twisted into a pitiful expression. Her lips and chin were trembling, as she wiped away her tears with her slender hand.

Why had the day become so unhappy and unbearable? She didn't know herself. She just felt that the time for first love had passed, her way of life was no longer interesting, something new should be coming. She was tired of being no one in the eyes of his parents and uncles and aunts, no one in the eyes of his friends and their girl friends. She wanted to become a wife and mother, but he couldn't see this. He was completely happy just as they were. But it was wretched and miserable compared to the first exciting time of their love, when everything had been so vague and undefined, so filled with the feeling of novelty, and mystery, and passion.

As she started to fall asleep, she dreamed an old dream of her adolescence again. The dream was about someone strong and manly who loved her. She loved him too but for some reason refused him. He went far away to the north, where he became a fisherman, and she suffered. He hunted on the hills beside the sea, went rock climbing, made up songs, went down to fish in the sea, but all the time he was thinking of her. When she understood finally that happiness for her was only with him, she gave up everything and went to join him. She was so pretty that everyone paid court to her along the road — the pilots, truck drivers, sailors — but she could think of no one but him. Their meeting would have to be so extraordinary that it terrified her imagination. So she kept on thinking up more and more ways to delay the great moment. She usually fell asleep without ever meeting him.

She hadn't thought of the dream or anything like it in a long time, but tonight for some reason she wanted to dream. But tonight, just as she was getting into the motorboat, her thoughts became confused and she fell asleep.

She woke up later because it was cold. He was squatting in front of the cold stove, kindling it. His face was sad and she felt sorry for him.

They were quiet the next morning, and ate their breakfast and drank their tea in silence. Then they cheered up, took their skis and went out. They climbed up the hills and skied down, each time choosing steeper and more dangerous slopes.

They warmed up later at the cabin, talking about trivial things, such as the fine winter they were having. When it began to get dark, they packed up, locked the door, and skied off to the station.

They were dozing as they approached Moscow that evening, but at the sight of the first apartment buildings with their rows of lighted windows, he realized that they'd be having to go their separate ways, and he suddenly imagined her as his wife.

Why not? His youth was over, the time had passed when everything is simple and a home, wife, family and all that aren't necessary. He was thirty years old and there no longer was any particular gratification in the feeling that she's beside you and she's lovely but you can always leave her for another because you're a free man.

All day long at the law office tomorrow he'd be writing appeals and applications, thinking about human unhappiness — including family unhappiness — then going home — to whom? Then summer, the long summer, all those trips, canoes, tents and again — with whom? And he suddenly wanted to be better and more human and to do everything to make her life good.

When they stepped out onto the platform, the street lights were on, the city was humming, and the snow had finally been removed. They both felt as if there'd been no trip, no two days together, and though they had to say goodbye now and go off to their own homes, they'd meet again, perhaps in two or three days. They both felt easy and natural and at peace. They said goodbye as they always did, with a hurried smile. He didn't see her home.

At the Station

IT was a cold, bleak autumn day. The small station's low wooden building was black in the rain. For the second day a stiff northern wind was blowing, whistling in the attic window, ringing the station bell, stirring the naked twigs on the birch trees.

A horse was standing at the broken railing, its head hanging, its swollen feet planted wide apart. The wind whipped at its tail, ruffled its mane and the hay on the cart, and tugged at the reins. But the horse didn't raise its head or open its eyes; it was brooding or perhaps just dozing.

A crew-cut young man, dressed in a leather coat, with a tough, pockmarked face sat on a suitcase near the cart. Rapidly inhaling a cheap cigarette, he spat, smoothed his chin with his red stubby-fingered hand, and stared gloomily at the ground.

A girl was standing beside him, her eyes swollen, a lock of hair come loose from her scarf. There was neither hope nor desire in her pale, weary face. She looked bored and indifferent, but her eyes hinted at something painful and unexpressed. Patiently shifting her weight from one small muddy boot to another, trying to get her back to the wind, she stared fixedly at the boy's thick-skinned ear.

With a slight rustle some leaves slipped along the platform, collected, whispered something in private, then, scattered by the wind, they spun over the damp earth, into a puddle, and touching the water, were silent. It was raw and chilly.

"Life has taken some turn, hasn't it?" the boy asked suddenly, with a shallow laugh. "*My* turn now. What's the collective farm mean to me anyway? A home? It can be home for my mother and sister, but not for me. I'll get away from here . . . They'll

give me a coach, an apartment in town. What kind of weight lift-
ers do we have? I was at the competitions, I saw: our best were
barely in first class. But I could have won with no trouble. Don't
you think?"

"But what about me?" the girl asked quietly.

"You?" The boy squinted at her and coughed. "We've gone
through all that. Let me get there and look around. For me it's
now or never. I've got to make a record for myself. I'll get to Moscow, and I'll give it to them there. I'm only sorry I didn't know
the mechanics of it earlier, or I'd have been there long ago . . .
What's it like there? They're already in training . . . But I'm
naturally strong, you wait, I'll walk all over everyone there.
I'll go abroad. I'll have a little life at last, God willing. And I'll
come for you . . . later . . . I'll write."

The vague faint sound of a train was heard in the distance: an
attenuated whistle broke the cheerless silence of the dismal day.
The station door banged and the stationmaster, all hunched up
in his overcoat, came out on the platform. He looked sleepy and
his red cap was covered with dark oily spots.

He glanced at the solitary couple, took out a cigarette, tamped
it, sniffed at it, and, looking at the sky, tucked it away in his pocket.
Then he yawned, rasping, "Which car?"

The boy slowly turned his short thick neck, looked at the stationmaster's new galoshes, and got out his ticket. "The ninth,
why?"

"Well," muttered the stationmaster and yawned again. "The
ninth you said? The ninth's all right. This weather's a bitch."

Turning, he stepped over a puddle and made his way to the baggage section. The train came out of the woods, moving fast. Then
it slowed and shrieked again, thinly and wearily. The boy got up,
threw away his cigarette, and looked at the girl; she tried to smile,
but her lips refused, and trembled.

"That's enough!" the boy snapped, grabbing his suitcase. "You
hear? That's enough, I said!"

They walked slowly along the platform toward the train. Searching the boy's face eagerly, the girl clung to his sleeve and said, stumbling over her words, "Take care of yourself up there. Don't lift too much . . . you'll bust something. Think of yourself and don't overstrain. And me? I'll wait. I'll look for you in the papers. Don't worry about me. I love you. Look at me, crying . . . I think . . ."

"Stop now," said the boy. "We've been through it. I'm coming back."

The engine passed them, rattling the platform and wrapping them in warm, wet steam. Then the cars, slower and slower, one, two, three . . .

"There's the ninth," the girl said quickly. "Let's wait here."

The train stopped gently beside them. Pale, rumpled passengers poured out onto the platform to look around. A fat unshaven man in striped pajamas stood behind the window, trying to yank it open, his chubby face contorted with the effort. It wouldn't budge, and he gave it a martyred look. When he finally got it open, he leaned out, smiled myopically at the station, saw the girl, smiled broadly and called out, "What station is this, young lady?"

"Lundanka," rasped the porter.

"Is there a market?" asked the man in pajamas, looking at the girl.

"No market," answered the porter. "This is a two-minute stop."

"Is that so?" The passenger was still looking at the girl.

"Close that window," ordered an irritable voice in the car.

The man in pajamas spun around, displaying his fat shoulders, and then, smiling sadly, he shut the window and suddenly disappeared, as if he had dropped through a hole.

The boy set his suitcase down on the step and turned to the girl. "Well, goodbye, I guess," he said slowly, stuffing his hands in his pockets.

The girl's face was covered with tears. She sobbed and buried her face in his shoulder. "I'll be so lonely," she whispered. "Write me often, you hear? Write me . . . Are you coming back?"

"I said I would." The boy sounded tense, frightened. "No crying now!"

"I'm all right," she whispered, taking a breath and wiping away her tears with a quick darting movement as she gazed tenderly at the boy's face. "I'll be here. Remember what we said?"

"I remember," he snapped, throwing back his head and looking away.

"I . . . my life is all yours . . . You know that?"

"I know," muttered the boy, staring at his feet.

The bell rang twice, cracked and thin.

"Citizens, all aboard please," said the porter, jumping on.

The girl blanched, and her hand flew to her mouth. "Vasya!" she cried, staring back blindly at the passengers who had turned to stare. "Kiss me, Vasya . . ."

"For . . ." the boy muttered, glancing over his shoulder and then bending down to the girl. He straightened up, as if he had just completed some heavy chore, and jumped onto the train. The girl gasped, bit her trembling lips, and for a brief instant covered her face with her hands.

The cars began to hiss, the engine gave a strained shriek up ahead, and a short, strained echo came back from the woods. Barely perceptibly, the cars began to move. The ties creaked. The boy stood on the step, frowning at the girl. Suddenly, he flushed and called out to her, "Listen, I'm not coming back! Listen . . ." He opened his mouth, took a deep breath, said something incomprehensible, awful, and picking up his suitcase, entered the car.

The girl dropped to her knees, her head hanging. The cars flashed past, the ties were steaming, something squeaked and creaked, but she was staring fixedly at something on the track, a shiny spot of grease. The wheels dashed over it, hiding it, revealing it. Thoughtfully, gradually, she moved toward the enticing, beckoning spot, straining, pressing her hand to the unendurable pain in her heart, her tender, almost childish lips gone white . . .

"Watch out!" A wild cry broke over her head.

The girl started and blinked. The spot flickered, the squeak of the ties broke off. Looking up, she could see the last car with its red emblem on the buffer steaming away into the distance, but she could hear nothing. Then, raising her head to the low, indifferent sky, she tightened the scarf around her face and began to rock to and fro like an old woman, howling drunkenly, "He's gone . . . !"

The train disappeared quickly into the woods. Silence. The stationmaster shuffled over, stopping behind the girl, and yawned. "Gone, eh?" he asked. "Yes, they're all leaving today." He was silent for a minute. Then he spat with great satisfaction, and rubbed his foot in it. "I'm going to leave soon. Go south. It's boring here, rainy. Down south there, the weather's mild and there're — what do you call them — cypresses." He glanced at the figure of the girl, studied his dirty boots at length and asked, without much interest, "You're not from the 'Red Lighthouse' farm, are you? You are? I see. This weather's a bitch, and that's a fact!"

He shuffled off, carefully avoiding the puddles.

The girl stood for a long time on the platform, staring straight ahead, seeing nothing, not the dark wet woods, nor the dimly shining rails, nor the storm-swept grass. Just the tough, pock-marked face of the boy.

Finally she sighed, wiped her face, and went over to the horse. She untied it and fixed the bridle, put back the hay blown off the cart and shook the reins. The horse stepped back, lifelessly flicked its tail, and with a great effort turned past the little flower bed, past the pile of hay, past some stacked ties, and out onto the country road.

The girl sat completely motionless, staring over the shaft. Then she looked back at the station one last time, and lay face down in the cart.

The Blue and the Green

"LILYA," she says in a deep throaty voice and gives me a small warm hand.

I take her hand carefully, squeeze it and let it go. At the same time I mumble my name. It seems I'd forgotten the possibility that I'd have to pronounce my own name. The hand I've just relinquished is lovely and pale in the darkness. "What an extraordinarily lovely hand!" I think ecstatically.

We're standing in a dark courtyard. There are so many windows in this dark square yard: there are pale blue windows, green, pink, and plain white windows. From a blue window on the second floor music can be heard. There they've turned on the radio and I hear jazz. I like jazz a lot, not to dance to — I don't know how to dance — I like to listen to good jazz. Some don't like it, but I do. I don't know, maybe that's bad. I'm standing and I'm listening to jazz coming down from the second floor, from the blue window. That's evidently an excellent radio they have.

After she says her name, there's a long silence. I know she's waiting for me to do something. Maybe she thinks I'll start talking, say something funny, maybe she's waiting for a first word from me, some kind of question so she can start talking. But I'm quiet, I'm entirely in the power of that extraordinary rhythm and the silvery sound of the trumpet. How nice that music is playing and I don't have to say anything!

Finally we go off. We come out onto a lighted street. There are four of us: my friend and a girl, Lilya and I. We're going to the movies. It's the first time I've been to a movie with a girl, it's the first time I've met her, and she gave me her hand and told me her name. A wonderful name — pronounced in a throaty voice! And here we are side by side, complete strangers to each other and yet friends somehow. There's no music to protect me any more. My friend drops behind with his girl. Panicky, I slow down, but they go even slower. I know he's doing it on purpose. That's not nice of him — to leave us alone. I never expected such treachery from him!

What can I say to her? What does she like? I sneak a look at her sideways: shining eyes, which reflect the light, dark, probably very coarse hair, thick eyebrows which are run together and give her the sternest look, but her cheeks are strained as if she were trying to keep from laughing. What is there to say to her anyway?

"You like Moscow?" she asks suddenly, and looks at me sternly. I start at the sound of her deep voice. Does anyone else have a voice like that?

I don't say anything for a while, getting my breath. Finally I collect my strength. Yes of course I like Moscow. I like the Arbat region especially. But I like other streets too. Then I shut up again.

We get to Arbat Square. I put my hands in my pockets and start to whistle. Let her think that knowing her isn't all that interesting to me. After all, I can go home, I live right near by, and I'm not obliged to go to the movies and feel bad because she looks as if she's trying not to laugh at me.

But we go to the movies anyway. There's still fifteen minutes before the showing. We stand in the foyer and listen to a singer, but it's hard to hear her, there are a lot of people around and they're all talking. The only ones listening and applauding are the ones in front, but behind everyone is eating ice cream and candy and talking. Deciding that you listen to a singer properly or not at all, I start looking at the pictures on the walls. I've never paid any attention to them before, but now I'm very interested. I'm thinking about the artists that did them. It wasn't such a bad idea to hang those pictures. It's nice that they're hanging there.

Lilya looks at me with shining gray eyes. She's so pretty! She isn't really pretty though, it's just those shining eyes and pink cheeks. When she smiles she gets dimples and her eyebrows come apart and she doesn't look so stern. She has a clear high forehead. Only once in a while a frown appears on it. That's probably when she's thinking.

No! I can't stand here with her any longer. Why is she looking at me that way?

"I'm going to smoke — " I say abruptly and carelessly, and I go into the smoking lounge. There I sit down and breathe more easily. It's strange but when there's a lot of smoke in the room, when the air is practically black with smoke, I don't feel like smoking for some reason. I look around: there are many people standing and sitting around. Some are talking quietly, others smoke quickly in silence, inhaling deeply, throw away their cigarettes without finishing them and go out. Where are they hurrying to? It's interesting, if you smoke fast, a cigarette tastes bittersweet. It's better to smoke without hurrying, and to take small puffs. I look at the clock: still five minutes to the showing. No, I'm probably a dope. Other people get to know each other so easily, they talk and laugh. Terribly clever people can talk about football or anything they like. They argue about cybernetics. I wouldn't talk about cybernetics with a girl for anything. Lilya is a hard person, I decide, she has coarse hair. I've got fine hair. That's probably why I'm sitting smoking when I don't feel like it at all. But I sit here anyway. What can I do in the foyer? Look at pictures some more? You know, they're bad pictures, and who knows why they hung them. It's a good thing I never noticed them before.

Finally the bell. I walk very slowly out of the smoking lounge, looking for Lilya in the crowd. Without looking at each other, we go in and sit down. Then they turn out the lights and start the film.

When we come out of the movie, my friend has disappeared completely. This makes me give up trying to think about anything at all. I just walk and don't say anything. There's almost no one on the street. Cars shoot past me. Our footsteps reverberate off the walls and can be heard way off in the distance.

So we get to her house. We stop again in the courtyard. It's late and not all the windows are lighted now, it's darker than it was two hours ago. Many of the white and pink windows have gone out, but the green ones are still burning. There's a light on in the blue window on the second floor but no more music to be heard. We stand for a while without saying anything at all. Lilya is behaving strangely; she looks up, looking at the windows as if she were counting them; she's almost turned her back on me. Then she starts to fix her hair. Then I say carelessly, just sort of by the way, that we ought to meet tomorrow. I'm very glad it's dark in the courtyard and she can't see my ears burning.

She agrees to meet me. I can come to her place, her window is on the street. She is on vacation, her family has gone to the country, and she's a bit bored. She'd love to go out.

I wonder if it's proper to shake her hand goodbye. She gives me her narrow hand herself, pale in the darkness, and again I feel how warm and trusting she is.

2

The next day I go to her house in the afternoon. This time there are lots of kids in the yard. Two of them have bicycles. They're going somewhere or have they just arrived maybe? The rest are just standing around. It seems to me they're looking at me, knowing perfectly well why I've come. I simply can't go into the courtyard, so I go up to her window on the street. I look in the window and cough.

"You home, Lilya?" I ask loudly. I ask it very loudly and my voice doesn't shake. That's absolutely amazing that my voice didn't break!

Yes, she's home. She has a girl friend with her. They're arguing about something interesting and I've got to settle the argument.

"Come quickly!" Lilya calls.

But I can't bear to go through the yard — I just can't.

"I'll come through the window!" I say decisively, and jump up. I jump up easily and gracefully, and only when I throw one leg over the windowsill do I notice the amazed amusement of the girl friend and Lilya's embarrassment. I guess right away that I've done something awkward, and freeze astride the windowsill: one leg in the room, the other in the street. I sit and look at Lilya.

"Well, climb in," Lilya says impatiently. Her eyebrows separate and her cheeks are getting red.

"I don't like to hang around inside in summer," I mutter, assuming a supercilious expression. "I'd better wait for you outside."

I jump down and go toward the gates. How they're laughing at me now! I know girls are all cruel and they never understand us. Why did I come here? Why do I play the clown? I'd better leave. If I run now I can get to the corner and turn before she comes out. Should I run or not? I think it over a minute: is this the moment? Then I turn and see Lilya suddenly. She and her friend are coming through the gates. She's looking at me, the laughter still hasn't gone out of her eyes, and her cheeks are dimpled.

I don't look at her friend. Why is she coming with us? What will I do with the two of them? I'm quiet and Lilya begins talking to her girl friend. They talk and I don't say anything. When we pass billboards I read them all attentively. Sometimes you can read billboards backwards, and you get funny guttural words. We get to the corner and the girl friend starts saying goodbye. I look at her gratefully. She's very pretty and intelligent.

The girl friend goes off and we go to Tverskii Boulevard. How many lovers have walked along Tverskii Boulevard! And now we're walking along it. True we're not in love yet. On the other hand maybe we are, I don't know. We're walking far enough apart. About a yard from each other. The linden trees have already blossomed. There are lots of flowers in the flower beds. They have no smell at all and probably no one knows what they're called.

We talk a lot. There's just no stopping us. We're talking about ourselves and our friends, we jump from subject to subject and forget what we were talking about a minute before. But that doesn't bother us, we've got a lot of time, a long, long night ahead and we can remember anything we've forgotten. It's even better to remember later on, at night.

Suddenly I notice her dress has come undone. She has on a marvelous dress. I've never seen one like it on anyone — tiny little buttons run from the collar to the waist. Now some of those buttons are undone and she hasn't noticed. But she can't go along the street in an unfastened dress! How can I tell her? Maybe I should start buttoning it myself? Make some funny remark and start buttoning as if it were an everyday matter. That would be nice! No, I can't do that, that's simply impossible. So I turn away, wait for a pause in the conversation and say that she's unfastened. Right away she's quiet. And I look at a great big sign hanging from the roofs. It says that everyone can win 100,000 rubles. A very optimistic sign. We should win sometime!

Then I light a cigarette. I make it last a long time. In general it's a good idea to smoke in difficult situations. It helps a lot. Then I look at her timidly. Her dress is buttoned, her cheeks are on fire, her eyes are dark and stern. She looks at me, looks as if I had changed greatly or had found out something important about her. Now we're walking a little closer to each other.

The hours pass, and we're still walking, talking, and walking. You can walk around Moscow endlessly. We go to Pushkin Square, from Pushkin Square to Trubnaya Square, from there we walk along Neglinaya Street to the Bolshoi Theater, then to Stone Bridge. I'm ready to walk forever. I ask if *she's* tired though. No, she's not tired, it's very interesting. The street lamps go on. The sky, awaiting darkness, falls, the stars grow bigger. Then the sun gently begins to set. Lovers walk along the boulevards clinging to each other. There's a couple on every bench. I look at them enviously and wonder if Lilya and I will ever sit like that.

There's absolutely no one in the streets but policemen. They all look at us. Several cough significantly as we go past. They probably want to say something but they don't. Lilya bends her head and hurries past. That seems funny to me for some reason. Now we're walking side by side. Her hand brushes against mine sometimes. It's just the smallest brush, but I feel it.

We part in her dark quiet courtyard. Everyone is sleeping, not a single window is lighted. We lower our voices to a whisper but our words still come out loud and it seems to me that someone is listening.

I get home at three. Only then do I feel my legs shaking. How tired she must be! I turn on the lamp and start to read. I'm reading *Castle Browdi* which Lilya gave me. It's a remarkable book. All the time I'm reading it for some reason I see Lilya's face. Then I close my eyes and hear her sweet throaty voice. I find a long dark hair between the pages. It's her hair — she must have read *The Castle*. Why did I think she had coarse hair? It's a soft silky hair. I fold it carefully and put it in the encyclopedia. I'll find a better place to hide it later.

It's quite light and I can't read any more. I lie down and look out the window. We live high up, on the seventh floor. We can see the roofs of many houses from our windows. In the distance, where the sun comes up in the summer, the star on top of the Kremlin Tower is visible. You can only see one star. I love to look at that star. At night when it's quiet in Moscow I listen to the Kremlin chimes. It's very nice to listen at night. I lie there, I look at the stars and I think about Lilya.

3

A week later my mother and I went up north. I had been dreaming about this trip since spring. But now life in the country had taken on special sense and meaning for me.

I went straight to the woods, the real, wild woods. I felt like an explorer. I had a gun — it was given to me when I finished the ninth class — and I went hunting. I could go out all by myself and never get bored. Sometimes I would stop and sit down to watch the wide river, the low autumn sky. August. It's often bad weather in August. But good weather or bad, I would leave home early and go to the woods. There I would hunt or gather mushrooms or just walk around the clearings looking at the white camomile flowers which grow a lot around there. There's not too much to do in the woods. If you sit quietly by a lake, ducks will fly up and drop down with a hiss right beside you. They'll just sit there at first, stretching their necks out straight, and then they'll begin to dive and splash and swim around. I'd follow them with my eyes, without turning my head.

Then the sun would come from behind a cloud, and break through the leaves over my head, sending trembling golden fingers down deep into the water. You could see the long stems of the water lilies and large fish swimming around in the stems. When they hit a sunspot, they'd stop cold, not a fin moving, as if they were sunning or sleeping. I had the queer sensation as I watched them of freezing up myself, and everything seemed a dream.

There's not too much to do in the woods. You can simply lie there, listening to the pine trees howl, and think about Lilya. You can even talk to her. I talked to her about hunting, about the woods and the lake, about the wonderful smell of gunsmoke, and she would always understand, though women usually don't like or understand hunting.

Sometimes I wouldn't go home until dark. I'd be a bit scared crossing the fields. Even with a loaded gun, I still looked around nervously. It was very dark. Owls would fly around in circles over my head. I could see them but I couldn't hear how many because I couldn't hear their wingbeats. Once I took a shot at them, and for a long time afterwards an owl flew around and around the clearing, hooting in the darkness.

After a month I returned to Moscow. I went straight from the station, just stopping off to leave my bags at home, to see Lilya. It was evening, her window was lighted, that meant she was home.

I went up to the window, crawled under the scaffolding — they were remodeling her building — and looked through the curtain. She was sitting alone at the table, reading by the table lamp. Her face was thoughtful. She turned the page, leaned on her elbows, raised her eyes and looked at the lamp, winding a lock of hair around her finger. What dark eyes! How could I have thought they were gray? They were dark, almost black. I stood there under the scaffolding, and it smelled of pine and plaster. The smell of pine was a distant echo of hunting, a reminder of everything I'd left in the north. Footsteps behind me. People going somewhere in a hurry, stepping loudly along the pavement. With their own thoughts and loves and lives. Moscow overwhelmed me. I had forgotten its noise, its lights, its smells, its crowds. And I reflected with quiet joy that, in an enormous city, it was good to have someone to love.

"Lilya!" I called softly.

She jumped, her eyebrows jumped. Then she got up, came to the window, raised the curtain, and leaned toward me. Her eyes were dark and delighted.

"Alyosha!" she said slowly. Two scarcely noticeable dimples appeared on her cheeks. "Alyosha! Is that you? Is it really you? I'm coming right out. You want to go for a walk? I want to. I'm coming right out."

I got out from under the scaffold, crossed the street and watched her window. There, the light went out, a short minute, and Lilya's figure appeared in the dark space between the gates. She saw me at once and ran across the street. She grabbed my hands and held them in hers a long time. She seemed browner and thinner. Her eyes were bigger. I could hear her heart thumping and her broken breathing.

"Let's go!" she said at last. And I suddenly realized that she'd been speaking to me in the familiar. I felt like sitting down or leaning against something — my legs were so weak. Even after the most exhausting hunt, they'd never shaken so hard.

But I felt uncomfortable walking beside her. I'd only dropped in to see her for a minute. I was so badly dressed. I had come straight from the train, in my old ski pants and boots. My pants were burned in several spots, because I had slept in them out hunting. When you sleep by the fire, you often burn your pants and jacket. No, I couldn't take a walk with her.

"What nonsense!" she said, unconcerned, and pulled me by the hand. She had to talk to me. She'd been all alone, her girl friends had all gone away, her parents were in the country, she was frightfully bored waiting for me all that time. What difference did my pants make? And why didn't I write? Maybe I liked making other people suffer?

And there we were again, walking around Moscow. It was a crazy night somehow. It began to rain. We ducked into an empty doorway, breathing hard from running, and watched the street. Water ran loudly down the drainpipes, the sidewalks glistened, the passing cars were wet all over, and sent red and white lines of light creeping over the wet pavement toward us. Then the rain stopped, we came out, laughing and jumping over the puddles. But it started to rain again with renewed vigor and we ducked back under. Drops of rain sparkled in her hair. And when she looked at me her eyes shone even brighter.

"You thought about me?" she asked. "I thought about you almost the whole time, not that I wanted to. I don't know why I did myself. You know, we don't know each other very well. Isn't that true? I read a book and wondered if you'd like it. Were your ears red? They say that if you think about someone a lot, that person's ears will get red. I didn't even go to the Bolshoi. My mama gave me a ticket, but I didn't go. Do you like opera?"

"Sure! Maybe I'll become a singer. They tell me I have a good bass."

"Alyosha! Are you a bass? Sing for me, please? Sing softly, and no one but me will hear."

I refused at first. Then I sang anyway. I sang romances and

arias and I didn't even notice that it had stopped raining, and that people on the sidewalk were looking at us. Lilya didn't notice either. She looked at me and her eyes shone.

4

It's terrible being young. Life goes quickly, you're seventeen or eighteen already and you haven't done anything. It's still unclear whether or not you have any talent. And you want such tremendous things out of life! You want to write poems that the whole country will learn by heart. Or to compose a heroic symphony and come out to conduct the orchestra, dressed in a tuxedo, pale, your hair in your face, with Lilya — and this was essential — sitting in the parterre! What could I do? What could I do so that life would not pass in vain, to make each day a day of battle and victory? The thought tortured and tormented me, I wasn't a hero, I wasn't an explorer. Was I capable of heroic feats? Was I capable of hard work, did I have the strength to accomplish great deeds? The worst thing is that no one understands. They all look, and pat your head as if you were a ten-year-old boy! Only Lilya, Lilya alone understood me, only with her could I be completely open.

We'd been in school a long time: she was in the ninth class, and I in the tenth. I decided to study swimming and become a soviet champion, then a world champion. I took lessons at the pool. The crawl — that seemed to be the best style, the most dashing style. I liked it very much. At night I liked to dream.

There's a brief moment in winter when the snow on the rooftops and the sky turn dark blue, purple even, at twilight. I would stand at the window, looking at the purple snow, breathing the light frosty air and dreaming of distant expeditions, unknown countries, unclimbed mountains. I would be hungry, I would grow a red beard, I'd be sunburned or frostbitten, I would even die, but I

would disclose one more of nature's secrets. That would be the
life! If only I could get on an expedition!

I began going around to the industrial firms and administrative
offices. There are a lot of them in Moscow and they all have mys-
terious-sounding names. Yes, there were expeditions going out.
To Central Asia, to the Urals, up north. Yes, they needed men. My
training? Oh, none. That was too bad, but they could do nothing
to help in that case. I had to be trained. Could I go as a laborer?
They hire laborers on the spot. Goodbye and good luck!

And so I went back to school and prepared my lessons. So what,
it was the fault of the circumstances. All right, I'd finish the tenth
class and enter the institute and become an engineer or a teacher.
But in me they were losing a great explorer.

December came. I spent all my free time with Lilya. I loved
her more than ever. I didn't know love could be so limitless. But
it can. Every month Lilya became dearer to me, there was no sac-
rifice I wouldn't have made for her. She would often call me on the
telephone. We'd talk for a long time, and after hanging up I just
couldn't get back to my books. Then the heavy snowstorms and
cold set in. My mother planned to go to the country but didn't have
a warm scarf. My aunt, who lives in the suburbs, had a heavy,
old-fashioned shawl. I was to go and get it.

I left on Sunday morning. But instead of going to the station, I
dropped in on Lilya. We went skating, and warmed up at the
Tretyakov Gallery. The Tretyakov is very warm in winter, and
there are benches where you can sit and talk. We walked around,
looking at the pictures. I love Serov's "Girl with the Pears" especially. The girl looks a lot like Lilya. Lilya blushed and laughed
when I told her this. Sometimes we'd get to whispering and looking at each other so hard we'd forget all about the pictures. Meanwhile it was getting dark fast. The Tretyakov would be closing
soon, and as we went out into the cold, I suddenly remembered that
I was supposed to go for the shawl. I was scared, and told Lilya.
Well, so what, that was just fine, we could go now.

And so we went, happy not to have to separate. We got out on a platform buried in snow and took a path through a field. Ahead and behind us were the dark figures of people, coming like us from the electric train. We could hear them laughing and talking, and we could see the glowing tips of their cigarettes. Once someone threw away a lighted cigarette butt, which was still burning as we approached, encircled by a ring of pink snow. We didn't step on it, we let it burn in the darkness. Then we crossed the frozen river, the wooden bridge creaking over our heads. It was very cold. We passed through the dark woods. Beside us the fir trees and pines were completely black. It was much darker than in the fields. The windows in several cabins sent out yellow bands of light on the snow. Many cabins were standing dark and lonely: there was probably no one living there in winter. There was the strong smell of birch buds and clean snow that you never get in Moscow.

Finally we reached my aunt's house. For some reason it seemed impossible to go in there with Lilya.

"Lilya, will you wait for me a minute?" I asked her uncertainly. "I'll be very fast."

"All right," she agreed. "Only don't be long. I'm frozen. My feet are frozen. And my face. And you flatter yourself that I'm glad I came with you! Just don't be long, all right?"

I went off, leaving her all alone in the dark clearing. I didn't feel very good about it.

My aunt and my cousin were surprised and delighted. Why was I so late? How I'd grown! Quite a little man. I would spend the night of course?

"How's your mama?"

"Very well, thank you."

"Your papa working?"

"Yes, papa's working."

"Everything the same there? How's your uncle?"

Heavens, a thousand questions! My cousin looked at the train schedule. The next train went back at eleven. I must take off my coat and have some tea. Then I must let them look at me and tell about everything. After all, I hadn't been there for a whole year — and that's a long time.

They made me take my coat off. The stove was going, the lamp burning brightly under its print lampshade. The grandfather clock struck. It was very warm and I would have loved some tea. But Lilya was waiting for me in the dark clearing.

Finally I said, "Excuse me, but I'm in a hurry. The fact is, I'm not alone. A friend is waiting outside."

How they scolded me! I was a completely unmannered person. Was it really possible to leave someone outside in this cold? My cousin ran out into the garden, and I could hear the crunch of her feet under the windows. A little while later the snow crunched again and my cousin brought Lilya into the room. She was completely white. They took off her coat and put her near the stove. She had tall warm boots on.

We warmed up a bit and then sat down to tea. Lilya was crimson from the warmth and her embarrassment. She didn't raise her eyes from her cup, but from time to time looked at me terribly seriously. Her dimpled cheeks were holding something back. I knew the meaning of that and was very happy. I drank five glasses of tea.

Then we got up. It was time to go. We got dressed and they gave me the shawl. Then they changed their minds, and made Lilya take off her coat, wrap the shawl around her head and shoulders, and then put on her coat again. She looked very fat and the shawl almost entirely covered her face, except for her shining eyes.

We went outside and couldn't see anything at first. Lilya held on to me very tight. As we got away from the house, we began to make out the path. Lilya suddenly began to laugh. She even fell down twice, she was laughing so hard, and I had to pick her up and brush her off.

"What a face you made!" she said, barely able to get the words

out. "You looked like an ostrich when they brought me in!"
I roared with laughter.

"Alyosha!" she said, suddenly terrified. "They might hold us up!"

"Who's they?"

"Anyone . . . Bandits . . . They might kill us."

"Nonsense," I said loudly.

A little too loudly perhaps. And I suddenly began to feel the
cold. It seemed to have gotten colder while we were drinking tea
and talking.

"Nonsense," I repeated. "There's no one around."

"But what if there is all of a sudden?" Lilya asked quickly, looking around.

"You scared?" she asked in a loud voice.

"No, although . . . Are you?"

"I'm terribly scared! They'll rob us for sure! I have a presentiment."

"You believe in them?"

"I do. By the way, I'm still glad I came."

"Really?"

"Really. Even if they rob us and kill us, I won't be sorry. And
you? Would you die for me?"

I didn't answer. I just squeezed her hand harder. If only something would happen so I could prove my love!

"Alyosha . . ."

"Yes?"

"I want to ask you something. Only don't look at me. Don't
you dare look at my face! So, what did I want to ask? Turn away!"

"All right, I've turned away. You look at where we're going. Or
else we'll stumble."

"That's nothing. I've got the shawl on. I don't mind falling."

"So?"

"Have you ever kissed anyone, Alyosha?"

"No, I never kissed anyone. Why?"

"Absolutely never?"

"Well, once, but that was when I was in the first class. I kissed some little girl. I don't remember what she was called."

"Really? You don't remember her name?"

"No, I don't."

"Then it doesn't count. You were still a little boy."

"Yes, I was."

"Alyosha, do you want to kiss me?"

I stumbled, and started watching the path more attentively. "When? Now?" I asked.

"No, no. If we get to the station without being killed, then I'll kiss you."

I didn't answer. It didn't seem so cold. I couldn't even feel it. My cheeks were burning. It was hot. Were we walking that fast?

"Alyosha."

"Yes?"

"I've never kissed anyone."

I looked at the stars without replying. Then I looked ahead at the haze of yellow light over Moscow. It was fifteen miles to Moscow but the haze was still visible. Life was wonderful after all!

"Kissing is probably a shameful thing. Were you ashamed?"

"I don't remember, it was so long ago — I don't think I was particularly ashamed."

"Yes, but that was a long time ago. It's probably shameful."

We'd already reached the field. This time the field was empty and we were all alone. Not a soul to be seen ahead or behind. No one throwing lighted cigarettes into the snow. Only the loud crunch of our feet. Suddenly there was a glow up ahead, a pale glow, like a candle from far off. It flared, flickered a moment, and went out. Then it flared again, closer this time. We watched it and finally realized that it was an electric lamp. Then we made out some small black figures, coming from the station. Maybe they'd just arrived on the train? No, the train couldn't have come, we hadn't heard a sound.

"There they are," Lilya said, pressing closer to me. "I knew it. Now they'll kill us. Those are the bandits."

What could I say? I didn't say anything. We were slowly getting nearer. I looked and counted the black figures — six men. I felt around in my pocket for my key, and I suddenly felt a hot wave of courage and excitement. I was going to fight them off! I coughed nervously, my heart beating wildly. They were talking loudly, but when they were twenty feet away, they fell silent.

"I'd better kiss you now," Lilya said sadly. "It's too bad . . ."

We met at last in the middle of the empty field. The six men stopped and lit their lamp, its weak reddish light passing over the snow to fall on us. We squinted. They looked at us in silence. Two of them were wearing their coats open. One hurriedly finished a cigarette and spat in the snow. I waited for the first blow to fall, or a yell. There was no yell. We passed each other.

"That girl wasn't bad," someone remarked regretfully. "Hey, boy, don't be scared. We'll make it."

"Were you scared?" Lilya asked a little later.

"No, just about you."

"About me?" She slowed down and gave me a strange, sideways glance. "I wasn't one drop afraid! I was just sorry about the shawl."

We said no more until we reached the station. At the station Lilya stood on tiptoe and broke off a pine twig, bringing down a flutter of snow, and put it in her pocket. Then we went up on the platform. No one else was there. There was one lamp burning in the ticket office and the snow on the platform glistened like salt. We began stamping our feet — it was cold. Suddenly Lilya walked away and leaned against the rail. I stood at the very edge of the platform, over the rails, craning my neck, trying to see the lights of the train.

"Alyosha," Lilya called. Her voice sounded strange.

I went to her. My legs were shaking. I was afraid suddenly.

"Hold me, Alyosha," said Lilya. "I'm frozen."

I put my arms around her and hugged her, my face practically touching hers, and I saw her eyes up close for the first time. Her eyelashes were covered with frost, as was the hair that had crept out from under the shawl. What a frightened look in those big eyes! The snow crunched under our feet. We were standing still, but the snow was crunching nonetheless. Suddenly there was a sharp crack of wind behind us. It rolled over the signboards, with a sound like ice cracking in the river, and died out somewhere at the end of the platform. Why didn't we say anything? We just didn't feel like it.

Lilya's lips moved. Her eyes were completely black.

"Why don't you kiss me?" she asked in a faint voice. The steam of our breath blended together. I looked at her lips. They moved and parted. I bent over and gave them a long kiss, and the world silently began to spin. I saw as she kissed me that she loved me.

So we kissed for the first time. Then we stood motionless, her cold cheek pressed against my face. I looked over her shoulders into the dark winter woods behind the platform. I felt her warm childish breath on my face and I listened to the quick beat of her heart as she was probably listening to mine. Then she moved and caught her breath. I bent and found her lips and kissed her again. This time she closed her eyes.

There was a low whistle in the distance, and a dazzling flash of light. The train was coming. A minute later we entered the warm, lighted car, slamming the door behind us, and sat down on the warm wooden bench. There were very few people in the car. Lilya was quiet and looked out the window the whole way, although the glass was frosted over and there was absolutely nothing to see.

5

It's probably impossible to pick out the exact moment when love comes to you. I can't decide when I fell in love with Lilya. Maybe when I was wandering alone in the north? Or maybe during the kiss on the platform? Or when she gave me her hand the first time and sweetly told me her name, Lilya? I don't know. I only know that at one point I couldn't get along without her. My whole life divided into two parts: before Lilya and since. How did I live and what was the point without her? I didn't even want to think about it, the way I didn't want to think about the death of people close to me.

Our winter passed wonderfully. Everything, everything belonged to us: the past and future, joy and all of life to the last breath. What a happy time, what days we had, what giddiness!

But in the spring I began to notice something. No, nothing specific, I just had the painful sense that there was something new coming. It would have been hard to say what it was. It just turned out that our characters were different. She didn't seem to like my funny looks any more, she laughed at my dreams, laughed cruelly, and sometimes we quarreled. Then . . . Then, everything went downhill, faster and faster, worse and worse. More and more often she wouldn't be home, more and more often our conversations were unnaturally gay and stupid. I felt her getting farther and farther away from me.

How many seventeen-year-old girls there are in the world. But when you're in love you know just one, you look just one in the eyes, see their sparkle, their depth, their wetness; only her voice moves you to tears. It's only her hands you're afraid to kiss. She talks to you, listens to you, laughs, is silent, and you see that you're the only one she needs. That she lives because of you and for you, that she loves you alone, as you love her.

But you notice with horror that her eyes that used to give off their warmth, their sparkle, their life just for you, are now indifferent, withdrawn, and she has withdrawn to such a distance that you can't find her, a distance from which she won't return. Your most holy aspirations, your proudest, most secret dreams, are not for her and you yourself in the complexity and beauty of your soul are not for her. You chase her, you reach and strain, but everything's gone, everything's wrong. She has escaped and withdrawn somewhere into her own wonderful unique world and you aren't to be admitted. You're a sinner — heaven is not for you. What despair, regret and pain grip you! You're ravaged, deceived, humiliated and unhappy. Everything is gone and you're standing there with empty hands, ready to fall down and cry out to some unknown god about your pain and helplessness. But when you fall and cry out, she looks at you with fear and wonder and pity in her eyes — with everything except what you need; you don't receive the one look you want; her love, her life are no longer yours. You could become a hero, a genius, someone who'd be the pride of the nation, but you still would never get that one look. How unbearable and painful it is to be alive!

And so it was spring. Sun and light, blue skies, the linden trees on the boulevards were becoming fragrant. Everyone was cheerful, and full of high spirits, preparing for the First of May. So was I. I was given a hundred rubles for the holiday, and was therefore the richest of men! Three free days. Three days to spend with Lilya — if only she weren't studying for exams then! No, I wasn't going to go anywhere, I didn't need company, just her. It had been so long since we'd been together.

But she couldn't be with me. She had to go see a sick uncle in the country. Her uncle was sick and bored and wanted to spend the holiday in the family circle. So they were going, she and her parents. Excellent plan! Very good to spend the holidays in the country. But I'd wanted so much to be with her. Maybe the second of May?

Second? She thought a minute, wrinkling up her forehead and blushing slightly. Yes, she could probably get away. Of course she wanted to! We certainly hadn't been together in a long time. So, the night of the second then, at the Telegraph Building on Gorky Street.

I was standing at the Telegraph Building at the appointed hour. So many people everywhere! There was a globe hanging over my head. It was still daylight, but the globe was already lighted — blue with yellow continents — and was swaying slightly. There was a blaze of fireworks, golden wheels, blue and green sparklers.

In the light of the fireworks everyone's face looked beautiful. I had a hundred rubles in my pocket. I hadn't spent them the day before, I still had them. But there wasn't much we could do on the second. We could go to the park or to a movie. I waited patiently. Everyone else was scurrying about, but I was amazingly calm.

Crowds of people were walking in the middle of the street. So many boys and girls, all singing, shouting, and playing accordions. There were flags on all the houses, slogans, lights. They were singing and I wanted to sing too, because I have a good voice. I'm a bass. I once dreamed of becoming a singer. I once dreamed a lot of things.

Suddenly I saw Lilya. She was coming toward me, climbing the steps, and everyone was looking at her, she was so pretty. I'd never seen her so pretty. My heart began to pound. She looked around at everyone, her eyes running over their faces, looking for someone, looking for me. I took a step toward her, just one, and suddenly a sharp pain struck me in the chest, and my mouth went dry. She wasn't alone! A boy in a cap was with her, and looking at me. He was good-looking, that boy, and he was holding her hand.

"Hello, Alyosha," said Lilya. Her voice trembled a little and she looked embarrassed. Not much embarrassed, just a little bit. "Have you been waiting long? I guess we're late . . ."

She looked at the large clock under the globe and frowned. Then she turned her head and looked at the boy. Her neck was lovely as she looked at him. Did she look at me that way?

"Let me introduce you . . ."

We shook hands. His grip was firm and sure.

"You know, Alyosha, our date today didn't work out. We're on our way to the Bolshoi. Do you mind?"

"No, I don't mind."

"Will you walk along with us for a while? I guess you have nothing to do now."

"Sure, I will. I really haven't anything else to do."

We mixed in with the crowd and moved down toward Okhotny Row. Why did I go? What should I have done? Everyone around us was singing. Playing accordions. Loudspeakers thundering out on the housetops. I had a hundred rubles in my pocket. A crackling, brand-new hundred-ruble note. Why was I going? And where?

"Well, how's your uncle?" I asked.

"Uncle? Which uncle? Oh, you mean about yesterday?" She bit her lip and took a quick look at the boy.

"He's better. We had a good celebration, very gay. We danced. And you? Did you have a good time?"

"Me? Very good."

"I'm glad."

We turned toward the theater. We were walking along in a row, all three of us. Only, I wasn't holding her hand. That good-looking boy was. She wasn't with me, she was with him. A thousand miles away. Why did my throat tickle? And my eyes sting? Was I coming down with something? We got to the Bolshoi and stopped. We were silent. There was absolutely nothing to say. I saw the boy squeeze her elbow.

"Well, we'll be off. Be seeing you!" said Lilya and smiled at me. Such a guilty, and at the same time such an absent smile!

I took her hand. It was still a nice hand. They turned and walked off slowly toward the columns. I stood looking after them. She'd grown a lot in that last year. She was seventeen already. She was slender. When did I first become aware of her figure? Oh yes, in the black space between the gates when I came back from the north. That was when I was first struck by her figure. And I had loved her in the Hall of Columns and at the Conservatory. Then at the dance . . . a marvelous winter dance! Now she was going off without even looking back. She always used to look back. Sometimes she would even come back, give me a long look, and ask, "What was it you wanted to say to me?"

"Nothing," I'd answer, glad that she'd come back.

She'd look around quickly. "Kiss me," she'd say.

And she'd smell of the cold as I kissed her, standing in a square or on a street corner. She loved those fleeting kisses on the street.

"What do they know about it?" she'd say about the people who would see us kissing. "They don't know anything. We might be brother and sister. Right?"

But this time she didn't look back. I was standing and people were passing me, as if I were a thing, or a column. There was the sound of laughter. People were walking in twos and threes and whole groups — no one was alone. A street on a holiday is an unbearable place to be alone. The other people who were alone were probably sitting at home. I stood looking. Lilya and the boy had already disappeared through the lighted entrance. All evening long they would listen to the opera, enjoying being near each other. I would have flown into the violet sky if those four winged horses in front of the Bolshoi had only known how. And I had a hundred rubles in my pocket. A brand-new note which I hadn't spent on the First of May.

6

A year passed. The world wasn't destroyed, life didn't come to an end. I almost forgot about Lilya. I did forget her. Rather, I tried not to think about her. Why should I? Once I ran into her on the street. True, my spine froze, but I controlled myself. I'd lost all interest in her life. I didn't ask what she was doing and she didn't ask about me. Although a lot new had happened to me in that time. A year — you know, that's a lot!

I was studying at the institute. Studying hard, with no distractions, no dates. I was doing a lot of public service work, and working on my swimming. I was first rate already. I'd finally mastered the crawl, the most dashing of all styles. But then, that's not important.

And then I received a letter from her. It was spring again, May, gentle May, and my heart was light. I love spring. I had passed my exams and was now a second-year student. And then, this letter from her. She wrote that she was getting married. She went on to say that she was going to the north with her husband and asked to come see her off. She called me "sweet" and signed the letter, "Your old, old friend."

I sat for a long time looking at the wallpaper. We have very pretty wallpaper, ingeniously drawn. I love to look at it. Of course I'd see her off if that was what she wanted. Why not? She wasn't my enemy, she'd done me no wrong. I'd see her off, all the more because everything was forgotten; there was a lot more to life. You can't remember everything that happened a year ago.

And so I was at the station on the day and the hour she wrote in her letter. For a long time I couldn't find her on the platform, and when I finally did I was so startled that I jumped. She was standing in a bright-colored dress with bare arms and her face and arms were already slightly burned. Her arms were still lovely. But her face had changed, it had become the face of a woman. She wasn't a girl any more — no, not a girl. She was standing with her family and her husband, that same boy. They were talking loudly and laughing, but I noticed that Lilya was looking around impatiently, waiting for me.

I went up to her. She took my hand.

"I'll just be a minute," she said to her husband, with a sweet smile.

Her husband waved to me with an affable look. Yes, he remembered me. He shook hands magnanimously. Then Lilya and I walked away.

"Well, I'm grown up and going away. This is goodbye, Moscow," she said sadly, looking at the station tower. "I'm glad you came. It's strange to see you though. You've grown a lot. How are you?"

"Fine," I answered, trying to smile. But I didn't achieve a smile, my face had gone wooden for some reason. Lilya looked at me attentively, her forehead broken by a frown. That was always her way when she was thinking.

"What's the matter?" she asked.

"Nothing. I'm just glad for you. Have you been married long?"

"A week. It's such happiness."

"Yes, it's happiness."

Lilya laughed. "How do you know? But you're making a strange face."

"It just seems I am. It's the sun. And I'm a little tired, I'm taking exams, you know. German."

" 'Damned German'?" she laughed. "Remember, how I helped you?"

"Yes, I remember." I moved my lips into a smile.

"Listen, Alyosha, what's wrong?" she asked, alarmed, moving closer. And I saw her beautiful face up close again. It had lost something. Yes, she had changed, she was quite strange to me now. Whether she was better or not I couldn't decide.

"You're hiding something," she said reproachfully. "You didn't used to!"

"No, you're mistaken," I said firmly. "It's just that I didn't sleep much last night."

She looked at the clock. Then she looked around. Her husband waved to her.

"I'm coming!" she called to him and took my hand again. "You know, I'm so happy! Be happy for me! We're going to work up north. Remember how you told me about the north? Are you happy for me?"

Why, why did she have to ask me that! Suddenly she started to laugh.

"You know, I just remembered. Remember the winter we kissed on the platform? I kissed you and you were shaking so hard the platform creaked. You had such a stupid look!"

She laughed. Then she looked at me with those gay, gray eyes. During the day her eyes were gray. They only seemed dark at night. There were dimples in her cheeks.

"What fools we were!" she said lightly and looked affectionately at her husband.

"Yes," I agreed. "We were fools."

"No, not fools, that's not right. We were just stupid kids. Don't you think?"

"Yes, we were stupid kids."

The green light had gone on up ahead. Lilya went to her car. They were waiting for her.

"Well, goodbye," she said. "No, be seeing you! I'll write you for sure."

"Good."

I knew she wouldn't. Why should she? She knew it too. She looked at me sideways and flushed a little.

"I'm glad you came to see me off. And without flowers of course! You never gave me a single flower!"

"No, I never gave you anything . . ."

She dropped my hand, took her husband's arm and they climbed up on the train. We stood below on the platform. Her parents asked me something, but I didn't understand a thing. Up ahead the engine gave a long low whistle. The cars moved. It was amazing how gently they moved! Everyone smiled, waving handkerchiefs and hats, calling, running alongside the train. Two or three accordions were being played in various places, and in one car they were singing loudly. Students probably. Lilya was already a long way off. She was holding on to her husband's shoulder with one hand, and waving to us with the other. Even from afar you could see how lovely her arms were. And you could see how happy her smile was.

The train passed. I lit a cigarette, stuffed my hands in my pockets and moved off in the crowd toward the square. I clenched the cigarette in my teeth and looked at the silver paint on the lampposts. In the sunlight they were so bright they hurt my eyes. I looked down. Now I could admit it: the whole year I had had hope. Now everything was finished. So I was happy for her, really I was, happy! Only there was a pain in my heart for some reason.

An ordinary occurrence, a girl gets married — it happens all the time. Girls getting married — that's a good thing. It's just too bad not to be able to cry. The last time I cried I was fifteen years old. I was now twenty. My heart was in my throat and climbing still higher — pretty soon I'd be chewing on it and still I couldn't cry. It's a very good thing — girls getting married.

I came out on the square, the face of the clock on Kazan Station jumped out at me. It has strange figures instead of numbers — I couldn't make them out. I went into a soda fountain. At first I asked for a soda, and then I changed my mind and ordered plain water. It's hard to drink soda when your heart's in your throat. I picked up the cold glass, and took the water in my mouth, but I couldn't swallow. I swallowed some finally, in one gulp. I felt a little better, I thought.

Then I went down into the subway. Something had happened to my face. I noticed that people were staring. At home, I thought for a while about Lilya. Then I began to study the patterns in the wallpaper again. If you look at them you can see many curious things. You can see jungles and elephants with wounded trunks. Or strange cloaks and berets. Or the faces of friends. But not Lilya's face.

She was probably passing that platform where we first kissed right now. Only now the platform was surrounded by green. Would she look at it? Would she think of me? But why should she look at it? She'd be looking at her husband, loving him. He's very good-looking, her husband.

7

There's nothing constant in this world but sorrow. Life doesn't stop. No, life never stops, it just absorbs your soul and all your sorrows, your little human sorrows, dissipate like smoke by comparison. Such is the excellent construction of the world.

Now I'm finishing the institute. My youth is over, gone far, far off, forever. And that's good: I'm grown up and can do anything I want, no one pats me on the head like a boy. I'll be going up north soon. I don't know why, but something calls me north. Probably because I went hunting and was happy there. I've forgotten Lilya completely, so many years have passed! It would be very hard to live if you didn't forget. No, happily, a lot has been forgotten. She has never written of course. I don't know where she is; I don't even want to know. I don't think about her at all. My life is good. It's true I haven't become a poet, or a musician, but we can't all be poets. Sports, conferences, vocational training, exams, all have kept me very busy. I haven't had a free moment. I have learned to dance, and have gotten to know a lot of pretty and bright girls. I go out with them and fall in love with some of them, and they fall in love with me.

But sometimes I dream about Lilya. She comes to me in my dream and I hear her voice, her sweet laughter, I touch her hand and talk to her, about what I don't know. Sometimes she's sad and glum, sometimes joyful and her dimples flash, so small that a stranger wouldn't notice them. And I cheer up and laugh and feel young and bashful, as if I were seventeen again and in love for the first time in my life.

When I wake up the next morning I go to my lectures at the institute, preside at the trade union meeting, speak at the meeting of the Young Communists. But the day goes badly for me for some reason, and I want to be alone and sit somewhere with my eyes closed.

It doesn't happen often — four times a year maybe. But then, those dreams. Those dreams, those uninvited dreams.

I don't want them. I love it when I dream about music. They say if you sleep on your right side, you stop dreaming. I've started sleeping on my right side. I'm going to sleep soundly and wake up happy in the morning. Life is an excellent thing after all!

But oh God, I don't want dreams!

On the Island

THE steamship on which Inspector General Zabavin was arriving gave a low, vibrating whistle, turned, rolled to one side, and moved into the remote northern harbor. After three days on the dirty white ship, three days of the groan of the winches on the docks, the roar of the engines, the short-legged captain, the old mate with his lewd, insolent face, the rude waitress and the endless drunkenness in the third-class bar, Zabavin was too fed up to watch.

The more Zabavin traveled around in the north, the more and more commonplace and boring it became; he had even stopped noticing the beauty of the dark hills, the beauty of the sea and of northern nature, although he'd once loved it all very much. Even in the launch, he paid no attention to the queer silhouette of the island, which resembled a beast hunched over with its head in the water, nor to the dark green rocks under water, nor to the gay chatter around him; he was feeling irritated, mean and unshaven and all he wanted was to get to shore as soon as possible, and into a warm room.

When the launch had made its way through the many cutters and motorboats, and pulled up to the wooden pier, Zabavin was the first to get out. He stood there blinking, enjoying the sensation of hard ground under his feet.

The pier was crowded with drying bales of brown and lilac seaweed, barrels of cement, and near the wall of a one-story warehouse, rusty piles of tubing and rails. The seaweed smell was strong and stupefyingly sweet, and then there were the milder odors of fish, ropes, crude oil, wood, hay, the sea — all the smells of any harbor wharf.

Yawning, Zabavin walked aimlessly through the slag past a cannery — the noise of the machines was deafening — past the boiler rooms sending warm drafts of air out into the morning chill. The soil was poor, encrusted with whitish moss and gray stones, and the horses and cows roaming over the moss were thin and pitiful-looking, abandoned on a wilderness island that had no use for them. Frowning and sighing, Zabavin asked directions at the cannery office; they showed him and he went there directly, observing nothing and thinking of nothing but getting to sleep as fast as possible. The last night on ship he had had almost no sleep at all.

They showed him to his room and he had a good sleep. When he woke up, he shaved, rubbed on some eau de cologne, and carefully combed his hair until it shone. Then he drank some strong hot tea in a slender glass and enjoyed a cigarette. Finally he got out his folder of documents, and straightened his tie, glad now to be there, glad to be feeling so well and neat and clean, relieved to be rid of the repulsive odor of salted cod which he'd gotten so thoroughly tired of while on board ship. Feeling fresh and cheerful and pleased with himself, smelling of eau de cologne and good tobacco, he went to the office, to get down to the business that had brought him.

All that day and the two successive days Zabavin spent working punctiliously, going through fat folders of documents, checking and verifying complicated figures. He inspected vats of produce, slicing machines, storehouses and laboratories. Throughout he was cool, respectful and businesslike with the cannery director, who was so delighted to see a new face that he bustled about, chattering incessantly, eagerly asking questions about Archangelsk. Dressed in a skullcap, his eyes popping under their bulging lids, deep pouches hanging from his fleshy cheeks, the director took Zabavin about, moving heavily and unsteadily on his statuesque legs, short of breath and perspiring. Next to the enormously, unpleasantly fat director, Zabavin — thin, dark-haired, dressed in fashionably narrow trousers — seemed like a boy. The director said that he was going to retire soon and recited Fet's verses in a tremolo, gazing mournfully at the ocean. When he invited Zabavin to eat "God's gifts" with him — and at these words his eyes filled with tears — Zabavin, feeling the openly envious eyes of the younger workers upon him, became even colder and more respectful in manner.

2

Then one day Zabavin had to telegraph to Archangelsk, so he went over to the radio station. He found it without any trouble by the tall transmitter that was wired to the ground on all sides by cables. Climbing up on the porch, Zabavin knocked. Nobody answered so he opened the door and went in. He found himself in a large empty room. It was clean and warm, with a painted floor. There was an aneroid in a long wooden box and a table standing near the window. On the table lay a chronometer in a velvet case, a pair of binoculars, and several magazines lying open. There were three or four doors in the room, one of which flew open suddenly, and the radio operator looked in. He was a confident-looking young man, with a thin neck, a prominent Adam's apple, large ears, and long hair. On seeing Zabavin, his face became suspicious.

"Who are you?" he asked, trying to sound authoritative though he was obviously frightened and didn't know what to do with his large hands. Without hearing Zabavin out, he told him rudely, frowning and blushing, that the boss wasn't there and that without her he couldn't take any telegrams, and anyway they could only get through to Archangelsk in the evening.

Zabavin smiled, said he'd come around that evening, and went out on the porch, feeling the young man's scared and uncertain gaze on the back of his neck. Delighted by the good weather and the unexpected free time, he started off to wander the island.

He climbed up toward the white lighthouse tower. Looking around, he noticed for the first time how beautiful the ocean was, how it lightened and darkened in the sun. Near the lighthouse he came upon a boarded-up wooden chapel, and a bit beyond that, an old cemetery. Sighing, he went in and began to wander through the sunken mounds with their dark gravestones. On one Zabavin managed to make out: "Beneath this stone lie the ashes of Second Lieutenant and lighthouse keeper Vasily Ivanov Prudnikov, born in the province of Smolensk, in the city of Byela. He lived in all 56 years. He passed away after a trip to the Solovyers Monastery in the year 1858, the sixth day of September. Lord, accept his spirit in peace."

Yes, Zabavin thought with a touch of sadness, one hundred years ago. One hundred years.

He tried to read some other stones, but they were even older and more covered with moss, and it was impossible to make anything out. Then he sat down on one of the stones and watched the water for a long time, giving himself up to the melancholy charm of autumn and of the forgotten cemetery, thinking about the people who had lived there perhaps more than a century before. Then, in a pleasantly pensive mood, he walked slowly down to his room to sleep.

But he slept badly, and woke up again almost immediately. Sitting at the window, he saw that a fog had come in while he was asleep. The fog was so heavy that nothing was visible: the radio station's transmitter, the lighthouse, the long dark pier, the cannery, the factory smokestacks, nothing. Some goats were huddled in an unmoving knot under the window. Life on the island, it seemed, had come to a halt, the fog drowning out all sounds, except an ominous, melancholy howl of wind from the north.

Since his visit to the cemetery Zabavin had developed a strange feeling for the island — for its lighthouse keeper who had lived and died one hundred years ago when life had been probably even gloomier than it was now — which he couldn't shake. The fog, the howling wind, the knot of goats were suddenly too much for him, and he wanted conversation, music, people. He pulled himself together quickly and set out for the radio station, finding the road with some difficulty in the fog and the early autumn twilight.

The head of the radio station was a twenty-six-year-old girl with the unusual name of August. She was small, with slender legs, a short haircut which made her neck look especially sweet and fragile, a round dark face, large eyes and long lashes that gave her face incredible spirituality. Everyone on the island called her Gusta. When she smiled her cheeks flushed hotly and her small ears turned pink. One look at her moved and touched Zabavin; he wanted to take her, stroke her fluffy hair and feel her sweet warm breath on his neck.

When he had given the radio operator the text of his telegram, he gave Gusta a long hard look, his dark eyes brilliant, and asked her permission to stay and listen to the radio. She quickly assented, and even seemed delighted to take him to her own small room, where she turned on the table lamp and went to put on some tea.

While she was getting down the cups, setting the table, her slender hands clattering the spoons, and pouring sugar in the sugar bowl, growing more and more nervous all the while, Zabavin was sitting with his legs crossed, smoothing down his narrow trousers in a habitual gesture. He turned on the radio, which lit up with a dark garnet light, and found a close Norwegian station. He lit a cigarette, smacking his lips in satisfaction.

With unusual attentiveness he examined in great detail both his gentle hostess and the small room, with its own window facing south, the dozen books on the shelf, the rug, the narrow, carefully made and — from the looks of it — very hard bed. Remembering the frankly envious stares of the cannery workers and trying not to smile, he began thinking about the island, the cemetery, the darkness and fog outside the window. But strangely enough these thoughts failed to alarm or depress him; on the contrary, he was greatly enjoying the thin, bright music, the crackle of the stove in the big room, and watching his hostess without having to say anything.

"Amazing! Who would have thought or guessed that such an evening was in store for me?" he began loudly and cheerfully. "You know, when you're traveling, always the weak tea, the stale rolls, the loneliness — if you could just take your wife with you! They're useful on days like today."

"Oh?" Gusta spoke, lowering her eyes. "You're married? Been married long?"

"A long time," Zabavin answered, a touch of sadness in his voice. "I even have children, two of them. It's terrible, but I just can't get used to the idea that I'm married, that I'm in my thirty-sixth year, everything goes so fast . . . When you're traveling, or sitting in some hotel room, you think to yourself: you, who have dreamt so long about love and some extraordinary kind of happiness, you're just wasting your time, going around as an inspector, you're just getting away from your family . . . But my wife's a good soul . . . Others live worse."

Suddenly Zabavin saw a strange look cross Gusta's face. He caught himself and blushed.

"Forgive me," he muttered, filled with sudden self-disgust. "What's the matter with me? You're not interested. I just got carried away. I haven't talked to anyone for a whole week and it was just such a fine night . . ."

"Never mind," answered Gusta quickly, giving him a sad smile. "It's all right, don't apologize for that . . ."

"For what then?"

"Men away on business usually don't love their wives," said Gusta ironically, pouring Zabavin's tea. "Here, drink this."

Zabavin laughed, and took his cup. They began to talk, and he found out that she had worked on the island a long time, she had already doubled her salary, that she was bored and wanted to go to Archangelsk or Leningrad. From talking about boredom, they got on various other general subjects and began talking about love and happiness. They both became animated.

"You're talking about love as if it were rational," Zabavin suddenly said bitterly, although Gusta hadn't said a word about love being rational. "People discuss love, make decisions about who should love whom. Writers write about it, readers organize discussions and argue whether he's worthy of her or she of him, which one is better, purer, more rational, more suited to the century of socialism. But not one of us can really say what love is. The more I think about it, the more convinced I am that the qualities of intelligence, talent, purity, etc. play a very small role in love. What's important is something quite different, something that can't be named or understood. What's the point of trying to understand it? I know one guy — an insolent, drunken fool, a man without honesty or conscience — and can you imagine it, women love him. Smart, intelligent women. And knowing they love him, he goes after them for their money. He drinks, treats them like dirt, and they cry over him. I've seen them! Now why?"

"You probably don't see in him what they see," Gusta answered gravely.

"What is there to see in him? Intelligence? Talent? Breadth of soul? No, he's a fool, an insolent, lazy fool. His face isn't even a face, it's just a bloated snout! God strike me dead if I ever understand it!"

There was a squeak in the operator's room, a key turned and stopped in a keyhole, and then there were footsteps.

"I've sent all the wires, and the reports are on the table," called the radio operator, slamming the outer door. "See you tomorrow! I'm running over to the club!" he shouted, stamping across the porch, and the house was silent.

The expression on Gusta's face changed suddenly, as if something had frightened her. She looked out the dark window, then fixedly and gravely at Zabavin, blushed, and immediately dropped her eyes. And Zabavin, as if he weren't thirty-six years old, as if he didn't have the army, his wife, children, his work behind him, felt the same sudden shooting tremor, the same dryness in his mouth that he had felt as an adolescent when he'd been in love with some schoolgirl and kissed her during the white nights of summer.

"Then there's the kind of happiness," Zabavin began quietly, and because as he said this she understood that he was going to say something serious and fine, she relaxed and smiled, her beautiful velvet eyes resting on his face, "that puts all its hopes in the future," Zabavin continued quickly, gulping his tea, aware of the darkness beyond the window and the cold breath of the sea. "People who put their hope in the future live shallow and uninteresting lives. They live unaware of anything good around them, blaming life, sure that when the time comes, happiness will come. Everyone does it, you, me. But happiness is everywhere, in everything, it's happiness that you and I are sitting drinking tea and that I like you and you know I do . . ."

Zabavin hesitated, took a breath and smiled at himself. Blushing deeply, Gusta didn't dare raise her eyes.

"We'd like it if someone strong and wise came and made us look around. But the longer we live, the more we live, the less happiness there is. Mankind is always young, but we get old . . . I'm thirty-five and you're . . ."

"Twenty-six," whispered Gusta, raising her blazing eyes at last, and looking straight at Zabavin.

"So, in a year I'll be thirty-six and you'll be twenty-seven. We'll both be a year older, some of our strength will be gone — a certain number of cells will be dead forever, and so on, year after year. But the most important thing is that it isn't just our bodies that age, just that we get gray and bald and acquire various diseases that we don't have now, no — it's that the spirit gets old, little by little, imperceptibly, but it will — then where's happiness? No, there isn't any then, and I don't understand people that are always waiting: summer's coming and I'll be happy, but when summer comes they're not as happy as they think they should be. Well, winter's coming, and I'll be happy . . . What's the use?"

"Where is happiness?" Gusta asked quietly.

"Where? I wonder where it is too. Now you want to get away from the island, you're waiting for something, you think in a year or two or three you'll be happy. No! You're happy now, infinitely, enormously happy, because you're not sick, you're young, you have beautiful eyes, because now when you're twenty-six, your eyes are a pleasure to look at, because you have an important job, because of the sea, the island . . . think of all the reasons!"

"It's easy to say," said Gusta uncertainly.

"Of course the world is big, there are many excellent places in it, and why, in the last analysis, should you be on this particular island? Of course, Archangelsk is a more interesting place than this island. When you think and when I think of Archangelsk or Moscow or Leningrad we think of theaters, lights, museums, exhibitions, noise, movement, all the rest, in short, we think of *life!* Right? But when I'm there, at home, I don't see any of it, I begin to think that only when I'm away from it. When I'm in Archangelsk, I discover that my son is sick, that there's an evening meeting I must attend, that they want my report in a hurry . . . And I begin to spin around like a squirrel in a cage on wheels; I don't think about the theaters or any of the rest of it. How do I live any better than you? In the ultimate sense I mean? I don't, I don't, you're much happier than I am. You're twenty-six and I'm thirty-five!

"Oh you'll be leaving sooner or later, you'll live in Leningrad and see the Neva River, the bridges, Isaac's Square . . . But believe me, when you leave here, you'll remember this island, its people, the sea, the smell of seaweed, the fleecy clouds, the sun, the thunderstorms, the northern lights, the gales, and in a few years you'll come to understand that you were really happy here."

"I don't know," Gusta said thoughtfully. "I hadn't thought of it that way somehow."

"Well it almost always is that way. We regret the past, because it's easier to see it from a distance."

Zabavin looked excitedly at Gusta and thought despite himself how good it would be to be married to her. He tried to stop thinking such thoughts, knowing them to be out of place, knowing his powerlessness to change his life in any way, yet he couldn't not think them, any more than he could leave her, although it was late.

It was only when the radio operator came back from the club and went to his room, whistling as he looked for jazz on the radio, that Zabavin got ready to leave. Gusta went out on the porch with him and they stood for a long time, getting used to the darkness.

"I'll go along with you for a while, there are lots of wires to trip over here," Gusta said, taking his hand. Her hand was rough and warm and trembling. Good sweet thing, he thanked her silently, but the thought of himself brought back sadness.

The fog had lifted and the howling had stopped. Small bright stars burned overhead, and the milky way spilled down, split in two clear streams. Already accustomed to the darkness, Gusta went on ahead, Zabavin behind, barely able to make out her brightly colored skirt, feeling his way unsurely along the stony, moss-covered path. They walked several minutes in silence, then Gusta stopped and Zabavin saw a few scattered yellow lights in the village below.

"Here you are," said Gusta. "Now you can make it, you won't get lost. Goodbye."

"Stay a bit longer," said Zabavin. "I'll just have another cigarette."

Gusta thought a moment. "All right," she answered. Taking his hand, she went several steps farther and stopped near a fence. Leaning against it, she turned her face toward Zabavin. Zabavin lit a cigarette, trying and failing to make out the expression on Gusta's face in the matchlight.

The surf broke evenly beneath them, the tide was going out, and it was getting colder. The wind carried an especially melancholy breath of autumn water. The water was deep and inscrutably black.

Zabavin noticed suddenly that Gusta's face was intermittently lighting up and disappearing in the darkness. He looked, and three or four seconds later he saw the high white star of light from the lighthouse blazing up brightly and then going out. Again it blazed up and went out, and again. The mute, flashing light was strangely comforting.

Zabavin turned to Gusta. "You're a beautiful girl," he whispered gently, and with a detached, censorious feeling of shame, he bent and gave her still cold lips a long hard kiss.

Gusta turned away without saying anything, so small, so dear, and lonely that Zabavin's throat caught. He took hold of her thin shoulders and led her into the darkness, through the rustling grass and short prickly underbrush which smelled so sharply of autumn, over the hard cold stones covered with soft moss, out of the light from the lighthouse. Finally they stopped, ahead of them only the density of night and the roar of the sea.

"Why, why?" she asked. "You don't even know me. But more important, why?"

And he began kissing her face and hands, knowing already that this was the happiness and love that they had been talking about earlier.

"No more, let's go back," she said in a quiet voice.

"Don't be angry with me," Zabavin asked just as quietly, and followed her obediently. At the fence where they'd kissed the first time, Gusta stopped suddenly, burst into tears and buried her face in Zabavin's cold mackintosh.

"I'll see you tomorrow," she said at last, wiping away her tears. She sighed. "Now I won't sleep all night. Why, why all this?"

Pushing him away, she walked off so quickly that she was nearly running. Zabavin stood for a long time, watching the flashing light in the lighthouse and the warm light in Gusta's distant window. His face was hot, his throat burned, and he coughed, but he couldn't make himself leave. His heart was beating slowly and heavily.

3

The ship Zabavin was supposed to take back to Archangelsk was due at the island in a week. Seven impossibly wonderful happy days before them! But the next morning the radio operator came to the office where Zabavin was working and silently handed him a telegram. On the blank, written in unsteady, uneven lines were the words: "Await your immediate arrival in Archangelsk stop Don't wait for ship stop Today or tomorrow schooner *Suvo* will arrive at island stop Maximov."

Zabavin froze. The radio operator left. Zabavin wanted to go on working, but he couldn't understand a thing that was said to him, nor could he remember any figures. He finished up somehow, wrote his last reports, told the director about his orders and went home.

That evening as Zabavin was getting ready to go and see Gusta for the last time, shaving and combing with unusual care, trying to put on his tie with numb fingers, the schooner arrived. It appeared suddenly, like destiny. They were warned of its arrival by its mast lights — green and white — and by the radiogram that was received first at the lighthouse and then at the radio station. Zabavin sent an anxious reply and the schooner stayed at anchor until morning.

All night long Zabavin and Gusta walked around the island, scaring up partridges which would fly away with a strange heavy rustle whenever they stopped to sit down. All night long they held each other, more and more painfully in love, while the lights on the schooner went on blinking, to remind them of their imminent separation.

Then they went back to the radio station and again the radio glowed with a soft garnet light, music played softly and there were mumbled announcements. Again they drank tea and talked, unable to take their eyes off each other.

"What is it we have?" asked Gusta. "Is this happiness? Tell me!"

"Yes, it's happiness," Zabavin answered bitterly.

"My god," she said, and there were tears in her eyes.

Zabavin was ready to give up everything — his family, his work

— and stay with her forever. But at the same time he knew it was impossible. Gusta understood it too, which made things worse. And so they spent their first and last night together.

The sun came up reluctantly and stingily. The window gradually grew light. Zabavin got up, catching a glimpse in the mirror of a long pale face, frightened and unhappy, and went to the window. Wiping it off with his hand, he saw that the sky was a light blue, and thin as glass, while the sea looked full and enormous and peaceful. A few hundred feet from shore the dark schooner stood at anchor like a statue, pale lights still burning on the mast. As far as the eye could reach, over the water and on shore, everything was frozen still — silent, unpeopled, dead. Suddenly a large black dog came out from behind some rocks and trotted past, its tail flying straight out behind it. It was so unexpected that Zabavin jumped.

He turned away from the window and looked at Gusta. She was sitting at the table, her hands folded across her chest, her eyes closed, her small pale face so calm she might have been asleep. Cautiously Zabavin pulled on his whispering and crackling mackintosh. Then he thought a minute, and took his eau de cologne out of his bag, poured some in the hollow of his hand, spilling some on the floor, and rubbed it briskly on his face.

"Gusta, it's time," he said huskily and lit a cigarette.

"What, already? Wait. I'll be ready in a minute. I'll go with you," she said quickly.

Zabavin turned again to the window, hunching over as he heard Gusta's uncertain breathing as she moved about the room.

They went out on the porch together. Zabavin breathed in the sharp cold air and shivered. The sun was coming up and the moss, gray with frost, crunched under their feet. The dog reappeared and started following them.

The tide was out and the rowboat seemed a long way from the water. It took them a long time to push it into the water. When they were finally in and shoved off from shore they were flushed and panting. Zabavin took the oars and began to row out slowly. The dog stood on shore, sniffing intently and then he began to whimper softly, scraping his paws in the sand. Gusta sat in the stern, her skin looking especially dark at this hour, and stared blankly over Zabavin's shoulders, pulling on the stern oar.

The water was extraordinarily clear. Rocks, sand, leaves and sea-weed in the shape of horse tails passed underneath them. From time to time Zabavin would stop to look at a dark red starfish, amazed to find himself taking an interest in anything at such a moment.

The boat bumped heavily against the schooner. The captain immediately appeared on deck in a blue jacket and high boots. He was bareheaded, his hair long and sunbleached, and his young high-cheekboned face was puffy with sleep.

"Comrade Zabavin?" he asked in a broad accent, grabbing the side of the boat. "Let's have the rope."

Zabavin handed him his suitcase and tossed the rope. Then he turned to Gusta, and swaying, took three steps toward the stern. Gusta got up, looking at Zabavin through her tears.

They gave each other a long and painfully hard kiss. Then Zabavin turned away and climbed on board the schooner. The captain watched them gravely as he helped Zabavin aboard, then he went below.

A moment later sleepy-looking sailors began to climb out, pulling on their jackets. The schooner came to life. The frost on the deck was broken by dark footprints, the motor began to knock and the anchor chain rang out. A slight wind came up, ruffling the smooth water. A lock of hair fell in Gusta's face, but she sat unmoving, not bothering to fix it.

The captain took the wheel, watching Zabavin as he put the schooner into low gear. Gusta and the rowboat began to move away from them. A tousled sailor stood in the bow, pulling in the anchor, shouting "Eight, seven, seven and a half!"

The greenish rocks, the dark blotches of seaweed and starfish were still visible in the water.

Zabavin stood at the rail and watched the boat and shore move away. Gusta was still sitting motionless in the stern of the boat. The bow, high out of the water, turned slightly in the wind toward shore. Watching the island and the boat, Zabavin heard a strange thin sound in his head. His eyes were dry and burning.

Having come through the danger area and out into open sea, the schooner picked up speed. The captain gave the wheel to a sailor and came out of the wheelhouse and stood beside Zabavin.

"We'll be in Archangelsk tomorrow evening," he said in a low voice.

The island was now only a thin blue line, they could make out the white tower of the lighthouse, nothing more. The strong swell of the open sea began and the schooner shook from the power of the diesel. Finally even the blue line disappeared. They were surrounded by water — smooth waves all the way out to the horizon. The sun came up, but some clouds came from the east at the same time so it wasn't very light.

"A wind's coming up," the captain said, yawning. "Get the instruments going!" he shouted suddenly in a sharp voice. "And won't you please come below with me?" he invited Zabavin.

Down in the crew's quarters, they sat at a narrow table opposite each other and smoked.

"Who was that, your wife?" asked the captain.

"No," answered Zabavin and his lips trembled.

"Lie down and rest," suggested the captain. "Here's one of our empty bunks."

Zabavin lay down obediently on the hard narrow bunk, and put a lifesaver under his head. The cabin rose and fell. Overboard the sound of water rang out. Well, this is happiness, thought Zabavin and saw Gusta's face. This is love . . . How strange . . . love.

And he lay there, biting his lip, thinking of Gusta, the island, seeing her face and eyes, hearing her voice, and he wasn't sure if it all hadn't been a dream and a reverie. The ringing sound of water overboard was like the sound of a gaily running brook, a brook that would never be stilled.

PARENTS AND CHILDREN

Along the Road

THE end of winter came as usual. The snow suddenly disappeared, leaving the ground smoking and steaming in the sun. The stallions kicked at the sides of their stalls and gnawed at the grooms' hands. Then the bulls began bellowing, shaking the oaken beams of the barns where they had been chained for the winter. The thrushes did stunts at the edge of the forest, the starlings whistled at sundown, the cherry trees in the ravine began to blossom drunkenly. The countryside, stripped shamelessly naked by winter, secretly began to cover itself with berries, birches, and lilacs.

And the fields were already a misty green, and the road was already awash, the dry summer was already on its way when Ilya Snegirev packed up again for Siberia.

He had decided to go in February.

One night, worn out from driving all day, Ilya had come out of the office of the tree farm and crossed the forest clearing covered with fallen branches, going toward his truck. His truck — like his jacket, his boots, his hands and his hat — smelled of gas. But Snegirev was aware of no odors, except the smell of dust in the summer and frost in the winter.

That particular February night the thaw had begun. Above him the sky was turning green, above the forest it was glowing darkly; the trees were black and swollen. Spring was clearly in the air. Ilya smelled, listened, blew his nose, and getting into the cab, he made up his mind.

It was not the first time spring had torn him away. Last year he'd been in Siberia — suffered through a whole summer there — and had returned in the fall deeply disappointed. He didn't like barracks life and he loathed Siberia with its vile taiga, and the distant noise of trucks straining along the roads.

When Snegirev had returned that fall the ground was streaked with blackish snow. The woods were naked and dead. The grass hummed and trembled in the wind, and the first dustings of snow melted overnight. But then the real snow fell, to freeze and thaw, and Snegirev settled happily back to work.

His job kept him driving night and day — to the station, the woods, to neighboring regions. He'd stop for the night anywhere, getting up at dawn to heat water, fill the radiator, and start the motor. Then he'd have a quick glass of tea and exchange a few words with his host, all the while enjoying the roar of the engine in the street.

He loved driving the lonely roads at night, when it seems you're the only one in the world who isn't sleeping, and the truck wavers and drowses, and the blinding spot of headlight leaps ahead toward the horizon.

Alone at night, thinking idly about the past, he began to forget his grudge against Siberia; the bad part grew so dim it was as if it had never been, and all that remained were the power and beauty of the mountains, of the raging, un-Russian rivers, of the heavy concrete contours of the dams.

So having decided to go there again, Snegirev began to settle his affairs a week before his departure in May.

2

He wakes every morning in a holiday mood. Nights, he dresses up and goes around saying goodbye to his neighbors. He has the quiet air of someone celebrating something special, but gradually, he begins to talk about Siberia. He talks long and well, and his friends' faces begin to cloud with envy, they'd also like to see Siberia.

Ilya gets home late every night, taking off his shoes and walking around in his stocking feet, thinking his mother asleep. The last evening he spends at home packing, having said all his goodbyes during the week. For the first time he notices the sadness in his mother's face, her tearful eyes. In bed, thinking about Siberia and about leaving his mother alone, he is alternately happy and sad. He smokes furtively and just can't get to sleep.

Ilya leaves the next morning, not especially early. No one is seeing him off but his mother because he doesn't like to be seen off. His mother has been crying all morning and now, walking along with her son, she sighs, but keeps up a conversation about this and that.

Leaving the farm, where the road turns sharply to the right past the thicket, they run into the truck bringing a load of bricks from the station. Mishka Firsov, Ilya's friend and neighbor, has taken Ilya's place at the wheel.

The Snegirevs step to the side. Covering them with a light coat of spring dust, Mishka calls something to them. Putting on the brake, he jumps out and comes back.

"You mean you're really going?" he asks, shaking hands.

Mishka smells of gas now.

"I'm going," says Ilya.

"Look here, maybe you won't like it this time either."

"I'll like it all right," Ilya mutters tensely. He's listening to his mother starting to breathe unevenly.

"Ekh, I guess we've had our fun, the two of us," says Mishka, looking at the truck. The motor is still running. "Here, have a last cigarette."

They smoke for a while without saying anything.

"And what about Tamara?" Mishka remembers. "Is that all over?"

"What about her?" Mishka answers indifferently. "If she wants to, she'll come."

"Oh. Well, let's shake on it then!"

"Right."

They'd like to embrace, but are too embarrassed. They simply shake hands.

"Going straight to the train?" asks Mishka.

"We'll just about make it," says Ilya, shifting impatiently.

"And I've got to be back at the station in half an hour. Well, *gudebye!*"

Mishka hurries into the truck and Ilya and his mother go on. A minute later they hear Mishka stepping heavily on the gas.

His mother doesn't say anything for a long time, shielding her eyes from the sun with her scarf. Finally she says, absently, "I tell you, Tamara is *perfection* next to your other girls." She pronounces "perfection" with great care and is evidently satisfied with the result. "Yes, and she really loves you too, not like all those flirts."

Ilya doesn't say anything, but his mother needs to talk. So she speaks of Tamara, of how they'll put a new roof on the house this summer, of when it will be her turn to tend the farm's kitchen garden, and again of Tamara. Ilya takes a look at his watch and quickens his step. His mother hurries, and stumbles. Her thoughts are confused.

"Well, son . . ." she says and stops.

Ilya also stops, looks at the fading, myopic, loving eyes of his mother, and begins to scratch his nose. His mouth is drooping, he feels numb all over, but he thrusts out his chin, and cocks his eyebrows, assuming a casual expression.

"Let me . . . you . . ." his mother murmurs, making the sign of the cross. "Go on now, go on, you've got to go . . . I . . . I'll follow for a little bit."

"I'll write you, Mama," Ilya says in a thin voice, kissing her awkwardly. "Don't get sick."

"Don't you stay too long, and dress warmly. Maybe it's still cold there in Siberia," his mother says, trying not to cry.

"Now stop this, Mama," Ilya answers too cheerfully. "Is this the first time I've gone away or something? You take care, write me everything. And I'll send money as soon as I get some."

He hugs her again and turns and walks quickly down the road. He snuffles, his eyes sting and his throat is full. He relaxes after a few hundred feet and begins to breathe more easily. The bridge of his nose is no longer throbbing and his face takes on the same look of intense concentration it has had all week.

He looks up at the lacy clouds, the muscles in his face move, and he swallows, already seeing the river, flowing through Enisei, the rocky hills, and the taiga, and the pale electric lights of the towns at work on a white night.

Another hundred feet and he looks around. His mother is still following him, shielding her face with her hand. Ilya stops, takes out his handkerchief and waves. His mother doesn't respond.

Doesn't see me, he thinks in disappointment. Sighing, he goes on.

And just as he is beginning to walk faster, and with more determination, his mother stops and waves to him with a radiant smile. It seems to her that her son has turned and is looking at her. She can even make out his features. She's amazed how well she can see through her tears.

Far off in the fields, a spot is moving on the horizon — a girl is running along the edge of the forest. That's how my mother ran once, he thinks sadly and tenderly. When he looks back, his mother is so far behind that he can't tell whether she has stopped or is still following.

She is, she can't make herself turn back. Tears are running down her face, and she wipes them away with the ends of her scarf. She has no need to hold herself in any more, along there on the road. *Oh God,* she thinks. No use for their own homes. On the go. Always on the go. The country's all torn up these days. He used to run around in just a shirt and his little bare feet, holy mother of God! And now he's gone, flown away . . .

She stops, sobs, and raises her hand to her eyes. Ilya has been out of sight a long time, dissolved in the azure horizon, but it seems to his mother that she can see him. He has turned and is waving goodbye. She takes a deep fluttery breath and limply waves in answer.

The Smell of Bread

THEY received the telegram on New Year's Day. Dusya was in the kitchen at the time and so her husband went to the door. Dressed in his undershirt and suffering from a hangover, he couldn't hold back a yawn as he signed for it, wondering who could have sent them a New Year's greeting. And so he was yawning as he read the short doleful announcement of the death in a distant village of Dusya's seventy-year-old mother.

What a time for this to happen, he thought, afraid to call his wife. Dusya didn't cry, she just paled slightly, returned to their room, straightened the tablecloth and sat down. Her husband stared dully at the untouched bottles on the table, poured himself a glass and drank it. Then he thought a minute and poured one for Dusya.

"Drink this," he said. "God knows, *my* head is splitting. Oh well, we all have to go. Are you . . . going there?"

Dusya didn't answer. She ran her hand over the tablecloth and picked up her drink. Then, moving blindly, she went to the bed and lay down.

"I don't know," she said, a minute later.

Her husband went over and looked down at her full round figure. "Well, what can you do? What will you do?" Not knowing what else to say, he went back to the table, and poured himself another drink. "Kingdom of heaven, we all have to go!"

All day long Dusya wandered aimlessly around the apartment. Her head was aching and she didn't go out. She wanted to cry, and yet why should she? It was sad, but Dusya hadn't seen her mother in fifteen years. Since she'd left the village, she had almost never thought about her past life. If she thought about it at all, it was usually something from her early childhood or adolescence, or perhaps about someone who had once walked her home from the club.

Dusya went through her old snapshots and still couldn't cry: they all showed her mother with a strange tense expression, bug eyes, and dark, work-coarsened hands.

That night in bed Dusya talked with her husband for a long time. "I'm not going," she said at last. "Why should I? It's cold there now. And her stuff, such as it is, has probably been grabbed up by the relatives already. No, I'm not going."

2

The winter passed and Dusya forgot all about her mother. Her husband had a good job, they had all the conveniences, and Dusya filled out and grew even prettier.

But at the beginning of May she received a letter from her cousin's son, Misha. The letter had been dictated and the handwriting ran in oblique lines across the page. Misha relayed greetings from various relatives and wrote that Grandmother's house and things were still intact and that Dusya must come.

"Go," her husband said. "Go on! Don't make a big thing of it. Just sell everything that's there as fast as you can. The rest can go to the collective farm."

And Dusya went. She hadn't traveled anywhere in a long time, and it was quite a trip. But she managed to enjoy it by getting acquainted with her traveling companions and conversing with them.

She'd sent a telegram that she was coming, but for some reason no one met her. She had to go on foot, but the walk was a pleasure for Dusya. Lining the narrow, rutted road were her native Smolensk fields, blue-green copses running along the horizon.

She reached the village in three hours. She stopped on a new bridge over the river and looked around. The village had grown

up a lot, and had widened out so with white farmsteads that it was
hardly recognizable. Dusya didn't care for all the changes.

She walked along the street, looking hard at everyone she met,
trying to guess who they were. She recognized almost no one,
although many stopped to greet her, exclaiming over how she had
grown.

Dusya's sister was overjoyed to see her. She burst into tears and
ran to put on the samovar. Dusya unpacked her gifts. Her sister
looked at them, cried some more, and hugged Dusya. Misha sat
on a bench and wondered what they were crying for.

As the sisters sat and drank tea, Dusya found out that the relatives had divided up many of the things. Her sister had taken the
livestock: a pig, three lambs, a goat, and a chicken. Dusya was a
little annoyed at first, but she got over it; not so much because a
great deal was still left but because, more important, the house remained. When they finished their tea and had talked themselves
out, the sisters went to take a look at the house.

Dusya was surprised to find the farmland plowed, but her sister explained that the neighbors had plowed so the land wouldn't
go to waste. The house didn't seem as big as Dusya remembered
it.

The windows were shuttered and a lock hung on the door. Her
sister worked at the lock a long time, then Dusya tried, then her
sister again, and finally they managed to open it.

Almost no light was coming through the shutters and it was dark
inside. The house was damp and had an unlived in look, but it
smelled of bread, a smell familiar from her childhood. Dusya's
heart began to pound. Her eyes grew accustomed to the darkness
as she walked around the room, inspecting it. The low ceiling was
a dark brown. Photographs were still hanging on the walls, but
the icons, except for one worthless one, were gone. The embroidered scarves for the stove and chest of drawers were gone.

Left alone, Dusya opened a chest — it smelled of her mother
— and found some dark old-womanish skirts, sarafans, and a

threadbare sheepskin coat. Dusya took them out, looked them over, and walked all over the house again. As she looked out into the empty yard, it occurred to her that she had had a dream about all this a long time ago and now she had returned to that dream.

Hearing of the sale, the neighbors began to come to see Dusya. They went over everything left in the house with great care, feeling everything, but Dusya wasn't asking much, so it all disappeared quickly.

The house was most important. Dusya inquired about prices on homes and was amazed and delighted to find that they had gone up. Three prospective buyers showed up immediately, two from her village and one from a neighboring village. But Dusya didn't sell right away; she was afraid her mother might have money hidden away somewhere. Three days she looked for it, pounding the walls, feeling the mattresses, climbing down into the cellar and up to the attic, but she found nothing.

When she'd settled on a price with the buyer, Dusya went to the regional seat, notarized the sale, and deposited the money. Then she went back, bought her sister some more presents and began to pack for Moscow. That night her sister returned to the farm, but Dusya decided to visit her mother's grave. Misha went along to keep her company.

They went through the meadow at sunset. The dandelions were out already, and the grass was fresh and green. The second half of the day had been hazy and misty, but the storm clouds had disappeared toward evening. Now only a rosy bank of clouds, so vague and distant that it appeared to be behind the sun, remained on the horizon into which Dusya and Misha were walking.

A mile from the village, the river turned sharply and the graveyard sat in the loop, on the high peninsular right bank. The graveyard had been surrounded at one time by a brick wall, with a tall arched gate at the entrance. After the war, however, they'd used the bricks for construction elsewhere, leaving only the gate. Now paths ran all over the graveyard from every side.

As they walked Dusya quietly and calmly questioned Misha about school, about the working day, about the chairman of the collective farm, about the harvests. But then the old graveyard appeared in the red light of the setting sun. At its edge, where the wall had been and sweetbriar now grew, were the older graves, which had long since ceased to look like graves. Next to them the common graves could be seen through the branches, with freshly decorated fences and high wooden obelisks.

Dusya and Misha went through the gate, turned to the right, then to the left, through the blossoming birch trees, through the pungent sweetbriar. Dusya was becoming paler and paler, her mouth half open.

"There's Granny," said Misha and Dusya saw a mound, sparsely covered with grass, revealing the sandy soil underneath. Its small blue cross, unstained by winter, had already slipped to one side.

Dusya went completely white. It was as if a knife had suddenly entered her chest at her heart. Her soul was struck by such black misery that she gasped, trembled, shrieked, fell down and crawled on her knees to the grave, sobbing and scaring Misha with the words that suddenly came to her.

"Ohh," she moaned softly, falling face down on the grave and digging her fingers into the wet ground. "My precious Mama . . . My darling beloved Mama . . . We'll never see each other again on this earth, never, never! How am I to go on living? Who'll love me, take care of me? Mama, Mama, what have you done?"

"Aunt Dusya, Aunt Dusya," whispered the frightened boy, taking hold of her sleeve. But when Dusya only bent again and beat her head against the ground, he tore off to the village.

An hour later, when night had nearly fallen, they came for her from the village. She was still lying there, nearly unconscious, unable to cry, unable to speak or think, just moaning through clenched teeth. Her face was black with dirt and awful.

They picked her up, rubbed her temples, tried to talk with her and soothe her as they took her home, but she understood nothing, staring at everyone with enormous swollen eyes — life, it seemed, was night. When they got her to her sister's home, she staggered to bed, barely making it, and was asleep instantly.

The next day, all packed for Moscow, drinking a last cup of tea with her sister, she was gay and talked about what a nice apartment and all the conveniences they had in Moscow.

So she departed, gay and calm, giving Misha another ten rubles. Two weeks later new people opened the old woman's house, washed the floors, brought in their things, and settled down to live.

Smoke

THEY spent the night sleeping on dead leaves in the attic of an abandoned cabin. Peter Nikolaevitch woke up when the first weak rays of light began to come through the holes in the rotting roof. His son Alexei rolled over and buried his face in his coat, his arms, bare legs and great big feet all sprawling. The butt of his gun was sticking out from under him.

Peter Nikolaevitch pulled on his boots and very cautiously descended the outside ladder on the few rungs that were left. Straightening up at the bottom, he looked at the brightening east, the trees, their branches still and heavy with dew, and then walked slowly around the cabin.

There had been a cattle enclosure here formerly and the cabin had been used by the herdsmen. Then it had smelled of smoke and milk and manure, and the ground had been trampled and slippery with cow dung. But it had been abandoned five years ago when the herd was moved and now there was nettle, with its great pale green leaves, growing all around the cabin. It had that look of total abandonment and desolation and loneliness that only a place of former human habitation can have.

The cabin door had been broken open and Peter Nikolaevitch went in. There were no panes in the windows, just one dim fragment left, gray with age and rain and sun. There were piles of leaves in the corners, and the oven door was gone, revealing a cold, black, gaping emptiness inside. Why did they leave? Where did the herd go to pasture now?

Peter Nikolaevitch sat on a pile of leaves in the corner and smoked slowly, his sorrowful dark eyes following the smoke as it rose to the window and lost its way in a large, dusty cobweb. The cabin smelled of the dried-out clay oven, and of rotting wood. From the window came the wistful smells of new grass and fresh air, and as his cigarette went out, Peter Nikolaevitch sat brooding about the time he had hunted here as a very young man.

He'd been twenty years old. For a whole month, either alone or with his father, he had wandered around, wild as a young stallion and almost crazy with happiness, in this melodious expanse, sleeping in the lean-to or in a haystack, sleeping the deep sleep of youth, waking at dawn with the feeling that his whole life lay before him — untouched, unlimited, and full of joy. He had wandered around the lakes and ponds and gloomy pine forests, unspeakably happy in his youth and strength, ready to swim through icy water after a teal, ready to cover dozens of miles on the chance of finding snipe. And also, and this was probably most important, he'd been in love then. He had thought about her and longed for her constantly, feeling at the same time that this was not real happiness yet, he was still too young, but that a far greater, ineffable happiness still lay ahead.

So much had passed and gone from memory since then, but this bright quiet spot and the time he had wandered about here came back now as the best and the purest he'd had in life. And he remembered all the days he'd had good hunting, the trees and hidden springs that marked the good places, and he even remembered what he had been thinking about on those lucky days.

Now he had come again, not alone this time, but with his son. He'd been terribly excited at the thought of seeing it all again, but now he was finding it painful, everything was so changed and faded beyond recognition. This was wrong, that was wrong. Only the dawn, the dew on the grass, and the smells remained eternally, forever the same. And it was strange and wonderful to think of the thousands of people — some as yet unborn — who would wake and look at the sunrise, the mist on the lake and smell the strong sad smells of earth.

2

Pretty soon his son woke up and began to bang around in the attic. The ladder squeaked and then there was a thud of feet.

"Father!" Alexei called softly.

Peter Nikolaevitch sighed, ran his hand over his face and went out. Alexei, his long, ski-pant-clad legs spread wide apart, was looking up at something, his face scared and thrilled.

"Shh." He grabbed his father's arm. "Hear that?"

"No, what is it?" asked Peter Nikolaevitch, straining for every sound.

"You can't hear that?" Alexei asked in an excited whisper, looking at his father, his eyes round with delight. "Wasps! There are three nests over there. I missed them yesterday in the dark, but I bumped one accidentally just now and the noise they started to make! You hear?" Alexei looked up with the same thrilled, scared look.

"Yes, they certainly are noisy," Peter Nikolaevitch agreed, smiling.

But he couldn't hear a thing and he felt depressed. My hearing is going already, he thought and mumbled hurriedly, before he got in a really bad mood, "Well, let's go, let's go. It's late already. Rucksacks, rifles, where are they?"

"Coming right up," his son answered and climbed the ladder without another word. Still without saying anything, he solemnly handed down to his father first one rucksack, then the other, the rifles, and the heavy cartridge bags. Then he pulled on his boots, climbed down, and caught his breath.

"Let's go," Peter Nikolaevitch said cheerfully, and set out ahead of his son across the wet grass to the place where he knew a path ought to be.

They didn't find it for a long time and got soaked, making their way by guesswork toward the tall dark pine woods. Their legs got tangled in the grass, and the clearings were white with camomile flowers. I wonder how much good hunting is lost because they don't cut back this underbrush, Peter Nikolaevitch thought bitterly. Alexei stumbled along behind him, yawning, his rucksack banging as he went. The gentle rhythmic sound reminded Peter Nikolaevitch of something but he couldn't for the life of him think what it was.

They saw the old path the minute they entered the woods. The woods were dense and gloomy, but a timid blue light was beginning to force its way in from the other side of the pines, where the dried-up riverbed lay. And beyond, in the meadow, a bird began to sing a very simple song, just two notes, "Pii-pii, pii-pii."

Alexei yawned and stumbled again. "Still far to go?" he asked sleepily.

A wood grouse broke out of the darkest part of the woods, as if in answer to the question, and ran between the trees, clucking repeatedly. Startled, they both stopped, and Peter Nikolaevitch's heart turned over: there were still wood grouse here!

"Foo! You scared him!" he laughed. "Let's go on, there'll be more!"

But Alexei turned off the path without listening and moved stealthily across the silent moss and pine needles, through the cranberry bushes, his gun in hand. Peter Nikolaevitch stared after him, expecting any second to hear a shot. Then he straightened his gun, and quietly moved on.

He came out of the woods and sat down on a fallen tree to wait. In front of him there was a small field covered with mist, beyond the field more woods, beyond them another field probably, then a little sprucewood marker, then the rolling, swampy meadow with its tough sedge grass, and finally the lake — his old hunting spot.

Very shortly, Alexei appeared, coming toward his father getting his gun back on and wiping something from his face.

"Well, did you come across anything?" asked Peter Nikolaevitch.

"Nothing," Alexei answered cheerfully. "But what a wild

place! All the mushrooms, berries . . . is it nice! Are we really going to live here a whole month? That's wonderful!"

"We're going to live like kings!" Peter Nikolaevitch looked at his son affectionately. "You like it? I was afraid you wouldn't. You're my good boy!"

And they walked along the overgrown path through the meadow to some more woods, but this time Alexei walked ahead and Peter Nikolaevitch watched him, thinking what a big boy he had and how glad he was his son was with him.

3

The sun was high and the dew was still clinging only to the bushes in the shade when the hunters reached the lake. They had been in no especial hurry, enjoying the silence and seclusion and so had sat for long periods in the clearings, watching the sun come up, listening to the crystal call of the crane, the knock of the woodpecker, and the loud cry of the merlin.

They reached the lake and Peter Nikolaevitch took off his cap and stood looking around eagerly, smoothing back his thinning hair. How everything had changed!

The lake seemed smaller, as if it had shrunk with age. One narrow, shallow section was completely clogged with grass and weeds; the trees bent down in wilder profusion and there were more lily pads floating in the dark water.

Well hello, thought Peter Nikolaevitch, extremely moved. Hello bushes and trees and lake. Hello flowers and reeds, here I am again. You've been waiting for me a long time. I used to dream about you and I came back . . .

With difficulty Peter Nikolaevitch found what he thought to be the clearing where he and his father had kept a fire going almost continually, where they had dried out after a rain, cooked their soup, brewed their tea, loaded their guns, and harmonized softly together. But the clearing had become small and unfamiliar looking, and he couldn't decide if it was just the overgrowth, or if like almost everything else from the distant past it had grown larger than reality in his memory. Blinking back the tears he felt coming to his eyes, Peter Nikolaevitch grabbed his son's arm.

"Go take a walk along the lake. Look, over there. Go on!"

Alexei looked at his father closely, blushed and shuffled off hurriedly, hunching his thin back. Peter Nikolaevitch took off his rucksack, sank to his knees and ran his fingers through the grass. There has to be something left, he thought childishly, there were so many ashes and coals here. Even the lower branches of the pine were scorched! He glanced up at the pine needles silver in the sunlight, wrapped in an iridescent spider web, the hard, ripening, green-brown pine cones, a cluster of gnats. He raked the grass with his fingers, pushing aside the tough slender stems of the camomile flowers, but he found nothing but wet ground, rotted leaves, small patches of sticky substances, swarms of ants, and wild strawberries, glistening like drops of blood. It's the natural cycle, of course, thought Peter Nikolaevitch, confused and unhappy. Everything passes, everything changes. Is this the same spot at all? But wait . . . He got up and looked around. Their lean-to had been under a fir tree somewhere. Where should he look? It had been such a fine lean-to, cool during the day and warm at night. He and his father had done a good job. Where was that fir tree? Or was it all really just a dream?

The tops of the dense trees murmured, and the blue-white sky shone through. The bright undersides of the aspen leaves flashed, and a warm light flickered over the thick dark trunks and a kingdom of new-fallen birch branches on the ground.

Peter Nikolaevitch crawled around under the fir trees, scratching his face and hands, trying not to get too far from the lake. His gun got in his way so he took it off and leaned it against a tree. The air was full of the moist smell of all the mushrooms and berries and the spicy smell of fallen pine needles. Peter Nikolaevitch broke off a berry twig and chewed it mechanically, savoring its cool acid taste in his mouth and nose. Finally he came across a particularly fat fir trunk, and looked around at the clearing, then back at the tree. It might have been here. There should be a notch on the trunk, where it had supported one side of the lean-to, he remembered. But he could find no mark on the great sticky trunk. Then he dropped to his knees again, thoughtfully sifting through the twigs that had collected over the years under the tree. And he found what he was looking for, some blackened rotten sticks of wood, the ends broken off by repeated blows of an axe.

Yes! This was all that remained of their splendid lean-to — rotten sticks of wood.

Peter Nikolaevitch got up, brushed off his knees, and fought his way out of the underbrush. He looked up at the fir tree. How old it was! So much lichen! The top branches were already dead and before long what once had been a soft little green fir would dry up and die. And life would go on.

Finding his gun, he re-entered the clearing and stood staring at the camomile flowers, his mind a blank. Then he remembered how he and his father had signaled one another and he opened his gun, removed the cartridges, placed the barrel to his lips and a melancholy singsong sound flew out over the woods and died out somewhere beyond the lake.

"Yoo-hoo!" the boy's voice rang out quite nearby.

There was a rustle and Alexei, looking guilty, was coming toward him. Peter Nikolaevitch realized that he hadn't gone anywhere, he'd just sat nearby and waited for his father to find whatever it was he needed.

"How did you do that?" asked Alexei in an amazed way.

Peter Nikolaevitch showed him. Alexei broke his gun open immediately, blew with all his strength and again the disturbing sound from out of the past flew over the woods and the lake.

"So here's where we'll be living," Peter Nikolaevitch announced quietly.

"Is this where you and Grandfather lived?" asked Alexei, blushing.

"Get the axe, we've got to put up a lean-to," his father replied gruffly, searching through his rucksack without looking at his son.

4

Cutting the poles for the lean-to, driving them in place and getting them just right, and finally covering them with a double layer of fir branches, all took a long time. They were trying to get it in exactly the same place it had stood before. Peter Nikolaevitch remembered everything his father had done and did exactly the same, and his son watched and helped him in exactly the same way he had helped his father.

Around two o'clock, when the lean-to was completely ready, when the rucksacks had been unpacked and they had laid their coats and jackets over some fir branches and taken off their boots to rest, it began to look like rain. Dark clouds moved in fast, one by one blotting out the blue patches of sky. The woods darkened and were silent and it was nicer than ever in the lean-to. They were expecting a heavy rain, but it only drizzled timidly at first, and then came down warm and gentle and close.

The hunters sat inside feeling pleasantly tired, happy that they had managed to get the lean-to up and could wait out the bad weather in peace, listening to the barely perceptible rustle of the rain on the leaves. Soon everything became damp and close, but there was no longer the clean nostalgic smell of dew that there'd been in the early morning, but the smell of mushrooms and wet earth, of bitter aspen roots and birch leaves.

Alexei curled up in the corner of the lean-to next to the thick trunk and fell asleep. Peter Nikolaevitch moved closer to the entrance and began watching the birch branches hanging wet in the rain and the camomile flowers in the clearing. He sat as he used to sit, with his arms around his knees, singing softly to himself. He sang sad old Russian songs, the ones that tell of separations, death, unrequited love, rolling fields, of sorrow and lonely nights. He sang and remembered many things from the past, dreaming his private dreams as he watched the sullen sky and the quiet peaceful woods. Then he stopped singing and thought about his son. He didn't know which was the greater part of his feelings, elation or envy.

Though he dozed off, conquered by his exhaustion, with his head on his knees, the feeling of longing and regret for something forever wasted had not quit him. His arm went to sleep and hung lifeless. And the rain went on drizzling and rustling in the aspen leaves and in the grass, everything grew wetter and wetter, and the lean-to under the fir tree was the only dry place around.

When they awoke that evening the rain was over and they took their guns and went into the damp woods. The branches were dripping, and the larger drops could be heard in the distance, tuk, tuk, tuk! The sun was setting, sending weak yellow rays through the woods, and a transparent golden mist was everywhere. The birds were singing their last songs of the day. There was a mist on the lake. There was a flash of white in the reeds and rushes, the water rippled: there were ducks there somewhere.

"Wait, let me, let me," Alexei pleaded in a whisper.

Peter Nikolaevitch turned, remembering asking his father the same thing, and being given permission. Alexei balanced his gun on a branch, his elbows twitching. "Toch-tiou-tukh!" the echo rang out, and the smoke settled in a ring on the water.

No longer having to be afraid of noise, the hunters pushed through the rustling underbrush to the shore, in time to see three ducks starting up from the lake. Two were still in the water. One was lying absolutely still, its yellow belly exposed, and the other was bobbing on its side, trying to dive under, but it could only get its head in the water, its wing flapping weakly. The gunsmoke blended with the mist and formed a shroud over the water.

"Wait, we'll cut a board!" Peter Nikolaevitch said excitedly, taking off his gun and getting out his axe.

But Alexei wasn't listening. Keeping his eye on the duck which was still alive and thrashing, he pulled off his boots and foot wrappings and began to undress. Peter Nikolaevitch put down the axe and sat down patiently on a log. He lit a cigarette.

The boy undressed, his long thin body shivering, covered himself quickly with goose grease and went in. He walked out carefully, feeling for the bottom, shoving lily pads out of his way. When he stumbled and couldn't catch himself, he dove in and started swimming. He swam out to the ducks and turned a radiant face toward shore.

"Father!" he shouted, gasping from the shock of the cold water. "Come on in! The mist smells so good! Like hydrogen and tobacco!" he laughed, and dove under ecstatically, wiggled his feet and came up again, coughing and choking. Then he swam over and collected both the ducks.

And with a shudder Peter Nikolaevitch remembered suddenly how he had shot a duck on such an evening as this on another lake a mile from here, and he had gone in after it while his father sat smoking and resting on the bank. The smell of gunsmoke and tobacco had spread over the water, thrilling him so that he had also called to his father and begun to splash about in ecstasy.

Yes, things were the same. Life was as beautiful as ever, and always would be — there'd always be swimming, sunsets turning to red and green, the gentle light of sunrise, flowers would bloom and grass would grow, and new people would come to the old hunting spots.

His heart constricted with joy and sadness. He couldn't sit still any longer, so he threw away his cigarette and went off, ignoring the path, through the wet grass, into the depths of the dark silent woods.

His son splashed around for a long time, slapping his palms against the water, calling out in different voices and listening to the echo, watching the opposite shore, already blue in the mist of the dying day. Then he got out blue and shivering and dressed quickly, hopping about on one foot. He patted the warm ducks, looking at their wet feet, their half-closed turquoise eyes and the drops of blood on their bills. Then he noticed the cigarette and after looking around furtively, he smoked it, coughing as he inhaled, blinking his eyes and smiling in his as yet untarnished happiness.

THE RENEGADES

The Mendicant

HE was walking along a side road looking at a bank of summer clouds which seemed to be lying on the gentle line of hills up ahead. He was walking into a stiff wind, and it ruffled his fine, sun-bleached beard. Wiping his teary eyes with a rough grubby finger, he stared at the mirage without blinking. Automobiles passed him, whining madly on the asphalt, but he didn't deign to move aside, sending a dark straight shadow down the middle of the oily gray road.

He was young, tall, a bit stoop-shouldered, and he took long, firm strides. His rubber boots, torn winter hat, the knapsack on his back, his warm threadbare coat, all sat on him easily, without seeming to burden him or get in his way.

Was he thinking about anything as he passed the villages, woods, rivers, green fields and fallow? His bloodshot, dark blue eyes looked at nothing carefully nor rested on anything long; lost in the distance, they would cloud with tears, and then stare blankly again. His grass-stained walnut stick tapped loudly on the asphalt. The bushes sneaked up on the highway, and the tall old birch trees approached, but silently and pensively disappeared, knowing it was not in their power to hide the vast expanse of the fields.

At high noon the sun grew hotter and dryer, the wind brought the smell of warm hay and burning asphalt, but the mendicant kept on briskly, tapping his stick, not knowing where he was going, nor how long it would take him to get there.

Finally he noticed the white shape of a church tower far off to his right. Seeing it, he slowed down and turned onto a dusty country road. Reaching a clear blue river, he sat in the shade of a bush, took off his knapsack, and taking out eggs and bread, began to eat. He chewed slowly, carefully inspecting each bite before he put it in his mouth. When he was full, he crossed himself, wiped the crumbs from his mouth and beard, and got up slowly. Going to the river, he drank and washed his face, and then he came back, walking deeper into the bushes. He put the knapsack under his head, pulled up his collar, covered his face with his hat, and fell instantly into the deep sleep of a very tired man.

2

He slept for a long time and when he awoke the sun was already behind the hills. Rubbing his teary eyes, he yawned and scratched for a while, looking around, not knowing where he was or how he had got there. His face, swollen with sleep, expressed nothing but boredom and indolence.

A milk truck was going along the road toward the highway. The mendicant watched the truck and his face sprang to life. Quickly he put on his knapsack, got back onto the road, crossed the bridge over the river and went toward the village he'd seen earlier in the day.

To his right lay a field of dry green oats, turning brown, and then a double line of fir trees. The sun disappeared, leaving behind only a narrow ruddy strip shining through the black firs. The effect was sinister. The mendicant hurried, kicking up dust. He was afraid of the dark and didn't like nighttime.

The smells were different now. There was the wet grass, the dust on the road, the heavy fragrance of clover, the sweet smell of snuff from the yarrow grass, and from the fir trees a strong breath of resin. The sky, clear and deep, grew pensively dark, revealing a milky white new moon.

The road began to loop around woods and ravines. The mendicant walked faster. He was snorting in animal fear, his nostrils quivering. He tried to sing once or twice, but stopped, stifled by the twilit silence.

At last there were smells of human habitation and livestock. He walked more calmly, but still stared ahead vigilantly. Presently the bushes and trees began to scatter and drop behind, and he saw a village, with a river running below and a church on the hill above. The entire river bottom was taken up by grazing land and life could be felt there, despite the covering darkness, the way it is felt in a beehive at night.

He'd almost reached the threshing barn when the mendicant noticed a woman walking from pasture to town, and he stopped to wait. The mendicant took off his hat as she approached, and made a low bow, looking up into her face searchingly.

"Hello, mother! God keep you." His tone was deep and significant.

"Hello yourself," she echoed, slowing down, straightening her scarf and licking her cracked lips.

"Are you from around here?"

"Me? Around here. And you're . . . ?"

"From afar, I am. I visit holy places. A mendicant."

The woman looked at him curiously, wanting to ask him something, but she was too embarrassed and walked on in silence. The mendicant walked beside her, maintaining his stern and significant expression.

"Is the church open?" he asked, looking at the red-gold cross on the bell tower.

"The church? Are there any open churches? There're no services in there, just the machine tractor station. There used to be a Father there, an old priest, but he died twenty years ago."

"Meaning you live without faith?"

The woman was uneasy. She straightened her scarf again, took a deep breath, and dropped her eyes. The mendicant looked at her sideways. She was not yet old, but her face and hands were dark and roughened by the wind. Her thin shoulders protruded through her faded jacket, but her flat breasts were almost invisible.

"What else?" she said sadly. "You know how our young people are today, they don't believe. We have our farm work all year around here, there's no time for anything else. When a Father comes around, we have a service at the cemetery, that's about it."

"So." The mendicant drew the syllable out mournfully. "Oh you people, you people! My heart is sick that my eyes have looked on you. You're swarming right toward the pit . . ."

The woman was silent. The pond water glistened in the dark. The last of the ducks were swimming along in the weeds, greedily eating duckweed, trying to fill up for the night.

"Is there at least one believer here who will give shelter to a man of God?" the mendicant asked pathetically.

"You mean spend the night? Well of course, you can stay at my house, it's just for the night."

Neither the mendicant nor the woman said another word until they got home. Only as she was unlocking the door did she ask, "What's your name?"

"Johann," answered the mendicant in the same stern, significant tone.

The woman took a deep breath, thinking of her sins perhaps, and opened the door. They went through a dark smelly passageway and into the house.

"Take off your things and rest," she said and went out of the room.

Johann took off his knapsack and coat, and then began to pull off his boots. He took a long time, gravely smelling his foot rags, scratching his large flat feet, and looking around.

When his hostess came back again, Johann was sitting in his shirt, digging around in his knapsack. He drew out a gospel and a flat notebook with a cross on the cover called "The Memorial Book of Saint Johann." Groping around, he found a stub of a pencil, and opened the notebook. He thought a minute and asked sternly, "Have there been any deaths in this house?"

The woman winced, and turned to stare at the strange bearded man.

"Yes," she said softly. "My boy died this spring. He worked as a driver on the collective farm, he started across the river . . ."

"Name?" the mendicant interrupted her severely.

"What?" She hadn't understood him.

"The name, the name. The name of your son." He raised his voice in irritation.

"My boy? Fedya he was called. They told him, don't go across . . . The stuff won't spoil . . . It's just parts for the machine tractor station . . . Go around, or over the bridge . . . The ice is breaking now . . . He didn't listen, he was a hothead . . . He drowned . . . My boy . . . drowned . . ."

"I'll pray for him," Johann interrupted, writing "Fyodor" in large letters in the notebook. "What's your name?"

"Nastasya."

"So, Na — stas — ya. You live alone?"

"There are two of us. A daughter. Not my daughter. Fedya's wife . . . We . . ."

"Did you have a husband?"

"Of course. He was killed at the front. In '42."

"Name?"

"Mikhail."

"So." Johann was silent. "And your daughter-in-law's name?"

"Lyuba. That means love."

"I know," the mendicant said, writing. "Is she a good girl?"

"What?" Nastasya didn't understand.

"Well behaved? Does she believe in God?"

"No, she doesn't believe in God, she's a Young Communist leaguer. All the same, it's not a sin to say she's a good girl. She finished the zoological institute, and now she works here on the farm, they even made her club director. The club is near and she spends her evenings there. She gets tired being there night and day, and I don't blame her, it's boring for her alone, she's young, they only lived together a year. My boy, Fedenka . . . He came out of the army, 'Mamunya,' he says to me . . . 'Mamunya' . . ."

Nastasya's face wrinkled up, her cracked lips trembling, and tears ran down her dark, thin cheeks. The mendicant was sternly silent.

"Sit down, get ready for bed," Nastasya said through her tears. "I'll go start the samovar."

"Do you have any icons?"

"Yes, 'Myrrh-bearing Women,' and 'Theothokos with Three Arms.'"

"Where? Bring them to me."

"They're over here, come . . ."

She opened the door to an empty room. Johann clumped along the floormats with a bored expression, holding his memorial book.

"Leave me," he said, looking at the icons. "I'm going to pray."

He bumped down onto his knees and pulled his beard. Nastasya slipped out.

"Oh Lord," Johann exhorted in his deepest voice, "Lord!"

And then he was silent, lost in contemplation of the apple trees, motionless outside the window. Nastasya was setting the table, rattling the dishes. The gentle sounds, the long summer twilight pleased and touched him, pulling gently at his heartstrings. How many towns had he seen, where hadn't he spent the night? Everywhere things were different — the people, the customs, the talk. Only the twilight, the bread, the smells and sounds of domesticity — these were everywhere identical.

Johann looked out the window, craning his neck: beyond the gardens below was the river, and beyond the river the fields and woods. The fog had already crept out of the woods and was covering the meadow in milky waves, rolling slowly down to the river.

"Oh Lord!" sighed Johann as he listened again to the gentle clatter of the dishes and looked out the window into the distance.

Nastasya peeked cautiously into the room and saw the disheveled, long unclipped head, the dark neck, the wide strong shoulders, the large feet, the bent legs.

"Please come and eat," she called softly.

But the mendicant didn't answer or move, lost in thought, his long hands resting on the floor. Nastasya went out, put the samovar on the porch and began to milk the cow.

A minute later the mendicant heard light footsteps in the passageway. The girl, he thought, turning quickly. The door slammed, and the footsteps died on the threshold of the room. Johann pulled on his beard and crossed himself broadly, studying the dark faces of the icons; the new arrival, he knew, was watching him from behind.

Silence. Then the quick footsteps in the passageway again. Johann got up and went silently over to lay his sunburned ear to the door.

"Mama!"

"What?" The steady flow of milk into the pail stopped.

"Mama, who's that man?"

"That's a wanderer. A mendicant, looking for the faithful, asked to spend the night."

"A mendicant? Is he old?"

"He has a beard, but he's not old. His eyes are young."

"Maybe he's some kind of criminal?"

"What do you mean? Christ be with you! A godly man, a prayerful man."

Silence. Only the gentle grunting of the pig. Then the quick steady flow of milk into the pail again.

"Have you fed the pig yet?"

"No I haven't. I've mixed it, it's behind the stove."

"I'll feed her."

Johann turned away from the door, worried. The bitch! he thought angrily. They could still kick me out, not let me spend the night.

But the gentle domestic noises went right on. In the corners where darkness had accumulated it was already impossible to make out the icons, the photographs, or the official documents on the walls. Everything was falling into darkness, over everything an air of mystery. When it was completely dark and the moon shining over the forest had begun to peep in the window, they brought in the bright hot lamp, and the samovar on the table began to hiss. The mendicant came out of the empty room, slipped the gospel and the memorial book into his knapsack, sat on a bench and followed Lyuba through half-closed eyes.

3

They sat down to eat. The mendicant was greedy and ate a lot, making loud gulping noises, his beard and ears twitching.

"Eat, eat," said Nastasya, pushing food in his direction.

Each time he raised his bloodshot, dark blue eyes from his plate he would gaze at Lyuba, and, becoming aware of his gaze, she would blush, and fidget and frown. She was pretty in a dark subdued way and still had something of a young girl about her: her angular movements, her elusive eyes, her timid breasts . . .

The mendicant watched her. There was something about her he liked. He began thinking it might be a good idea to shave his beard, work on the farm, marry a girl like her and sleep with her in the hayloft, kissing her until the first roosters crowed. The thought made his head swim and his heart swell.

"Eat, don't be bashful," Nastasya begged. "Here's some mushrooms you must try. We get our mushrooms early here."

When he had finished, he crossed himself, made a bow to his hostess and to Lyuba, and moved back from the table. He wanted to belch, but was embarrassed and managed to do without it. He started to roll a cigarette, spilling some tobacco as he did so and scraping it up.

"Here I am smoking," he said regretfully. "It's the temptation of the devil. How many times I've repented and given it up, but I can't."

Lyuba burst out laughing suddenly, and turned and went to the stove. Nastasya moved nervously, straightened up and gazed at the mendicant imploringly as she snapped at the girl, "What's the matter with you? Have you gone out of your mind or something?"

Lyuba didn't answer; she'd closed her eyes, holding in her laughter.

"Yes," the mendicant raised his voice. "People have become too smart for religion but the devil is still the devil . . . Life has become stupid and trivial, there's no real thought, the machine is everything . . . It has devoured man! It is all written in the apocalypse."

Lyuba laughed in his face.

"What are you looking at?" Johann asked roughly, half playful, half nasty. "Don't you like what you see? Ever seen the like? Maybe you're sorry you sat at the same table with me?"

"Of course not, bless you!" Nastasya was frightened.

"I'm not sorry about sitting at the same table, nor about sleeping in the same house," Lyuba said in a clear voice. "That's Mama's business. But frankly . . . you amuse me. Why are you a wanderer? Aren't you ashamed? You've grown a beard. Do you think you get saintliness from a beard? Honestly, it's just like our amateur theatricals!"

"And you don't attend such things?"

"Me? No, I love my work."

"Work . . ." The mendicant sniffed and stared into the corner. "You're a stupid girl. What's work? You don't believe in God but He exists and will eternally exist! Work . . . Ekh, you . . . I get around, I see things . . ."

"That sounds easy," she came back quickly.

"I get around, I see things," the mendicant went on louder. "What are you doing? How do you live? Is life on earth better today? No, worse! I tell you verily! There are more thieves today, more depravity. I read the gospel. Here it is," he patted his knapsack, "you won't find it in your technical institutes. No sir!"

"And it's not needed," Lyuba answered with a yawn. "We get along fine without it. I'm tired. I'm going to bed. Thank you, Mama."

She turned away from the stove and took something from the chest of drawers. She passed the mendicant, leaving the clean healthy smell of her womanly body behind her, and went into the passageway, slamming the door behind her.

"A proud girl," the mendicant's voice caught, and he laughed. "She's got character!"

"You know young people." Nastasya's look was placating as she cleared the table. "They understand things differently. They speak up. Don't be angry with her. Her life isn't easy. She's young, pretty, and a widow."

"Hmm," the mendicant muttered thoughtfully. "God must have willed it so. Now I didn't intend to become a mendicant, although of course I was always interested in life on the other side. I'm from Pscov, from the village of Podsosna, ever hear of it? My parents were killed in the war and went to the heavenly kingdom. I was left alone, how was I to live? I knocked around, worked at various jobs, I worked as a mine clearer and one exploded and wounded me in the stomach, right below my lung. I just barely survived and I became an invalid. So what is there for an invalid? Just a little light work perhaps? With no education it would have taken a long time to learn to be an engineer or an agronomist. I didn't care for the collective farm, it was boring and my soul is insatiable. I was called by the distant hills. Although I hadn't believed before, I began to turn to God. There was an old man on the collective farm — he worked as a milk

driver — he was a godly man. He gave me guidance, books to
read. And that's how it happens. 'Go, my son,' that's what he
said to me. 'Go,' he says, 'to holy places, pray, save yourself and
all of us from destruction.' And I went, and this is now my fifth
year of wandering. There are lots of others like me — all clean,
holy people. My life is no longer a burden. I am close to God and
I shall not leave my chosen path. No I won't!"

"Are you going far now?" Nastasya asked sleepily.

"Yes, tomorrow I'll get to Borisov, and I'll kiss the life-restoring
cross I've heard so much about. Where haven't I been? I lived
on alms in the Kiev monastery, I have been in the holy
Kiev-Pecherski caves — wonderful place! I have offered up so
many prayers! I was in Troitse-Sergievski, in Estonia, in Vetlug.
Now there are people I don't love, gloomy, sectarians without
priests, parasites who won't give alms . . ."

She must be sleeping in the passageway! There was a sweet
pain in his heart as he suddenly thought of Lyuba. "Ekh Mama-
sha," he said, feeling warm and gay, excited that everything was
turning out so well, that his hostess was becoming converted, and
that a young widow was sleeping in the passageway. "Ah, Mama-
sha, I've walked the world over, and to speak from the soul, as before the one true God, there's no better place on earth than our
Russia! You walk through Russia and the skylark sings, fluttering and flickering, there's clover in bloom, camomile flowers, good
people talk to you, ask you in for the night, feed you. Or you
walk in the forest — our forests are inspiring! — and the bumble-
bees are buzzing and the wasps whispering. Oh it's sweet and
good! Nobody ordering you around, no laws, you can come and
go as you please. What about people? Which people? I've a bad
memory, and I forget everyone. I don't remember anyone. No,
absolutely no one. I sleep somewhere, I get up and pray, I thank
my host, and I'm off. There are some who won't take me in, they
say I'm a swindler. That hurts me, God bless them, it does. But
there are lots of good, religious people who'd give me a home; 'live

with us!' they say. But I can't live in one place, there's something
pulling and drawing me on. Especially in the spring. No, I can't."

The mendicant stopped, lost in thought, his hands resting on
the bench. His hostess began to doze off, swaying, twitching, blinking. The clock ticked loudly in the passageway. Everything was
quiet.

"I'm kind of sleepy," Nastasya said shamefacedly, yawning.
"Up at dawn tomorrow . . ."

She pulled herself up with an effort, pulled off the cover on the
wide wooden bed, laughing at herself apologetically and mumbling, "It's my job to see to the cattle before daylight, I'm the first
one up around here. Get in, God bless you, you're probably tired."

"Oh no, I'll manage somehow on the floor. You go ahead," the
mendicant said resignedly, looking enviously at the feather bed.

"Get in, get in, don't think twice about it. I don't sleep here, I
don't like it, it's too wide. Lyuba sometimes sleeps here, but I
sleep on the stove. Get in!"

"Well all right, Christ save you," Johann said, with a show of
reluctance, but secretly relieved. He began to undress.

Nastasya moved around a bit more, rearranging, straightening,
casting a large sleepy shadow on the wall. Disturbed, the flies on
the ceiling began to drone. Then Nastasya went to the table, put
out the lamp, and the house was dark.

4

Is she sleeping in the passageway? The mendicant thought
about Lyuba, struggling with his desire. Sleep didn't come; he
turned over and watched the patches of moonlight on the floor.
Finally, he got up, in his long undershirt, a pale figure in the darkness.

"I forgot to go outside," he muttered, fumbling for the door. He
stood for a moment in the black passageway, getting used to the
dark. Cocking his ear, he heard Lyuba's steady breathing. She's

here! he thought joyfully, and crossing the passageway, he opened the bolt and went out on the porch.

The village was dark and quiet, but somewhere someone wasn't asleep, a light was burning. Someone was talking and laughing in the distance. The moon was full and low, the shadows of the houses stood out clearly on the road. The stars twinkled feebly and it grew colder. A tractor was whirring in a field somewhere, but he couldn't make out where. The voices and laughter came nearer, so close now he could see lighted cigarette ends. The mendicant shivered, crossed the passageway again, and entered the house, leaving the door ajar behind him. I'll wait a bit longer, till the old woman is sleeping soundly, and then . . . He lay down and closed his eyes.

Then, the sound of low voices and an accordion being played quietly outside the window. A slight tap on the pane. Stretching, Johann saw the figures of two girls. They rapped again, quietly, surreptitiously. No one in the house stirred: the two of them were heavy sleepers.

"Well?" said a male voice. "Is she asleep? Tap louder then."

The boy knocked so hard the window frame rattled. Then he burst out laughing and jumped back.

Johann was annoyed. Little devils!

Bare feet padded along the passageway and Lyuba came quietly into the room, dressed only in a nightgown. She opened the window.

"What do you want?" she asked angrily.

"Lyubushka," a girl's voice pleaded, "we thought you weren't sleeping . . ."

Someone burst out laughing.

"That's what we thought, really. Will you give us the key to the club so we can dance?"

"Come on, Lyubushka," a second gay and pleading voice took up with the first. "We're just drying up here in the summer, no movies, nothing to see."

"No I won't," Lyuba said sternly. "Go to bed."

The mendicant didn't move. Holding his breath, he examined her figure in the moonlight, her strong arms and shoulders, her breasts.

"No movies, no amateur theatricals, nothing . . ." the second injured voice went on.

"Just for an hour, Lyubushka?" the first begged again. "It's still early."

"Early! It's practically light!"

"Where it's light, it's light," came back quickly from the other side of the window. "What time is it, Kolya?"

"Twenty of eleven," said someone with a husky voice, and burst out laughing.

"I won't give it to you!" Lyuba said severely. "The chairman has given me no permission. We discussed that question at the board meeting today. Dance all night and you can't get up for work. You have to sleep!"

Lyuba closed the window and went out into the passageway, her white calves flashing.

"Wouldn't she give it?" someone asked outside the window.

The accordion played and a cracked falsetto voice rendered a couplet of a tedious popular song. Then the voices scattered, faded, and it was quiet. In the yard, the rooster crowed three times. The mendicant sat on the bed, took out a cigarette and lighted it cautiously in his cupped hand, dropping the ashes on the floor. Putting out the stub in a flowerpot, he got up, and went quietly over to the stove. He poked Nastasya and listened: she was snoring softly.

Johann walked quickly out into the passageway and closed the door tight behind him. Quaking and cold in his legs and stomach, he felt his way to the place where Lyuba was sleeping.

Feeling about for the bed, he touched its edge and pulled off the light blanket. He wet his lips as he slid his hands under her nightgown. Lyuba woke up, squirmed out from under his beard and screamed, hitting the mendicant on the chest. Johann fell full length on top of her and covered her mouth, whispering, "There now, there now, don't be afraid, I . . ."

"Let me go, you hobo! Let me go, you devil's pilgrim!" she hissed, pulling away. She sat up and pulled her gown over her knees.

"Wait, I'll marry you . . . don't make any noise, listen to what I'm saying," he whispered. "I'll marry you tomorrow. I'll shave off my beard, I'll work on the collective farm. I'll go to the baths," he added, remembering that he hadn't had a bath in a long time. "Come to me, I'll be tender . . ."

"Mama!" Lyuba cried, jumping up and running to the wall. "Will you get away from me, you filthy devil?" she screamed, trying to hide her terror in insults.

"I'll love you," the mendicant pleaded, becoming aware that nothing would come of this. "I'm healthy, young, at the height of my powers. I'll shave off my beard right away! Think it over, there aren't many young people on the collective farms these days, you'll just die or marry a widower with children . . . Come here, won't you? Do you want me to go down on my knees?"

"Mama!" she cried again. "I need help!"

"Keep quiet," the mendicant hissed. "I'm going, I'm going, you damned witch, Satan . . ."

He got up, fumbled for the door and walked unsteadily into the moonlit room.

"Who's that?" the woman called sleepily from the stove. "Who's there?"

The mendicant lay down quietly on the bed, trembling all over, grinding his teeth, tears of pain and frustration in his eyes.

The woman turned over on the stove and then was quiet, snoring gently.

"Bitch!" whispered the mendicant. "Bitch! Tramp! Tease!"

Something creaked and rolled and came down with a crash in the passageway; footsteps were heard on the ceiling, another creak, and silence.

"She's climbed up to the attic, the little bitch," he whispered to himself furiously, "and taken the ladder up with her. So go to the devil, you damned anathema!"

He had another cigarette, not bothering to cup it in his hand, cursing under his breath. Time passed, the moonlight shifted, it began to get light, but the mendicant couldn't fall asleep, tossing on the soft feather quilt.

5

The rooster woke him in the morning, crowing right under the window. He yawned and combed his hair, not bothering to wash. Then for a long time he sat still, trying to remember his dream, but he couldn't remember. The sun was baking hot, the room was stuffy and smelled sour, there were flies everywhere. Everything seemed tiresome and ordinary; the mystery of the night before was gone. Johann got dressed and sat down at the window, smoking and thinking.

The door slammed loudly, and Nastasya came in. Giving Johann a strange, nasty look, she went to the stove and picked up the tongs. Bending over, she banged the oven door open, her sharp shoulder blades moving quickly and angrily. The girl must have told on me, Johann supposed. Ekh! now she won't feed me. I'll have to leave.

He got up slowly, his face deliberately sad and penitent, put on his coat and picked up his knapsack. Nastasya watched him silently, holding the tongs, her lips compressed into a tight line. At the door, the mendicant cheered up suddenly. He smiled. Making another deep bow, he said solemnly, "Christ save you. May God love you and save you. I'll pray for you all."

"You red-eyed dog," Nastasya said quickly, her face reddening splotchily. She turned her back.

The mendicant put on his hat and left the room.

It was always the same, whenever he set out for somewhere. He began to feel happier and happier. The road called out, yesterday faded and was forgotten. Night after day, *away, away!* he said to himself joyfully as he went down through the gardens to the river. At the river, he found the ford and crossed. Climbing the gentle slope into the hills, he entered the forest from which the milky clouds of mist had come rolling down to the river the evening before. Losing his way in the forest slightly, the mendicant came out on the road and took it west.

Where the road would come out, he didn't know. But his spirits were high and joyous again; again he was walking with the fluid stride of a man used to walking, rustling his stick through the grass and underbrush, tapping the trees, quietly singing a little tune. Only the memory of last night's failure, and a faint yearning for some unknown thing, sometimes stabbed faintly at his heart.

And so he walked the whole day, and that evening he requested lodging in a distant town.

Adam and Eve

An artist named Ageev was staying in a hotel in a northern city, where he'd come to paint the fishermen. It was a broad city, with squares, streets and boulevards all so broad that they made it seem empty.

It was autumn. Low fleecy clouds were hanging over the city and the gray-brown, frost-covered forest to the west; it rained ten times a day, and the lake rose like a leaden wall. Ageev lay in bed for a long time in the morning, smoking on an empty stomach, looking out the window. Sheets of rain played against the glass, and the rooftops of the houses below shone gloomily, reflecting the sky. The room smelled heavily of tobacco and of hotels in general. Ageev's head was aching, his ears wouldn't stop ringing, and he had a pain in his chest.

Ageev had been talented since childhood, and at twenty-five his face was full of contempt — in his heavy, dark, downcast lids, in his lower lip, in the lazy, arrogant look in his dark brown eyes. He always wore a velvet jacket and a beret, and he walked hunched over, his hands in his pockets, staring blankly at anyone he met as if he hadn't noticed them, just as he looked at anything his eye happened to fall on, but he remembered everything, with unbearable, painful, clarity.

He had nothing to do in town, so either he'd sit at the table, his head in his hands, or he'd lie down, waiting for the bar to open. Finally, he'd grope his way downstairs, never failing to give the painting in the hall a look of loathing. It depicted a local lake, the fiords, and some unnaturally purple mountains sprinkled with some unnaturally orange birch trees. It was also autumn in the painting.

Ageev ordered a cognac in the bar and carried it carefully to a table, afraid of spilling it. He lit a cigarette and drank slowly, watching the goings on at the bar, impatiently waiting for the burning shock of the drink to take effect. Then he knew everything would be fine, he'd love life, people, the city, and even the rain.

Then he went out and wandered the city, wondering where he could go with Vika, what he was going to do in general, and how he was going to go on living. In two hours he was back at the hotel, feeling sleepy, so he lay down and went to sleep. When he woke up, he went downstairs to the restaurant.

The day was already over. Outside the window it was growing dark, evening was coming on. In the restaurant they were beginning to play jazz. Heavily made-up girls, smelling of singed hair, came in and sat down in pairs, hungrily eating the repulsive, waxen food, drinking vermouth, and dancing, if anyone asked them, delight with their lives of luxury written all over their faces. Ageev looked around the huge smoky room with disgust. He hated the girls and the foppish boys, those dreadful musicians shrilly blowing their trumpets and thumping their drums, the horrible food, the vodka shot glasses which the barmaid never quite filled.

When the restaurant closed at twelve, Ageev barely made it to his room on the third floor. Snuffling and muttering to himself, he couldn't get the key in the keyhole, so grinding his teeth and moaning, he took off his coat and collapsed into darkness until the following day.

So Ageev spent the day. Around two the next day he went to the station to meet Vika. He was early. With a brief glance at the passengers with suitcases on the platform, he went off to the bar. Some time ago he'd begun to get palpitations and wanderlust at the mere sight of a railroad platform or train tracks.

In the bar a red-haired waitress brought him his vodka.

"Brilliant wench," he muttered, running his eyes over her appreciatively. "*Khello,* old girl," he said when she came back. "It just so happens I've been looking for you all my life."

The waitress smiled noncommittally. Almost everyone said something like it. They'd come into the bar for half an hour or so, murmur something to her, usually something disgusting, and then they'd go out again, never to think of that station or the red-haired waitress again.

"I must paint you," said Ageev, getting tipsy. "I'm an artist."

The waitress smiled as she put his drink on the table. This was rather pleasant.

"Listen, I'm a brilliant artist. I'm known in Europe. Well, what do you say?"

"Artists don't paint us." The waitress spoke with an accent.

"How do you know?" Ageev asked, looking at her breasts.

"What they need is fishermen. Workers, haun . . . hunters. Or else the island and the wooden church. They all go over there. From Moscow, Leningrad. And they all wear berets, yes?"

"They're all idiots. We'll see each other again, all right?" he asked quickly, hearing the sound of the incoming train. "What's your name?"

"Call me Janna, please," said the waitress.

"What are you, not Russian?"

"No, I'm Finnish."

"Ahhh, damn good," Ageev muttered, finishing his vodka, and coughing.

He paid, gave Janna a hug, and strode out on the platform. What a waste of a good woman, he thought. But when he squinted at the blue express train already flashing past him, the motion of the train combined with his tenseness made him so dizzy that he turned his back. I shouldn't have had a drink, he thought vaguely, and he suddenly felt scared again: Vika was coming. He lit a cigarette.

People were already getting off the train. Ageev sighed, threw away his cigarette and started to look for Vika. She saw him first and shouted. He turned to see her coming toward him in a black wool coat. It was unbuttoned and her round knees poked out from under her dress as she walked.

Shyly she gave him her mesh-gloved hand. Her hair, bleached and cut short from summer, was mussed and tumbling into her face. Her tartar-shaped eyes peered timidly up at Ageev, but her mouth was tight and red, her lips chapped and half opened, like a child's.

"Hello!" she said, panting slightly, wanting to add something, some gay remark prepared in advance perhaps, but she stammered and said nothing.

Ageev was staring blankly at the thin scarf around her neck, looking like a frightened little boy. Then he grabbed her card-board suitcase, and they left the station and walked down the broad street.

"Your face is a little swollen . . . How are you?" she asked, looking around. "I like it here."

"*Gyeah.*" He made an ugly sound in his throat which he always made when he wanted to express his contempt for something.

"Are you drunk?" She stuck her hands in her pockets and bent her head. Her hair fell in her face.

"*Gyeah,*" he said again, squinting at her.

Vika was very pretty, with something indefinably Muscovite in her clothes, her tousled hair, her manner of speaking, that he had forgotten while he'd been in the north. They'd only met a couple of times in Moscow and hardly knew each other really. Her vacation and trip here — which Ageev knew had not been easy to arrange — and the readiness for the worst which he also sensed in her were odd and somehow surprising.

I certainly have good luck with women, he thought in crude, delighted amazement. He stopped, supposedly to put on his gloves, in order to look at her from behind. She slowed down and half turned, giving him a questioning look, at the same time gazing absently at the passersby and the store windows.

She was pretty from behind too, and the fact that she had not gone on ahead, but was hanging back, giving him a look that expressed her dependence, made him terribly glad she'd come, although a minute before he'd felt nothing but awkwardness and shame. He understood remotely that he'd had a drink so he wouldn't feel so awkward.

"I brought you some newspapers," said Vika when Ageev caught up with her. "They're pretty harsh on you, you know? There was quite an uproar at the show. I was there."

"*Gyeah*," he said again, feeling deeply pleased. "Did they take down the collective farm woman?" he asked anxiously.

"No, it's hanging," Vika burst out laughing. "No one understands, they just shout and argue, bleary-eyed kids with beards, running around in blue jeans . . ."

"Did you like my woman?" asked Ageev.

Vika gave a vague smile that infuriated Ageev. He frowned and snorted and thrust out his lower lip, his eyes slack and puffy. He decided to get drunk.

The whole day he treated Vika like a stranger as they wandered about the city, yawning and mumbling indistinctly in answer to her questions. He waited for her while she was inquiring at the dock about boat schedules, but that evening when Vika didn't invite him in he locked himself in his room and got drunk. Knowing that Vika was alone and miserable in her room with nothing to do pained him sharply, but he just sneered and went on smoking. And he thought about Janna, the redhead.

The telephone rang twice. Ageev knew it was Vika, but didn't pick up the receiver. Go hang, he thought.

The next day Vika woke Ageev up early, made him wash and get dressed, packed his rucksack for him, got his exercise book and spinning reel out from under the bed, checked the bureau drawers and threw out the empty bottles. She was decisive and cool, and paid no attention to Ageev.

Just like a wife! he thought in wonder as he watched. Frowning, he began to think how quickly women attach themselves, how quickly they become as cold and imperious as if they'd been living with you a hundred years.

He had a headache and wanted to go down to the bar, but remembering it was still closed, he coughed and groaned and lit a cigarette. On an empty stomach it made him feel worse. Vika had paid downstairs in the meantime and had called a taxi. The hell with it, Ageev thought diffidently, going outside and getting into the taxi. What the hell. He sat down and closed his eyes. The morning rain had begun already, that meant it would rain all day. There was even some snow. Heavy and wet, it was falling fast, barely touching the sidewalks before melting.

At the dock Ageev began to feel very badly indeed. He dozed off exhausted, not knowing where he was going, or why it was necessary to go there, listening to the wind whistling, the water splashing around the pier, the engines as they rose to a high note, held it awhile and died out. Vika too seemed sad and withdrawn. Her former decisiveness had disappeared without a trace. She was sitting next to Ageev, looking around helplessly, wilted, dressed in short tight slacks, her head uncovered as usual. The wind tousled her hair and she looked as if she might have received a telegram summoning her to a funeral.

She's wearing slacks, Ageev thought biliously, closing his eyes and trying to get more comfortable against the wall. Where the hell am I being taken? Ai-ai-ai, this is bad!

They could hardly wait to get on board and they watched impatiently as the boat loaded, hissing and squeaking and knocking against the pier, chipping off little white splinters of wood.

But Ageev felt no better on board. Down below things were bubbling and seething, pistons were working up and down in the hot grease, and it was warm, but in the cabins in the bow it was dark and cold and musty. The wind howled outside, the waves splashed against the sides, the boat lurched, and glass tinkled nervously. It was dusk. Outside the window, the trees, already stripped bare of leaves and dark from the rain, and the buoys with their tattered flags began slowly to move away. Ageev shivered and left the cabin.

Walking along the iron planks on the lower deck, Ageev found himself near the engine room, not far from the bar. It wasn't open yet either, though they had started cooking some salted cod in the galley, and the stench was awful. Ageev climbed up on a warm metal box, leaned against the shiny satin bark of some birch firewood, and began to listen to the even breathing of the engines, the splash overboard, the discordant talk. As usual, the passengers who had been seen off were the last to quiet down, and they were still shouting and joking. Someone in the front of the boat was playing the accordion, stamping his boots, shouting "Ekh! Ekh! Ekh!"

The rest had filled their mugs and cups from the samovar and were sitting on their suitcases in the warmest spots they could find, drinking and eating hunks broken from their long loaves of bread, gazing calmly at the water as the wind whipped it into dark disorderly waves. The women removed their kerchiefs and the children were playing and running around.

The lamps went on warmly under the frosted shades, and immediately everything outside seemed even colder and darker. Ageev looked around lazily. The passageways were all littered with bags of potatoes, baskets, pickle barrels, and other such things. These were all local people, headed from some place called Mala Guba. The talk was local too: livestock, the latest government decisions, mothers-in-law, the fish catch, the forest industry, the weather.

This isn't so bad, thought Ageev. Just one day of this, and then the island, some sort of place to stay, quiet, solitude . . . not bad!

At last the bar opened, at the same moment that Vika appeared. She looked at him sadly, and smiled.

"You want a drink, poor thing?" she asked. "Well, go on!"

Ageev went and brought back a small bottle, some bread, and some pickles. Vika got up on the box beside him, and gave him a searching, worried look. He uncorked the bottle, had a drink, and took a bit of pickle. Feeling his spirits soften, he looked at Vika with slightly renewed interest.

"Eat something," he muttered, and Vika also started to eat.

"Tell me, what's the matter?" she asked a bit later.

Ageev took another drink and thought about it. Then he lit a cigarette, staring at Vika's dangling suede shoe.

"I'm just blue, old girl," he said quietly. "It's just that I'm probably a no-talent fool. I paint and I paint, but everyone says it's not right. And why not? 'Immature in his outlook!' 'Weak in his approach!' 'Alien to the people!' As if The People were standing over *their* shoulders, nodding approvingly!"

"Dopey!" Vika said affectionately, smiling suddenly and pulling his head down on her shoulder. Ageev rubbed his cheek in her hair; it had a strange, bitter smell. He blinked.

She was suddenly very close and dear to him. He remembered the first time he had kissed her in Moscow, standing in the hall at a fellow artist's house. He'd been drinking and was feeling good; she'd been quiet, overwhelmed by him. They'd talked for a long time in the kitchen, and he'd told her, feeling very sure of himself, that he was a genius and everyone else so much dross. When they'd left the kitchen he'd kissed her in the hall and he'd told her that he loved her madly.

She hadn't believed him, but she'd gasped and blushed, her eyes growing dark and her lips beginning to tremble. The rest of the evening she had talked and laughed with the other girls there, but she hadn't looked at him again. He had joined the boys in another room where they were looking at drawings and discussing them.

Vika had talked and laughed with her friends and with whomever came and went, happy all the while because he was sitting in a chair talking to someone in another room. She admitted this to him later.

Yes it was good, sitting somewhere in the north, suddenly to remember that not so distant evening in Moscow. It meant they had a history. They had no real love for each other, there were no bonds between them, they were still seeing other people, they had yet to spend the night together, but they did have a past. That was very good.

"Seriously," Ageev said. "I've been thinking about my life since I've been up here. You know, it was lousy here without you, rainy, nowhere to go. I just sat in my room or in the restaurant, drinking and thinking . . . I'm tired. When I was a student I used to think I'd turn the world upside down, I'd kill them with my paintings, I'd travel, live in the mountains like some kind of Rockwell Kent, don't you know. But the closer you get to the diploma, the more abuse you get, you get called this, that, and the other name. Once those dogs learn how to attack, they don't leave off. The further you go the worse it gets. You're called an abstractionist, a nonrealist, a formalist, you have every kind of fault . . . Well, we'll see."

He moved away from Vika slightly and took another drink. His headache was gone and the reason he felt like sitting and talking and thinking at such length was that Vika was beside him listening. Ageev glanced at her sideways. Her face was animated and serious, and her eyes, cloaked beneath her lashes, were wide and black. He looked again, they really were black. He saw those chapped lips, and his heart began to pound. Vika pulled her feet up on the box, opened her coat, put her chin on her knees and looked up into Ageev's face.

"You look bad," she said, touching his chin. "Black and unshaven."

"And smelly." He smiled, and began watching the lake. "I compare myself to Van Gogh all the time. Do I really have to croak before they'll take me seriously? Are my colors, drawings, people really worse than those of the political types? I'm fed up."

"The political types don't even acknowledge you," she said quickly, almost parenthetically.

"Why not?"

"Because. Because if they were to acknowledge you, it would mean admitting they've been wrong all their lives."

"Oh." Ageev stopped to light a cigarette. For a long time he sat smoking, staring at his feet, and rubbing his sallow face. The bristle crackled under his fingers. "Three years!" he said. "I have to do illustrations to make money. Three years since I finished the institute, and everyone envies me: oh, you're so famous, you're known in Europe! Idiots! What is there to envy? That with every picture I . . . That I haven't been given a studio yet? You paint a picture of spring, your spring is wrong. Don't you see you've made it too 'biological'? Hmm? You don't get into the art shows, the commissions are all given out to others, and if you explode over something unimportant, so much the worse. Criticism! They talk a lot about contemporary life, but their understanding of it stinks! And how they lie . . . what a lot of demagoguery behind those wise words!"

"And there hasn't been one true word about you?" Vika asked thoughtfully. Breaking off a birch twig, she began to chew on it.

"You schoolgirl!" Ageev went white. "You don't know what they're like, you haven't clashed with the right books, dialectical materialism, practical experience, you're still on the sidelines. When they talk about 'man,' it's always with a capital letter. To their clear vision, Man represents the nation, a thousand years, the cosmos! One man isn't enough for them to think about, they have to have millions! They hide behind those millions and the ones of us who are actually doing something get called names. Spiritual hooligans — that's us! Heroics!" said Ageev with a sarcastic smile. "The masses! There they are, the masses!" Ageev nodded his head toward the other passengers. "I love them. I don't want to cover them with ecstatic spittle. I love them in the flesh — their hands, their eyes — you understand? Because the soil of the earth clings to them. That's the whole thing. The people are good only if each person is good, I tell you. I think about it night and day. I'm in a bad way, I have no commissions, no money, but to hell with them, they're not important. I'm right, and they can't teach me anything. Life is teaching me. As far as optimism and faith in the future and in the masses are concerned, I can give all my critics 100-to-1 odds!"

Ageev snorted. His nostrils flared and his eyes darkened.

"You don't need to drink any more," Vika said quietly, looking him up and down pityingly.

"Wait a minute," Ageev rasped. "Have I got asthma or something? I can't seem to get a deep breath."

He relit his cigarette, but when he inhaled, he began to cough. Throwing it away, he put one foot down and stamped it out. Then he turned to Vika with a wry face.

"Oh well, I'm going to bed." With a mean expression he slid off the box and went to the cabin.

The heat had been turned on while they were talking and now the cabin was so warm the windows were steamed over. Ageev sat down by the window and wiped it off with his sleeve. His left eyelid began to twitch. His only salvation was in Vika now, and he knew it. But something about her drove him crazy. She'd arrived so fresh, pretty, in love — oh hell! Why, why did he have to prove something? And to her of all people? On the train she'd probably been numb with excitement, her heart in her throat, as she thought about him, their first night together, being in his arms — the arms of a drunken devil! Ai-ai-ai! And she could have been too, if only she'd just agreed with him, and told him, yes, you're right. He would have gone out of his mind, he would have carried her off to a cabin in the fiords, and set her down by the window so he could paint her, that tiny face, those wide eyes, that sunbleached hair, her chin resting in her hand. He might have painted better than he ever had in his life! Ai-ai-ai!

As he began to get undressed, he was so overcome by solitude and self-pity that he was on the verge of tears. It doesn't matter, he thought, it doesn't matter, it's not the first time. And he winced when he remembered everything he'd told Vika. He should keep his mouth shut and do something besides talk.

When he finished undressing he lay down on the upper berth and turned toward the wall. He fidgeted around with the pillow-case for a long time, trying to get comfortable, but he couldn't.

The boat reached the island that evening. A gentle sunset glowed in the distance, and it was beginning to get dark as the boat passed through countless rocks jutting out of the water. Already the dark, many-turreted church could be seen shifting on the horizon as the boat approached, first to the right, then to the left, and once it even appeared to be behind them.

Vika looked obstinate and resentful. Ageev whistled, gazing around nonchalantly at the flat rocks and noting with some interest that the larger ones resembled Viking ships.

When they were all the way in, they could see a windmill, a splendid old house, and some storage buildings — all as empty and lifeless as if they'd been on display in a museum. Ageev sneered.

"Just the thing," he muttered, giving Vika a look, half gay, half malicious. "You might call it the forefront of the seven-year plan, mightn't you?"

Vika didn't answer. Her expression indicated the issue was closed. It was as if she had come alone, following a long-standing plan, and this was the way it was supposed to be.

No one got off at the island but the two of them. And no one was on the wooden dock, only one sentry lantern, although it was not yet dark.

"So here we are, Adam and Eve." Ageev smiled again, stepping onto the wet dock.

Vika still did not reply.

A smiling woman dressed in a quilted jacket and peasant boots appeared on shore.

"Just two of you?" she shouted, hurrying toward them, looking

from one to the other. When she got up to them, she took Vika's
bag from her and spoke as if she'd been expecting them a long
time.

"Well thank God," she said, speaking rapidly and affectionately.
"I thought it was all over, and that there wasn't going to be anyone more this year. I was getting set for winter. Come to the
hotel."

"Hotel?" asked Ageev in his nastiest tone.

The woman laughed. "Everyone is surprised, but this is my second year here. I had a husband, but he died, and now I'm alone.
It's a real hotel! For guests and artists. They come here a lot in
the summer to draw."

Remembering his lonely ordeal in the hotel, Ageev sighed and
frowned. He'd wanted to live in a cabin, in some musty little place
smelling of cows and hay.

But the hotel turned out to be quite cozy. It was just three big
rooms, including a kitchen with a stove, and one other strange-
looking room with pillars carved in the old Russian style supporting the ceiling in the middle. On three sides, there was a great
picture window from floor to ceiling. It was like a glass hall.

The rooms, all unoccupied, were furnished with a bed, suitcase
nets, and crude little night tables.

Ageev and Vika took a room with a stove and a southern ex-
posure. The walls were hung with framed watercolors. Ageev
looked at them, thrusting out his lip. They were all well-meaning
and amateurish. They all depicted either the church or the windmill.

The woman brought in sheets and pillows and pillow slips. The
clean linen smelled good.

"Here you are," she said happily. "Now everything's nice. Have
you come for long? It's boring here now, but in the summer it's
nice. The artists are fun. But I'm the only one here now, can you
imagine it, on the whole island."

"How do you get food?" asked Vika.

"You won't starve," the woman answered cheerfully from out in the hall somewhere. "There's a village near the other end of the island where you can get milk or anything you want. Then there's a store on Pug Island which you can get to by boat. Where are you from, Leningrad?"

"No, Moscow," said Vika.

"That's nice. They're usually from Leningrad. I have firewood, and various other odds and ends. This summer they restored the church, there was still so much left inside. I have the keys and if you want, just tell me, and I'll unlock it for you."

She went out, and Vika fell on the bed with an exhausted sigh of happiness.

"It's too much!" she said. "This was a stroke of genius! My sweet Adam, this was simply a stroke of genius! Do you like fried potatoes?"

Ageev sniffed, thrusting out his lip, and went out. Slowly he circled the graveyard surrounding the church. It was quite dark and when Ageev walked along the eastern wall of the church, it rose up in magnificent silhouette above him, the light coming through the open spaces between the onion-shaped cupolas and the flying buttresses. Two birds were flying around in slow, identical circles above him. The air smelled strongly of grass and autumn cold.

So this is the end of the world, thought Ageev, going past the church and along the shore of the lake. Then he went down to the dock and sat on a piling facing west. Two hundred yards away there was another island — flat, uninhabited, overgrown with willow trees. Behind it another island, where the village was evidently; an occasional light could be seen through the branches. Presently the high shrill sound of a motor came up from that direction, roared for a time, and suddenly broke off after a few knocks.

Ageev was lonely, but he kept on sitting and smoking, getting used to the silence, the clean smell of water, and the freshness of autumn. He was thinking about himself and his paintings, thinking of himself as a Messiah, a great artist sitting in solitude God knows where, while his critics were sitting with their girl friends in restaurants on Gorky Street in Moscow, drinking cognac and eating hot Georgian dishes. Wiping their greasy mouths, they'd be saying various beautiful high-flown things, all lies, because they weren't really thinking elevated thoughts — just how to get the girls to sleep with them. And in the morning, after they'd gotten rid of their hangovers with coffee and stimulants, these critics would write articles about him, telling more lies, because there wasn't one of them who believed in what he wrote, not one whose only thought wasn't how much he'd be paid, not one who had ever sat on a wet dock alone, looking at a dark uninhabited island, preparing himself for a real creative effort.

These thoughts made Ageev feel pleasantly bitter; he had such thoughts often. They had a sweet bite that he enjoyed.

Suddenly the old countess's song from the *Queen of Spades* came back to him for no reason and he started singing to himself. The ghostly music, the gloomy timbre of the clarinets and bassoons, the agonizing caesuras, could still terrify him just as it had years ago when he'd heard it played by the full orchestra. It was the music of death.

Suddenly he had a sharp, painful longing for the smell of tea, not hot tea in a glass, but the smell of dry tea. He remembered the tea canister from his childhood, made of frosted glass, decorated all around by a sweet little landscape. He remembered how he had dreamed of living in the little house with its red roof; he remembered how the tea had poured out with a gentle whisper when his mother had opened it; he remembered how dark the muddy opal glass had looked when it was filled.

He remembered his mother, her love for him; her whole life had been in him and for him. He remembered himself as he was then — so lively and quick, with such bursts of causeless joy and high spirits. It was hard to believe now that he could ever have been that way.

With belated regret he remembered how often he'd been rude

to his mother, inattentive, and insensitive. He regretted the many times he might have listened to her stories of her childhood, of things past and forgotten, and hadn't. He regretted the many times in his childish egotism he had failed to understand or value her love, such love as he'd had from no one since, never.

Remembering all these things, he began to have doubts about himself. Perhaps his critics were right, and he was wrong and the things he was doing not at all necessary. He realized that he'd probably never had a firm foundation of ideas for his work — ideas in the highest sense. Too often he'd been arrogant about his talent, cold and indifferent to everything unrelated to him or his talent. To have these doubts now!

He remembered with helpless bitterness all the arguments he'd had as a student, with other artists, art critics, with everyone who didn't accept his paintings and drawings and colors. He wondered if his failure to convince them and prove to them the truth of his messianic vision was due to his lack of ideas. What good a prophet without ideas?

So for a long time he sat there, until he heard Vika come outside, take the boardwalk down to the shore, and stand looking around, calling to him softly. He didn't move or answer. Yet he loved her, his heart beat fast when he thought of her! The two of them, like Adam and Eve, on a dark, uninhabited island, alone with the stars and the water. It hadn't been easy for her to come. How unhappy she must have been alone in the hotel room when he'd gotten drunk and left her!

A bitter feeling of estrangement, alienation from the world came over him. There was nothing, and no one, he wanted. He remembered that sick animals hide in inaccessible and remote corners and either cure themselves on secret herbs, or die. He was sorry that it was autumn and cold now, sorry that he had to be in boots and a sweater, or he'd find such a corner on this or another island with rocks and sand and clear water. Then he'd lie whole days in the sun and think about nothing. And go barefoot. And fish. And watch the sun set. He felt infinitely tired, tired of himself, his thoughts, his doubts, his drunkenness. He felt completely sick.

I should go south, to the sea, he thought sadly as he rose to leave. Turning away from the lake, he again saw the great old church with the little hotel hiding in its shelter. Lights were burning warmly in the hotel, while the church looked closed and dark and forbidding. But there was something powerful in the church that aroused thoughts in him about the genius of the people, about history, about peace and solitude.

"Seg Pogost." Ageev remembered the name of the island and of the church. "Seg Pogost."

He climbed to the house and stood in the darkness on the porch, trying to guess how long life — real life, of the land and water and people — had gone on here without him. But he could make out nothing but the dim radiance of the water all around, and a few light shreds of clouds in the sky. Then he went in.

The room was lit by a kerosene lamp. The stove was humming and crackling and there was the smell of fried potatoes. Vika was bustling about, all flushed, and the room had taken on a nice, lived-in look. Her blouses and skirts had been unpacked and thrown on the bed, her black gloves and a compact with a streak of lightning on it were on the night table. The presence of a young woman was to be felt in everything, and the room smelled of perfume.

"Where were you?" Vika asked at length, raising an eyebrow. "I looked for you."

Without answering, Ageev went to the kitchen to wash. He looked at his bristle for a while in the mirror, and thought about shaving, but all he did was to wash, enjoying his clatter in the basin. Then he wiped himself with a soft warm towel and went back to the room to lie down. Putting his feet up on the bed, he stretched and lit a cigarette.

"Come and eat," said Vika.

They ate in silence. It was obvious that Vika liked the place a lot and that there was only one thing bothering her — Ageev. The stove crackled and the teakettle whistled.

"Have you got a long vacation?" Ageev asked suddenly.

"Ten days," said Vika with a sigh. "Why?"

"Just asking."

Three days gone already.

And again they said nothing for a long time. When they'd finished with tea, it was time to get ready for bed. Vika flushed hotly and looked desperately at Ageev. He averted his eyes and frowned. Then he got up, lit a cigarette, and went to the window. He was glad Vika couldn't see that he was also blushing. Something rustled and whispered behind him. Finally Vika could contain herself no longer, and said in a pleading voice, "Please put out the light."

Ageev blew out the wick without looking at her, undressed quickly and lay down on the bed, facing the wall. Just you try coming any closer, he thought. But Vika didn't try. She was lying so absolutely still that she didn't even seem to be breathing.

Twenty minutes passed. Neither of them was asleep and they both knew it. It was dark in the room, and outside the window the sky was black. A wind came up, and there was a brief flash of light on the window curtain. Ageev thought someone must be passing along the wall outside, throwing a lantern light on the curtain, but three or four seconds later, there was a soft roll of thunder.

"A storm," said Vika softly and sat up to look in the darkness. "An autumn storm."

Another flash, a roll of thunder, then the wind died down and it started raining hard. The drainpipes began to hum.

"Rain," said Vika. "I love the rain. I love to think when it's raining."

"Can you be quiet?" Ageev lit a cigarette and blinked as the flame made his eyes smart.

"Do you know what? I'm leaving," said Vika in a voice that told Ageev how much she hated him. "I'm taking the first boat

back. You're nothing but an egotist. These last two days I've spent
trying to figure you out — who are you? Who? And what's wrong
with you? And now I know — you're an egotist. You talk about
art and the people but you're thinking only of yourself — no one
else. You don't need anybody. You're repulsive. Why did you
send for me? Why? I know why, so I could reassure you and flatter you. Well I won't, my sweet; find yourself some other fool. I'm
ashamed of how I went running to the dean's office, the lies I told
about Papa's being sick."

Vika gave a loud sigh.

"Shut up, you little fool," he said with an effort, realizing that
this was the end. "Get out then, go on, leave!"

Ageev got up and sat at the window, resting his elbows on the
night table. It was still raining. There was something large and
dark and shimmering under the window. It was a long time before
Ageev realized that it was a puddle.

Ageev felt like crying like a child, burying his face in his sleeve
to wipe the tears away, but it had been a long time since he'd been
able to do that.

Vika lay with her face in the pillow, sobbing and choking, but
Ageev didn't go to her; he just sat crushing cigarette butts and
matches in the ashtray, feeling tremulously numb with disgust,
almost at the breaking point of depression. Then this passed and
he felt elevated, released from pettiness, sad and at peace, full of
compassion for every individual pitted against the irresistible force
of the mass of humanity. And yet in the depths of his soul he was
seething, feverish and in pain. He couldn't remain silent, he
couldn't smile cynically and withdraw behind his *"gyeah."* He
should say something.

But he said nothing, he sat thinking. Not so much thinking
really as simply existing in silence, staring out the window at the
dark shimmering puddle. There was a ringing in his head that
comes with fever during an illness, and he pictured an endless file
of spectators in a gallery walking silently through the halls, with

something indefinably mysterious and sorrowful written on their faces. He stopped at that, at the vision of sorrow, and wondered: why should their faces be sorrowful, I must be wrong. Then he was distracted by the thought of something higher, of what seemed to him the highest thing of all.

He thought that in spite of everything he'd do what he had to do. And that no one could stop him. And that then he'd have to be reckoned with.

He stood up. The veins were standing out on his temples. Without bothering to dress, he went out on the porch and stood there, his mouth filled with sweetish saliva. He spat. There was a lump in his throat that was strangling him.

"It's all over," he muttered. "To hell with it. It's all over."

All the next day Ageev lay in bed, his face to the wall, dozing and waking, listening to Vika move around the room. She called him to breakfast and lunch, but he just lay there, his lips twisted into a nasty expression, his eyes closed, until he drifted off again. Toward evening when his body started to ache and it became impossible to lie their any more, he got up. Vika was nowhere around. Ageev went to see their hostess.

"Will you give me the key to the boat?" he asked. "I've got to row over to the store for some cigarettes."

She gave him the key, told him where to find the oars, and showed him where to go.

The boat was as heavy as it was pretty to look at, and rowing into the wind, with the heavy awkward oars, Ageev managed to blister his hands before reaching the other island.

He bought some cigarettes, a bottle of vodka, a few things to eat, and started back. He was already going through the wet meadow when a thickset, bowlegged, red-faced fisherman dressed in an overcoat caught up with him.

"Hello there, brother," said the fisherman, coming alongside and looking up at Ageev. "You an artist? From Seg Pogost?"

With both hands he drew some bottles of vodka wrapped in newspaper out of his coat. "We're having a party today. After we go to the baths," he informed him happily, as if they were long-standing acquaintances. "Shall we have a drink for the road?"

The fisherman climbed clumsily into his boat. His motor had a bright green cover. He put down the package and took out the bottles. There turned out to be four of them — two had been in his trousers pockets. Three he wrapped in tarpaulin and laid carefully in the bow. The fourth he opened, and feeling around for a jar, he rinsed it out in the water and poured Ageev a drink. Ageev had a drink and started munching on a cracker. The fisherman poured himself a drink and got out of the boat.

"To our friendship," he said happily. "Been here long?"

"Arrived yesterday," said Ageev, watching the fisherman with amusement.

"Going to do the church?" asked the fisherman, winking.

"Whatever I find."

"Come see us in the fleet, then," proposed the fisherman, getting rapidly drunk. "Have you a girl? We have" — he spread his hands — "like that! You get me? You can draw girls, can't you?"

He stepped back into the boat, got the unfinished bottle, and poured Ageev another drink.

"Shall we finish it?"

"Yes, and here's a bottle of mine," said Ageev, getting out his bottle.

"We'll drink yours when you come," said the fisherman. "It's not far from here, you just say the word, and I'll come for you in the motorboat. We like artists, they're not bad guys. An old professor from Leningrad lived with us and he said, people like you, he says, you don't meet anywhere else in life." The fisherman burst out laughing. "You know what sig fish are? We'll give you sig fish soup. We have fun, the girls laugh a lot, sometimes we're at it all night long!"

"Where do you fish?" Ageev asked, smiling.

"We fish on Kizhme Island, don't worry, I'll take you myself. If you can remember it, ask for the Stepanov fleet. That's me, Stepanov, see? Just go left past the lighthouse and you'll see the island. Go on the right side, they'll tell you there."

"I'll come for sure," said Ageev, delighted.

"That's the stuff! You respect me as an equal, don't you, man-to-man? Hmm? All right then. All right. Are we agreed? All right. Goodbye, I'm going, the boys are waiting for me."

He got in his boat, untied it, shoved off, and started the motor. As soon as the motor began to buzz, he jumped into the bow, but it still rose out of the water. By pulling a rope connected to the tiller, he guided the boat into deep water and was gone, leaving a white arc in the water behind him.

Smiling, Ageev got in his boat and rowed back. Now he was rowing into the sunset and whenever he had to stop to rest, he watched the colors of the sky reflected in the water. Halfway to Seg Pogost there was a small island, and as Ageev rounded it, the wind died, and the water took on the still, heavy look of gold.

Surrounded by total silence, Ageev laid down the oars and looked at the church. To the east of its practically black wall was a rain-cloud, to the west, the sun was shedding its last rays and everything in its light — the island, the church, the ancient house, the windmill — was by comparison with the cloud a sinister red. Far out on the horizon, from the direction of the raincloud, the rain hung in dark sheets, and an enormous rainbow shone mournfully.

Ageev settled himself more comfortably in the boat, and after another drink and something to eat, he looked at the church again. The sun set and the raincloud moved in, covering nearly everything. It was already raining on Seg Pogost. The boat drifted imperceptibly toward the island.

Around Ageev it was quiet and still, and the sky was bright in the west. A wide band of misty beauty surrounded the setting sun.

Ageev examined the church and had the urge to draw it. He

thought it must be more than three hundred years old. It was as old as the stones, as old as the earth itself. The high-spirited fisherman was still in his mind, and he had the urge to draw him too.

When he turned to the west, the sun had already set. The rain came finally, and Ageev pulled up his hood and grabbed the oars. It was a hard, warm rain, and for some reason felt very nice. The fish were jumping all around him.

Rowing rapidly into shore, Ageev saw Vika. She was standing in the rain, a plastic raincoat over her shoulders. She watched as Ageev tied and locked the boat, picked up the oars and his bundle of purchases, and stuffed the opened bottle of vodka into his pocket.

Look at me, look at me! Ageev thought gleefully, heading silently for the hotel.

But Vika wasn't looking at him. She was standing on the dock, looking at the sunset in the rain.

Entering the warm room, Ageev saw that Vika's things were all packed and a suitcase was standing by the door. *"Gyeah,"* he said and lay down on the bed. The rain was pounding on the roof. The drinks had made him feel relaxed and good. Ageev closed his eyes and dozed. When he came to again a little later, it was not yet dark. The rain had stopped, and the sky had cleared. It was alight with a cold radiance.

Ageev yawned and went to see his hostess again. He got the key from her and entering the graveyard through a wooden gate, he walked among the ancient graves, unlocked the door to the tower, and started up the dark, narrow, creaking staircase.

It was dark at first and smelled of birds and rotten wood, but as he climbed it grew lighter and the air fresher. When Ageev finally reached the top, his heart was beating fast and his legs felt weak.

As he climbed out of the hatch, the first thing he saw was the sky, with a few fluffy clouds, the first bright stars, and behind them,

just the last blue rays of the sun, which had disappeared itself long
since.

When he looked down he saw another sky, as enormous and
bright as the one above. The endless expanse of water all the way
out to the horizon was radiant with reflected light, the islands dot-
ting it like clouds.

Ageev sat on the railing without moving, holding on with one
hand, until it was dark, until pearl-white Cassiopeia was not
quite out in full constellation. Then he climbed down and walked
around and around the church, studying it from all angles and
sighing.

When he got home, the stove was crackling and Vika was preparing dinner. She was quiet and withdrawn.

"Your boat coming soon?" asked Ageev. "Did you find out?"

"At eleven apparently," Vika said after a while.

Ageev's spirits faltered. He wanted to tell her something, ask
her something, but he didn't. He got his exercise book out from
under the bed and started packing cartons on the bed and windowsill with his paints and bottles of turpentine. He sorted his brushes
and put an easel together. Vika stared at him in amazement.

They sat down to eat in silence, just as they had the night before,
and their eyes met. Ageev looked at Vika's chapped lips and suddenly her face was so very dear to him that his spirits faltered again.
It was time to say goodbye.

He got a bottle of vodka out from under the bed and poured a
drink for himself and Vika.

"Well," he said hoarsely, and coughed. "Let's drink to parting!"

Vika put down her glass without drinking. She leaned back
and watched Ageev through half-closed lids. Her face moved, a
vein throbbed in her neck and her lips trembled. Ageev couldn't
look at her. He felt hot. He got up, opened a window, and took
a deep breath of the strong night air.

"It's stopped," he said, returning to the table. "It's not raining
any more."

"Do you need any money?" asked Vika. "I have some extra, I brought a lot, thinking . . ." She bit her lip, with a pathetic smile.

"No, it's not necessary," said Ageev. "I'll be giving up drinking now."

"You're still wrong," Vika said bitterly. "That's all that's the matter with you. Give up drinking for good, and everything will be fine."

"Oh?" Ageev sneered. "A one-man show straight off? Cheers!" he said and took another drink. "And the political types will understand all at once that they're not artists, is that it?"

"Where were you this evening?" asked Vika, after a pause.

"Up there," Ageev made a vague gesture with his hand. "Way up. With God."

"You won't be coming back to Moscow soon?" she asked, looking at the paints and brushes and easels strewn around the room.

Ageev yawned and stretched, and lay down on the bed. He lit a cigarette. It was easy to breathe again and his fingers were twitching the way they always did when he wanted to get to work.

"No," he said, thinking of all the fishermen he'd meet, their legs, their shoulders, their eyes. How they looked when they were at work, their teeth clenched, pulling nets into their sunburned arms. "In a month probably. Or later. I'm going to paint the fishermen. And the water." He paused. "And the sky. That sort of thing, old girl."

Vika went to see if she could hear the boat.

"No, it's still too early," she said, coming back and looking at herself in the mirror. She got a scarf out of her suitcase and put it on, tying it under her chin. Then she sat down and folded her hands on her knees. She sat with her head hanging, not saying anything, as if she were sitting in a railroad station with someone she didn't know. Her thoughts were far away. Her hair shone golden through her transparent scarf. Ageev lay there, squinting at her curiously and smoking nervously.

"I can't stay here any longer," Vika said with a sigh. "I'm going down to the dock."

With another sigh she stood up and stood staring straight into the lamp without blinking for several seconds. Then she put on her coat. Ageev slid his feet off the bed and sat up.

"Well," he said. *"Gude bye,* old girl! Should I come with you or something?"

Vika went to get her passport from the woman. Ageev had a quick drink, choking and making a face, and started getting dressed, studying his trembling hands and listening to Vika and the woman talking on the other side of the wall. Then he picked up the suitcase and went out on the porch. The porch, the railing and the boardwalk down to the dock were still wet from the rain. Ageev waited until Vika came out and then stepped down off the porch. Vika followed, her heels tapping on the boardwalk.

Ageev set the suitcase down on the dock. Vika sat on it, curled into a lifeless ball. Ageev shivered and turned up his collar. The high, cheerful sound of an airplane was heard in the dead unnatural stillness of the night. The sound came nearer, rising, growing stronger, at the same time dropping to a lower, more muffled and velvety tone, as if someone were gradually retuning a bass, slowly drawing the bow over one of its strings. Finally the plane moved away, with a sound like a stomach rumble.

Dead silence once more. Ageev stamped around on the dock and then turned and climbed up the bank. He stood for a moment and then moved off toward the southern end of the island.

The stars burned overhead and the red and white buoy lights among the rocks blinked off and on.

The stars shimmered and suddenly it was as if the sky had taken a deep breath. It darkened, rose and fell again, and then it was filled with a shimmering blue light. Ageev turned around to the north and saw the source of the light immediately. In the mute darkness behind the church, rays of pale golden-blue northern lights were spreading out in waves of rising and falling light. As they grew stronger they illuminated everything around them — the water, the shore, the rocks, the wet grass, the sharp silhouette of the church. Then they shrank and went out, and everything shimmered into darkness.

The earth turned. Ageev felt its movement suddenly, in his legs and in his heart. It was flying around with its lakes, cities, people and their hopes, turning and flying endlessly, enveloped in that terrible radiance. And he was on an island on that earth, in the silent light of night, and she was leaving him. Eve was leaving Adam, and it was happening not in some vague distant time, but right now. This was like death, something that can be sneered at from a distance, and unbearable when it's next door.

Unable to stand his thoughts any longer, he hurried back to the dock. He felt his boots getting wet in the grass, and he knew, though he couldn't see them, that they were black and shiny.

When Ageev got back to the dock, there was a kerosene lamp on a piling and a woman caretaker was standing yawning on the steps. From behind the hill to the north, a new ray of light was coming up, shimmering too, but warmer in color. Just as it appeared the distinct sound of paddles was heard and the high shrill whistle of the boat echoed in the islands.

"Did you see the northern lights? That's what they were, weren't they?" Vika asked in a half-whisper. She was no longer sitting on her suitcase, but standing excitedly at the rail.

"I saw them," Ageev said and coughed.

The boat moved around a bend in the shore and they could hear it better. In the bow a bright searchlight flashed and lit up the dock. The wet planks glistened. Then the engine was shut off and the boat moved into the dock on its own momentum. The woman was watching something on board, shielding her eyes against the bright light. Ageev turned his back and saw the searchlight smokily lighting up the splendid old museum piece of a house.

The boat came nearer. The searchlight turned and flooded the

dock again with a blinding white light. Ageev and Vika watched
the boat tie up in silence. A sailor threw the caretaker a line and
she slowly looped it around a piling. The sailor leaned and pulled
on the rope; it tightened and creaked; the dock heaved and gave.
Then the boat knocked gently against the dock fenders. The sailor
jumped onto the gangplank to check in the light the ticket of a
passenger getting off. Finally he checked him through and
turned to Ageev and Vika.

"Are you getting on or anything?" he asked uncertainly.

"Off you go!" said Ageev, giving her a careless hug. "Have a
good trip!"

Vika's lips trembled. "Goodbye," she said and went aboard, her
heels tapping on the plank.

The boat seemed almost empty, the lower deck only dimly
lighted, and the cabin windows dark. Either there was no one in
them or everyone was asleep. A clear mist rose from the water between the boat and the dock.

Without turning around Vika disappeared quickly into the back
of the boat. There was one long whistle, then three short. The
woman slid the rope from the piling, they took up the plank and
slammed the passage shut. The sweet warm breathing thing, the
only thing alive in the cold night moved off, its paddles churning,
and turned sharply to the right.

The woman yawned again and muttered something about the
lights being early this year because of the cold. Taking her lamp,
she went up the bank, throwing a pool of yellow light ahead of her
and a great shadow to the left of her which swayed with the motion
of the lamp from the dock to the bank to the water.

Ageev stood there finishing his cigarette, and then he returned
to the warm hotel. The northern lights were still blazing up,
weakly now, and there was just one color — white.

The Old Guys

THE watchman's hut stands right next to the warehouse which is, you will see if you climb up there, the highest point in town. The long stone building, sunken over the years, sits tilted on the slope, now covered with short dusty grass, but where they say a rampart was in the old days. The steep run from the warehouse down to the river is covered with ancient gardens, ravines, and crooked streets. From there you can see church towers, rooftops of the old merchants' houses with their balconies, carved fretwork, and attics; the marketplace, rows of stores, the green stadium field, the ship repair yard, the chimneys of two small white factories, the creeks, the landing dock, the river; and beyond the river, the fields running off into the distance where all summer long the winds play and dark cloud shadows wander about.

In the summertime a whitish dust from the trucks on the highway rises to hang over the city; it is hot, the river sparkles, the winds are dry; in the evenings, long, deep crimson sunsets blaze through the mist of intense heat on the steppes. In the summertime trucks overheat their engines climbing to the warehouse and by the time they get there, their hoods are sizzling hot, but the warehouse has the cool smells of soap, pine boards, matting, gas and dry dust.

In winter everything is buried in snow, snowdrifts pile up in the streets at night, to be trampled down all over again in the morning by the horses. The city seems cozier, cleaner, happier. The sleighs squeak and squeal in the snow, the truck chains jingle, the marketplace on Sunday is yellow with manure, black with sheepskin coats, and red with bloody sides of meat. The warehouse seems to hunch up and sink in winter, when the snow drifts up almost to its carved latticed windows, and its odors are stifled by the frost. Then the only path to it is the one up to the two wide iron delivery doors, cleaned and worn down by the trucks.

The town is ancient and remote. Long ago religious dissenters and priestless sects chose the area for its remoteness and built their hermitages — one more austere and secretive than the other — in the woods; in town they lived behind shutters, skulked inside their meetinghouses, and hung their wells with locks of iron. In those days even the densest, most backward of merchants went to Moscow and Petersburg to barter, do business, and have a spree, but they all had their own house, their own little nest to go home to die in. In those days they built nothing but churches and they produced nothing but cast-iron pots, wooden spoons, and baskets made of bark. The town was primitive and Asiatic, dull and dusty and forgotten. To this very day the nightwatchman goes around at night, to this very day they bury the old men according to ancient rites, the enormous wheels of the primitive, bottomless wells, dug in the days of Yuri the Long-armed, stand out on the hills, to this very day the old women hurry to the marketplace to listen, entranced, to the prophecies of Koli the Fool, a dirty, sunbaked, cackling old whiner.

Last year they began construction of a dam ten miles down the river, and they've been bringing up stone from the quarry night and day ever since. About ten years ago, an enormously wealthy collective farm suddenly sprang up on the other side of town, and foreigners on their way to visit the farm in limousines always have to stop off, always have to get out and stretch their legs. Dressed in narrow trousers, high overshoes, short full overcoats, elegant hats, they always whip out their cameras in amazement, and sometimes stop in for a quick look at a nearby church. But the townsmen pay no attention to the foreigners, they're used to it.

2

During the day, while the warehouse watchman Tikhon, dressed in a parka and mittens, checks the inventory, the district truck drivers warm up and have a smoke in the hut. The walls in back of the benches where they sit and the benches themselves glisten with grease. In the corner there's a pile of bitter-smelling aspen wood which Tikhon's relief, one-armed Fedor, brings from the village. There's a shelf nailed over the table, covered with cans of salt and tea, greasy black nuts and bolts, weights for the warehouse scales, opened packs of tobacco and cigarettes left behind by the drivers.

The ceiling is sooty, the floor is littered — neither watchman is an enthusiastic sweeper. The small stove, plastered with dark, unwhitewashed clay, is noisy, the iron range a raspberry red, filling the air with a hot golden light. In the heaviest weather, the chinks in the warehouse door are crusted with curls of frost, and frost collects on the windowpanes two fingers deep. During the thaw the windowsills leak and have that damp smell of uninhabited places, and the door swells so that you have to throw the whole weight of your body against it in order to open it. A sawed-off rifle hangs in the corner near the door, its steel barrel stuffed with a rag against the damp. Sometimes when he has nothing else to do, Tikhon takes the cartridges out of the magazine and cleans the gun. The cartridges are filled with good-size shot and are greasy, heavy, and pleasantly cooling in the hand.

Tikhon loves to sit on a log and stare into the open stove. At these times his broad face is still, his pupils contract, and his eyes shine. At these times his thoughts are heavy, old man's thoughts, and he chain smokes until he gets palpitations and spits a thick stream of phlegm onto the brightly burning coals.

In his youth Tikhon was extraordinarily, almost unnaturally strong. Working as a stevedore, he could hoist 150-pound bales and still move about easily, taking tremendous strides. He was extraordinary and he did queer things, like eating his meat raw, just like the thickset, flat-faced, mustachioed Tartar stevedores. He'd buy two pounds of raw beef at the slaughterhouse, sprinkle it with salt and devour it between his great white teeth, blinking his eyes and crunching on the bones, red saliva running onto his beard. Oh, he was a terrible sight!

As a young man he was always alone, he had no friends, no one to whom he could bare his soul; he was taciturn and morose. Then he disappeared from town once and dropped out of sight for two years. He returned with a darker complexion, a shaved head, a full reddish beard, dressed in an embroidered silk shirt and some worn-down Moroccan boots. He told no one where he'd been or what he'd done in those two years, he only said he'd been in Persia. Long afterward, looking even more morose and inscrutable than usual, he was likely to drop into the conversation strange sharp guttural words.

Our people love the extraordinary, the strong, the powerful, but they didn't love Tikhon, they were too astounded by him and afraid of him. He had a reputation for being extraordinary, but it was a wild, dark reputation. Sober, he wasn't frightening, or even especially interesting; but he was ominous when he was drunk, and inclined to do wild and violent things.

He drank infrequently, and when he did drink a lot, he became not drunk but stupefied: his eyebrows quirked, and his heavy-lidded stare became glazed and crazy. And he'd sing strange word-less, tuneless songs, throwing back his head, his Adam's apple quivering, his soft eyelashes coming down over his inflamed eyes. He wouldn't sing actually, he'd wail, in a falsetto, although his normal voice was low and resonant.

Sometimes when he'd been drinking since morning, he'd come out of the tavern at noon, stooped and glowering at everyone he met, his hands crammed into the pockets of his baggy, dirty trousers, and go to the market. Some distance behind, the curious would tail after him, giggling nervously. At the market, his face purple, without a word, he'd rattle the reins of all the sleeping horses to frighten them. Then, covered with sweat, his eyes wide and mean, a crazy ominous smile on his lips, he'd go up to one of the wagons. "Well now, what do you want? Well?" the owner of the wagon would mutter, turning white. "Hey! Brothers! Fellow Christians! What's going on here?" Tikhon would lean down, grab a wheel, arch his broad back bent over from hoisting bales and bags, and overturn the wagon. Then, wiping his tar-stained hands on his trousers, taking a deep breath and looking around sourly at the men approaching, he'd go back to the tavern. "Blockhead! Crazy devil!" they'd shout after him, but they were too afraid to shout it very loud.

Tikhon was drunk when he got married. During the ceremony he managed to control himself, but he was sweating when he kissed the bride to the accompaniment of much shouting. Then, rolling his drunken watery eyes, he turned over a table with a roar, and kicked out all the guests, ramming them through the passageway. That night, trampling over the vegetable garden, the guests came back and whistled and beat sticks against the window of the room where Tikhon was sleeping with his young bride. Then they crashed through the fence and scattered in all directions. All night long Tikhon was roaring around the village, chasing them.

He had two children, but they both died: one as a child of cholera, the other drowned as an adolescent, diving from a barge.

Tikhon didn't grow old like other people either: not gradually, or all at once, but in spurts. In half a year he'd age five years, developing deep wrinkles, cramped, bowed legs, a beard that was streaked with gray. Then he'd go ten years without changing, until the time came again, and his beard would turn completely gray, his hair turn white and fall out.

Only rarely did he ever think about Persia. Then he'd close his eyes and there it was — the unbearable white sun beating down, the noise of the marketplace, the smell of hot dust, the dirt of the narrow dark streets, the blue smoke as drops of lamb fat dripped onto the red-hot coals, the men sitting on carpets in the coffee houses, chewing on hard little cakes, drinking coffee and bitter green tea, smoking, their amber squirrel eyes squinting, their smoke-ringed faces shining with sweat. And in the evenings, the old worn-down hearthstones giving off the warmth of a day's accumulated heat, the swift un-Russian sunsets, the minarets shining pink against the violet sky, the haunting throaty sound of the muezzin's call, and everywhere the faithful falling, falling to press their faces to the dusty stones.

And remembering all this, remembering the dark oily water of the bay, the smell of cinnamon, of rusty iron, the dark echoing ships' holds, the blue-emerald immensity of the sea, the crowd of stevedores, with their sharp smell of sweat: Persians, Greeks, Armenians, Azerbaijanians, Russians — Tikhon would clench his teeth, lay his hand on his heart and think with helpless longing about getting away.

But there were some good moments in Tikhon's life. Every year, two weeks before St. Peter's Day, he'd get his old scythe that he had wrapped up so carefully the previous year out of the closet, put on a pair of tough new sandals, take a knapsack and some bread, and set off to do some haying.

He'd go to the farthest, most remote places, into the black earth regions, the regions of the old believers. And no sooner had he settled himself on the echoing lower deck, next to the firewood smelling of forests, ravines, and mushrooms, next to the engines with their steel pistons evenly thumping in the yellow grease; no sooner did he feel the quick throb, noise, and splash of the paddles overboard, and the shiver of picking up speed, than his old life disappeared and was forgotten, and the beckoning call of the endless dusty roads, the river pools, the hot drowsy woods, all those ancient things so familiar and natural since childhood, all seemed painfully sweet.

The whole time he was out haying, Tikhon would be more talkative and tolerant of people, and he wouldn't drink at all. Starting right in at daybreak, he'd mow in the cold and the wet, working eagerly, using a broad, uninterrupted stroke, growing flushed, breathing deeply the oppressively fresh smell of the hay, the sweet clover, the dense spicy damp of grassland.

It was the freedom of wide open space that he loved, the lonely trill of the skylark in the red-green morning sky; the sight of a foal racing with a quick clumsy trot through the bushes wet with dew, its short fluffy tail flying out behind him, was enough to make him quiver with delight; he loved the shy barefooted children with their sunbleached hair, trotting back from the village to the fields after their afternoon snack; but most of all, probably, he loved the long summer twilight, the grass dropping with a crunch at the smooth sweep of the scythe; he loved to think of vague, good things and listen to the slow mournful sound of the bells in the distance, the neighing of the mares in the meadow, the thin singsong voices of the old women in the village; he loved to sleep the short light sleep of summer on the warm and fragrant threshing room floor; half awake, he loved to watch the radiance of the countless stars, the rye ripening in the darkness around him.

But the haying would come to an end, and Tikhon would go back to the dust and swelter of the town, to the stench and dirt of the village; once again he'd strain his back until it snapped walking up the sagging gangplank; once again the shout of orders and the smell of matting and tar on the barges, the slimy musty river carrying down manure and urine from the taverns and tea shops above; and once again Tikhon would begin to drink, growing stupid and noisy and quarrelsome; again they would call him Crazy One and again he longed for Persia.

But as the years passed, the widower and landless peasant calmed down and became a nicer person, easier to get along with, more open; he grew a yellowish, patriarchal beard, but he was as strong as ever. He never lost his terrifying strength, his iron constitution, or his reputation as a fabulous strong man.

He became one of the sights of the region; people started loving him and taking pride in him; suddenly they began to find intelligence and Russian shrewdness in him; suddenly it turned out that they had been electing him to the city council for the last twenty years. On seeing his enormous figure, now the regional secretary will always stop, leap out and greet him, eagerly inquiring after his health, apologizing in advance for the problems and confusions of the work plans, but never neglecting to brag about the accomplishments either. Tikhon likes all this interest in himself, and all this respectful attention, and he stands there frowning playfully, wiping his runny eyes, smoothing his beard with his great bluish hand, breathing deeply and enjoying the view, the streets, the people, the sky, the river down below.

Then, delighted with his encounter with Tikhon and their practical chat, feeling happier, and better somehow, the regional secretary gets back into his car, and Tikhon walks on, unbuttoning his sheepskin coat as he goes, looking everyone straight in the eye. They greet him, stop to talk, and invite him to the tea shop. Tikhon replies to everyone at great length in a loud resonant voice, but he goes to the tea shop only with his oldest friends. There he takes off his cap, opens his coat still more, pushes his feet in their tall stiff boots under the table, and orders a small bottle of vodka and a couple of glasses of tea to make himself "a bit of punch." Young people come up to him, factory and shipyard workers, and ask to drink with him, if they can buy him a drink, and he drinks it down straight, without tasting it, making a slight show of his toughness and strength.

Tikhon loves to vote. Before an election he goes to the voting place practically every day and reads the magazines and newspapers, and listens to the speeches attentively, his ear cocked to one side. He's always the first one to vote; if he's on duty that day and can't come, they bring the ballot box to him first thing in the morning. Putting on his glasses, he reads the ballots over at length, asks all about the candidate — who he is, where he's from, who his father and mother were — and then he orders them to come into the booth, and holding the ballot carefully in his fleshy fingers, he drops it into the box.

3

It's a short winter day. The muted sunset dies out quickly, the pinkish snowbanks fade from view, there's one last golden flash on the windowpanes, the roofs and chimneys glow, and twilight descends on the town and the river.

Tikhon goes on duty around nine. He checks the locks with the man going off duty, yawns, and gets ready for the long night. After starting the stove in the hut, he takes his gun and goes out as usual to take a look around. The sky is dark and clear, and a few stars burn with a greenish light. Tikhon tramps around in the circle thrown by the lamplight, looking down at the wide dark river, smelling the ice on the river, the frozen iron doors, his sheepskin coat. The snow crunches and sparkles under his feet, dazzling him. When Tikhon walks directly under the light, his shadow is short and dense, but with every step it widens and lengthens, until it becomes enormous, flickering as it falls on the roofs of the houses below.

Everything around is frostbound, still, and dead. The only movement is a dark wisp of smoke climbing out of the chimney hut up toward the black sky, throwing a faintly moving shadow on the snowy roof of the warehouse. Down by the river, at the landing and loading docks, the street lamps are lighted, but only the spots of light on the snow can be seen, not the lamps themselves. A few last trucks are coming in, moving along the river, the high roar of their motors sounding distinctly, their headlights casting a ghostly light on the housetops and the road. The town is sleeping, buried in snow, but in the darkness there's a dull metallic light over everything: the streets, the ravines, the yards, the sheds, the gardens. But not on the warehouse doors and the windows of the nearby houses; they are black as slate.

Suddenly a small sleigh comes flying and screeching out of the path of fir trees above him, swerving and stopping under the light. Tikhon looks and recognizes the district policeman coming toward him. His strong little horse, his girth covered with curly gray hair, immediately drops his head meditatively. The policeman starts to get out, but changes his mind for some reason, and dropping the reins and taking off his mittens, dives into his pocket, looking for cigarettes.

"Hello, Tikhon Egorich!" he says in a loud cheerful voice, coming down hard on the "ich." "Any trouble here?"

"Do I ever have any trouble?" Tikhon answers with a grin.

"You better not. We have enough as it is," the policeman says emphatically, with some satisfaction. "For the time being at least." They smoke in silence, sending up a cloud of smoke. They both spit. "As it happens, I'm on my way from a case."

"Oh? Where?"

"At Bondarev. One kid attacked another, both mechanics. Nine wounds. The son of a bitch stabbed him with a penknife."

"Was it fatal?" Tikhon asks, distressed.

"He's still alive. Raving away, it's a laugh to listen to him."

"Did you get 'im?" Tikhon is very interested.

"Got him. He's being held in the village council building. We're sending a car over for him tomorrow morning."

"Good work!" Tikhon pauses. "What was it about?"

"A girl," the policeman frowns, putting on his mittens. "A girl. They say she's pretty. It was over her."

"What's going to happen to 'im?"

"Well, we won't be easy on him. If he lives, they'll give him ten years. If he dies, they'll send him to the wall! That's fair, I think."

"Yes . . ." Tikhon shifts his weight to his other foot, straightens his gun, the snow squeaking under his feet. "And all that for some wench! How many poor guys have died for 'em . . . It's beyond me!"

"Don't say that!" the policeman objects excitedly, settling in a more comfortable position. "Don't say that! Just a case of one person's stupidity and lack of morals — that's all . . . Did you know I was married?"

"No!" Tikhon breaks in. "First I heard of it! Been married long?"

"Two weeks, going on three."

"Did she have a dowry?"

"Dowry? She's an orphan, but you wait, I'll probably get a bonus for this business, and we'll have a real wedding ceremony.

I've been meaning to ask you something, Tikhon Egorich, wore a pin so I'd remember to drop in on you: will you be best man and all the rest of it?"

"Why not, if she's a good girl?" says Tikhon, brightening up, and taking one of the policeman's cigarettes smokes it hurriedly.

"You said it!" the policeman says quickly, watching him smoke, and taking the pin out of his coat, feels around in his side pocket. "No, I must have left it at home. I wanted to show you a photo. How did I ever get along alone? Now I get off duty and the apartment is warm, there's hot soup on the stove and lace curtains in the windows! The cold really knocks me out, my nose practically freezes, you know, so now she's making me an overcoat. An overcoat she's making me."

His voice rings out ecstatically, and he elongates and repeats his words, trying to prolong the pleasure of his own story. "Overcoat," he pronounces "ooo-vercoo-oat."

"Helps me wash up, dotes on me, fusses over me."

The policeman bursts out laughing and can't go on. Tikhon grins too but a little scornfully — his boots have crusted with ice and his nose is running. The sleigh is packed down with hay, and clumps that have fallen on the runners and down into the snow are tipped with white. There is a tender breath of summer in the frosty air.

"That's how we live and you talk about wenches!" the policeman finishes huskily and coughs, looking at the distant glow of the fire at the dam site. "They're building everywhere," he comments in another, more everyday tone of voice. "They're really coming to the people! That's how it always should have been!"

"There are more thieves these days," Tikhon comments, smiling.

"Ekh, Tikhon Egorich, that's not the point!" The policeman leans over to collect the reins. "The point isn't to catch thieves, it's that life is better. Well, I'm off. But I'm expecting you at the ceremony!"

He adjusts his pistol holder, blows his nose with an extraordinarily sharp, clear sound, first one side and then the other, and takes up the reins. The restless horse, its shaggy muzzle covered with frost, moves gratefully, and the frozen runners shoot forward with a crack. The thin squeak of the sleigh and the crunching zheek-zheek-zheek of the horse's hoofs die out in the distance. The policeman rides off, dragging his feet, his heels leaving a line in the snow on either side.

Tikhon goes back to tramping up and down under the light, thinking about the policeman's young wife, laughing to himself. Looking down at the town, he stops and listens for a moment. Then he shivers, and beating his arms against his sides, he goes to the hut for some tea.

4

Right near the river in the town below, another old man is living — a former millionaire, steamship captain, and miller — named Krugloff. Winter or summer he goes around in a sheepskin coat, cracked and shiny with age; summer or winter he never takes off his cap or felt boots, or lets his silver-plated walking stick out of his hand.

Krugloff is the same age as Tikhon and was also known in his youth all over Russia. Only he was known for something different: his mad drives in his troika, his gypsies, his debauches; his was the kind of total wildness found only in such remote, god-forsaken places. Thin and gypsylike, with burning black eyes and extraordinarily thick black hair, Krugloff was as insatiable in his drinking bouts, abominations and depravity as he was insatiable for work when they were over. He'd go on an orgy to Moscow, to Petersburg, even to Paris, astounding the civilized French with his troika, the enormity of his daily spending in restaurants and public houses, embarrassing them by his homesickness, his tears, his dancing, his crazy practical jokes.

But his debauches aside, as an owner and an entrepreneur, Krugloff was hard, intelligent, and cold-blooded. Almost the whole area was under his control, and he lived in the remote town purposely so that the governors, council members, merchants and even gendarmes who wanted to pay their respects to him had to travel great distances over terrible Russian roads.

When he got married, Tikhon took a wife with a small dowry, and thinking they'd settle in the country, he bought a mill near town and moved there to live. But that year Krugloff dunned him and cleaned him out, leaving him with nothing but debts, and Tikhon had to move back to town, meaner and crazier than ever. Whenever Krugloff would see Tikhon on the dock, he'd doff his high hat with its snow-white silken lining, make a deep bow, to the appreciative guffaws of the shop assistants and ask, "How do you do, your Excellency?" Tikhon would just scowl back.

To Krugloff the revolution came as a storm on a sunny day. He was just forty at the time, but he'd already calmed down a bit, and was harder, tighter, more of the implacable businessman than ever. His capital ran into the millions. But with entrepreneurial shrewdness, he suddenly began to understand that the old way of life wasn't coming back, that all this was too deep and too wide, and that he'd better run for it. And he almost made it: he'd just gotten his passport (English), just packed up his gold and diamonds, and informed his wife — a simple, dim-witted woman, very unlike him — when the Red Army arrived, confiscated his gold, kicked his family out of his house and imprisoned him for three months. He came out of prison another man: thin, dark, outwardly simple and calm, but inwardly bitter. To the end of his life he never forgave his wife for his unhappiness, and for fifteen years he didn't say a word to her. When she died he paid his last respects at the church, and kissed her corpse at the services, but he didn't go to the cemetery. When he went later to honor his parents, he never visited her grave; he didn't even know where it was.

As he got on in years, Krugloff became converted to evangelism, retired to live by himself, and was forgotten. Now on Saturdays he goes to the meetinghouse where he reads the Bible, finding great satisfaction in all the references to the imminent end of the world. He has a fierce hatred of the Soviet government and he refuses to take part in elections. "Governors used to stand at attention in my presence! I'm a British subject!" he says with pride to the election officials, willing to joke with them, but if they harass him too much, he goes white with rage and stamps his walking stick.

He had a stroke and has a tic now: first his left eye flicks like a bird's, then his right eye slowly closes. His dirty dark beard is continually quivering, his bald bony skull and sunken temples are as shiny and yellow as a dead man's. He has the dirtiness and untidiness of senility, and he smells bad even in the cold. But he still hasn't lost his temper. Even now when he's humbled, frightened, and decrepit, he'll suddenly open his thickened cloudy eyes, throw back his head, and fly into a rage, his feeble body trembling — and it can be difficult sometimes to bear up under his gaze.

Human consistency can be astonishing at times. There is a man in town whom Krugloff has hated for years, whose very name is enough to make him tremble with helpless rage. What wouldn't Krugloff give, what wouldn't he do, to see his enemy humbled and trampled on, in order to enjoy once more his feeling of excellence and superiority! During how many sleepless nights does Krugloff torture, punish, and burn him! This enemy, naturally enough, is Tikhon.

Krugloff has hated and despised him so hard for such a long time that the feeling has become for him his special passion, his soul's delight; he can't stay away from him, he can't stop talking to him and teasing him. So here it is winter, when the evenings are especially long and lonesome for Krugloff. Three times a month or so Tikhon hears the sharp tap of Krugloff's stick and in a few minutes sees the familiar hated figure. Krugloff approaches and stops under the light.

"Well?" asks Tikhon.

"I was at my . . . my grandson's," says Krugloff, breathing hard
and running a trembling hand over his sheepskin coat. "I was on
my way home, and I had a seizure. Thought I was dying. My
mouth tastes sweet."

Looking at Krugloff sideways, Tikhon doesn't answer. He
scowls: he doesn't like sick people, he's afraid of feeling sorry for
them.

"My legs are giving out," Krugloff goes on, after he catches his
breath. "My legs, my poor old legs . . . Twice already! I'll probably be dead soon . . . To whom should I give your greetings?"

"What do you want from the warehouse?" Tikhon interrupts
him roughly.

"Nothing. Just let me stand here . . . It's good to see our own
things again. You know, this was all mine," says Krugloff with
elaborately simple modesty. "My very own warehouse."

"Yours?" Tikhon clucks in mock sympathy. "How do you like
that? All yours!"

"Shut up, fool," Krugloff rasps and plunges his stick in the
snow.

Tikhon doesn't say anything.

"Still don't think you're going to die?" asks Krugloff, calming
down a little, looking at Tikhon's great frame. "Maybe not.
You've got twenty years maybe. But I'm afraid," he says quietly,
blinking. "I'm afraid of death. Here I am, talking to you, and
you're nothing but a bum. All of *Rawsha* knew me, and I'm talking to you. Now why is that?"

"All *Rawsha* knew you, but forgot you, that's why," Tikhon
sneers.

"That's a lie, you fool! I'm afraid to go home, that's why. You
get there, lie down, and your head starts to swim and your heart
starts to pound. Pound as if the earth were falling. That's death
letting you know. I believe in God, so I light the candles. *Lord
God!* I think to myself. It's all right during the day, but at night
. . . I lie there and listen, the clock strikes, strikes one, my poor

little birds flutter in the cage . . . I've got some goldfinches, they're the only things . . ."

"You mean to tell me you love live things?"

"That's it! I love to have living things near me. When the old lady was alive, she used to snore. But I'm alone now, can't hear anyone breathing, only my own heart. And it wheezes so! Oh, my poor old heart tortures me, *tortures* me! I don't like to listen to it. I wonder, should I buy something? A cat? I don't like cats, I can't respect them. There's blackness in them, bestiality! I had a dog, Damka, she was a little devil! Healthy bitch, ate a lot, could she eat! A carload of food was nothing to her. Well, I killed her."

"Killed her?"

"Strangled her!" Krugloff senses the hate in Tikhon's question, and laughs. *Here we go,* he thinks. "I tried to drive her away, but she wouldn't go, she was used to me. But what was I supposed to feed her? Under your soviet regime you can't even feed yourself! I couldn't feed a mutt like that. So I called her to the shed, 'Here Damka!' I say. So we went, that is, I looped a rope round her neck and dragged her. She looks at me, she understands, that's obvious, she whines, and I . . ."

"You mean you didn't take pity on her?" asks Tikhon, looking gravely at Krugloff's unnaturally jovial face.

"Fool!" Krugloff answers with great satisfaction. "Think! What's it to her? You know no mutt worries about death, it's just something that happens, they strangle, get clubbed, go mad . . . That's the fate fixed for them by God!"

"You're a wicked one," Tikhon comments quietly. "You look like a cockroach and you're mean to poor innocent brutes. You've a rotten soul."

"Ah-ha!" Krugloff has finally reached the point he came for, and all at once he starts shivering with blind hatred. "Ah-ha! He's remembered about the soul! And when you stripped me clean, did you think about my soul? Huh? Does that make you squirm, you bastard, you bum? Krugloff lived and he let others live. Didn't I give you good-for-nothings enough to eat and drink? Who owned the poorhouse, where the technical institute now is? And who built the church you destroyed? Huh? Who brought in the goods? And the local ladies, our little wenches? Didn't they get a lot out of me? I gave them up. I gave them up, but I didn't abandon them, I built a house for them. In those days we used to live, really live! No thanks to you, you antichrists, you pure sons of bitches, you fools! I used to sweat for it, sparks in my eyes!"

"Those sparks in your eyes were from being drunk," Tikhon is delighted to put in gloomily.

"From being drunk! You know when a fool is smart? When he doesn't say anything. So shut up — from being drunk! I drank, but the whole town got rich off me. How many thousands did I put into it, and where are they now? I don't sleep nights wondering what we were ruined for. For nothing, that's what for. Was life any worse than life today? When I start thinking about it, I itch all over. Just you think about it and you'll cry your eyes out!"

" 'You think about it!' " Tikhon mimics him, laughing vindictively, and slapping his coat sleeves against his sides. "You're crying your eyes out. Go drown yourself in your crocodile tears! Don't you think about anything else?"

"Certainly I think about something else," Krugloff says, raising his trembling hands. "I think that soon, *very* soon, the end is coming for all of you. You haven't got much more time for bloodsucking. The Bible will make good on its prophecies! yes it will. Oh you'll all burn, it won't go easy for you. What do you think the atom is? Just an atom, yes? No! It's all there in the Bible! Brothers will rise up against each other, fathers against sons, sorrows will multiply, the heavens will crack and the earth and heavens will burn . . . Oh yes, you'll be eating each other, like Arabian jackals eating their own heads, you'll set fire to your own curs-ed selves! Then you'll remember Krugloff! Then you'll remember who gave you food and drink and who predicted a dog's death for you! You robbed Krugloff, that's that, but I have a place prepared for me . . ."

"A place is prepared for you in hell!" shouts Tikhon, aroused at last by Krugloff's words. "You're weeping over your money? And how did you get it? By giving your father arsenic? By drowning your nephew? Why don't you say something, you snake in the grass? How many souls did you let go begging, how many orphans' tears were shed on your account? And whose fault was it I drank, whose fault I used to be a crazy fool? 'We really lived!' We would have if you hadn't! You remember Paris, but hunger and cholera you don't remember, your children didn't die of it. It was out of sweetness that I worked for you, breaking my back, my body all covered with boils? Who devoured my life, my youth, if it wasn't murderers and mother-f——'s like you, huh? I remember nothing — my whole life is like a single day — and why? You moan at night, weeping over the past, and I stand in the hut here and can't remember a thing. We didn't shoot many of you, but we should have, should have tortured you in the name of the hungry, in the name of all of us, we should have gotten to the root. You — slobbery devil! I'll kill you! Don't come here, I'll kill you, you'll drive me to it, you know me, you remember me the way I was. Don't bother me, don't open up my wounds . . . I'm so sorry I could chew my arm off that I didn't get you and exterminate you in '17. Listen merchant, listen, on your holy cross, I'll kill you!"

Tikhon grabs Krugloff's collar and drags him away from the light, his face terrible. The collar tears and Krugloff comes meekly, calm and quiet, his beard quivering.

"You wait, the dam will be finished in the spring, it'll flood you, you damned bastard." Shrieking, panting, wheezing, Tikhon shoves Krugloff to the ground.

Slowly, Krugloff gets up and turns toward Tikhon, gurgling and whistling in his throat.

"It won't fl-flood me!" he cries, choking and stammering with rage.

"It'll flood you!" Tikhon trumpets cheerfully. "Your days are over, you'll soon breathe your last, merchant, your Excellency! 'How do you do, your Excellency?' Huh?" he suddenly remembers. "Huh? Ho ho ho!"

"It won't!" sobs Krugloff. "I'll outlive you. My blood is immortal!"

Tikhon bursts out laughing with special glee and vindictiveness. Krugloff raises his chin, and throws back his tearstained face to the black sky.

"Lord God!" he pleads desperately, mumbling inarticulately, "Boo-boo-boo . . ."

And he goes off into the darkness, pitiful, blind with tears and wild despair, torturing himself with memories of his former strength and power and pride and influence. He goes off to pray, assuring himself again and again of the imminent end of the world, despising everything new and young and incomprehensible, trembling and gasping at the imagined sight of Tikhon's enormous shape in the shadows. He goes off, only to return to the warehouse two weeks later, like an alcoholic, like a man obsessed.

And coming back, staggering and stumbling with weakness, he'll lean against the lamppost, damning and threatening Tikhon and everyone else along with him who is building a new life. And he'll torture himself, desperately, rapturously recalling the past — his life, his successes, his wealth, even his past failures. And everything past will seem sweet and wonderful and full of truth, while everything new will seem alien and hostile, incomprehensible and unfair. And again Tikhon will be aroused at last to shout and laugh at him cruelly and push him to the ground.

And the townspeople, knowing about the feud, so amazingly persistent that it has become a legend in town, knowing the old guys, remembering Tikhon when he was young, his wildness, his crazy temper, are sure that disaster is inevitable: someday Tikhon will kill Krugloff. They're so sure that they even justify the murder in advance — Krugloff, they say, asked for it himself.

Silly-Billy

WORN OUT by the heat, full of underdone, undersalted fish, Egor the buoy keeper is sleeping in his shack.

His shack is new and bare. There isn't even a stove, the floor is only half laid, and the passageway is cluttered with bricks and wet clay. The walls are hung with tow ropes, the unsealed glass in the window frames rattles in answer to every train whistle, and ants crawl on the sill.

When Egor wakes up the sun is going down, a misty radiance has settled all around, and the river is golden and still. He yawns, and becomes absorbed in its sweet torment, twisting and straining almost in a convulsion. His eyes half shut, his fingers limp, he hurriedly rolls a cigarette and lights it. As he smokes he stretches luxuriously, and a sobbing sound escapes his lips. Voluptuously he clears his throat and gives his chest and side a good hard scratch. His eyes moisten, go vacant, and a pleasant languor pours through his body.

Having finished smoking, he goes to the passageway and in the same avid way he smoked, he takes a drink of water. It is cold and smells of roots and leaves, and leaves a sharp pleasant taste. Then he takes his oars, kerosene lamps and goes down to his boat.

The stern of his boat has settled and is swimming with water and trampled weeds. Egor thinks about bailing it out, but feels too lazy. Sighing, he looks at the sunset, then up and down the river and then, planting his feet and straining harder than necessary, he shoves off from shore.

Egor's stretch of river is not large. His job is to light the lamps on four buoys, two above his shack and two below. Each time he spends a lot of time trying to figure out where it would be better to start: upstream or down. He's pondering this right now. Then, settling himself, he grabs the oars, tramples down the weeds, shoves the lamps away with his feet, and begins to pull against the current. It's all just silly-billy nonsense, he thinks to himself, warming up with each short stroke, pulling quickly back and forth, watching the rosy, darkening reflection of the bank in the calm water. The boat leaves a dark trail behind in the golden water, and neat little waves lick at the sides.

The air is growing cooler, the swallows skim right over the water, screeching shrilly, and fish splash near the bank. Egor's expression at each splash is as if each fish were an old friend of his. From the shore come the smells of wild strawberries and hay and dewy underbrush, and from the boat the smells of fish, kerosene, and weeds. A mist is rising imperceptibly from the water, bringing with it the smell of the inscrutable depths.

One by one Egor lights the red and white lamps, places them on a buoy, and then almost without using his oars, he lazily, gracefully, moves on to the next. The buoys burn brightly and are visible far off in the gathering darkness. But Egor is already in a hurry to get back upstream to his shack. He washes up, inspects himself in the mirror, puts on his boots and a fresh shirt, slaps on a tight-fitting sailor cap at a jaunty angle, crosses the river, ties the boat in the bushes and walks off into the meadow, intently studying the sunset ahead of him.

The meadow is covered in mist already and smells damp.

The mist is so dense and white that at a distance the meadow looks flooded. As in a dream, Egor moves, rather swims, along, up to his shoulders in mist, able to see only the tops of haystacks and the black line of the woods, under the soundless heavens, under a dying sunset.

Egor stands on tiptoe, craning his neck, and finally catches a glimpse of a pink kerchief above the line of mist.

"Hey!" he calls out in a loud tenor.

"Ahh!" comes faintly back.

Egor walks faster, and then he crouches and runs like a quail. Turning off the path, he falls to the grass, staining his elbows and knees, his heart pounding, to watch the place where he'd seen the pink kerchief.

A minute passes, two, but no one comes, no steps are heard. Egor can't sit still. He gets up to look. As before, he can only see the sunset, the line of the woods, the tops of haystacks, vague and gray around him. She's hiding! he thinks, rapturously impatient, and crouching down again, moves on. He takes a breath and holds it until the blood rushes to his face. The tight sailor cap is beginning to pinch his forehead. Suddenly he sees someone approaching and jumps in surprise.

"Stop!" he roars. "Stop or I'll shoot!"

Stamping his boots, he runs after her and she runs away, squealing and laughing, dropping something from her purse as she goes. Quickly, he catches up to her and they fall together in a fierce happy embrace onto a soft molehill smelling of fresh earth and mushrooms. Then they get up, find the thing she dropped, and wander slowly back to the boat.

2

Egor is very young, but he's a drunkard already.

His wife — a shabby little wench many years older than Egor — had also been a drunkard; she died in the autumn freeze-over. She had gone to town for vodka, which she drank on the way back, singing songs as she went. By the time she had reached the river across from the shack, she was drunk.

"Egor, you old louse," she called. "Come out and look at me!"

Overjoyed at her return, Egor had thrown on a sheepskin coat and come out, his feet wrapped only in footrags, and had seen her dancing in the middle of the river, waving her purse over her head. He was just going to shout to her to hurry when before his eyes the ice broke, and she went under.

Tearing off his coat and footrags, he ran barefooted across

the ice. It cracked and heaved gently under him as he ran, and falling down, he crawled on his stomach to the hole and looked down into the black steaming water. Closing his eyes, he howled and crawled back. Three days later, he locked up the shack and went to spend the winter a mile and a half away in the village on the other side of the river.

When the ice broke in the spring, he ferried young Alenka from Trubetskoi across the river. When she tried to pay him, Egor suddenly said, "Forget it, that's just silly-billy. Come home with me. I live alone and I'm bored. It could do with a cleaning too, you get lousy dirty without a woman around, and I'll give you some fish."

Two weeks later when Alenka, on her way back from somewhere to her place in the village, happened to drop in on him one evening, Egor's heart began to pound so hard it scared him. For the first time in his life Egor fussed over a girl. He ran outside, got some kindling, started a fire going in the bricks, and put on the sooty teakettle. He started to ask Alenka all about her life, but stopped in the middle of the sentence, embarrassing her to tears and getting embarrassed himself. It was already night when he washed and changed into a clean shirt in the passageway, and took her across the river, walking her all the way across the meadow.

Alenka comes to see him often now, and each time stays three days or so. When she is with him he is carefree and joking. When she isn't, he gets bored and doesn't know what to do with himself. Nothing turns out right. He sleeps a lot and his dreams are bad and disturbing.

Egor is strong but a little sluggish, has a prominent Adam's apple, and is slightly pigeon-toed. His face is broad and gentle, dreamily expressionless, and hooknosed. He is burned almost black by the summer sun, and his gray eyes seem blue by contrast. "They never quite finished the job on me," he complains when he's drinking. "I was fathered by the devil, out of a drunken she-goat!"

This spring he's staying home on the May First holiday. He planned to go to town for the celebration, but didn't for some reason, he doesn't know why not. He thrashes around on his rumpled, unmade bed, whistling gloomily. At noon his sister had run down from the village and called out thinly to him from the opposite shore.

"Egor!"

Egor comes sullenly down to the water.

"Egorka, they say you have to come . . ."

"Who does?" Egor shouts back.

"Uncle . . . sia and Uncle . . . edya."

"Why don't they come here?"

"They can't, they're drunk."

Egor's face is the picture of regret. "Tell them I have work to do!" he shouts, although he doesn't of course. Ekh, aren't they having a time in town now, he thinks gloomily, and pictures his drunken relatives, his mother, the tables of appetizers, the pies, the incessant music, the sparkle of home-brewed beer, the dressed-up girls, the houses hung with flags, the movies at the club. He spits sullenly in the water and climbs back up to the shack.

"Egor . . . come!" her voice rings out from the other side, but Egor isn't listening.

Egor reacts to things with scorn and indifference; he's extraordinarily lazy, but he has plenty of money because it's easy to get. There's no bridge in the vicinity and Egor ferries everyone across, charging a ruble — two rubles if he's in a bad mood. His work as a buoy keeper is easy, old people's work really, and has definitely spoiled and corrupted him.

But sometimes a vague uneasiness comes over Egor. Usually this happens in the evening. Alenka will be sleeping and Egor will lie beside her, recalling his days up north with the navy. He'll remember the buddies with whom he has long since lost all contact. Vaguely, idly, he'll remember their voices, their faces, and even conversations he had with them.

He'll recall the low dusky shore, the Arctic ocean, the eerie northern radiance of the land in winter, the stunted blue-gray fir trees, the moss, the sand; recall the lighthouse at night, throwing its blinding, smoky light over the dead forest. Even the thought of all these things leaves him impassive and cool.

But sometimes he is gripped by a strange trembling, and strange queer thoughts creep into his head. He imagines that his river shore is the Arctic shore, that it is lined with slate-roofed barracks, that the lighthouse light is flashing. There are sailors in the barracks, double-decked beds, the crackle of the wireless, conversations going on, letters being written, the smell of cigarette smoke. Everything is just as it was, only he's not there. It's as if he'd never lived there, or worked there, and everything is just an illusion, a dream!

Then he gets up and goes out to sit or lie under the bushes, wrapped in his sheepskin coat, listening intently, watching the reflections of the stars and the brightly burning buoys in the dark river. In these moments he's not pretending for anyone, and his face goes pensive and sad. His heart is heavy, and he wants something, somewhere to go, some other life.

A deep, velvety, three-toned whistle slowly rises and falls over the water from the direction of Trubetskoi. Presently a brilliantly lighted steamboat appears, smacking the waves, hissing steam. It whistles again. The noise, the splash, the whistle resound against the trees alongshore and shimmer back across the water. Egor watches the boat and feels an even stronger longing.

He pictures the journey ahead, the perfumed young women sleeping in the cabins, on their way to some unknown destination. He imagines how the engine room smells, of steam, polished copper instruments, and the intimate warmth of the engines. The deck and railings are wet with mist, and yawning deck officers are standing on the bridge, manning the rudder. On the upper deck, lonely passengers are sitting wrapped in their coats in the darkness, looking at the buoy lights, the occasional glow of a fisherman's campfire, or of a factory or power station; and it all seems so wonderful to them that they'd like to get off at any of the small landings and stay awhile in the cool, misty stillness. And there's bound to be someone sleeping on a bench, his coat pulled up around his ears, his legs drawn up, who'll be awakened by the steam whistle or the fresh air, or the touch of the boat at the dock.

Life is going past him! What is the ringing in his heart and over all the land? What agitates and beckons him in the still hours of evening? Why is he full of longing and why is there no pleasure in the misty fields and quiet water, no pleasure in his easy, care-free, casual work?

After all, he still has his wonderful homeland — the dusty roads he's tramped since childhood; the towns, each one an individual, each with its own talk, its own girls; the towns where he'd gone so often to spend the evening, kissing in the rye fields, getting into bloody fights, being knocked out even; the bluish smoke of the campfire over the river was wonderful, the buoy lights; spring with its violet-colored snow on the fields, the immense, turbulent spring floods, the cold sunsets in a lowering sky, the rustling piles of last year's leaves along the bank! And autumn was wonderful, the boredom, the rain, the fragrant evening wind — how cozy to be in the shack then!

Why does he wake up, who calls him at night, as if the stars were crying out, "Egooor!" He feels chilly and afraid, called by far-off places, towns, noise, lights. He longs for work, real work, work that will bring exhaustion, happiness!

Dragging his sheepskin, he goes back to the shack and lies down beside Alenka. He wakes her, and hungrily presses close to her, wretched, aware only of her, like a child on the verge of tears. Closing his eyes, he buries his face in her shoulder, growing weak with his feeling of joy and passion and tenderness, feeling her quick, responsive, sweet kisses on his face, thinking of nothing and de-sirous of nothing except to stay like this forever.

Then they whisper together, though there's no need to whisper, and Alenka always tries to persuade him to settle down, give up drinking, get married, go somewhere where there's real work, so that people will respect him, so they'll write about him in the news-papers.

Half an hour later, feeling calm, languid and joking, he grumbles and calls her "silly-billy" but absent-mindedly, not trying to offend her, secretly hoping that she'll keep on and on trying to persuade him to start a new life.

3

Oftentimes people going up and down the river in motorboats, canoes, or even on rafts, spend the night in Egor's shack. It's always the same thing: the visitors switch off the motor and someone climbs up to the shack.

"Hi there, master of the house!" he'll say with excessive heartiness.

Egor doesn't answer, muttering under his breath as he cleans a willow fish basket.

"Hello?" the visitor repeats, a little less heartily. "Can we spend the night with you?"

Again the only answer is silence. Egor isn't even breathing, he's so busy with his basket.

"How many are there of you?" he asks at length.

"Just three. Anything will do for us," the visitor says hopefully. "Don't worry, we'll pay."

Slowly, apathetically, pausing frequently, Egor asks who they are, where they're from, where they're going. And when there's nothing more to ask, he'll give his permission with a great show of reluctance.

"All right, you can spend the night."

Then everyone gets out of the boat. They find a good spot to empty the boat, and then they drag it up and turn it over. Then carrying the motor and their rucksacks, canisters, and pots, they go up to the shack. It begins to reek of gasoline, travel, and wet boots. The air is close. Egor becomes more animated, and shakes hands with everyone, gaiety coming over him in advance of the forthcoming drinks. He begins to bustle about and talk non-stop, chiefly about the weather. He orders Alenka about and builds a great bright bonfire near the shack.

But when they pour the vodka, Egor drops his lashes and his eyes shimmer with tears, scarcely daring to breathe, he's so scared that there won't be enough to go around. Then, taking his glass in his strong brown fingers with their jagged nails, he says in a loud gay voice, "To our acquaintance!" and drinks and his face hardens.

He gets drunk quickly, happily, and easily. And when he's drunk he begins, with great ease, pleasure, and conviction, to tell lies. He tells lies for the most part about fish, because he is for some reason convinced that his visitors are only interested in fish.

"Fish," he says carefully, as if he had just inadvertently tasted one, "are all kinds around here. True there's just a few of each kind left, but . . ." he giggles, pauses, and lowers his voice. "But if you know how . . . Yesterday, by the way, I got a pike. Not a big pike, to tell the truth, just thirty-five pounds. I was tending the buoys in the morning, I listen, there's a splash under the bank. Right away, I cast, while I'm still holding the buoy, and it bit: the hook was all the way into the belly!"

"And where is this pike?" they ask him.

"I took it to the farmers' market and sold it," Egor replies without batting an eye, and describes the pike in detail.

And if someone doubts his story, and they always do, and Egor waits impatiently for them to do so, he flares up, reaches for the bottle as if it were his, pours himself a neat five-ounce drink, and downs it quickly. And then he raises his drunken, dumbly desperate eyes to the doubter, and says, "Do you want to go fishing tomorrow? What are we arguing for? What kind of motor do you have?"

"LM-1," they answer.

Egor turns around and looks at the motor leaning in the corner for a minute.

"That? That's a silly-billy motor. My boat *Slavka* has a Bollinder motor, mine, I brought it back with me from the navy and put it together myself. Now there's a brute of a motor: ten miles an hour she'll go! And that's against the current. What do you say? Let's put my Bollinder up against your silly-billy motor! Well? Only one other person has made a bet like that with me; he lost his gun. Want to see my gun? Made to order, a real killer, I used it this winter, and," he thinks for a minute, his eyes glassy, "I got three hundred and fifty rabbits! Well?"

And the guests, cowed and slightly embarrassed, try to pique him a little by asking about the stove.

"So, friend, you get along without a stove?"

"Stove?" Egor is shouting already. "Who knows how to build one? Do you? Build me one then! There's the clay, bricks, all your materials, in short. Go ahead, I'll give you a hundred and fifty rubles for the job. Well? Build one for me!" he persists stubbornly, knowing his request won't be fulfilled, and hence, the victory is his. "Well? Go ahead!"

And then, noticing that there's still some vodka, and that his guests are laughing, he goes out into the passageway, puts on his sailor cap, rips open his shirt collar to show his navy T-shirt, and comes back in.

"You will permit me?" he asks with elaborate drunken deference, standing at attention. "Boatswain of the Northern Fleet at your service! Requests permission to congratulate you on the anniversary of this socialist and communist holiday. All forces of the camp of peace are called to struggle with the enemy. And requests that you give him a drink in honor of the occasion!"

They give him a drink, and Alenka, in an agony of embarrassment, begins to make the beds for the guests, tears burning in her eyes, waiting with near-wild impatience for the moment when Egor will astonish his guests. And Egor does astonish them.

Suddenly, he sits down on a bench, totally bleary-eyed, and leans against the wall. Settling his shoulder blades and legs more comfortably, he coughs, raises his head, and begins to sing.

And at the first sound of his voice, all conversation stops; everyone looks startled and unbelieving. He doesn't sing popular or contemporary songs, although he knows them all and hums them constantly. He sings in the traditional, drawn-out Russian style, somewhat forced and harsh, the way he heard old men sing when he was a child, with endless "oooos" and "aaaas" that sear the very soul. He sings softly, a little playfully, a little coyly, but there is so much penetration and such power, so much of authentic Russia, of ancient Russia, in his gentle voice that after a minute everything is forgotten: Egor's crudeness and stupidity, his drunkenness and boasting. The day's fatigue is forgotten. It is as if the past and the future had come together in this extraordinary voice clouding the brain as it rings out and shimmers in the air. You want to listen to it forever, your head bowed, your eyes shut, your breath suspended, not holding back your tears.

"You should be in the Bolshoi Theater! The Bolshoi Theater!" everyone shouts the minute he is finished, and in great excitement, their eyes shining, they all offer to help him, everyone wants to write off somewhere: to the radio, the newspapers, or they want to telephone someone. Everyone feels joyful and festive, but though pleased by the praise, Egor is tired and already cooling off. His manner becomes casual and joking once more, and again his broad face is expressionless.

He has a vague image of Moscow, the Bolshoi, its statue of four galloping horses, the glittering hall, the sounds of the orchestra; he's seen all that in the movies. He gives a lazy shrug and mutters, "That's just silly-billy . . . there are lots of other theaters there."

But so great is his glory now, so powerful and incomprehensible does he seem to his guests that no one takes offense.

But that's not the whole of his glory.

4

That's not the whole of his glory, it's just a quarter of it. His real glory comes, as he says, when he "gets the urge." He gets the urge once or twice a month, after he's been feeling especially bored and lost.

He has the blues from early morning on, and from early morning on he drinks. True, he doesn't drink much, and from time to time he asks lazily, "Well, come on, huh?"

"What?" Alenka pretends not to understand.

"Let's sing a duet or something, all right?" he asks dully, with a sigh.

Alenka laughs casually and doesn't answer. She knows that the time hasn't come yet, that Egor isn't really ready. And she moves around the shack, dusting this, washing that, going down to the river to rinse out some clothes, coming back.

Finally the time comes. It usually comes toward evening. Egor doesn't request a duet this time; he gets up, rumpled and frowning, looks out one window, then the other, goes outside for a drink of water, comes back and pockets a bottle of vodka and grabs his sheepskin coat.

"Do you plan to go far?" Alenka asks innocently, beginning to tremble inside.

His face is pale, his nostrils distended, the veins stand out on his temples. Alenka walks beside him, coughing as she tightens her wool scarf around her throat. She knows just what Egor will do. He will walk first to the riverbank, look up and down the river, think for a minute as if he didn't know where he was going, and then he'll go to his favorite place, to the flat-bottomed boat, the one full of holes and turned over in the birch trees down by the water. And there he will sing with her, not quite the way he sang for his guests; for them he sang carelessly, playfully, and not with his full voice, not by a long shot.

And Egor indeed stops on the bank and thinks a minute, then walks silently to the boat. Here he spreads out his coat, sits down, leans against the side of the boat, drawing up his legs and setting the bottle between them.

The sunset is beautiful, the mist has flooded the field. On the horizon the black line of the woods and the black tips of the hay-stacks. The birch branches above are still, the grass is wet with dew, the air is warm and peaceful, but Alenka feels cold and clings to Egor. He takes the bottle in his trembling hands, takes a swig, winces, and clears his throat. His saliva tastes sweet.

"Well," he says, turning to cough. "Watch me for your part," he whispers.

He fills his lungs, tenses, and begins in a mournful and trem-bling, clear, high tenor:

> Down by the sea
> The deep blue sea—

Alenka frowns, trembling as she waits her turn, and joins him, low and clear:

> Swims the swan and his mate—

But she is not listening to herself; she's not even aware of her own low, ardent voice. She can only hear Egor's voice and feel his gentle, grateful hand squeezing her shoulder.

Oh, it is sweetness, this song, and torment! His voice now low, now swelling, now hoarse, now metallically clear, Egor sings, as they have been sung for hundreds of years, the wonderful, extraor-dinary, simple folk words:

> Swims the swan so smoothly
> And the smooth soft yellow sand —

How was it? Why was it so painful, so familiar, as if she had already known all this earlier, as if she had lived some time long ago, and sung and listened to Egor's wonderful voice. In what distant place, on what ocean had she drifted? It had been with him, with Egor, that she had gone through the meadow at sunset before, in the mist under the stars, as in a dream or under water, full of joy, drunk without wine!

And the blue-gray eagle comes . . .

Egor moans and sobs, giving himself up to the song's agony, his head bent, and half turned away from Alenka. His Adam's apple quivers, his lips are mournful.

Oh that blue-gray eagle! Why, why did he throw himself on the white swan, why did the grass wilt, why was everything covered in darkness, why did the stars fall! Let there be an end to these tears, to this voice, to this song!

And they sing, knowing only that now their hearts will burst, that now they'll fall dead on the grass, not to be revived by cool water or anything, not after such happiness and after such torment.

And then they finish, exhausted, devastated, happy, when Egor silently lays his head in her lap. Breathing hard, she kisses his cool pale face and whispers breathlessly, "Egorushka, sweet. I love you, my wonder, my precious."

Oh you silly-billy, he wants to say but says nothing. His mouth tastes sweet and dry.

THE SPIRIT OF THE FOREST

Kabiasy

Zhukov, the club director, was held up late at the neighboring collective farm one afternoon in August. He'd gone there on business, and had been all over, talking with everyone, but even so it had been an unsuccessful day — it was hot and everyone had been in a hurry.

Just a boy really, Zhukov had worked in the club only a year and was still quite vague about his duties. He'd been named to the post because he played the accordion well and because he always took part eagerly in local sporting events. He was on the soccer team for Zubatov, his home town, even though he was living in Dubka now, in a small room in the club.

He should have gone straight home, and there was a truck going to Dubka, but he changed his mind and went instead to see an old former teacher of his with whom he wanted to discuss the volleyball team and other cultural matters. But his teacher, it turned out, was hunting and should have been back long ago; he was late for some reason. Zhukov sat down despondently to wait, knowing it was stupid and that he ought to leave.

So he stayed for two hours, sitting at the window smoking and chatting aimlessly with his hostess. He would even have slept, except that voices awakened him. The old women were shouting as they drove the herd to pasture.

Finally there was no sense waiting any longer, and angry at the bad break, Zhukov drank a glass of kvass for the road that set his teeth on edge, and took off for home. It was a six-mile walk.

On the bridge Zhukov caught up with old Matvei, the night watchman. He was standing, in a torn winter cap, a dirty sheepskin coat, his feet wide apart, a gun under his elbow, rolling a cigarette and watching Zhukov sullenly as he approached.

"Ah, Matvei!" Zhukov recognized him although he'd seen him only twice before. "You out hunting too?"

Matvei walked on without answering, squinting at his cigarette. He got out some matches, lit the cigarette, inhaled a few times and coughed. Then, scraping his coat with his nails, he tucked the matches away and said finally, "Hunting! I'm on nightwatch. In the garden."

The taste of kvass in Zhukov's mouth was nauseating. He spat, and lit a cigarette.

"You probably sleep all night," he said absently, thinking how stupid he was for not going earlier with the truck, saving himself the walk.

"Sleep!" Matvei retorted emphatically. "I'd sleep, but they don't let me . . ."

"What won't let you, thieves?" Zhukov inquired ironically.

"Thieves!" Matvei sneered, suddenly beginning to walk more freely, straddling the road like a man who has been cooped up for a long time and finally comes out into open space. Without so much as a glance at Zhukov, he stared sideways at the twilit fields. "They don't come to thieve, brother, but they come . . ."

"Well? Are they girls, or what?" asked Zhukov and burst out laughing. He'd just remembered he was going to see Lyubka tonight.

"They . . ." Matvei muttered something indistinctly.

"Out with it, old man!" Zhukov spat. "Who are they?"

"Kabiasy, that's who," Matvei pronounced with an air of mystery, squinting at Zhukov for the first time.

"So that's it!" Zhukov said mockingly. "Tell it to your old lady. What kind are these 'kabiasy'?"

"You know the kind," Matvei answered sullenly. "You'll recognize them when you see them."

"Are they devils or what?" asked Zhukov, pulling a serious face.

Matvei squinted at him again. "They're sort of black," he growled uncertainly, "and greenish." He took two copper cartridges from his pocket and blew off some tobacco.

"There, see," he said, pointing out two paper wads stuffed in the cartridges.

Zhukov looked and saw a cross scratched in ink on each wad.

"Magic," said Matvei with satisfaction. "So I can handle them!"

"You mean they bother you?" Zhukov mocked, but checked himself, and pulled another serious face to show he believed it all.

"Not too much," Matvei replied seriously. "They never get that far. But they come out of the dark, see, one by one, and crowd under the apple trees, they're tiny little things standing this way, right next to each other." Matvei looked down the road, and pointed. "They stand and play songs . . ."

"Songs?" Zhukov couldn't contain his laughter. "You're doing no worse than we do at the club — amateur theatricals! What kind of songs?"

"Oh different kinds. Sad ones sometimes. And then they tell me, 'Come here Matvei, come here!'"

"And you . . . ?"

"I tell them, 'Listen you mother-f——, get out of here!'"

Matvei laughed delightedly. "Well then, they start toward me, I load my gun with my magic cartridges and yell . . ."

"Do you get them?"

"Get them!" Matvei exclaimed contemptuously. "*Kill* an evil spirit? No, I just keep them off until morning, until the rooster crows."

"So!" Zhukov said thoughtfully. "Bad, very bad."

"What?"

"My work in atheistic propaganda has been bad, that's what!" said Zhukov, making a face at Matvei. "You're telling that stuff around town, scaring the girls?" he asked sternly, suddenly remembering that he was club director. "Kabiasy! You're the kabiasy!"

"What?" Matvei repeated again, his face angry and resentful. "Will you go into the forest?"

"Of course I will!"

"Go ahead then. You won't hardly make it home!"

Matvei turned without saying goodbye and quickly crossed the field, heading toward the dark garden, the intensity of his anger apparent even in his retreating figure.

Left alone on the road, Zhukov lit a cigarette and looked around. Twilight was falling, the light was fading in the west, and all that could be seen of the collective farm were the darkening rooftops and the electric windmill jutting above the poplar trees.

To the left he could see the birch forest, running toward the horizon. It was as if someone had drawn a line along the darkness with a white pencil. At first just a few trees, then more farther on, the thin white line passed into the twilit horizon.

To the left he could also see a lake, bright in the darkness, brimming over the banks, and yet so still that it seemed to have been soldered into place. A bonfire burned on the lake shore, sending smoke over the road. The dew had already fallen and the smoke was damp.

To the right marched the great mast timber, from hill to hill, through the gloomy meadows and forest clearings. They resembled a file of enormous mute creatures thrown down from some other world, silently marching west with upraised arms toward their homeland, the inflammable green stars.

Zhukov looked around again, still hoping for a passing car. Then he set off down the road, keeping his eye on the campfire and the lake. There was no one to be seen near the fire. Not a soul on the lake either, and the solitary fire, built by some unknown person for some unexplained reason, made a strange sight.

Zhukov walked haltingly at first, turning around, half expecting a car or another pedestrian. But there was no one to be seen, ahead or behind, as far as the horizon and finally Zhukov began really to move along.

He had gone two miles when it became completely dark. Only

the road, cutting through the mist, was light. The night had come on warm, but in the mist, Zhukov was gripped by the cold. Then he would hit a warm spot again, and the shifts from cold to warm were quite pleasant.

We certainly have a backward peasantry, thought Zhukov. He was walking with his hands in his pockets, knitting his brows as he recalled Matvei's face, how furious and contemptuous he'd become when he'd been laughed at. Yes, he thought, we'll have to step up our atheistic propaganda. Superstition must be ripped out by the roots! And more than ever he wanted to have a talk with someone about culture and intellect.

Then he began thinking that it was time perhaps for him to move to a city somewhere to study. He could imagine himself directing a chorus, not in a collective farm club, where they didn't even have a proper stage and the kids smoked and fooled around during rehearsal, but in Moscow where he'd have a chorus of one hundred — a real, academic chorus.

Such thoughts revived his spirits as they always did, and he strode along, oblivious to everything around him, paying no attention to the stars or to the road; clenching and unclenching his fists, knitting his brows, letting himself laugh and sing, unafraid of being seen. He was even glad to be walking by himself without any company. And so he reached the empty shed near the road and he sat down to smoke and rest.

A little farm had been here once, but it had been torn down when the collective farm was organized and only the shed remained. The shed was dark and empty. It appeared never to have had a door. It sat at an angle and its interior was pitch-black. Zhukov sat with his back to the shed, facing the road, his elbows on his knees, smoking and slowly relaxing. He was thinking not of the conservatory now but of Lyubka, deciding how to kiss her more masterfully, when he felt the eyes of someone behind him.

He realized suddenly that he was sitting all alone in the dark empty fields, surrounded by shadows that might, or might not, be bushes.

He remembered the cruel fear on Matvei's face in the end, the mute, deserted lake and the unexplained fire.

Holding his breath, he turned around slowly to look at the shed. The roof was suspended in midair, and he could see stars through the aperture. And just then the roof settled again and there was a patter of running feet behind the shed and a low droning "Oh-oh-oh!" faded into the distance. His hair standing on end, Zhukov jumped up and ran for the road.

Well, he thought, as he hit the road, I'm done for. The wind was whistling in his ears, the cold breathing down his back, and something cracked and snuffled in the bushes by the side of the road. Cross yourself! he thought, feeling cold fingers trying to grab him from behind. *Lord, in your hands . . .* He crossed himself, unable to run any farther, and stopped and turned around.

There was no one on the road or in the fields. He could no longer see the shed. Without taking his eyes off the road, he wiped his face on his sleeve and called out "Ha!" so shrilly that he startled himself. Then he coughed, listened, and called out again, trying not to let his voice tremble, "Ho! Hey!"

When he'd caught his breath, Zhukov moved on hurriedly, intensely aware of the distance he still had to go, aware of the night and the darkness around him, aware of the forest to which Matvei had pointed so mysteriously up ahead.

The road dipped down to the stream, and Zhukov took the bridge over the black, willow-clogged water in a couple of great leaps. There was a noise under the bridge but Zhukov couldn't figure out if it was real or imaginary. Just wait till I get you, Matvei, he thought as he climbed to the top of the hill where, he knew, the forest began.

The air became damp and dewy. From the heart of the forest a strong wind was blowing, bringing to the warm meadow air the smell of mold and mushrooms, of water and pine needles. On the right, in the forest, it was pitch-black. On the left, in the field, there was some light. Above, the stars were coming out; more light smoked across the sky, bringing the trees into sharp silhouette.

With a slight rustle an owl flew down from a branch somewhere in the darkness and settled again right in front of Zhukov. He heard the owl but didn't try to locate it. All he could see was the branch where the owl had been, blotting out the stars as it swayed.

He scared the owl a second time as he approached, and it began flying around in circles, out to the edge of the meadow and back into the gloom of the forest. The horizon behind the fields was still alight with the last of the sunset, or perhaps it was simply that there the sky was washed and clear, and against it the circling owl threw a dark, silent stain.

Watching the owl, he stumbled on a root, and his thoughts were unkind. He dared look neither into the forest on his right, nor behind. But when he looked ahead, a chill went down his spine: on the road up ahead, and a little to the left, the kabiasy had come out of the forest and were standing waiting for him. They were small, just as Matvei had said. One of them giggled, another made the same moan he'd heard earlier behind the shed, "Oh-oh-oh!" and a third cried out in a taunting singsong voice, "Come here, come here!"

Zhukov clamped his teeth together and froze. He couldn't raise his hand to cross himself.

"Ahhhhh!" his yell penetrated the entire forest before he realized suddenly that what he was seeing were baby fir trees. Step by step he went toward them, quivering like a dog in point. There was a rustle and a nervous screech in the field.

A bird! Zhukov straightened his shoulders and took an ecstatic breath. His shirt was wringing wet. Getting past the baby firs, he took out a cigarette and was going for his matches when he suddenly knew that if he lit a match he'd be seen. He didn't know by whom, and didn't want to know, but he knew he'd be seen.

Zhukov sat down, looked around and pulled his jacket up over his head to light his cigarette. I'm going into the field, he decided. He just couldn't take the forest road any longer. The field was bad enough, but not like this.

He scurried past the walnut trees at the edge of the forest and came out into the open. He walked along beside the forest, his head averted, generously avoiding all shadows on his path. The owl was still flying around, rustling and hooting, somewhere in the heart of the forest. The noise that came back, not quite a shriek, not quite a moan, hovered and rolled like an echo along the edge of the forest.

But the forest ended at last, and again the dusty moonlit road wound in front of him. Zhukov got onto the road and broke into a dead run, squealing in terror, his elbows tight to his sides like a professional runner. He ran, the air rushing in his ears, and the forest began to move farther and farther away until it was only a faintly visible dark line. Zhukov decided not to look back any more and was just beginning to feel good again and chant in monotonous rhythm with his running feet, "Ti-ta-ta! Ti-ta-ta!" when once again he was suddenly brought up sharp and staring.

What he had seen this time was not a tree and not a bird, he was accustomed to them, and it was something alive, moving in the roadside shrubbery. It didn't look like a man, nor a cow or a horse, it was indescribable. Zhukov distinctly heard a soft rustle and a gentle tapping in the tall grass.

"Who's there?" a loud voice rang out.

Zhukov didn't answer.

"Someone there, no?" The voice, now on the road, asked nervously.

Zhukov finally realized that there was a *man* coming toward him wheeling a bicycle and calling to him, but still he couldn't answer. He just started breathing again.

"Zhukov?" the man inquired uncertainly, coming up and looking right in his face. "Hey? Why didn't you answer? I couldn't imagine who it was. You have any matches? Here, have a cigarette."

Zhukov recognized Popov, of the regional Young Communist League. Zhukov's hands were shaking so hard that the matches rattled as he handed Popov the box.

"Where have you been?" asked Popov, lighting up. "You know, I got lost? I was coming to see you, and got to thinking and missed the turn. I got all the way to the road to Gorki — What's the matter?"

"Wait a minute," Zhukov croaked, feeling weak and dizzy. "Wait a minute."

He stood there, with a sheep-faced smile on his face, unable to shake his dizziness. He staggered and took a deep breath. There was the sharp smell of dusty weeds in the air.

"You sick or something?" Popov asked, frightened.

Zhukov nodded.

"Get on," Popov ordered, pointing to his bicycle. "Hold on to the handlebars."

Popov ran the bicycle forward jerkily, jumped on the seat, and blowing the hair out of his eyes, started pedaling hard for Dubka.

Zhukov sat on the handlebars, uncomfortable and embarrassed. He could feel how difficult the dusty road made pedaling. Popov was breathing hotly down his neck, stabbing him with his knees.

Almost the whole way they said nothing. When the lights of the collective farm finally appeared, Zhukov sighed and said, "All right, you can stop now."

"Stay on, stay on!" Popov gasped. "A bit farther and we'll be at the clinic."

"No, no, stop!" Zhukov grimaced and dragged his feet on the ground.

Popov put on the brakes with a sigh of relief. They got off and stood silently for a while, not knowing what to say. They were near the horse barn, and hearing voices, the horses got nervous and began shifting around noisily. A strong pleasant odor of tar and manure came from the barn.

"May I have a light?" Popov asked again. He lighted a cigarette and wiped the sweat from his face and neck, slapping his neck under the collar.

"Well," he asked hopefully, "feeling any better?"

"Much," Zhukov said quickly. "I drank some kvass. That was probably it."

They walked along slowly, listening to the sounds of daily life quieting down for the night.

"How are things at the club?" Popov asked.

"Not so bad. You know, harvest time, people are busy," Zhukov answered absently. "Say, do you know the word 'kabiasy'?"

"What? Kabiasy?" Popov thought. "Never came across it. Why? From a play or something?"

"Just came into my head," Zhukov answered evasively.

They shook hands at the club.

"Take the matches," said Zhukov. "I've more at home."

"All right." Popov took them. "And you drink some milk. It'll help your stomach."

He rode on to see the collective farm chairman, and Zhukov went through the dark passageway and unlocked the door to his room. He drank some cold tea, smoked a cigarette, listened to the radio for a while in the darkness. Then he opened the window and lay down.

He was almost asleep when it all came back to him. This time it was as if he were watching from above, from the hills: he could see the twilit fields, the deserted lake, the dark file of mast timber with upraised arms, the solitary campfire, and he listened to the whole tremendous expanse alive in the still of night.

And he began to relive the entire walk, only this time he was happy, in love with the night, the stars, the smells, the bird rustlings, the cries.

And again he wanted to talk to someone about culture, about higher things, about the eternal; he thought of Lyubka and, jumping up from his cot, he ran around barefoot getting dressed. Then he went out.

Fog

A HIGH shrill noise rang out in the fog. Somewhere in the distance someone was pounding on something metal and the sound came back round and reluctant: tiou, tiou, tiou.

"You hear that?" asked Kudriavtsev.

"Uh-huh," replied the agronomist. "It means we've come the right way. Let's have a cigarette."

Heaving a great sigh, he sat down, put his gun beside him, and rolled over on his side to get a cigarette from his back pocket.

Kudriavtsev, an engineer, had gone hunting with the local agronomist, but things had gone badly. They had stood at the evening duck flight for hours, staring into the west until their eyes ached, until almost dark, but they'd had no luck.

Then a heavy fog had come in and they had forced their way through the soaking underbrush, slogged and rustled their way through the swamp and had very nearly gotten completely lost.

Then when they heard the pounding so close by they both realized at once that the noise must be coming from the workshop at the edge of the collective farm. Feeling better, they sat down to smoke.

"Do you see any stars?" asked Kudriavtsev after a pause. He was nearsighted.

The agronomist raised his head and looked up. "No," he said presently, yawning and lying back. "It's a good healthy fog. But it should clear."

He lay back, his belly making a mound over his cartridge belt, cleared his nose and lit a cigarette, inhaling deeply from time to time.

Kudriavtsev had also been lying down, but suddenly he sat up, breathing hard, and slapped his thigh.

"What is it?" asked the agronomist.

"I don't know. All of a sudden everything seems wonderful." Kudriavtsev burst out laughing. "Are we going to have a drink later?"

"Definitely!" the agronomist sprang to life. "I was just thinking about that duck. I must have gotten it. It's a shame we couldn't find it. Did you see me get it?"

"No, all I could see was the splash of your struggle with the weeds," Kudriavtsev chortled.

"You never see anything. There were three of them, flying along the bank over the trees. I was within a hundred feet of them, two of them escaped and the third fell right into the reeds! If only we'd had a dog!"

The distant pounding rang out reassuringly in the fog, again and again. Kudriavtsev didn't say anything, overwhelmed by his unexpected and incomprehensible joy. Perhaps it's the fog, he thought vaguely. Or because we're out hunting. Or because of the pounding, it's always good to know there are people up and about, working nearby . . .

He thought of his wife, with whom, it seemed, he had quarreled for the last time. He had broken off with her completely, to the point of ceasing even to notice her. For days on end, he'd say nothing to her, going out at night to drink with the agronomist or the tractor drivers. One look at her resigned face and he was seized with anger, telling her things so awful that he shocked himself.

But that was all over now. Suddenly he wished to be kind himself, and that everyone around him be happy and nice to each other.

"Well, let's go," said the agronomist, standing up. "It's too bad we're going back empty-handed. It would have been nice to have a little duck as an appetizer."

"I feel good all the same," said Kudriavtsev, following the agronomist, eying his enormous shoulders.

Now that they were sure where they were going, they chatted

loudly about the summer, how hot it had been, the harvest on other collective farms, and suddenly they came out on the road.

The road was slick from yesterday's rain, the first rain in a long time. All summer it had been very hot. The wheat, the flax, clover and peas had all dried out. The still languor of drought had hung over everything, and the dust had been three inches deep on the roads.

It was now the end of August. Though the sun was actually less strong, it seemed even hotter. There was something feverish in the heat, something bitter and furtive and urgent, like Indian summer, though that was still a long way off.

The nights had become foggy, cold, and wet. The moon came up over the trees, big and red in the mist. But summer hung on, hot and dusty, until finally yesterday, a heavy freezing rain, and suddenly autumn was coming, the first yellow leaves appeared and the lonely overgrown roads turned a reddish brown.

Kudriavtsev had walked along this road three days earlier and the flax — a reddish color shot with chocolate-brown — had been rustling in the dry wind.

But today the flax had already been cut, and as they passed the birch and aspen grove, there was the smell of a hothouse, while the flax fields smelled of wet wash.

"Listen!" Kudriavtsev said to the agronomist's enormous shoulders. "I feel just like a young kid! I could leap off the ground! I listened to that pounding, the fog all around, I looked at you and watched you smoking, and I found something."

"What did you find?" Uncomprehending, the agronomist slowed down so they could walk side by side.

"Happiness I guess," Kudriavtsev said uncertainly, laughing at himself. "It's like autumn. In the most abominable weather there'll suddenly be a blue opening in the clouds and you look up at that pale blue sky and down at the puddles shining on the road, and you remember all the springtimes and all the happiness you've had!"

"Hmm," said the agronomist, thinking. "Living means remembering. I should have gone on looking . . ."

"What did you say?" Kudriavtsev hadn't heard.

"I say I should have gone on looking for that duck!"

The hunters walked on for a long time before they realized that that glowing flickering light up ahead was a campfire.

The campfire had been laid near the workshop. The tractor drivers were sitting around in their greasy clothes, throwing long shadows in every direction. There was a caterpillar tractor with a broken tread standing nearby, the tread rubbed to a glossy velvet by the swampy terrain. Three men were at work on it, one lying underneath it with only his feet showing, the other two, their shadows one, were working on the tread, hammering it together, only to have it fall apart again.

"Good work, boys. You need any help?" Kudriavtsev asked heartily, feeling himself go out to these men at work in the darkness.

"Who's that?" asked the one under the tractor, sticking his head out for a minute. "Oh, hi! No, another half hour's work and we've done it . . ." and his voice was muffled by the tractor.

"Have you gotten to the Kharitonovski section yet?" asked the agronomist, lighting a cigarette in the fire."

"Well, we started on schedule," someone answered after a while.

"Better watch out," the agronomist warned, "the representative of the regional committee is coming tomorrow night."

The hunters stood awhile, watching the fire, enjoying the smell of oil and metal, and then they went on. On the outskirts of the village, they lowered their guns and began to walk faster.

The feeling of happiness and joy was still with Kudriavtsev. His fatigue had gone and for some reason he kept thinking more and more tenderly about his wife. He decided to go home and make peace.

"You know what?" he said to the agronomist. "I'll go on home today, I just don't feel like drinking somehow."

"Hmm, suit yourself," said the agronomist, slightly surprised.

They were nearing the club and they could hear the scratchy music of the old-fashioned victrola. There was a bright light on on the porch.

"Shall we cross to the other side?" asked Kudriavtsev.

"There's light enough here," growled the agronomist, pulling down his cap and stumbling a little as he walked.

There were couples sitting on benches and standing by the fence near the club. None of them were talking for some reason, listening to the music perhaps, and they turned to watch the hunters approach.

"Did you kill anything, comrade agronomist?" someone called out raucously.

"Just his feet," answered another and everyone laughed.

"As if you'd ever killed a flea," said the agronomist after a while, huffing in embarrassment.

The friends parted abruptly at Kudriavtsev's house. The agronomist turned to Kudriavtsev. "So you're not coming over?"

"No, I'm going home," said Kudriavtsev.

"Well, see you then."

Kudriavtsev stood on the porch smoking, scraping his feet on the step. His gun shoulder was sore, but his body felt light.

Happiness, he thought, why happiness all of a sudden?

When you're in love, yes, or lucky or successful, when your work and everything else is going well, then it's not surprising. But for no reason, at the most hopeless, Godforsaken moments, your heart suddenly begins to pound and you know it'll be a long time before you'll forget this day. Akh, what a lovely night, how good to be alive!

"Zoya!" he called out to his wife, "come here!"

And while he was waiting for his wife to find something, gently shuffling around inside, waiting for her to open the door and come out, he stood drawing in the coolness of the fog and the strong sharp odor of the herb leaves, listening to the distant music at the club, thinking about the men working on the tractor in the glow of the campfire.

"Look at this fog," he said to his wife, putting his hand on her shoulder. "Do you see any stars?"

For some reason he wanted to see the stars.

Antler House

SHE has already been living several days in a rest home on the seashore. She came after a long illness and for the first three days didn't go out at all, but sat on the cold echoing veranda, gloomily watching the squirrels leaping around in the pine trees.

It's the fourth day and she wakes up early, when the half light of a lazy spring dawn is still outside her window. She dresses and goes out on the porch and begins to grow ruddy from the cold, the smell of March snow, from the sight of the pine-covered hills, and from the freshness and silence of morning. Stepping out carefully onto the road which thawed yesterday and froze again last night, she takes a few steps, balancing with her arms. The ice crunches and crackles under her feet, and the sound, loud and wet, reminds her of something long since forgotten, something achingly sweet and secret. Without looking around she walks on farther from the rest home, climbing into the hills, where she can see the freezing ocean with its dark line of unfrozen water along the horizon, where she can watch it gradually grow light all around, until the sun is fully up at last, still weak and white and dim. She returns, smelling of the cold, and when she goes to breakfast, she exchanges greetings with the others, and then bends her head to hide a smile, to hide her dazzled eyes.

She's moody like all convalescents, and her happy moods are especially poignant because she is sixteen years old, because her eyes are dark and limpid and enigmatic, because she's alone and free, and her imagination naïve and romantic. And because everything around her seems extraordinary and fantastic.

Every morning she goes into ecstasy over the announcer's deep jolly voice on the loudspeaker: *"Rune Riga! Pareis Laiks!"* Every morning, her heels crunching in her own tracks from yesterday, she walks toward the hills, stretching out occasionally, her thin face upturned, for a willow branch to take home and put in a vase. Every morning she goes a bit farther into the pine woods, until she finally comes out on the sea. Terrified, she walks way out on the ice and stops finally, not daring to breathe or move, feeling the ice rock beneath her.

Then she goes back, gazing curiously and thoughtfully at the empty houses in the woods, which are boarded up for the winter. For some inexplicable reason they make her feel gay and at the same time terrified, as if she were entering the fantastic world of the fairy tales which she still reads in secret. She has made no friends at the rest home. She just says hello in a polite little voice, sitting on the edge of her chair like a schoolgirl, blushing, confused, and afraid to look the person with whom she is speaking in the face.

She is getting to like her solitude, her freedom, and her walks so much that she's afraid even to think of the time when she'll have to leave. The more she cuts herself off, the more grown up and stern she wants to seem, the more apparent it is that she's just a young girl.

One day she met a young man on skis. He slowed down to a stop and watched her with great interest but she hurried past, staring fixedly at her feet. He has come often since that day, skiing down out of the hills and looking around for her, but he has never run across her again.

There are houses standing in the woods, each one prettier than the last. When the sun is shining, the fences and trees have blue-green shadows, the squirrels leap from pine tree to pine tree, and yellow-green moss covers the concrete fence posts. At night the church bell tolls slowly, there's the occasional two-toned whistle of the electric train, the rest home creaks, ice rustles in the drainpipe and the roar of the sea can be heard in the distance. The smell of the dry snow, the pine bark and the linden buds is sharp and biting. Every evening the sunset is longer and more crystalline, the sky colder and deeper, the stars in the east bluer and clearer. And when the sunset dies out, going yellow, then green, then lilac, the tree trunks, the houses with their empty verandas, and the cross on the church all seem black by contrast.

At night the girl flies over the hills in her dreams, hearing distant music, her heart aching with fear and ecstasy. She wakes up with a light dizzy feeling and makes a serious effort to understand what is happening to her. But what is happening to her is too extraordinary, too totally incomprehensible. She almost never answers her letters. She's in love with the lonely pine forests, the distant music, the solitude. She loves the desertion, the silence, the quiet sunny clearings, the red willows, the silver-gray Canadian elms, the gloomy stone grottos in the hills.

In the evening, they light a fire in the fireplace in the living room of the rest home. The birch logs crackle, crimson shadows dance on the walls and the ancient furniture, there is a slight smoky smell, and the large frozen windows that face west are bright with light.

This is the moment she has been waiting for, and she tiptoes into the living room, settles herself in an armchair and stares into the fire, her enormous eyes sparkling. Sometimes, looking back at the windows and listening to the conversation at the far table, she goes over to the walnut piano and opens it. The piano keys are stiff and cold and dark with age. Pressing down the squeaky pedal, she timidly strikes a note. She'd like to remember the music she heard in her dream. She picks out a chord, her fingers growing cold, and shivers. It seems that might be it . . . But no, not right, not it, not even close. Carefully closing the piano, breathing in the smell of dark varnish that still remains here and there, she goes back and curls up again in the armchair. Once more she stares absently into the fire, listening to the crackle, enjoying the homey, strangely melancholy smell of birch smoke. What's the matter with me? she wonders. Why am I in pain? And why is the pain so sweet?

Eventually one of the empty houses catches her attention. It stands under the trees on a large plot of land, nearly hidden by its fence. The doors have been hammered shut and the windows are shuttered. It has a dark tiled roof, high and pointed, and the porch and steps are covered with snow, all except the top step where the snow has melted. Polished brown antlers are nailed just under the second floor window, which is not shuttered for some reason . . . It and the veranda windows below palely reflect the sunset. The snow surrounding the house is unbroken and clean, making the clearing seem especially large and especially remote. The fence is tall and solid, except for some broken slats in one place where dogs have dug a hole. The deep clear dogtracks run toward the thick-trunked pine tree and from there they fan out toward the back of the clearing.

Antler House — that's what the girl calls the house and its clearing. And now she goes nowhere else but Antler House, delighting in the discovery of her own footprints from yesterday, convinced that no one else has ever been there. She finds a stump to sit on, and tucking her coat around her knees, she falls into a trance.

She's thinking about the house. She can picture its empty, echoing, shadowy rooms, the silence at night when the thin moonbeams force their way through the shutters.

But the clearing is brilliant with light. The sun is baking down so hard that the sap runs down the sunny side of the pines, and the willows are sweating, standing in dark, melted pools, and their supple dark gray branches are already in bloom.

2

It happens on an especially warm and fragrant spring day, when she's feeling especially lightheaded, dizzy, and heavy-hearted; suddenly the girl gasps, covers her mouth with her hands and gapes at the house. Up on the second floor the window has opened and a little man is looking out!

He sits on the ledge, feeling around for the antlers and takes a firm hold with his feet. Then a long rope ladder is pushed through the window. The little man grabs it and climbs down on the porch. Another little man follows. They must be trolls, she guesses with a shiver of sweet terror. Magic dwarves! They live in a spellbound house! Crouching down, her mouth gaping, her eyes aglow, she watches.

They are dressed in old-fashioned clothing: long stockings, short pants, lilac-colored vests, and red-tasseled caps. They are both bearded and pompous-looking and they are both smoking old-fashioned Dutch pipes. They sit down side by side on the warm and dry top step, their legs dangling, and silently lift their faces to the sun. From one mouth and greenish beard, and then from the other, come puffs of smoke.

The smoke wafts in the hiding girl's direction and in it there is the unfamiliar odor of the South, the fragrance of the tropics. She breathes deeply, again and again. The air trembles and sings, there are rustling sounds heard on every side, and clumps of snow fall from the pines and firs. Suddenly the trolls get up, very business-like, and follow each other across the bluish snow to the willow tree. There they stand sniffing for a long time, and then they dig up some little roots and bringing them right up to their eyes, examine them closely. Then they wipe off their hands and start playing together, throwing willow buds at each other, running around at an unhurried, dignified pace, never dropping their pipes from their mouths, their faces never losing their thoughtful pompousness. When they finish their game, they go back to the porch, climb the ladder to the window and pull it in after them. The window slams shut and once again the house seems to be empty.

Scarcely breathing, feeling pleasantly faint, stupefied by the sun and the trolls' smoke, quiet, tight-lipped, the girl goes home, more than anything afraid that they will know from her face that something has happened to her and will try to find out by asking questions. The whole day she's not herself, and her eyes are quite wild-looking. She's tormented by doubts, she can't believe what she saw, and she can hardly wait for nightfall.

She goes to bed that night fully clothed, and lies awake thinking about the trolls. She's already sure that something magical and inconceivably fine must be happening to her. She can't sleep, her forehead is hot and her lips are dry and cracked. The church clock strikes, the rest home is still, but she seems to hear someone going from room to room, from window to window, and testing the piano keys in the living room.

Exhausted finally by fear, nerves, and chills of ecstasy, she gets up, and stands listening, her eyes darting around frantically. She goes out on the porch, and the silence, the clear blue stars and the smell of snow seem as sharp and painful as they were the very first time she went out.

Breathlessly she runs through the park and the village, past the sleeping houses, the shuttered stores, under the lampposts, her heels clattering on the flagstones. Then at last she turns toward the sea, the woods, and Antler House.

The lampposts are behind her and suddenly it's dark, everything around her turns dense and blue, the black pines and firs move in on the road, and the moon comes out. Deep shadows lie by the fence, and the snow glistens as if it were steaming.

She approaches Antler House on tiptoe, peering between the branches of the dark, dense trees. Her heart stops and she catches her breath: there is a faint light coming between the shutters. As in a dream she moves along the fence to the broken slats, drops to her knees and crawls through. She takes a few giant steps along the path made by the dogs and then turns toward the house. The dry, tightly packed snow crunches under her feet, with a sound like a watermelon being opened.

She stops as she approaches the house. There is a light on inside, a thin wisp of smoke climbing from the chimney, and faint shadows moving across the snow. Inside they are playing a flute and a stringed instrument she has never heard before. The sweet hollow sound of the flute, then a soft chord sung out by the strings, and they are playing a slow and graceful ancient melody. But that was the same music she'd been hearing in her dreams! And suddenly she recognizes everything from these enchanting dreams, she remembers flying here, leaping from hill to hill, floating through the pines, through the smoky rays of the moon, remembers hearing this fantastic and beautiful music . . . Who was playing it now?

Trying not to make any noise, she goes closer and through the shutters she can see a flickering orange light throwing weird shadows down from the ceiling. Her hand clenched tightly to her heart, she looks inside.

There is a ruby blaze in the great fireplace, and a rough-hewn table and tall clumsy chairs to match standing in the middle of the room. On the table there's a small wine cask, some pewter mugs, and a round cheese. The trolls are sitting around the table. There are a lot of them, and they're all bearded, with mock-serious, pompous expressions. They're sitting around, drinking, eating, playing cards and smoking. Others, with equally pompous expressions, are sitting on stumps near the fire. The oldest of them, his hat over his eyes, is playing the flute, leaning to one side, his fingers crooked sharply; the rest are gravely picking at the strings of their lutelike instruments. Only the faces of the dancers have any animation. Their dancing is old-fashioned, with rounded, fluid movements, and graceful, deferential bows. The room is filled with smoke and illuminated by narrow red candles in copper candlesticks. What does it mean? the girl wonders. What is this enchanted house? What will happen if I go in?

She turns away from the window, climbs the porch, and tries the door. To her astonishment, the door gives, and the music becomes louder and more distinct. The house itself seems to be playing the music, the old beams singing, the furniture dancing.

The girl crosses the veranda with its colored glass windows, feels her way along the corridor, and timidly opens the door where the trolls are. Immediately the fire dies on the hearth, the music breaks off, trembling in mid-air, the dancers come to a halt. The trolls give her a wild, menacing look. She wants to say something friendly and wonderful to them. She moves her lips, but she can't say anything, or bring out a single sound. Her eyes sparkle, she blushes in embarrassment, curiosity, and joy, everything in her going out to them. And all at once they relax again.

But the secret of their lives has been violated. They get up, collect their cards and clear the table for her, put out the candles and the fire, and open the trapdoor in the floor. Then they each make a slow, serious bow to their uninvited guest and descend through the trap.

There's just one troll left, the oldest, most pompous and ugliest one, and she looks at him, questioningly and pleadingly, waiting for him to say something to her. But he doesn't say anything. He just goes to the trapdoor with the last candle in his hand and starts to descend. At the last minute he turns and fixes her with a look. In his look there is hidden goodness, and the promise of something wonderful and extraordinary to come. He is telling her something with his eyes, with his face full of the wisdom of a thousand years, telling her of his prophetic knowledge of the sorrow and joy of life, but she doesn't understand. He puts his finger to his lips, gives her a meaningful nod, blows out the candle and drops the door shut over his head.

She barely makes it to the porch and sits in the darkness on the steps. Why didn't he say anything? she thinks bitterly. Oh, that's right, they can't talk to us. But he wanted to, I could see that.

Suddenly feeling something behind her, she turns and sees the old troll again. He's looking at her with the same thoughtful benevolence, and his face in the moonlight is even fuller of hidden meaning, wisdom, and prophecy. But he's so little and frail that she has the urge to smooth his beard and straighten his cap. He nods to her silently, and jumps down the steps; then he turns and beckons to her. She gets up and follows him obediently. He goes to the window where she first peeked in at the troll's party through the shutter, and points. Frozen with presentiment, she looks through the slat and cries out.

Instead of a room, she sees a sunny day, the hills, the lush pines, and the skier, gliding silently from hill to hill. She sees his flushed, resolute face, his strong, thin body. She sees him fling out his skis and bring his poles down sharply in the snow.

When at length she turns back to the troll, he's no longer there. Silence and bright moonlight all around her. The emerald stars raise their shaggy eyelashes and blink, and caps of snow hanging on in the moonlight by a powdery feather fall from the pines and the firs.

3

She wakes up late the next day, when the sun is already beating through the window and lying in pale yellow squares on the floor. The new day, the voice over the loudspeaker — *"Rune Riga!"* — the fresh cold air coming in through the vent, the smell of coffee, the warmth of the house, all strike her as unspeakably wonderful. All morning long she sings and dances when no one is watching, in imitation of the trolls, falling face down on her pillow at each onset of uncontrollable laughter.

At noon, unable to wait any longer, she goes to Antler House, but is afraid to look or even turn her head in its direction. She thinks the trolls will get mad at her if they see her there. Uncertainly, she whisks the morning's new snow from a stump with her red mitten and sits down, taking several deep breaths to gather courage. Then she raises her eyes to the house.

There is no one there. The shutters are closed, the antlers shining dully in the sun, and the window on the second floor is closed. The trolls aren't there! She looks around for last night's tracks, but there are none to be seen, and her heart aches with bitter disappointment. Did it mean she hadn't been here?

She jumps up, runs toward the fence, through the hole, and bends down scanning the blindingly smooth snow. She touches it — no, nothing. Only the frozen dogtracks toward the pines. She goes to the house and walks around it. She tries the door. She finds the window the troll had pointed out and looks for a loose slat, but the shutters are tight and the door boarded up. There are no tracks anywhere, or any trolls, or music or candles or blazing fireplace. For the first time she feels sick and unbearably alone. She cries, wiping the tears with her mittens.

The skier appears in the pine trees, rushing headlong downhill, raising a fine dust of snow, coming up another, going down again. Breasting the third hill, he comes out on the rising and falling sea.

She recognizes him at once and hides behind a corner of the house, watching him and sobbing. No longer sure of anything, she wipes away her tears when he's gone and goes to see if he has left any tracks.

Climbing the hill, the snow collecting in her boots, she sees the soft deep track of the skis and the sharp round pole marks. She turns back in astonishment and recognizes everything the troll had showed her: the fine March day, the blue fir trees, the dark green pines, the sea, and she becomes ecstatic; she can believe in miracles, dreams and fairy tales again. She smiles and raises her rosy face, opens her throat, raises her wet lashes and cries, "Ay-a-hoy!" and listens in ecstasy to the sharp clear echo.

Hearing the triumphant cry, the skier digs his poles in and stops. He turns his flushed face back to look, not expecting to see anything. Then he throws his skis around, scattering the snow, and races back along his own track.

But she's hidden in the pines, heart pounding, waiting and listening for an answer. In her red cap almost like the trolls', her coat open, her thin neck bare, she's happy, her eyes large and dark, her face glowing.

What answer does she expect from the pines, the sea, the spring? Why does she dream of music, why does she fly in her dreams? Why was it so staggeringly important to her what the troll would say? Why does she look that way, why that smile with which she meets each new day, why is she so passionately and confidently waiting for something?

And who will find her, who will guess what she's waiting for?

Teddy
(The Tale of a Bear)

THE big brown bear was called Teddy. All the other animals had names too but Teddy just couldn't remember them, and he always mixed them up. But he was sure of his own name and always came if he was called and did what he was told.

His life was monotonous. He worked in a circus, and had worked so long that he'd lost count of the days. He was usually kept in a cage although he'd been tame so long a cage wasn't necessary. He'd become indifferent to everything, interested in nothing, and only wanted to be left in peace. But he was an old and experienced artist and they didn't leave him in peace.

In the evening they let him out into the brightly lighted ring where a tall man with a powdered face was slowly strutting around in the middle. The man wore white pantaloons, soft black boots, and a purple jacket decorated with gold braid. The pantaloons, the jacket, and the pale, indifferent face always made a great impression on Teddy. He feared those eyes more than anything.

Back in the days of his youth Teddy had several times raised a wild, frightful rumpus. He'd howled, rattled the bars of his cage, and couldn't be calmed by even the harshest measures. But then the man with the pale face had come, stood near the cage and looked at Teddy, and each time Teddy had quieted down under his gaze and within an hour allowed himself to be taken to rehearsal.

Now Teddy wasn't rebellious any more, and he performed obediently all manner of awkward, unnecessary, often even unpleasant tricks. The man in the white pantaloons no longer terrified him with a look, and whenever he spoke of the bear, he spoke with great tenderness in his voice, and he never called him anything but "good old Teddy."

Teddy came into the ring in a leather muzzle, and bowed to the spectators, who responded with noises of delight. He was given a bicycle. Putting his paw on the saddle, he pushed off and then taking firm hold of the handlebars and coming down on the pedals, he circled round the ring. The music played loudly and the spectators laughed and clapped.

He knew how to do several other amusing tricks: dance on big balls on all fours, climb up and balance on a narrow metal plank, wear boxing gloves on his front paws and box with another bear. Teddy lacked a sense of humor, or more accurately, his animal's sense of humor was different, and he couldn't understand why those people were so happy when, with great distaste, he performed his awkward, unpleasant tricks.

He often didn't sleep at night. In the corridor a small lamp burned dimly and the old watchman who always smelled so good snored loudly. The animals growled and squealed in their sleep. The strong odor of animals came from all the cages. The corners were dark. Great impudent rats ran about and sat up on their haunches, throwing long shadows across the cage.

After tossing around and thinking for a while, Teddy would begin to occupy himself with his toilet. Slowly and carefully he'd go over his paws and stomach and when they were completely wet and sticky, he'd begin on his side and back. But it was hard to get at his back, so he'd soon grow tired of it and give himself up to melancholy musings.

He could remember his mother, a beautiful bear with soft paws and a long warm tongue. But he remembered almost nothing of his childhood, only a small stream with sandy yellow banks: the sand was fine and warm. He recalled the sharp sweet smell of ants, which he had yet to taste.

He also recalled the tasty meals they sometimes gave them in the circus. A little donkey had gotten sick once and groaned all night in his stall and finally stopped in the morning. Then stern-looking people had come and taken the dead donkey away. That evening they hadn't given Teddy his usual oatmeal, but a whole basin of fragrant boiled meat, and the next day had been a holiday.

He thought about a lot of other things. Sometimes his visions would fill him with anger and bitterness and he'd feel like growling and going somewhere and doing something of his own, like an animal. All night he'd breathe hard, and the next day he'd be especially sluggish and gloomy, and he'd go to rehearsal unwillingly.

2

One day, the circus went somewhere far away by train. Teddy went too. He'd traveled so much in his day that he wasn't surprised by anything. He just hated the way the trucks smelled of gas.

Everything took place as usual. At the station they'd loaded the animal cages onto the train, shouting, swearing, hammering, and there was a great deal of noise. Finally they clapped the doors shut, and they were rocking and swaying along, and all the animals felt like sleeping. Two days they rocked and swayed, and then everything was quiet. When they opened the doors, and unloaded the cages from the train and reloaded them onto trucks, everything around looked and smelled different, but that didn't surprise Teddy.

It was decided the animals should be fed before going any farther. An attendant came and cleaned the cages, and then he brought food. Shoving Teddy's boiled potatoes, bread and basin of oatmeal into the cage, the attendant was distracted by something and went off, forgetting to close the cage.

Without noticing the open door, the bear greedily ate his potatoes and oatmeal, grunting a little he was so hungry. When he finished, he cleaned up and started pushing the dish toward the door as was his habit and only then did he notice that it wasn't closed. Very surprised, he stuck his head out and looked this way and that. Then he yawned, backed up, lay down and closed his eyes. But a minute later he got up and stuck his head out again. He sniffed and looked as if he were trying to remember something. Then he thought a minute, stuck his head out again and jumped to the ground. He stretched luxuriously and began to wander curiously around the truck.

The driver was coming toward the truck, holding his cap under his arm, and eating something. The wind was coming from his direction and Teddy caught the scent of sausage and went toward the driver. Seeing the bear, the driver stopped eating and froze in his tracks. Teddy got up on his hind legs and turned around appealingly. The driver dropped his cap, turned, and ran for a long low building with some kind of sign on the door.

"Help! Help!" he screeched in terror.

Teddy got down and retired to the sidelines. He had even turned to get back in his old cage when people started pouring out of the building, yelling wildly. Teddy turned in bewilderment, looking for a familiar face, but there wasn't one. Teddy became frightened and ran. He tore past the horse van. Seeing him, the horses shied and whinnied. Teddy roared back and went on.

He ran through a kitchen garden, jumped a fence, crossed a field, and ran toward the woods. He ran fast, his ears back, snorting and experiencing a sharp, unfamiliar feeling of pleasure. He was out of breath when he reached the underbrush, so he stopped and looked around in terror: there was no station, people or trucks to be seen, only the naked field and the roofs darkening in the distance.

The bear began to miss the circus, and he wanted to be back in his dark cage, listening to the snores of the good-smelling watchman. But he was afraid to go back, so with a low growl, he got up on his hind paws and rocked back and forth.

Then he turned and looked at the forest, snorted several times to clear his nose, and sniffed. There was the sweet smell of pitch and mushrooms and many other exciting things. Teddy went toward the forest. He walked slowly through the brush, looking around at every clearing in hopes of seeing an attendant or the man in the white pantaloons calling to him gently, "Teddy!" But no one appeared, no one called him, it was still. The powerful call of the forest grew more and more distinct. With a feeling mixed of fear and curiosity, Teddy entered the forest.

3

Teddy was unlucky. He landed in a part of the forest where people had been. The lumber industry had been there, cutting down great areas, and everywhere the eye was struck by unpleasant things: a pile of scraps of narrow-gauge cable, greasy rags, much-trampled roads and echoing boardwalks. There were almost no birds or animals in the place and sounds could be heard at night inimicable to the forest and silence: the sound of motors, pounding metal, the thin hoot of a steam engine.

The forest was wild and unfamiliar to Teddy and his first impulse was to find some people. But at the same time something kept him from going in the direction of the motors. He was exasperated, he hadn't eaten, had almost no sleep, and he was very thin. Several times he tried going through all the tricks he had ever learned, in the hopes that someone would come and feed him.

He circled the clearing on his front paws, waving his back paws as if he were balancing a ball. Then he did a somersault, danced, played dead and got up quite pleased with himself. He looked around, expecting his reward. But there was no one to be delighted and praise him, his oatmeal didn't magically appear, and the bear's small eyes filled with pained astonishment. Desperate finally, he turned from the incomprehensible forest world to the human world, but there something happened that hardened his fear of man.

One morning, wet with dew, Teddy was sulkily scouring the ravine looking for weeds he could eat. Raising his head, he was suddenly confronted by the gaze of a man standing over him. Surprised, Teddy started to get up on his hind legs. He grunted with joy. But the man wasn't overjoyed and didn't call "Teddy!" as the bear expected. The man blanched, grabbed his gun from his shoulder, and raised it. There was a flash of fire, a sharp clap of thunder, and something lashed painfully across Teddy's ears. He bellowed, rolled on his back, and waved his paws. His was a roar of pain and shame and surprise. Having done this wicked thing, the man turned and ran, and over the sound of his own roars, Teddy could hear the quick thud of his feet and the racket he made as he ran.

After a minute or so Teddy was overcome by a violent rage and tore after the man, but he had managed to hide so Teddy didn't find him. From that moment on, Teddy was afraid of people, and he was more determined than ever to find someplace remote and deserted.

But in order to get into the heart of the real forest, the bear had to cross a river, and he didn't know how. His situation was becoming desperate. Several times he went down to the river and watched the logs floating by on the water, felt sorry for himself, and then went back into the forest.

4

So two days and two nights went by. The third night Teddy went down to the river again and stopped in amazement: a big raft with cabin was moored to the bank. A bright moon was shining, and there were white barracks with dark windows standing along the shore. There was no one around, not a sound to be heard except the water murmuring sleepily around the floating logs. Teddy got up on his hind legs and sniffed. From the cabin on the raft came a tantalizing odor of bread and potatoes. Teddy licked his lips and danced on his hind legs. As he was dancing, he weighed his alternatives.

He was afraid of going where the smell of food was since he knew there'd be people whom he hated and who would hate him. His painful ears hadn't let him forget about that. But the temptation was so great that the bear went down to the shore just opposite the raft, as it happened, and tested the water with his paw. Oh it smelled wonderful!

The raft was connected to the shore by a gangplank, but Teddy didn't even see it. Impatiently he threw himself into the water and right up on the raft. Unsure of his footing on the logs, Teddy crossed to the cabin and walked around it. A loud snore was issuing from within, and remembering the circus watchman, Teddy took heart. He looked inside and saw nothing. He shoved the door open and the instant he had squeezed through, he swallowed a gush of sweet saliva — the smell of dirty socks and bread and potatoes was so good. The bread and potatoes were on the table. Teddy went to it, removed the warm steamy plate from the iron pot, tipped it up and started right in, growling and gulping down bread simultaneously.

"Hey!" The man on the bunk stopped snoring and suddenly shouted. "Who's that? That you, Fedya?"

The bear was so frightened he sat down. Then he got angry and beat his paw on the table, growling. The pot and the plate fell to the floor. Then something bearing no resemblance to a man came down off the bunk and whisked past him on all fours, through the door, along the gangplank to shore.

Teddy realized this meant trouble, but went on hurriedly eating, chewing, snarling, his saliva dribbling to the floor, knowing all the while that he was committing a crime against man.

When the bear had eaten the last piece of bread, a loud noise was heard on shore. He knew he must leave but he was still hungry and there were still several potatoes lying on the floor that he grabbed before making for the door. Squeezing his way out, he saw a lot of people coming. Seeing the bear, they all shouted, just as at the station, and Teddy stopped in confusion: he was cut off from shore.

He was going to jump over the side and skirt around the edge of the raft, but he was intercepted by a protracted flash of light. A shot rang out. Startled, the bear turned back toward the cabin. the people ran after him and circled him into a corner. Another shot skimmed the bark off the floating logs and lashed Teddy in the stomach. Roaring, he took a leap and splashed into the water, raising a silver spray in the moonlight. He had never swum in his life and his head went under. He surfaced, not knowing what to do, but his paws began to move of their own volition. He paddled with all his might, pushing his nose up out of the water toward the stars, the water buoying him slightly. The people on the raft were still shouting at him and he paddled harder, sneezing, panting, shoving his nose out of the water.

He swam for half an hour in the warm silver water. Then quite nearby he saw the forest — dense and dark. It was not the same stretch of forest from which the bear had just come. It was a stretch of forest without clearings, without the lumber industry, without human habitation.

Feeling bottom, Teddy slowly dragged himself onto shore. Water streamed from his coat. Looking far upriver he could make out some faint lights, barely whitening the darkness, and he understood that that was where the people and the barracks and the raft were; he understood further that it was dangerous and noisy there, but here it was quiet and good. Remembering the shots and the potatoes lying on the cabin floor, he growled, shook himself off thoroughly, and climbed the steep hill toward the still and enormous pine trees.

5

The forest was vast, stretching five miles along the river. To the east it ran all the way to the Urals, to the north, all the way to the tundra, climbing into the hills, spreading around lakes and fields, around occasional villages and cabins. It was a remote section, rarely visited by people, so there was real freedom for the animals and birds.

There were many wolves and foxes here, squirrels, rabbits, elk, and yellow-eyed, enigmatic lynx. There were spots so densely overgrown that they were impossible to reach, where trees had fallen and lain for years gradually turning gray and rotting.

There were fires here, started by unknown causes, seemingly spontaneously. They would come in waves, raging over enormous areas, burning trees and grass and killing thousands of animals, and then gradually die out, also seemingly spontaneously, leaving black coals and ash and scorched trunks in their wake.

Soon afterwards coarse red grass would begin to grow over the burned area, wild strawberries and cranberries would appear, and then new birches and pines. Then the sweetbriar and the raspberries would come up around the rim of the forest and the burned area would no longer be a strange and frightening place to the animals, but an inexhaustible pantry for the dusky little wood grouse, the timid hazel grouse and the black grouse. Elk would come too, leaving deep tracks in the soft white moss.

Life in the forest seethed on, undarkened by the presence of man. True, there was a continual struggle going on, under the rule of fang and claw, and the nooks and crannies of the beautiful place were littered with bones and feathers. But a dangerous struggle here was not a hopeless struggle, as it is with man.

Only very rarely did the sound of a shot ring out, and when it did, it echoed in the hills a long time, flying over the river, reverberating against the other bank, and returning, faint and drawn out. Then the squirrels would drop their pine cones and scamper to the tops of trees so they could look on in unlimited curiosity; the rabbits froze on their haunches; the elk pricked up their ears to listen and moved off quietly to another place; the lynx, drowsing in the thicket, would half open his sleepy yellow eyes and shake the branches nervously from his ears; only the wolves, best of all acquainted with man, would drop everything and streak for the hills, casting gray shadows as they ran, sniffing in terror, trying to locate the hated smell of man.

6

All night long Teddy headed north, clinging to the riverbank as the sailor clings to his compass. He was afraid to plunge into the forest, since the forest was filled with the unknown, while the river was a friend that had saved him once, and he trusted it. Sounds and smells were coming at him from all sides, and he had to learn what they were. Twice he crossed paths with a lynx, and he remembered the circus lynx, although it had had a sharper odor: captured animals always have a stronger odor. Then he frightened some hazel grouse spending the night on the lower branches of a large fir tree, who frightened him in turn, but he relaxed the minute he realized they were just birds. He also recognized fox tracks immediately.

But finally the abundance of new impressions which had kept him continually on guard so exhausted the bear that he chose a dry place in the overgrown hollow of a small fir tree, lay down, and slept until morning.

Strange how completely helpless this large beast was in the forest. Over the many years he'd been away from the forest he had forgotten the little he'd managed to learn as a cub. All the instincts given to him by nature were dormant, and he was confused by anything demanding the least kind of decision on his part. Accustomed to lots of satisfying food, his stomach was empty and painful; he was hungry all the time. The attendants who had fed him in the circus weren't there; he had to search for his own food, but he didn't know how this was done or what he should eat.

Probably no one knows what mother means as well as the wild animals. The mother teaches her young how to hide, fight, run. She explains who is an enemy, and who a friend. She knows where to find the berries and ants, the strawberries, tasty succulent roots, the mouse holes, the fish and the frogs. She knows where the fresh water is, the safe places, the sunny clearings where the tall soft grass grows. The secrets of scents and migrations are open to her. And she knows, finally, that no forest animal ever reaches a grand old age, that something frightful will befall all of them, that each must be deft and daring and clever in order to protect himself and his children after him as long as possible.

If Teddy hadn't grown up first in a zoo, and later in the circus, among people, if his teacher in life had been a she-bear fierce to the world but infinitely kind to her young, then he'd have been a powerful brute, knowing everything that wild brutes should know. But Teddy had learned about life from the man in the white pantaloons; his indomitable brute spirits had been crushed since childhood. He had managed to learn many things too difficult and too frightening for the denizens of the forest: he was certainly more experienced and wiser than any of his fellows in the city, but what was all his worldly knowledge worth where he'd gotten to now? In the forest he was just a pitiful helpless cub again, knowing nothing, afraid of everything. The only difference was that he was no longer a bit of a cub, but a huge bear with yellow fangs and a bald patch on his behind from living in a cage, with no wise, good mother to protect and teach him.

7

The birds awakened Teddy, although the small things were just barely audible, fluttering in the dew-wet branches. The sun was coming up behind the hills far to the east. A clear mist hung in the pine trees, the dew glistened and the air was fresh and clean. Coming out of his refuge for the night, Teddy hobbled on farther to the north. On the second day, unused to wandering in the forest, his paws were aching, but he went right on, as if he were trying to get away from something he didn't like. Without thinking about it, he headed north, just as birds collect into flocks for the migration without thinking about it. His instincts took him into unknown territory, but where there'd be lots of sun and food, fresh water and silence.

The bear was crossing a sunny clearing at noon when his nose discovered an unusual smell that stirred up a swarm of memories in him. What was the source of that nice sweet smell? Going on, Teddy turned east and the smell disappeared. He turned back, disturbed and excited: again the alluring smell! Teddy circled, taking his time, looking for an anthill. The smell, which he had recognized after so many years, was the smell of ants.

The ants were delightful. Is there anything as delicious, fat, sweet, tickling, that arouses and satisfies both the thirst and the appetite? He could eat endlessly!

Teddy stuck his nose in the anthill and the wonderful smell was so strong he grunted with pleasure. Closing his eyes, he went in deeper, stuck out his wet tongue and took a mouthful. In an instant the big red ants were all over his muzzle and climbing in his ears, but Teddy just shook his head, put his tail between his legs and took another great mouthful. Finally it became unbearable and he sat on his haunches to catch his breath. Just then he remembered something he'd forgotten and he plunged his paw into the anthill. Immediately the ants were all over his paw and all he had to do was lick them off. This was incomparably more comfortable. He was no longer getting ants in his nose and ears and dirt and pine needles in his mouth. When Teddy left the anthill there was nothing left.

Teddy turned and moved on. He climbed a broad hill covered with dead fir trees, their tops naked, and descended into a ravine where he discovered a raspberry patch that he didn't leave until evening.

Teddy was frightened at first by the sounds of the forest, by the hazel grouse and the wood grouse, by the flash of fish in small ponds, by the crash of passing elk. Slight strange smells, sharp and unfamiliar, frightened him. But he conquered his fear and followed out all sounds and smells so that he'd know next time whether it was something to be tracked down, or avoided, or generally ignored.

There was one happy fact about his life now that he couldn't

have predicted: he didn't have to be afraid of anything but
man. He wasn't afraid of any of the terrible creatures that are the
bane of the small animals and birds — the wolves, the lynx, the
weasels. No one bothered him. He didn't have to hide or run
away, listening to the light step of his pursuer behind him. On the
contrary, everyone here in the forest suspected and was afraid of
him, the strongest and most dangerous animal.

But he didn't understand this until one day when he happened
to run across the body of a little elk being devoured by a big pair
of wolves. Seeing the wolves, the bear stopped in confusion.
Snarling in helpless rage, the wolves turned and ran, leaving the
place to the bear. And the whole time Teddy was enjoying the
elk, the wolves circled nearby, not daring to come any closer. This
delightful realization of his own power led him to return several
times after he'd eaten his fill, just to see the wolves jump away and
disappear on his arrival.

8

Stopping in one spot for a day, in another for two days, Teddy
kept on going north. The pine trees became higher and thicker,
there were more berries and strawberries and cranberries, and
fewer tree villages. With the endless wild beauty, the undisturbed
density and serenity all around, what else did he need? But Teddy
had fine and vague memories from a practically forgotten youth
that told him nothing was quite right yet — he was going to find
his own country, his own bear's paradise.

Whenever he found someplace especially nice from his point of
view, Teddy would begin making the rounds, rooting out the rotten stumps, destroying the mouse and squirrel nests, turning over
the white moss-covered stones, looking for slugs and worms.

Teddy had learned a great deal in two weeks. He began sleeping
with his head in the direction from which he had come; he knew
that the most delicious mushrooms grow near roots and berry

bushes. He no longer ate everything he came across uncritically as he had at first; he knew the most succulent roots grow in wet places; he began to drink only clean running water and he learned to make use of the wind; his senses were getting keener: he could already distinguish between a fresh and an old smell. From bitter experience he knew that not everything in the forest was edible, that there were berries and mushrooms that it was better not to touch.

He grew stronger and got less tired. The soles of his feet which had hurt him so at first were tougher now, and the claws which had been cut in the circus had grown out. He could walk quietly, almost without a sound. He broke things that fell in his path only for fun, and then the crash would resound through the forest.

At first Teddy slept mostly at night, as he had in the circus. But then he noticed that life in the forest was more interesting at night than during the day. The tracks made by the weasels and rabbits and foxes were fresher at night, things rustled in the grass and underbrush, there was the sound of footsteps running through the ravines and across the clearings, and strange cries sprang up in the silence. Furthermore, the flies and horseflies that annoyed Teddy by day disappeared at night. So more and more he began going out at night, and sleeping in hidden places by day.

9

One night Teddy happened on a small oat field near an abandoned road to a village. He understood this immediately to be connected somehow with man; the oat field hadn't simply grown there.

Teddy went to the edge of the field. The oats tickled him, a pleasant sensation. When he'd circled the field without finding anything interesting, he left, but came back a bit later and went right into the heart of the oat field and lay down in a soft moonlit island. He chewed some oats and recognized the almost forgotten taste of oatmeal. He started by eating everything, stalks and all, but then he sucked and ate just the oats. He left at dawn, leaving a great bare patch in the field behind him.

He liked oats a lot, and a day later he came back and feasted all night. He was on his way the following night, but got distracted coming through a small bog when he awakened two or three dozen frogs. He went after them and got so muddy that he spent the whole morning getting clean.

Teddy didn't know that that morning people had come in a cart along the old road, looked the field over carefully, arguing with each other, and then left. Toward evening they had returned with hatchets and boards and had spent some time, trying to pound quietly, putting up something on an old pine tree.

"Made to order!" one of them kept repeating, and nasty smiles appeared on all their faces.

Then, smoking and dropping ashes in the grass, the people went back to the cart for their guns. Two of them climbed the pine tree, and the third went off somewhere in the cart, singing as he went. A pail jingled under the cart and for a long time after he'd gone, the jangling pail and the song could still be heard.

The moon had come up over the forest when Teddy woke up. He lay quietly for a long time in the total silence, moving only his head to sniff. Then he got up, yawned and stretched. Remembering the oats, he shambled off impatiently toward the field. Every now and then he stopped, distracted by a smell, to stick his nose in the grass and pull up some sweet tender root to crunch on. He still didn't know how to eat quietly.

He was almost at the field, just ten or fifteen feet to go, where he could look between the pale lines of oats and see the dark patch in the middle, the place he had spent two nights, when he suddenly stopped.

No, he hadn't heard or smelled anything, but he had a faint hint of something, some kind of shadow had fallen over him. His instinct told him that something had changed since he'd been here.

Teddy turned to the right and circled the field, going through the forest without taking his eyes off the faintly shining rows of oats. The fur on his back was standing on end, but he didn't growl as usual, something told him it was better not to. A wind came up from somewhere, barely ruffling the grass it was so slight, but the smell of oats grew stronger and Teddy's nose became cold and wet.

But Teddy didn't lick his lips or open his mouth, he just quietly swallowed his saliva, and went onto the lighted road, crossed by the dark shadows of the trees. The hair on the nape of his neck suddenly stood on end. His nose had just caught the faint, cutting odor of tar, horses, tobacco, and people. He stopped and sniffed. He realized finally that people on horses had stood here, smoked, and left. Feeling a little braver he went on down the road, crossed it and found himself on the other side of the field.

He was already sure that the people who had been there that evening had left, but the sense of danger didn't leave him, strangely enough, and the hair on the nape of his neck didn't go down. He wanted to get away completely from a place that aroused such terror in him — everything unknown is terrifying — and he had turned toward the forest when he detoured slightly and came back.

Teddy had no mother, no one to teach him that anything he didn't understand he should leave in a hurry. So he came back and stood for a while in the shadow of the fir trees while the smell, the sweet delicious smell of oats, stifled his feeling of fear and drew him on, lulling and killing caution.

Little by little the bear came out of the shadows and made his way toward the field, but just then there was a loud click and something moved over his head. Before Teddy had the chance to jump aside or even raise his head, there was a great flash, a terrifying shot pealed out in the dark stillness, something stung his left front paw, tripping him, and Teddy fell.

There was another click and Teddy realized that he'd been trapped by his most dangerous enemy, man, and that no matter how angry he was, he must run away. He jumped up and made for the dark protective forest, as fast as he could. To his surprise, on the second bound he fell again. Two more shots rang out of the scrubby pine trees, humming and cracking distinctly around and ahead of him.

But he wasn't afraid of the bursts or the shots now, only of the fact that he had fallen and couldn't run. He got up again and jumped clear of the oat field. Again something incomprehensible and frightening happened to him, and he fell with his nose in the dirt. And only then did Teddy understand that it was as if his front paw wasn't there, it was numb and paralyzed, and he couldn't stand on it. So he shifted the weight of his body to the other paw and ran faster and faster, without looking where he was going, making a terrible crash, snorting in terror, stumbling and falling — anything to get away.

He kept on running for a long time, always thinking that someone was behind him, catching up. He exhausted himself trying to go faster and when finally he simply couldn't run any longer, he stopped, growled, and turned to face his enemy. Growling, he sat down with his ears laid back, and lifted up his now unbearably painful paw. His eyes were on fire, his sides heaving, and the hair on his back and sides standing up in fear and rage. He could hear nothing over the noise of his own breathing, so he stopped breathing to listen. Still hearing nothing, but distrustful of the silence, thinking his enemy must be hiding, Teddy growled again, turned and went on, looking back continually.

But no one was following him, the forest was quiet, stilled by his roars. There was no sound to be heard. Teddy licked his paw as he ran. The warm blood excited him, the pain subsided somewhat, and he kept on licking diligently, experiencing a strange new pleasure.

And that's what saved him. At dawn, the hunters followed the bloody tracks and figured it all out: where he'd gone crashing through the underbrush, digging into the earth with his claws and spattering blood on the grass. They figured that the place where there was an especially large amount of blood and where the grass was trampled and sticky was where he had sat down, facing in their direction. But then the tracks became fainter, less bloody and soon they disappeared altogether. Losing the tracks, the hunters searched the nearby ravines and returned to their village, empty-handed.

10

Meanwhile Teddy was lying in agony far off in a dry little island in the dark forest. His paw was painful and swollen and all day long he couldn't move.

Night fell but the pain in his foot didn't let him sleep. Furthermore he was alarmed about something new, but he couldn't make out what it was; he just kept sniffing, trying to guess the reason for his alarm. The forest was suddenly still, holding its breath, not the slightest sound was to be heard. The dead silence worried the bear even further and kept him on his guard.

Whatever it was swept the forest, the air was close. Infrequently at first, then repeatedly, summer lightning blazed halfway across the horizon. It flared up noiselessly and furtively, invisible from the depths of the forest, lighting up the tops of the pines with a pale ghostly light. Then, slowly, the far-off roar of thunder. Teddy roared back and thrashed around under his fir tree. The silence around him was sinister, and the cracks of thunder in the distance were becoming more and more distinct and more and more frequent. More than ever Teddy wanted to go hide somewhere. But there was no place to hide, so he moved closer to the tree.

The storm came up with astonishing speed; the stars in the treetops were trapped in blackness, the gloom cut only by white lightning striking somewhere in the neighboring hills. Something crashed and fell with a sharp, awful sound — Takh! Agrrbakh! — as if someone were coughing.

A wind came out of the clouds, and the tops of the pines and the firs responded with a hiss, but on the ground it was still, and nothing was stirring. The wind passed, and almost immediately afterward came the rain. This was no ordinary rainstorm with which Teddy was familiar, when the rain rustled gently in the leaves. This rain pounced on the forest, filling it with the roar of falling water, and nothing could be heard over the roar but the crack of thunder rising portentously, again and again.

The storm was over by morning and the forest, penetrated by the sun, grew warm again. Sparkling drops of rain fell from the upper branches onto the lower, and from there to the grass, to be drunk by the earth and all morning the forest was alive with rustling.

Poor, poor Teddy! Astonished by his pain, and by his fear of the storm and people, sleepless, wet and unhappy, he lay beneath the old fir tree, unable to enjoy the sun, unable to think even about going to look for food. And he lay helpless and alone all day, that night, and another day before the wound began to heal a little and a ferocious hunger drove him from his retreat.

Sulky and cautious, hobbling on three legs, he wandered the hills. Just tangling his wounded foot in brush, dry branches, roots or even tall coarse grass was enough to drive him into a rage. But after a few days the bear began to step cautiously on his foot and his melancholy mood gradually passed. He felt happy and cheerful again.

But he was fated to meet man once more. One warm night he was ambling slowly along the riverbank where there was an unusual number of berry patches, but Teddy was irritable: a grouse, groggy with sleep, was just in front of him. The grouse was flapping its wings in confusion, darting into the underbrush, colliding with trees and falling down. Teddy had almost had it several times, but the grouse had flown up into a birch tree and escaped. Then he got angry.

Going down into a ravine, the bear drank from a spring, came up the other side, and suddenly he heard the sound of human voices and smelled smoke. Slowly, he went in the direction of the smoke, and soon he came out on a clearing where there was a bright fire burning, a couple of tents, and some tethered horses grazing. This was part of a research expedition, although Teddy didn't know it of course. He was so astonished that he sat down to get a better look. People were sitting and moving around the fire, talking loudly, laughing, throwing great flickering shadows on the trees.

Teddy went around the edge of the clearing, closer to the tents, and suddenly, to his own surprise, he let out an angry roar. The horses snorted in fear and bunched together, and a dog jumped out from behind the tent and came leaping toward Teddy. Ten feet from Teddy, he stopped with a nasty, cowardly snarl.

Teddy backed up a little and tried approaching the tents from the other side, but the dog came around to meet him again. The people jumped up from the fire, and two of them ran into a tent and came out with guns. Seeing the fire reflected on the gun barrels, Teddy took to his heels. Ecstatic and triumphant, the dog went after him. Reaching the edge of the forest, Teddy turned in the direction of the swamp, and then stopped to face the dog. The dog stopped barking instantly and tore back to the tents. Teddy wanted to go and tear the camp apart, but remembering the guns, he headed for the river and resumed his search for food.

The bear had already covered about one hundred miles going north, never stopping anywhere very long. He was not as helpless now as he had been in the first few days. He was familiar with the smells, he was less and less often at a loss, more and more the master of the great mass of things and situations around him.

So he came to understand that in all circumstances he was to trust the jays and the magpies, although they number among the unworthiest birds in the forest. He learned to figure out the reason for their various cries. If he noticed a crow sitting high up in a tree, cleaning its beak with some magpies sitting quietly just beneath him, looking at the ground, he headed there at once, without question. For he knew that wherever there are satisfied crows, something profitable is sure to be found. He wasn't particularly good at climbing trees, but if he came across a comfortably low, spread-out pine tree, he never missed the opportunity to get his bearings on the whole vicinity from the top of the tree.

Having learned in a short period everything that he hadn't been able to learn his whole life in civilization, having become strong and wary, to an outsider, he might have seemed a real wild animal. But he wasn't, quite.

One morning, going to the stream for a drink, Teddy stopped as if he'd been struck by lightning: near the stream there was the smell of bear! It was an old smell, perhaps two days had passed since the other had been there. But the faint smell made Teddy so angry that for a long time he just stood there looking around, his hair on end. It seemed he was not the only monarch in the forest, there was another he must fear. From that day on, Teddy knew no peace.

More and more frequently he came across crushed anthills, half broken, eaten-over raspberry bushes, and eaten clumps of cranberries. Whenever he picked up the smell coming from a distance, Teddy would track it down, but it always turned out that the other one had gone, leaving only his smell. The whole forest smelled of the strange bear and it drove Teddy crazy. His anger piled up and grew so sharp and constant that it soon became clear that two of them couldn't live in this section of the forest, one had to leave. If it had been a bad section, Teddy would have left without giving it another thought. But it was nice here, with so much good food that Teddy decided to drive his enemy out. He began looking for a way to meet him. Sometimes he found fresh tracks, more often old ones, but he just couldn't locate the bear himself.

Their meeting took place unexpectedly. One morning Teddy was looking for a place to sleep and was crossing a tiny little clearing in the pines, covered with white moss, when he was suddenly struck by the repulsive odor of a bear quite close by. Raising his head, Teddy turned in the direction of the smell and saw his enemy at last. Oh, how he'd show this intruder! How he'd have it out with him! Disappearing momentarily behind the pines, his enemy entered the clearing.

He was an animal so monstrous that Teddy froze like a rabbit. Just a second before, he'd been a fierce wild beast, thirsting for battle. But what did his ferocity mean against the ferocity of this enemy? This was a real brute, shaggy, whiskered, with claws of steel, a mountain of muscle, with such ferocious eyes that Teddy, although strong himself, drew up in fear.

The bear's head was lowered, making him look humpbacked. He stood quietly, staring straight at Teddy. No sound or movement was made, and nothing was done, but Teddy understood that it was he who would have to leave this excellent place forever. How could he have even thought of rivaling this monster?

And as Teddy understood this, the other bear understood it simultaneously. He knew furthermore that Teddy understood. No, he didn't attack Teddy to kill him, he just growled softly. His growl was a whole octave lower than Teddy's lowest growl. All animal growls seem alike to man, whose ear can't distinguish the slight nuances in a growl. But Teddy knew immediately what the bear wanted. His low, almost contemptuous growl meant simply, "get out." To disobey that order would mean ending up on the white moss with a broken neck and a torn-open chest.

Teddy made no sound in reply. He turned quickly and left. When he was already almost hidden by the forest he turned around for the last time. The bear was still standing humpbacked and motionless in the pines.

Teddy took leave of this plentiful place of red ants and red cranberries forever, so as never to meet its whiskered sovereign again. He had emerged the weaker in a battle for life. He'd lost. It was a good idea to leave.

I I

The leaves had almost all dropped from the birch and aspen trees, and covered the earth like a heavy rustling blanket. The birds had migrated, the raspberries were gone, the plentiful mushrooms gone, and the first morning frosts had begun. Having crossed many hills, Teddy turned away from the river, along one of its tributaries and came out on a wide clearing.

Here there was a stream, pines murmuring softly, and the last camomile flowers were in bloom, hungrily turned upward to the sun. The soft golden sand along the bank of the stream was marked in several places by grouse tracks. The stream burbled constantly and melodiously. Teddy stopped in the clearing, suddenly realizing that he had found his promised land, that he had finally returned to his childhood country. He'd be drawn on no farther, there was nowhere else he wanted to go, his travels were over.

No, no, it wasn't home! But everything here was exactly the way it was long ago when Teddy had no name, when he was just a small stupid cub who'd made himself sick on berries and his mother had bathed him in the stream, holding on to his collar and licking his distended stomach clean with her long red tongue. That was a fine, ineffably happy time and now Teddy had returned to it. But that was wrong, of course. No, his childhood had been lost somewhere in the smoke of time, never to return, never to come to life again in the sunshine and the green grass. He'd have to be little again, and find his mother to cry beneath her soft warm stomach. What a pity it wasn't possible.

Wandering day and night Teddy gradually covered the whole area, noting the boundaries of his sovereignty. He followed the streams, inspected the bogs, the ravines, the meadow, the edge of the forest and all the remote places. He found old tracks of wolves, elks, squirrel, otters, and rabbits. Some made no difference to him, but some excited him and he began clawing and scattering the earth, tearing the bark from the trees, in order to establish his right to the land and the forest and the air itself.

Scattering the dry leaves in all directions, some grouse flew right under his nose with a great flapping of wings, but that couldn't trouble him now, he just accepted it as something familiar and inevitable. No longer did he sniff uneasily at every track. He simply noted them in passing, "there were elk here, three of them," or, "that was a fox, it was in a hurry, and was carrying a partridge."

His coat grew out nut-colored, fluffy and shining. His paw no longer hurt him when he used it to turn over a stump or a heavy fallen tree. He walked about a lot, working up a terrible appetite. There was freedom here, and he knew the enormous joy of feeling himself free and powerful as never before.

Freedom is a great thing! It is like the sun, like the enormous starry sky. It is like a warm gentle wind or quickly running water.

No need to be afraid of anyone, no need to do anything you don't want to do. You can get up when you want and go as far as the eye can reach.

You can stop and follow a flight of geese over the river; you can climb a hill blown by every wind; you can sniff at every smell and choose one to follow wherever it may take you!

You can go to a place where there are many dead trees, hollow and crawling with worms, and for the sheer pleasure of exercising your unfettered power, you can push the trees over — so dead and dry that they fall with a pitiful crash.

12

November, the month of heavy frosts and the beginning of the autumn mating season for elk. Wandering in the hills, Teddy was irritated by their roars. Several times he saw from afar a giant elk with great antlers wandering heedlessly through the brush, looking for mushrooms, snorting and trumpeting uninterruptedly. Teddy liked his noisy neighbors less and less. A cautious animal, Teddy forgot himself sometimes and was noisy, but excessive noise he couldn't stand. He grew to hate the elk, as he had once hated the bear.

One day he ran across some elk tracks and saw that they belonged to the giant elk with a herd of females. All day Teddy felt especially mean, possessed by the desire to get rid of them. He pawed angrily at the elk manure and followed after them. Cresting a hill, he lost the tracks, so he went back down, made a great semicircle and caught the scent again. Pretty soon he saw them. They were feeding on a thin little aspen, stretching their velvety lips up to the tenderest branches.

Teddy roared and went for them. The females jumped back and went leaping down the hill, but to Teddy's surprise the buck snorted and moved toward the bear. At any other time he would have thought better of it, of course, and gone with the herd. But now, after his many conquests, sexually gratified, he went to meet his enemy bravely. They met in the clearing and Teddy let out an angry roar. The elk answered with a sharp intake of breath. His whole body was quivering with desire for battle, his eyes shot with blood, his nostrils steaming. With enormous branched antlers, a powerful neck and graceful slender haunches, he was at the height of his powers.

Teddy was taken aback, he had not expected this response. He wasn't afraid, he just took a moment to think of the best way to attack. But the elk, interpreting the hesitation in his own way, lowered his head suddenly, snorted and bore down on the bear. Before Teddy managed to jump aside, he was hit in the leg. Then the elk reared up and started to come down on Teddy's head, which would probably have ended Teddy's life. But he came down not as he had intended, but on the shoulder instead. The bear's strong bones held out and didn't break, but it was a question now, not of fighting, but of merely getting out alive.

Seeing that he hadn't come down as he had expected, the elk reared again, but this time Teddy rolled away and the elk missed him completely. The elk lowered his head and made another dash for him. Teddy avoided him by jumping in a bush, and the elk was unable to stop immediately. By the time he turned back toward the bear, Teddy had turned tail and was limping as fast as he could down the hill.

This was an unprecedented victory for the great elk, but it didn't satisfy him. He wanted either to destroy his enemy or drive him away. So he went after the bear, catching up easily, and attacked several more times. Then suddenly he stopped, as if he had remembered something. Snorting, he returned to his herd. Completely beaten, Teddy dragged himself into the densest part of the forest. For a long time he lay there groaning, reliving the humiliation of defeat. Not long ago he'd been driven out by the whiskered bear, now by the elk. The worst of it was that now he had to avoid all elk: if he'd been beaten by one elk, that meant others could. From that day on, life became unbearable. He was constantly plagued by elk tracks. Going to the cranberry bog or to the stream to drink, he'd come across the tracks, and immediately turn and leave.

But the hopeless situation didn't go on for long. Atavistic instincts awoke in him, demanding he find his enemy and kill him. He began to wander the forest, tracking the elk, angrily clawing the ground and the trees, declaring his sovereignty. For hours he'd lie in ambush, without moving. And one day, coming on fresh elk tracks by the stream, he lay down in the bushes to wait.

He hugged the ground, watching the path through the branches. Wet yellow leaves lay in a thick layer everywhere. The trees were naked, and the dark dense fir trees stood out with especial clarity against the half-naked forest. There'd been a frost that morning, but it had melted. The day was sullen and cold.

In the latter part of the day there was a slight crunch and the sound of snorting. Teddy raised his head and sniffed. The air smelled of elk. His ears went back, his hackles rose. He crouched closer to the ground and drew his paws under his stomach. Once or twice the elk stopped. Teddy didn't know whether they'd stopped to listen or to eat, but lay patiently. Finally antlers appeared in the bushes, followed by the bull elk himself. There were three females with him. They stopped, peered around carefully, their ears quivering, then they started down to the stream for a drink, the elk first, followed by the females.

But the elk caught scent of the bear and stopped in his tracks. Teddy jumped from his hiding place. The elk snorted and turned on the bear, and was scratched as the bear jumped aside. The scratch turned out to be minor, glancing, but it had torn the skin and drawn blood. Smelling the blood, Teddy went wild. For the first time in his life he wanted raw meat, and to hear the death rattle of a victim. Meanwhile the elk turned and attacked again. The blow of the antlers threw the heavy bear like a kitten. Teddy rolled on the ground, but another wound was bleeding on the elk's neck. Teddy jumped up with his loudest roar, his whole body quivering, and made for the elk's side, recognizing the fact that the antlers were the kind of weapon against which he was powerless.

They fought for a long time, tearing up the wet grass and earth, breaking everything in sight. The elk was clearly weakening. Blood was pouring out of many wounds, and he was steaming all over in the cold. Finally, Teddy jumped onto his back. He clung to the powerful nape, tearing at the elk's sides with his back feet. Then holding on to the nape with his left claw and his teeth, growling though clenched teeth, Teddy dug into the elk's neck with his left paw and dragged the claws back, breaking the vertebrae. The elk fell and Teddy tore his chest open. But such was the elk's strength that even with a broken neck and gaping chest he tried to rise and attack. Growling and choking on his enemy's blood, Teddy was a long time coming to his senses.

Then, roaring uninterruptedly, the bear went off into the forest, only to return and try to drag the elk with him. It was hard and clumsy work, so he tried covering him with branches instead. Having covered his enemy after a fashion and piling dirt around him, Teddy left. No one had taught him this, and he had never done it before, but he knew now that he had to.

Two days later, having almost forgotten about the elk, Teddy happened to be passing by when the wind carried the sweetish smell in his direction. He remembered everything, and went and gorged himself.

Wolves had already been at the elk, Teddy saw from the tracks they'd left, so instead of leaving, he slept nearby.

He lived on the elk a whole week, sleeping nearby, master of everything around, knowing his territory to be as inviolable as the whiskered bear's.

13

But time passed and, like the last time, as his wound grew older, Teddy was seized with a new longing to see people. The strength of his longing, more powerful than instinct, chased him from the forest, to seek an encounter with man as he so recently had sought solitude and freedom.

Four days he went southeast before he came to open country. Before him was a high, half-naked hill. The winter crop shone green on the hill and along the edge of the forest where Teddy came to a halt, ran deep ruts, worn down by quick-moving automobiles and slow-moving carts.

Teddy half stood on his hind paws at the edge of the forest, rocking with loneliness and longing. He didn't need just any man, but the strong man in the white pantaloons. He wanted him to come and stroke him behind the ears and say gently, "Teddy," and thrust his strong hand into his mouth with a piece of sugar.

The bear stood a long time. But it was not the same Teddy. It was a Teddy relearning the great secret of life, and saying goodbye to the past forever. He didn't take the road toward man and he didn't repeat one of his killingly funny tricks he'd learned in the circus. He just mourned in silence. Then something turned over inside him, the last barrier fell, the last thread attaching him to man snapped, and he went back to the forest. In four days he was home.

Every day it grew colder. Teddy slept a lot now and seldom went out. In the mornings the small lakes and ponds closed over with singing ice. Teddy's constant master, hunger, left him suddenly and something else began to bother him more and more. They hadn't let Teddy sleep through the winter in the circus, because he'd had to perform. But here he obeyed the laws of the forest and of nature. He wanted to sleep. He went everywhere trying places out, but they were all either uncomfortable or unsafe.

Then one night snow fell, and in the morning everything was white, the hills smoky in the distance. Teddy wanted to sleep more than ever. Even his own tracks in the snow failed to interest him.

Once he tried settling down on some dry leaves under a fir tree and he slept for three days, but then he woke up and went off again, enviously watching the lively black crows in the white snow.

Finally he found what he needed. It was a deep hole covered by needles and leaves, sheltered not only by bushes, but also by a sawed-off fir tree. Some man had sawed off the top part but left branches that hung so densely over the hole that Teddy could just barely see the sky when he got inside. But things still weren't quite right. Getting out again, he began dragging over more dried underbrush and piling it on top, and he didn't climb back in until evening. Then he turned around and around, trying to find a comfortable position to lie in. Finally, everything seemed fine and he began cleaning himself off.

It gradually grew dark, and snow began to fall. When it was so dark that the snow on the tops of the pines lost all color, Teddy fell asleep.

What did he dream?

Did he dream about the circus and the long life of an artist, divided in two between the darkness of the cages and the blinding light of the arena? Did he dream about traveling, trains, the knock of wheels, the smell of coal and gas, people laughing and shouting angrily, about the man in the white pantaloons?

Or did he dream about his new free life, sweet ants, sparkling frost, streams, frightening storms, gunshots, the bear that had driven him out or his fight with the elk?

Did he dream of his youth? Did the sweet wise smells of the forest come to his den to lure him?

Who knows?

He didn't wake up the next day or the third. The snow covered everything, the branches became more fluffy with snow every day, the paths impassable, the pines and the firs totally white, and only the naked birch trees were visited by the partridges in the evenings. The heavy frosts struck, and real winter played through the forest.

Teddy's sleep grew more profound, his breathing slower and slower until it no longer sent up a swirl of steam. Only accidentally could anyone have guessed — from the small breathing hole and the yellowish frost on the twigs — that there was a den under the snow.